LISA JEWELL
Before I
Met You

arrow books

Published by Arrow Books 2013

8 10 9

First published in Great Britain in 2012 by Century

Arrow Books
Random House, 20 Vauxhall Bridge Road
London SW1V 2SA

www.randomhouse.co.uk

Addresses for companies within The Random House Group Limited can be found
at: www.randomhouse.co.uk/offices.htm

The Random House Group Limited Reg. No. 954009

A CIP catalogue record for this book
is available from the British Library

ISBN 9780099559535

Penguin Random House is committed to a sustainable future for
our business, our readers and our planet. This book is made from
Forest Stewardship Council® certified paper.

Typeset in Baskerville MT by SX Composing DTP, Rayleigh, Essex, SS6 7XF
Printed in Great Britain by Clays Ltd, St Ives plc

This book is dedicated to Amelie, Evie, Mia and Joy, four of the prettiest girls I know.

1

1983

The day, and, in fact the rest of Elizabeth Dean's life, had started at Weymouth at an ungodly hour, continued on to a damp, windswept ferry across the Channel and culminated in a silent drive across Guernsey and a walk up a long gravelled hill to a large house with grey walls and black windows. The house stood tall and wide, atop a hill of dense woodland. In front of the house was the sea. Behind the house was nothing.

Elizabeth thought, but did not say, that the house was clearly haunted and that she would not countenance spending as long as one night in it.

'Elizabeth, this is my mother, Arlette. And, Mummy, this is Elizabeth – or Lizzy, as we usually call her.'

'When she's being good!' Alison, Elizabeth's mother, interjected.

'Yes,' rejoined her mother's boyfriend. 'When she's being good. When she's not being good she's plain old Elizabeth.'

Her mother's boyfriend ruffled Elizabeth's hair and

squeezed her shoulder, and Elizabeth grimaced. She stared at the ground, at the brown and red tessellated tiles beneath her feet, cut and formed into the shapes of stars. She'd known this moment was coming for two weeks now, since Christmas Eve, when they'd got the call that had spoiled their Christmas Day. Two weeks ago Elizabeth's mother and her boyfriend had sat her down and explained that his mother, a woman called Arlette Lafolley, a person of whose existence Elizabeth had been blissfully unaware before that moment, had fallen in her house on an island called Guernsey and broken something, and had been advised by her GP that she should have someone living with her.

And so it had been decided, somehow, somewhere, behind some closed door or other, that the solution to this problem was for Elizabeth and her mother to leave the only home that Elizabeth had ever known, a neat, red-brick bungalow on the outskirts of Farnham in Surrey, and go to this island to live with this woman, for at least, her mother had told her, three months, and to do so within two weeks.

'Elizabeth,' said her mother's boyfriend, 'are you going to say hello?'

Elizabeth tried not to squirm, but it was very hard not to squirm when you were in a haunted house with your mother's boyfriend's hand on your shoulder, being introduced to a terrible old woman whose frail bones had conspired to crumble and break and destroy your life. Elizabeth lifted her gaze to the woman in front of her, but not before noticing, with some surprise, that the woman was wearing red silk shoes adorned with matching rosettes. Elizabeth's gaze also took in black lacy tights over shapely calves, and then a coat of full, luxuriant mink that hung from throat to mid-shin, and a face, round and elfin, like the face of a child, pink lips, pearly blue eyelids and a matching mink hat. On each earlobe a small chunk of diamond shone dully in the muted candlelight.

Elizabeth gulped. 'Hello,' she said.

The lady in the fur coat paused for a beat and then bowed down so that her head was level with hers and said, 'Hello, Elizabeth. I've heard a lot about you.'

It was impossible from her expression to gauge whether these things she had heard had been bad or good, but then her face softened and she smiled, and Elizabeth smiled back and said, 'I like your shoes.'

Arlette smiled too and said, 'Then you have very good taste. Now come in and get warm, I've lit the fire.'

Elizabeth and her mother exchanged looks. Elizabeth's mother had met this woman before, about two years ago when she and her boyfriend had only just started dating. She had described her then as 'colourful' but 'mean'. And someone 'not to be crossed'. She had probably not thought, as she'd passed these judgements upon her boyfriend's mother to her daughter, that one day she and her daughter would have cause to come and live with her. And she'd probably forgotten ever saying them. But Elizabeth hadn't forgotten. And she had come to this place with a full armoury of attitude and verve, ready to take whatever this lady had to dish up. And then been momentarily thrown by a pair of scarlet silk shoes.

But still, red silk shoes. Even on an old lady, that was rather spectacular. Elizabeth had had to endure all sorts of nonsensical after-school dance classes in order to get her mother to buy her interesting shoes. Slivers of flesh-coloured leather with silky ribbons for ballet, and chunky-heeled shoes with buttoning straps for flamenco and jazz. But never anything in red silk. Surely, she thought to herself, surely anyone capable of owning a pair of shoes that magnificent must be halfway decent.

She followed the old lady down the hall and into a room on the left. It was entered by a tall door with an ornately stained window in the fanlight.

'You'll have to excuse the damp,' said Arlette. 'I haven't opened this room up for quite a while. And it's too cold to have a window open.'

Elizabeth brought her arms around herself and shuddered. The room was tall and bare, with wood-panelled walls and pointy furniture, and everything was brown apart from a roaring fire in the hearth around which they all huddled on a tapestry-covered ottoman.

The adults were all having a conversation about the journey and about the delivery van and about the weather and about Arlette's hip (she had walked with a stick and a fairly pronounced limp down the hallway). Elizabeth got to her feet and went to the window. It was leaded and a touch baggy, and framed by dismal grey nets. Through it Elizabeth could see, in all directions, a vast expanse of blankness. She sighed and returned to the fire, the cold of the room seeping into the very marrow of her, the smell of damp firewood and unloved furnishings and cold, cold coldness leaching into everything.

'We've got blow heaters coming in the van,' said Jolyon, rubbing his hands together briskly. 'We'll plug them in when they arrive.' He said this to Elizabeth and to Elizabeth's mother in a perky, reassuring manner, but it was clear to Elizabeth and to her mother that it would take more than two cheap blow heaters to take the chill off this sad old house. 'And then,' he continued, somewhat desperately, 'I'll take a look at the heating.'

His mother threw him a disparaging look. 'Not necessary,' she said. 'The air will warm up pretty quickly over the next few weeks. Remember, we've the Gulf Stream here. By the time you've worked out how to fix the heating and found someone willing to come and sort it for a sum of money that will not make your eyeballs bleed, it will be summer again. Every room has a fireplace. And it's all a matter of wearing the right clothes. And keeping to just a couple of rooms. And, of course, lots and lots of hot drinks. Warming ourselves up from the inside out.'

Elizabeth stared at Arlette's furry coat and hat, and thought, well, yes, that is easy for you to say, you are practically wearing a *bear*.

Elizabeth was put in a room on the first floor that was papered with a green and blue vertical stripe that looked like old men's pyjamas. There were three small leaded windows overlooking the sea. It was even colder up here, and when she breathed out hard, her breath appeared around her like a wraith.

Her bed sat on the opposite side of the room to the windows. It was built from some kind of very heavy, darkly veneered wood and covered over with a cheap-looking duvet with a blue case. Atop the two biscuit-thin pillows sat a threadbare blue knitted rabbit that looked like he'd been left there to die.

Elizabeth thought of her bed at home. It was queen-sized, with a white powder-sprayed metal frame with curly bits in it and knobs made out of clear Perspex. Her mother had bought it for her for her tenth birthday; 'a double bed for double figures'. She also had a queen-sized duvet, clothed in a white cover embroidered all over with rose sprigs, and a pillowcase trimmed with lace upon which Elizabeth arranged all her teddy bears every morning before she left for school. She'd asked her mum if they could bring the bed, if they could squeeze it into the big van with all their other things, but her mum had smiled apologetically and said, 'Sorry, sweetheart, no beds. It'll still be there when we get back.'

And that had been that.

Elizabeth rested her rucksack on the floor and unzipped it with icy fingers. Inside she felt around for the soothing plush of Katerina's ears. She tugged at the fabric and pulled her free of the piles of books and games and notepads she'd packed this morning to relieve the boredom of an eight-hour journey. Elizabeth pulled the bear close to her face and breathed in the smell of her, and she felt her heart ache as the heady, honeyed scent of home filled her senses. With her nose still to the bear, she looked around the cold, spartan room, she gazed at the endless concrete grey of the sea through the mean little windows, and then she stalked across the room, picked up the ugly knitted rabbit, opened a window and hurled the thing as far as she could into the cold grey yonder.

2

It wasn't until the second week of February, five weeks after her family's arrival at her house, and ten days after the resurrection of the central heating, that Arlette and Elizabeth had any kind of meaningful conversation. They came upon each other in the hallway, as Elizabeth waved goodbye to her new best friend, Bella, and her mother, who had dropped her home after tea at Bella's house.

Elizabeth was still smiling when she turned to see Arlette standing on the bottom step, clutching her stick and wearing, not her fur, but a stiff black dress with a knife-pleat skirt, a white voile collar and three-quarter-length sleeves. With her tiny waist and shapely calves, she looked to Elizabeth like a fashion illustration from 1954 come to life. She descended the last step with the assistance of the stick she now used all the time and looked at Elizabeth.

'Who was that?' she asked.

Elizabeth paused for a moment, giving herself time to ensure that the question was not a trick or a trap. 'That was Bella,' she replied.

'Bella?' repeated Arlette, arching a pencilled-in eyebrow. 'Who's Bella?'

'She's my best friend.'

'Ah!' Arlette's face brightened. 'You have a best friend? Already?'

Elizabeth nodded proudly.

'Well,' said Arlette, 'in that case, I can stop worrying about you. Come,' she said, turning back towards the staircase. 'I've just made a pot of cocoa. Come and drink it with me.'

'OK,' Elizabeth said brightly, and joined Arlette as she walked slowly back up the stairs.

'You know,' said Arlette, pausing for breath at the top of the first flight, 'I went to your school. What's it called, these days?'

'Our Lady of Lourdes.'

'Yes, that's right. Not sure what Lourdes has to do with anything. It was called St Anne's when I was there. And it was all in one room. All of us, from four to eleven.' She smiled a soft smile and then continued up the stairs. 'Do you know how old I am?' she asked suddenly, stopping again, halfway up.

Elizabeth nodded. 'You're eighty-four.'

Arlette scowled at her. 'Who told you that?' she asked.

'Jolyon?' she replied breathlessly, lest it was somehow the wrong answer.

'Hmm.' Arlette twitched her nose and then carried on up the stairs.

'Are you?' asked Elizabeth, following her down the corridor. 'Are you eighty-four?'

'Yes,' said Arlette, stopping, but not turning to address

her. 'Yes, I am. I was hoping I might be able to fool you into thinking I was somewhat younger than that, but never mind.'

Arlette pushed open the door to her room and held it for Elizabeth. 'Come in, dear,' she said, with a hint of impatience.

Elizabeth stepped forward with a shiver of anticipation. She had assumed that she would never set foot in this room, or that if she did it would be at some point in the future when Arlette was actually dead. But here she was, suddenly and thrillingly, on the threshold of a mysterious new world.

And it did not disappoint.

Arlette's room was the loveliest place Elizabeth had ever been in her life.

A fire glowed and crackled in an ornate brass fire basket. Around the Gothically carved fireplace were red velvet club fenders. On a mantelpiece lined with creamy lace, which fell from the shelf in a tasselled, scalloped fringe, were silver-framed photographs of young men and women, of soldiers and babies and elderly people with severe haircuts. The floor was carpeted with something springy and bouncy underfoot, the windows were hung with pink silk curtains with shiny sateen fringed swags and billowy pelmets, and the walls were papered with fat, sugary roses growing amidst a pale green trellis. A standard lamp in the corner bore a lampshade that looked like a gold crinoline, wrapped in silk ribbon and dripping with black bugle beads. There were occasional tables in every corner, lit by glass-shaded lamps in shades of plum and peach. The room was full of things described by words that Elizabeth did not yet know: Chantilly, chenille, chinoiserie, chintz, chandelier.

'Sit.' Arlette gestured at a small blue velvet chair fringed with golden tendrils. Elizabeth lowered herself delicately onto the chair and tucked her hands beneath her bottom. Arlette poured cocoa from an ornate silver pot into a small rose-painted cup. She had a kitchenette – a small gas hob, a small fridge, a hotplate, a cupboard and some shelving stacked with antique china and dainty glasses. By Elizabeth's chair was a green leather globe, split in half horizontally and housing half a dozen decanters, a constellation of cut-crystal glasses and a small leather tub on top of which rested a tiny pair of silver tongs.

To the side of Arlette's four-poster bed was an over-sized armchair with a matching footstool, both of which faced towards a small TV set with an aerial on top.

Arlette had everything she could possibly need in here: warmth, nourishment, entertainment, sleep and gin. No wonder nobody ever saw her. No wonder she cared so little about the conditions in the rest of her home. Here she existed in perfect comfort, a deluxe studio flat, with a view.

'You know,' said Arlette, passing the rose-painted cup to Elizabeth, 'you're the very first person to join me in here for about ten years.'

Elizabeth looked up at Arlette but didn't say anything.

'Yes, I have lived in this house alone since Jolyon's father passed away. Just me. On my own.'

Elizabeth felt she should say something sympathetic but as she searched for words she saw Arlette's face twitch and then break into a smile. 'It's been bloody marvellous.' She stopped abruptly and the smile folded itself away. 'Anyway,' she continued, 'it's nice to have you about the place. Though I could do without the other two.' She shrugged her shoulders in the direction of her bedroom door and then shuddered delicately. 'No offence.'

Elizabeth smiled, feeling sure that none had been taken.

'I never wanted any children, you know,' Arlette continued.

Elizabeth glanced at her with surprise.

'It was a mistake really. They didn't have contraception in my day. But I wasn't stupid. I knew all the other ways in which one could prevent these things from happening. I took my temperature, kept charts . . .'

Elizabeth pursed her lips and wondered what she meant by charts, but said nothing, concentrating instead on keeping the delicate wide-mouthed cup balanced on the thin sliver of a saucer.

'We all did,' Arlette continued. 'Back in those days. Because we were all having so much fun and none of us was ready for babies. I managed to keep the babies at bay for eight years. Quite some feat, I can tell you. And then there it was, two days shy of my thirty-fourth birthday. A blasted baby. And once it was there, you know, bedded inside, well, all I could hope was that it would be a girl.'

She sighed, her fingertips held to the small of her throat. 'Ah . . .' she exhaled. 'Well, anyway, it most certainly was *not* a girl. It was him.' She shuddered lightly. 'My late husband was delighted. A son. To carry on the family name. All I could think about was having to handle his, well, his organs. I had a nursemaid. But she worked only days. So come seven o'clock it was all down to me. Ouf.' She sneered and brought her teacup slowly to her lips. Her hands did not shake. She seemed to Elizabeth not like an eighty-four-year-old at all, but more like a slightly etiolated fifty-year-old.

'So, I have to admit to being very curious about you, when I heard that Jolyon had taken up with a young widow. A little girl! I could not imagine my son having to play the father figure to a little girl. Or to anyone, for that matter. Selfish life he's lived. Takes after me,' she laughed drily. 'But he has become very fond of you. And now here you are. In my home. And I have to say, from the first time I saw you, I liked you very much.' Arlette smiled then and appraised Elizabeth with twinkling eyes. 'I'd like to call you Betty, if I may?'

'Betty?'

'Yes. In my day if you were Elizabeth, you were Betty. Or Bet. But Betty was more popular. And I don't know, you just look like a Betty to me.'

Betty.

Elizabeth rolled the name around her head.

She liked it. It was more fun than Elizabeth and less little-girly than Lizzy.

'Here,' Arlette got to her feet and crossed the room, 'do you like old photographs?'

Elizabeth nodded. She did like old photographs, very much.

'I thought you might.' Arlette walked to the other side of the room and brought down a few leather-bound books from a shelf. 'Here, my albums. Have a look.'

Elizabeth dutifully followed Arlette's instructions, while Arlette put a large black disc onto a gramophone player and slowly lowered a needle onto it. And there, in that moment, as the needle hit the vinyl and a crackle of static hit the air, followed by a flourish of piano, a log popping in the grate, the dusty aroma of old paper from the album on her lap, the smell of waxy candles and rich perfume, and the glimmer of a large paste brooch on Arlette's collar in the shape of a butterfly, Elizabeth felt herself open up and pull something into herself, something she'd never before encountered in her ten short years, something heady and fragrant and electrifying. And that thing was glamour.

Her home in Surrey had been modern and clean. Her mother spent a lot of time in jeans and polo-necks. Even when she went out to smart restaurants with Jolyon she would simply replace the jeans with trousers and sling a gold chain around her polo-neck. Elizabeth's mother wore no make-up. She listened to Radio One. She had a perm. She liked football. Elizabeth's mother was beautiful, but she was not glamorous. And before this moment, Elizabeth herself had had no real concept of the notion of glamour. She had swooned over Audrey Hepburn's dresses in *My Fair Lady*, and loved going into the jewellery section of the department store in Guildford and pretending she was going to buy herself diamonds. But this was different. In this room, with the inky light of a faded afternoon in the sky and the melancholy strains of Tchaikovsky's Symphony No. 3 in D in the air, Elizabeth turned the pages of an old lady's history and lost herself in nostalgia for a world she'd never known.

In this room, Elizabeth became Betty.

3

1987

At the ferry port, Betty's breath encircled her head and then floated out towards the sea, almost as though it were trying to find its way back like a cat abandoned far from home. She was not wearing enough for the weather. At fifteen, she was more concerned with her image than with her physical comfort, and knowing that they would soon be sitting on a train heading towards London, and that there might be real actual Londoners on the train, she did not want to look like someone who lived in a weird old house with a weird old woman on the edge of a cliff on a tiny island that was so small that it didn't even have a motorway. So she was wearing thick black tights, a very short denim skirt, blue suede moccasins and an elderly and very misshapen navy lambswool V-neck with a lace-trim vest underneath. Her hair was short and dyed black and her lips were painted a reddish black and lined with a slightly darker shade of old blood. She did not, she felt fairly certain, look like the type of girl who came from Guernsey.

Sometimes Betty forgot that she was a big, pretty fish in a small, not so pretty pond. She and Bella were the reigning queens of their small corner of the world. They were the prettiest, the coolest, the most popular. Everything, in the realm of fifteen-year-old life on the island, revolved around the pair of them. And sometimes Betty believed that she really was, well, that she was famous. Because, on Guernsey, with her smoky-brown eyes, her fashion-drawing legs and her wardrobe of cool and slightly quirky clothes collected from dark corners of charity shops and pilfered from Arlette's many wardrobes, she may as well have been famous.

But here, just a few miles from shore, all that fell away from her like discarded tissue paper. Here she was just a girl. A pretty girl, but no prettier than most.

It was the first time they'd been back to England since they'd left on that foggy January morning almost five years ago. Three months had turned into six months, six months into a year, and by then her mother had found the island quite to her liking. Betty had settled so well into her new school and someone had made a 'silly offer' for the house in Farnham, and they'd decided, as a family, to stay. Betty was delighted. From the minute she'd first set foot in Arlette's boudoir, she'd known that this was where she wanted to be now. The white powder-sprayed bed had been shipped across from England and Betty had settled down.

But they were back for Christmas, just Betty and her mother, two nights at Betty's grandmother's in Farnham, and time first for a bit of Christmas shopping in town. As she entered her teenage years, clothes shopping had become pretty much the only area of common interest between Betty and her mother, and they linked their arms together companionably as they made their way up Oxford Street.

It was nearly five o'clock; the December afternoon looked like deepest, darkest night and the whole road was bathed in the soft rainbow glow of the Christmas lights strung overhead. They had another hour before they needed to get a train back to Betty's grandmother's in Surrey. Betty could feel something deep inside her tugging her from the thoroughfare of Oxford Street, away from the homogeny and the brand names. She pulled her mother past the fairy-tale edifice of Liberty and on to Carnaby Street. Her mother kept pausing to admire a window, to exclaim about a musical showing in a theatre, to remember something she'd forgotten to buy. But Betty kept moving.

'Come on,' she implored, her hands on her hips. 'Come on!'

'What's the panic?' asked her mother. 'Where are we going?'

'I don't know,' snapped Betty, casting about anxiously, as she felt the day falling away from her. 'Just . . . *this way*.'

She didn't know what *this way* was. All she knew was that the day was dying and the night was giving birth to itself, and there was something electric, something magnetic pulling her down Carnaby Street, past self-consciously crazy boutiques, past grimy pubs, through the throngs of tourists and teenage girls *just like her*, girls from somewhere else with overblown ideas about themselves, girls having a special treat with dowdy mothers and bored fathers, a day in town with an early lunch at Garfunkel's, overfilled bowls from the salad bar, tickets for a West End show tucked away safely in Mum's bum-bag. It wasn't real. Even to Betty's immature, small-town eyes she could see through the fakery and the stage setting. There was something both murky and beguiling beyond this plastic street of Union Jacks and Beatles posters, something grimy and glittering. She wanted to find it and taste it right now before their time here in the West End was up and Christmas in a small cottage in Surrey swallowed her up for two whole days.

She walked urgently away from Carnaby Street and up side roads until the only lights were neon and the shops were small and anonymous.

'Oh God, where *are* you taking us?' said her mother, looking aghast at a middle-aged woman sitting on a bar stool in the entrance to a bar advertising a Live Girls Show, and dramatically underdressed for the weather in a gold boob tube and red leather shorts.

'I think it's Soho,' said Betty, her voice tremulous with excitement. *Soho*. That's what had been pulling her down these backstreets, of course it was. Soho. The centre of the universe. The Hundred Club. The Mud Club. The Blitz Club. Sex. Drugs. Rock and roll. Betty's favourite film of all time was *Desperately Seeking Susan*. She loved it for the setting, for the neon lights glistening on oily puddles, the alleyways and mysterious doorways, subterranean dives and shabby-looking people with secrets.

She turned to her mother and smiled. And then she looked upwards into the dark windows of a thin, grimy town house. 'Imagine living here,' she said breathily.

'No thank you,' said her mother, shivering in a blast of cold air.

Betty continued to stare upwards. 'I wonder who lives up there,' she said.

'French Model,' her mother read off the doorbell.

'Wow,' breathed Betty, picturing a woman who looked like Beatrice Dalle floating around a cool flat, talking loudly and crossly to her French boyfriend on the phone with a strong cigarette in her other hand.

'You know what that means, don't you?'

Betty shrugged uncomfortably, aware that her mother was about to flag up a shortcoming in her knowledge of the big wide world.

'It's a euphemism,' she said, 'for a prostitute. There's some poor girl up there having sex with an old ugly man. For money.'

Betty shrugged again, as if, really, what was so bad about that, whilst silently, invisibly, cringing at the very thought. But she still couldn't help but see a certain glamour in it. A dark, ugly glamour. If you were going to sleep with an old ugly man for money, then this, mused Betty, was the place to do it.

'Come on,' said her mother. 'It's nearly six. Let's get out of here. Let's go back to Grandma's.'

Betty let her gaze fall from the black eyes of the old town house, tore herself from her dreams of moody French models and Soho nights, and headed back to Surrey with her mother.

4

1988

'What did *you* do?' Betty asked Arlette, as Arlette searched her jewellery boxes for a particular paste brooch she knew would look just perfect with Betty's party dress. Betty did not want to wear a paste brooch, but she also knew that Arlette was rarely wrong about these things and that if she thought the brooch would go with the black taffeta off-the-shoulder dress she'd bought last week from Miss Selfridge, then she should at least try it on.

'What did I do when?'

'For your sixteenth birthday party.'

'Nothing,' said Arlette, 'absolutely nothing. We'd just gone to war. Nobody had any parties.'

'What was the war like?'

'It was bleak. It was terrifying. It was horrible.'

'And you lost your dad?'

'I did. I lost my father.' Arlette paused for a moment and sniffed. 'My lovely father.'

'And what did you do after?' Betty asked. 'After the war?'

Arlette sniffed again. 'Nothing at all,' she said. 'I stayed here and cared for my mother. I worked in a dress shop for a little while, in St Peter Port. And then I met Mr Lafolley.'

Betty sighed. It seemed such a waste. 'But didn't you ever want to go somewhere else? Didn't you ever want to have an adventure, go to London, travel?'

Arlette shook her head. Her demeanour changed for a moment. 'No,' she said. 'Bloody awful place, London. No thank you. No. Guernsey girl through and through. There was never anywhere else for me.'

She found the brooch and passed it to Betty. It was made of stones in graduated shades of cranberry and pink, in the shape of a butterfly.

'Yes!' said Betty. 'Yes. It is. It's perfect. Thank you.'

'You are very welcome, Betty, so very welcome.' Arlette squeezed Betty's hands inside hers and then carefully pinned it onto her dress. 'Awful cheap fabric,' she muttered, 'just awful, but there.' She stepped back to admire her. 'There you are, looking perfectly, perfectly beautiful. Only a beautiful girl of sixteen could make fabric that cheap look so good. Now go,' she said, 'go to your party. Go and be sixteen.'

Sixteen, Betty felt, should *sparkle*. Sixteen should glimmer and twinkle and gleam. It should involve taking off your shoes at the Yacht Club and cavorting, dancing, laughing, sitting on your best friend's lap and throwing knowing looks across the room to a tall, blond man with broad shoulders and a St Lucian tan, called Dylan Wood, who you've been in love with for, like, a whole *year*, before getting to your feet and dancing again with a sweet, spotty boy called Adam, who's been in love with you for, like, a whole *year*. It should involve sneaking outside to smoke cigarettes with a girl in your class who you've never really spoken to before, but who suddenly feels like your best friend, and watching two other boys in your class moon through the plate-glass windows at the assembled grown-ups before being hustled back indoors by an appalled manager. It should involve disco lights and glitter balls, and it should, at around two minutes to midnight, involve being given the bumps by thirty sixteen-year-olds and blowing out sixteen candles on a huge chocolate cake whilst *Sixteen Candles* played in the background. And then, at five minutes past midnight, the DJ must be instructed to put on 'Dancing Queen' and you must untie your raven hair and twirl round and round beneath the glitter ball while your friends all stand around and clap and sing 'only *si-ix-teen*' at the top of their voices every time Abba sing 'only seventeen'.

But sixteen could not be considered complete without a moment, somewhere between midnight and one, when the man called Dylan Wood, who you've been in love with for, like, a whole *year*, pulls you away from your party and onto a terrace overlooking the sea, and for a few minutes you both stare out together in silence at a view that could have been plucked directly from a pine-scented corner of the Mediterranean, with its yachts and its palm trees and the sound of music wafting across on a warm balmy breeze. This moment should involve some conversation and the exchange of observations such as, 'I've been watching you all night.' And, 'You've always been pretty, but tonight – I don't know – it's like you became beautiful.' And possibly even, 'Is it still all right to kiss you?'

Ideally the world should recede away from you at this point, the background noises become nothing more than distant buzz, and then Dylan Wood would cup your face with his hand, tip back your head and let his lips just brush yours, soft and gentle as butterfly wings so you're not quite sure if it really just happened or not, and then again, a little firmer, this time leaving no doubt whatsoever that he has just kissed you, that Dylan Wood has just kissed you, under the light of a pearly half-moon, with his hand in your hair and his thigh in your groin, and you should think then that you are sixteen and already your life is complete.

Sixteen shattered the following day into a thousand tiny, irretrievable little pieces. Betty knew sixteen was broken the moment her eyes opened at eight o'clock, as she felt the prickle of discomfort across her skin, the soreness of the skin around her mouth, the raw heat of devastation as she remembered Dylan smiling at her after their first shockingly passionate kiss and saying, 'Fuck, how the hell am I supposed to go back to London after that?'

'What?' Her voice had sounded flat and dull.

'I can't believe it,' he'd continued, his eyes on hers, his hands still clasped together behind her back. 'I've been stuck on this stupid rock for six years and just when I finally find something good about it, we're going.'

'You're going to London?' she whispered.

'Yes,' he said, 'didn't you know? I thought you knew. I thought –'

'No. I didn't know. When are you going?'

'Friday,' he said. 'We're going on Friday.'

'Oh. No,' she whispered. 'Why?'

He'd laughed then, as if there was something funny about the situation, the fact of their aborted union, his imminent emigration. But there was nothing funny about it, nothing whatsoever.

Betty pulled herself from her bed and opened the curtains. The sky was dense and grey. It didn't look like summer. It didn't feel like summer. Sixteen was dead and so was summer. Her black dress hung haphazardly from a wire hanger on her wardrobe handle, in stark contrast to the way it had been stored in the days running up to the party, in sheets of tissue paper and a plastic zip-up carrier, like a chrysalis. Now it was just a dress, deserving of no special treatment.

Betty sighed and let the curtain fall. She flopped backwards onto her bed and considered the ceiling while she pondered her feelings. The walls of her room seemed to close in towards her as she lay there; she could feel the shores of the island tightening around her like a corset, stifling her breath. She thought of Dylan, sitting on a double-decker bus, riding down Shaftesbury Avenue, on his way to some amazing new nightclub that everyone was talking about. Then she thought of herself, a tiny pinprick of a human being with no plans beyond sixth form and an interview next week for a Saturday job at Boots.

She hated being sixteen. She hated her life. She wanted to be nineteen. She wanted to get away from this stupid, pathetic island and get on with her life.

She let a few self-indulgent tears roll down her cheeks and onto her duvet cover.

And then she lifted her head abruptly at the sound of shouting coming from downstairs.

'Alison! Alison! Quick!'

It was Jolyon.

She heard her mother's voice in reply.

'What!'

'Call an ambulance! Quick! It's Mummy. She's collapsed!'

'What! Oh God!'

Betty raced to the top of the stairs and shouted down, 'What's happening!'

'I don't know!' her mother shouted back. 'It's Arlette!'

Betty fell down upon the top step and sat for a moment, listening to the sounds of chaos below, her mother's call to the emergency services, Jolyon panicking, doors opening and closing. She sat there for around thirty seconds before she could find it within her to get to her feet, because even as she sat there, her head full of fug, her cheeks still damp with just-spilled tears, she knew that whatever it was that was happening downstairs was going to impact her life in some terrible, weighty way. She knew that the future was being chipped and chiselled into some ugly new shape.

She breathed in deeply and slowly walked downstairs.

5

1993

You could hear it echoing down corridors and ricocheting off walls. It careered round corners and broke through the deep heavy silence of the night. Betty leaped out of bed, peroxide hair misshapen and on end, dressed in one of Arlette's vintage négligées under a big grey jumper, her feet in chunky oatmeal socks. She tried to fight her way out of the cloud of dreams that had swallowed her up.

'Coming,' she croaked. Then: '*Coming!*' louder, as her voice returned.

She stopped for just long enough to become aware that the sky was not pitch-black, that the time was 4.30 a.m. and that she had smoked way too many cigarettes the night before. And then she pushed her hair behind her ears and shuffled down the corridor, to Arlette's room. The noise was louder now, like a widow at a soldier's funeral, keening, wailing, scratching at the silence.

'Coming, coming, coming.' Betty pushed down on the handle and opened the door to Arlette's room.

'What's the matter?' She tried to keep the impatience from her voice, searched her sleep-addled soul for softness and compassion. 'What?' she said more gently, switching on the bedside lamp and sitting down on the edge of the bed.

'I can't see!' said Arlette, pulling her sheets up around her neck, her eyes darting around the room. 'I can't see where I'm going!'

Betty took her hand in hers, felt the skin shift and slither around against the bone and gristle. 'Where are you going?' she asked.

'I'm going to church. And I can't see! Help me. I'll be in so much trouble!'

'Who will you be in trouble with, Arlette?'

'With Papa, of course. He trusted me. He trusted me to go on my own. For the very first time. He gave me tuppence for the collection. And now I've lost it. Will you help me? Will you help me to find it? I dropped it here, in the dark.'

Arlette patted the top of her counterpane with both hands. Betty joined in, tap-tapping the counterpane, stifling a yawn. 'I'll get you another coin,' she said. 'Wait here.'

She went to the other end of Arlette's room and picked a two-pence coin out of a jar on her dressing table. 'Here,' she said, placing it in Arlette's hand, 'here, tuppence.'

Arlette's face softened and she smiled. 'I can see now,' she said. 'It must have been an eclipse or something, because first it was bright and then it was dark and now it's bright again. An eclipse. When the moon covers the sun.' She brought the coin closer to her face and examined it. 'I'll pay you back,' she said, 'next time I see you. Where do you live?'

'Next door,' said Betty. 'I live next door.'

Arlette squinted at her. 'And are you a boy. Or a girl?'

'I'm a girl,' she smiled. 'My name's Betty. I'm your granddaughter.'

Arlette let out a whoop of laughter. 'My grand-daughter!' she said. 'Well, that's nice. I always wanted a little girl. Never wanted a boy. Never wanted any children. But particularly not a little boy.' She shuddered. 'All their little bits. Used to change his nappy with my eyes shut, y'know?' She chuckled and glanced at Betty. 'Do you have a little boy?' she asked.

Betty shook her head and stifled another yawn.

Betty could hear the chickens stirring and clucking in the back garden of the new-agers up the road. The sun was warming up the leaden darkness of the room. Last night's vodka and limes were still sloshing about in the pit of her stomach. She felt a wave of nausea and winced at a sugary repeat at the base of her throat.

'No,' she said huskily, 'no. I don't have any children. I'm only twenty-one.'

'Quite so,' said Arlette, her eyes growing heavy again. 'Quite so. Too young for all that; should be out having fun. What did you say your name was again?'

'Elizabeth,' she replied patiently.

'Like our queen. She is still the Queen, isn't she?'

Betty nodded.

'Well, I shall call you Betty. You look like a Betty. Betty

Gable. Or was it Grable? Bette Davis. Elizabeths were always called Betty in my day. Where did you say you lived again?'

'Next door,' said Betty, 'I live right next door.'

Arlette's breathing slowed then and Betty watched her crêpey eyelids flicker and shut. She waited a moment to be sure she was asleep and then she left the room.

The house was waking up. It was almost five. Betty was dehydrated and too awake now to sleep. She headed downstairs, through the empty corridors and towards the kitchen. The debris of the previous night was still there on the kitchen table. Beer cans rammed with cigarette butts, congealing bowls of vegetable curry and rice, ashtrays brimming with fag ends and ring pulls and glitzy crumpled Quality Street wrappers. Someone's baseball cap sat amidst the carnage and someone else had left a full packet of Marlboro Lights in the middle of the table. Betty groaned and poured herself a glass of water.

Bella had stayed and was sleeping upstairs, in the spare bed in Betty's room, but everyone else had piled into Mitch's camper van at some time around one, and disappeared in a puff of Nirvana and raucous laughter.

Arlette was oblivious to the parties that happened almost nightly in her house. She was bedbound now, after her stroke five years earlier, the one that had stricken her the morning after Betty's sixteenth birthday.

Betty sometimes wheeled her to the terrace at the end of their corridor to feel the sun, but Arlette asked to be taken less and less these days, lived more and more inside her own head and in the endless corridors of her remembered history.

She had a carer now, a woman called Sandra, who turned her and cleaned her and medicated her. There had been talk, of course, of moving Arlette to a home. Jolyon and Alison had moved away last year, at Alison's insistence, after the heating had packed up for the fifth winter in a row. They lived in a small two-bedroom apartment overlooking the harbour at St Peter Port, clean, new and fitted out with all mod cons. They begged Betty to come and live with them, but Betty just could not find it within herself to leave Arlette in the care of strangers every night. Alison and Jolyon visited most days but Arlette had little idea who they were any more.

Betty had chosen to do an Art diploma here in Guernsey rather than a degree in London. And she had chosen to stay on in this big cold unwelcoming house with a ninety-four-year-old woman rather than find herself a room in a shared house with her friends. She had made these choices willingly and freely, in spite of the seventy-odd years that divided them, in spite of Arlette's irascibility and her misanthropy and her unshakeably grey-tinted view of the world, because she loved her.

Arlette had lived in this house for seventy years, had given birth in this house, grown old in this house, and Betty was determined that she would die in this house, surrounded by all her lovely things. The Alzheimer's had arrived shortly after the stroke, but Betty didn't mind the

Alzheimer's. In a strange way it had softened Arlette and made her more palatable.

Betty heaped two teaspoons of instant coffee into a mug and watched the kettle on the Aga slowly bringing itself to a wild and rolling boil.

'Morning,' someone croaked behind her. It was Bella. Her long brown hair was two curtains, half drawn across her elfin face. She was fully dressed in last night's clothes: baggy jeans that sat on her pointy hipbones, cropped marled T-shirt, red hoodie and socks. Her stomach was a slice of toned white flesh between her clothes. Her mascara was smudged around her eyes and she had a scab on her lip where a cold sore was healing. But she was still about the prettiest girl that Betty had ever seen.

'Nightmares?' she asked in a husky morning tone, balling her hands up inside the sleeves of her hoodie.

Betty nodded and yawned. 'Do you want one?' she asked, gesturing at her freshly poured coffee.

'Yes. Please.'

They took their coffees out onto the back step and rested the mugs upon their knees, staring out into the new day opening up across the distant gardens.

'I'm really going to miss this place, you know,' said Bella.

Betty sighed. 'Not as much as I'm going to miss you.' She breathed in deeply against encroaching tears. Everyone was going. Everyone had left, three years ago, gone to get their degrees in more inspiring places and then some of them had come back; back to save a bit of money, help out in family businesses, gird their loins, recharge their batteries, consider their positions. But now the returners were leaving again, peeling off one by one. Including Bella. Off to Bristol for a job as a trainee zookeeper at the zoo. She was to be paid five thousand pounds a year plus free accommodation and subsidised meals. She was leaving next month. If it wasn't for Arlette, Betty would probably be going with her. As it was, she was going nowhere. She wasn't even in a position to spend a night away from the house, let alone leave the island. Betty felt like the last plum left on the tree, overripe and splitting at the seams.

'I'll be back, you know?' Bella reassured. 'Any time off I get. And then, you know . . .' She trailed off. They both knew what that 'you know' meant. It meant: *When she's dead.*

The longest living resident of Guernsey was currently one hundred and five. The longest living in the island's history had made it to one hundred and eleven. These statistics filled Betty with cold dread. She was giving away her youth to a woman who often mistook her for a boy.

'How is she? Generally?' Bella asked delicately.

'Yeah,' Betty smiled stoically. 'Healthy. Relatively.' Her smile faltered. 'It's fine. It's good. I'm fine. It's the only way.'

'Your time will come,' said Bella, squeezing Betty's thigh. 'You'll be away from this place without a backward glance and the world won't know what's hit it. Seriously.'

The sun was on the horizon now and the sky was blood

red. Already the night chill was fading into the warmth of a hot July morning.

'You know,' said Bella, 'nobody would hate you. If you left now. Nobody would blame you.'

Betty shook her head. 'I can't explain it,' she said, 'and I know nobody really understands. But I have to stay until the end. Leaving her here is not an option.'

It was hard sometimes for Betty not to feel secretly disappointed by Arlette's continuing state of aliveness. It was hard for her to understand why Arlette was still alive when Freddie Mercury, for example, was dead. There was, as far as she could tell, no real advantage to Arlette's continued existence. If anything, it brought with it numerous disadvantages, not the least of which was the fact that in order to pay for Arlette's carer and the upkeep of the house, her personal effects and savings were being depleted at an alarmingly fast rate. All her good jewellery had gone. The few pieces of quality furniture, her car and a Wedgwood tea set dating from 1825 were gone. Consequently, Betty had absolutely no financial motivation for caring for Arlette the way she did. She knew the house would go to Jolyon, Arlette had told her that. 'I suppose there has to be *some* concession to him being my son,' she'd sighed sadly. There would be trinkets and baubles, she was sure of that, but no, she was not here for the money, she was here because she couldn't leave until she knew that Arlette no longer needed her, and she knew that Arlette would need her here until she drew her last breath.

Bella squeezed her thigh again. 'Saint Betty,' she said. She yawned widely and then blew air through her lips. 'I'm going back to bed. Wake me up if I'm still there at eleven. Off to Auntie Jill's for lunch today; promised Mum I wouldn't be late.'

Betty watched her pale, skinny friend head back into the house, heard her deposit her empty mug back on the kitchen table. And then she sat and watched the sun in the sky floating higher and higher like a big orange helium balloon. When it was high enough to turn the sky blue, she too headed back to bed.

She checked briefly on Arlette before turning in. She lay exactly as she'd left her an hour earlier, neatly upon her back, arms at her sides, face slack in repose, her heavy breathing the only real evidence that she was, in fact, alive and not newly expired and laid out as for a wake.

She was about to turn and leave when she heard Arlette's sheets rustling. Arlette was awake and she was smiling. 'Is that you, Betty?' she asked quietly.

'Yes, Arlette, it's me.'

She closed her eyes, still smiling, and just before she drifted back to sleep, murmured the words: 'I love you, very much.'

'Oh,' said Betty, her stomach lurching pleasantly at her words, her hand at her heart. 'I love you too.'

6

1995

THIS Last Will & Testament is made by me ARLETTE FRANÇOISE LAFOLLEY of LAURIERS HOUSE, LAURIERS MOUNT, ST PETER PORT, GUERNSEY, BRITISH ISLES, GY1 3DG on the 22nd day of SEPTEMBER 1988.

I APPOINT as executors and trustees of my will, JOLYON ADAM LAFOLLEY OF LAURIERS HOUSE, LAURIERS MOUNT, ST PETER PORT, GUERNSEY, BRITISH ISLES, GY1 3DG, and ALISON CATHERINE DEAN OF LAURIERS HOUSE, LAURIERS MOUNT, ST PETER PORT, GUERNSEY, BRITISH ISLES, GY1 3DG and should one or more of them fail to or be unable to act I APPOINT to fill any vacancy ELIZABETH JANE DEAN OF LAURIERS HOUSE, LAURIERS MOUNT, ST PETER PORT, GUERNSEY, BRITISH ISLES, GY1 3DG.

I GIVE
(1) My home, Lauriers House, and all its furniture, to

my son JOLYON ADAM LAFOLLEY.

(2) My MG Midget to my son JOLYON ADAM LAFOLLEY.

(3) All clothes – including in particular my mink coat which, at the time of writing, is on the top shelf of my middle wardrobe – all jewellery, personal effects, ornaments, photographs, books and ornamental furnishings to my son's stepdaughter, ELIZABETH JANE DEAN OF LAURIERS HOUSE, LAURIERS MOUNT, ST PETER PORT, GUERNSEY, BRITISH ISLES, GY1 3DG. I also give Elizabeth Jane Dean the sum of ONE THOUSAND POUNDS, to be paid to her in CASH and thereafter the sum of ONE HUNDRED POUNDS to be paid to her every year on her birthday, to be spent on champagne, designer dresses and parties.

(4) The rest of my estate, including all accounts held in my name, savings accounts, pensions and bonds, to CLARA TATIANA PICKLE a.k.a. CLARA TATIANA JONES of (last known address) 12 ST ANNE'S COURT, SOHO, LONDON, W1A 2DF. If Ms Pickle/Jones is deceased these monies will revert to her children. If her children are deceased these monies will revert to her grandchildren. If she is deceased and found to have no immediate family these monies will revert to ELIZABETH JANE DEAN. If the executors have been unable to trace Ms Pickle/Jones within a one-year period of my

demise, monies will revert to ELIZABETH JANE DEAN.

I WISH my body to be BURIED in the plot reserved for me at St Agnes' Church, beside my late husband. My son, JOLYON ADAM LAFOLLEY, has already been made aware of my requirements for the style and tone of my interment and subsequent celebration. I have given him written instructions and a sum of money to cover expenses. What I would now like to add to these requirements is that I should very much like there to be jazz and dancing.

Signed,
Arlette Lafolley

The lawyer looked from Jolyon to Alison and then to Betty.

'Clara Pickle?' said Jolyon, his large neck wobbling back and forth as he shook his head blankly. 'Who the hell is Clara Pickle?' He looked at Alison. Alison shrugged. He looked at Betty. Betty shrugged. He looked at the lawyer.

The lawyer said: 'So you don't know who this woman is?'

'Do I look like I know who this woman is? Here . . .' He put out his hand and the lawyer passed his mother's last will and testament to him. Jolyon read the document, once, twice, three times.

'St Anne's Court . . .?' he muttered.

'That's in Soho,' said Betty.

'Soho? What the . . .?'

He ran a hand through what remained of his hair and looked perplexed. 'This is crazy,' he said.

'How much money are we talking about?' Alison asked.

He shrugged. 'Not much, not any more. Ten thousand, fifteen, tops. Nothing life changing, but – you know – a nice amount. It's not the money, it's just, who the hell is this woman? And why am I only just hearing about her? You were with her when she set out this will,' he said to the lawyer. 'Did she say anything about this woman?'

The lawyer lowered his gaze to the table and shook his head. 'No,' he said, 'she just spelled out the names for me. She made no mention of her identity and I didn't ask.'

'I mean, Mummy never even went to London. How could she know someone there?'

Alison and Betty just shook their heads.

'Are we legally obliged to find this person?' Jolyon asked. 'Or can we just wait for the year to elapse and let Betty take the money?'

'Yes,' the solicitor said. 'There is a legal obligation on behalf of the executor to trace this person. She would be able to sue you if it was ever discovered that no effort had been made to trace her.'

'Yes, but who the hell is she? And how are we supposed to find her?'

'Well,' said Betty, 'we could start by writing to that address.'

The lawyer shook his head. 'Mrs Lafolley did mention that she had written to that address and been told that the address is no longer residential. It's now an office for a marketing agency, or something like that. If I recall, she said that it had not been in residential use since the nineteen thirties. So that is rather a dead-end road, if you'll excuse the pun.'

'Well, it's a starting point,' said Betty. 'There must be records, somewhere, of who lived there and when.' She had come to this lawyer's office with a heavy heart and now that same heart was fluttering with excitement. First a thousand pounds. Now mysterious legatees in Soho. Her imagination crackled with potential scenarios. She saw herself pacing sleuth-like through the streets of London in Arlette's Givenchy mackintosh and a pair of patent court shoes. She envisaged herself peering at sheets of microfiche in a high-ceilinged library, making phone calls to strangers. She knew Arlette and she knew what her intent was. She wanted Betty to find her heir. It was obvious.

'I don't mind doing it,' she said breathlessly.

Everyone turned to look at her.

'I'll be happy to go,' she said.

'Go where?' said her mother.

'To London,' Betty said. 'I'll go to London. I'll find Clara.'

'You don't need to go to London,' her mother replied hastily. 'We just have to put an ad in a paper, surely?'

'Well, yes,' replied the lawyer, 'an advert in the appropriate publication would cover your legal obligations.'

'Well, then,' said Alison, 'there you go. No need to go anywhere.'

Betty blinked at her, shocked that she could have missed the point so dramatically. 'Yes,' she said, 'but I want to.'

'But, why? Why would you want to find her? If you find her, you won't get the money.'

'I don't want the money.' The words flew out of Betty's mouth before she had even thought about it. Everyone looked at her in amazement. 'I don't want the money,' she said again. 'Really.'

'But ten thousand pounds, Lizzy,' said her mother. 'Think what you could do with that. That could be a deposit on a flat. A trip around the world. A wedding.'

'A *wedding*?' Betty sneered.

'Well,' her mother shrugged, 'maybe not a wedding. But something. Something worth having.'

'Arlette already gave me everything worth having,' she said piously. 'She gave me self-esteem, self-belief. I don't need her money.' Betty exhaled, conscious of the totally ridiculous melodrama of her preceding statement. It was only half true. The money would be nice. But not as nice as the notion of leaving Guernsey with a thousand pounds in her pocket and a burning mission to find a mysterious stranger. She was twenty-two years old and any ambition she may have had (and she wasn't sure there'd ever been one) had curled up and died in the wake of her responsibilities to Arlette over the past few years.

The last year, in particular, had been the toughest. Arlette had been nothing more than a terrified bag of bones, there had been no more 'I love yous', no unintentionally funny outbursts, Bella was gone, the carer left, the summer was a washout and for a while Betty had lost herself in a fug of night-time waking, wet afternoons and loneliness. She had really felt at times that Arlette might never, never die, that she might, in fact, be trapped in the house with her breathing corpse for another ten years. And then, one morning, twelve days ago, Betty had woken with a start, eyed her alarm clock and seen with a shock the improbably late hour of 09.12 blinking at her. Then she'd known immediately, without even a moment's doubt, that Arlette was dead.

She had cried, quite unexpectedly, when she touched the cold papery skin of Arlette's bunched-together hands a moment later. She did not know whether they were tears of sadness or tears of relief. Either way, they were heartfelt. She had sat with Arlette for a full thirty minutes before she called anyone, sat and made her look the best she could. She'd combed her sparse hair, tidied her nightdress, removed her unsoiled incontinence pants and pulled her nightdress down over her legs as long as it would go. She'd wiped a tidemark of dried spittle from the corners of her mouth, dabbed some pink lipstick on with her fingertips and coloured her cheeks with a coral-tinted powder. Then she'd sat, her legs crossed together, her arms wrapped round her knees and just stared at Arlette, feeling the essence of her; the glamour, the attitude, the sharpness of her mind and her thwarted attempt at living an unconventional life, feeling it all fill the room and fill her soul, reminding her why she had loved this woman and emphasising everything that she had given to her, rather than what the final years of her life had taken away.

But suddenly it was as though it barely mattered. Suddenly Betty could look back on these last few years and smile, knowing that she had done the right thing for the right reasons and that now, *exactly* now, was absolutely the perfect moment for these binds to be severed and for her adult life finally to begin.

She would not have been ready for it before, she would not have been equipped, and now she was. And here it was, not an ambition, as such, but a mission, a goal, a *raison d'être*. Ten thousand pounds would be nice, she mused, but having a reason to get up every morning now that Arlette was gone was even nicer.

Betty pulled the coat free of its tissue fillings and let it fall to its full length. It was a generous coat, constructed from more animals than it rightly needed. It fell in folds and drapes, and cascaded to just above the mid-calf. Betty pulled it on and turned to her reflection in Arlette's full-length mirror. She laughed. She looked crazy. A small child with white-blond hair, wrapped deep inside a tent of fur. She found shoes in the bottom of Arlette's wardrobe, kicked off her canvas pumps and squeezed her feet into a pair of patent courts with small gold buckles. There. Now she stood three inches taller, inhabiting the coat slightly more convincingly. From Arlette's dressing table she took a pair of ornate paste earrings and clipped them beside her silver hoops. She ruffled her white-blond hair with her fingertips and then tried to settle it back down again into something sleeker. Still, though, she could not take herself seriously inside this thing. Still the political incorrectness of it made her half want to rip it off with enraged disgust, half want to cry with laughter. But it was hers. It belonged to her, by law. Arlette's mink was now Betty's mink.

The mink wasn't the only thing that Arlette had left for Betty on the top shelf of her middle wardrobe. There was also a book. It was *Pollyanna*, a vintage copy with an illustrated cover of a small blond girl in a bonnet and a yellow plaid dress clutching a flower basket full of white peonies. Betty opened it to the title page and found an inscription:

> To Little Miss Pickle
> I do hope that you will be a glad girl
> Yours eternally,
> Arlette Lafolley

Betty blinked at the words. *Pickle?*

Clara Pickle.

The woman in the will.

Her breath caught.

Here was a clue. The first evidence that the woman in the will existed in a moment separate from the moment at which Arlette had placed her there. She stared at the inscription for a while, trying to read something more into it, some extra dimension, some brighter light, but failed to find any.

She put the book down and pulled the collars of the fur coat together, bringing them to her nose. The coat smelled of her room, Arlette's room. It smelled of old face powder and faded perfume. It smelled of Elizabeth's childhood, long afternoons sitting at Arlette's dressing table, trying on her paste necklaces, dabbing droplets of her heady scent onto her tiny wrists and wrapping herself up in shawls and gowns and rabbit-fur stoles. It smelled of a life that Elizabeth had both adored and detested, a life of duty and of crushed dreams.

Then she appraised herself once more in Arlette's mirror and spoke out loud. 'Don't you worry, Arlette,' she said, 'I'll find her for you. Whoever on earth she is, I'll find Clara Pickle and I'll give her her book for you. I promise.'

7

Betty checked the address on the letter again, and then the number on the door. Behind her, fixed to the exterior wall of a pub was a sign saying 'Berwick Street'. On the buzzer was a sticker with 'Flat D' written on it in black marker. She was definitely in the right place. She pressed the button again and waited. Still no response. Betty glanced around her. The market was packing up. The pavement was littered with old wrappers, cabbage leaves and rotten fruit. Men were shouting very loudly about fifty pee for a pound and everything must go, the sky was Quink blue and the air smelled of stale beer and old fruit.

She had been standing here now for nearly fifteen minutes. Her rucksack sat against the wall, looking as tired and wilted as Betty felt. It had been a long, long day. But more than the tiredness of travelling, Betty was feeling the sheer, wrung-out exhaustion of the years it had taken her finally to get to this place.

But for some reason, a girl called Marni Ali, with whom Betty had had a very animated and slightly confusing phone conversation just the night before, and who had promised to meet her here at exactly six o'clock with a key to let her in, was nowhere to be seen.

Gorgeous studio flat
Central Soho location
Adjacent to famous Berwick Street Market
£400 a month + bills

There'd been no picture. 'Adjacent' had suggested 'alongside', 'close to', 'a few metres from'. Not 'right in the screaming, squirming middle of'. Betty pulled her fur coat tighter around her body and shivered.

She'd taken the first flat she'd been offered by an agency she'd phoned the day after Arlette's funeral. They'd faxed across the details to her mum's office.

'Four hundred pounds a month!' her mother had exclaimed. 'That sounds an awful lot. Just for a studio.'

'Yes,' she'd countered huffily, 'but it's in *Soho*.'

'Well, yes, I can see that. But surely there must be something cheaper?'

'No,' Betty had said, snatching the fax from her mother's hand. 'This is fine. This is perfect. It's just been redecorated and it's available from next Wednesday. I don't want to wait another minute. I've waited enough minutes. I want this flat.'

'Well,' her mother had sighed, 'you're a grown woman. You can make your own decisions. But Arlette's money isn't going to last very long if you're spending that much on rent. When I lived in London I had a tiny room in a house out on the end of the Piccadilly line. And I could be in Soho in twenty-two minutes flat.'

'But you don't understand. When you're on a tube, you're *leaving* Soho. I don't want to leave Soho. I want to *live* there.'

Her mother had sighed again. 'So. You've got enough rent money for ten weeks. Then what happens?'

'It's fine,' Betty had assured her. 'I'll get a job. I won't need Arlette's money for long.'

'A job? In London? With a B.Tech in General Art and Design? And no work experience? Oh my God.' Her mother had clasped her ears as though trying to keep Betty's ill-thought-out plans from torturing them.

'It will be *fine*.' Betty folded her arms across her chest.

'There'll be thirty people lined up behind you for every job you apply for. All of them with more experience than you!'

'Yes!' she'd snapped. 'I know! But they won't be *me*, will they?'

She'd paused then, and stared at her mother for a second or two. She had shocked herself. She had always been a self-confident girl. Especially since moving to Guernsey and being picked out for special favour, first by Bella and then by Arlette. In all her years on that little speck of rock and soil in the middle of the English Channel, Betty had always floated somewhere above everything, in her big house, high above the sea, with her beautiful face, her quirky style, and latterly, of course, her saint-like commitment to the care of an age-ravaged lady right up until her final, unheard exhalation. Everyone knew who Betty Dean was. Everyone knew where she lived.

So it stood to reason, in Betty's opinion, that she and Soho were made for each other, that they were soul mates, a perfect fit. She had no concerns about being accepted and about fitting in. She was, she believed, entirely to the manner born.

Except that this girl called Marni didn't seem to have noticed. This girl called Marni was not here to greet her, to welcome Betty warmly and effusively to her new life. Instead, Betty was standing alone in the dark, invisible and slightly terrified. She breathed in deeply to stop herself crying and then scanned the street up and down for a payphone. She spied one to her left but it was at a critical distance from the flat. If this Marni girl arrived while she was on the phone, she would not know she was there and might just flit away again. She cast around helplessly, hoping for inspiration, and then she saw a man, late twenties, early thirties, hauling old LPs into boxes on the stall closest to where she stood.

'Excuse me?'

'Yes,' he replied, slightly impatiently.

'I need to make a phone call, but I'm supposed to be meeting someone here.' She pointed at the front door. 'Will you be here for the next few minutes?'

He looked at her uncertainly as though she had just spoken to him in Mandarin.

'What?' he said.

Betty sighed. She had had a very long day and she could see that charm and articulacy would be wasted on this man. 'I'm going to make a phone call,' she said abruptly. 'If a woman turns up here, can you tell her I'm over there? Please?'

She didn't wait for him to reply, just hitched her rucksack over her shoulder and stomped off to the phone booth.

The interior of the booth was rank, urine-sodden, damp and covered in graffiti. As Betty tapped in Marni's phone number, she looked at the patchwork of calling cards attached to the walls with blobs of Blu-Tack. Asian babes. Earth mothers. African queens. Busty beauties. Naughty schoolgirls. Basques, whips, boots, lips, stockings, nails, heels. A dazzling collage of commercial sexual opportunities.

'Oh, hello,' she began as the phone was answered by a man with an Asian accent. 'Is Marni there, please?'

'No, she's not, I'm afraid. Who is this calling, please?'

'My name is Betty Dean, I'm . . .' But she tailed off as a face appeared at the window of the booth and beamed at her. The face was dark and large-featured, kohled eyes, full lips, black hair hanging straight and glossy from underneath a cream pull-on hat, studded nostril and hoop earrings. She was clutching a folder under her arm and mouthing the word 'sorry'.

'Actually,' said Betty to the man on the phone, 'don't worry, it's fine.' She hung up.

'Oh God,' said the girl, 'I am *so sorry*. I got called away to an emergency. Another tenant. *A rat*,' she hissed con-spiratorially. 'But, oh God, I probably shouldn't have told you that. Seriously. You do not need to worry about rats. You're on the second floor. This one was in a basement. In Paddington. I hate basement flats. Never, ever live in a basement flat. Especially not in London. No light at all.'

'And rats,' said Betty, drolly.

'Well, yes, and rats. Anyway,' Marni beamed, 'I'm here now.'

'Did that guy up there tell you where I was?'

'Yes,' she smiled. 'He did. Told me there was a moody girl in a fur coat waiting for me up here.' She laughed.

'Oh,' said Betty, picking up her rucksack and letting the door of the phone booth close behind her. 'I think he'll find that he was the grumpy one, actually.'

She followed Marni back towards the flat, deliberately averting her gaze from the trader.

'She found you then?' he asked brusquely.

She looked at him and nodded, feeling a warm flush rising up her neck. 'Yes,' she said, matching him in tone. 'Thank you.'

'Come on,' said Marni, holding the door ajar for her, 'let's get you settled.'

Betty nodded and followed her into the downstairs hall, past a payphone on the wall with all its wires hanging out like entrails, and up a tight staircase painted buttermilk and streaked with mildew.

'Da-dah!' announced Marni on the top landing. 'This is it.'

She unlocked the door and pushed it open.

Betty didn't really know what she'd been expecting. She hadn't really thought beyond: FLAT IN SOHO. Or NEWLY DECORATED. She hadn't considered the possibility that NEWLY DECORATED might mean CHEAP WHITE PAINT SLAPPED ALL OVER LUMPY WALLS. And CORK FLOORING PEELING SLIGHTLY IN PLACES. And OLD METAL VENETIAN BLINDS GIVEN A WIPE DOWN WITH A DAMP CLOTH. Not to mention NEWLY REPLACED BARE BULBS HANGING FROM DUSTY LIGHT FITTINGS and NASTY AZTEC-PRINT SOFA COVERS GIVEN A QUICK SPIN AND SHRINKING SLIGHTLY BEFORE BEING STRETCHED BACK OVER TOO BIG SOFA.

Neither did her fantasies about FLAT IN SOHO really sufficiently prepare her for a living room that was, fundamentally, a low-ceilinged box with a kitchen counter glued to one wall and a small window on the other, with barely enough room to stretch out on the sofa without scuffing your toes against the skirting board on the other side of the room. This, she quickly concluded, was not a flat. This was a corridor with a piece of furniture in it.

Yet still the effusive Marni smiled at her with sheer delight, as though she had just shown her the presidential suite at the Savoy.

'Here's your kitchenette,' she said gleefully, pointing to the three cheap units screwed to the wall, an elderly brown microwave and a two-ring Baby Belling.

'Fridge here,' she announced, pulling open the rust-speckled door of a miniature fridge, just large enough to house two pints of milk and a box of eggs. 'And there's plenty of storage space.' She opened and closed a couple of flimsy doors, one of which almost fell off completely as she did so. 'Having said that, we do find that our tenants in this area tend not to have much need for kitchen space. Why cook, when you can eat out every night at a different restaurant?'

It seemed to Betty that this girl, Marni, had looked neither at her nor in any detail at this flat. If she had, Betty pondered, it would be immediately obvious that she had just stepped off a ferry, that she had all her worldly possessions in a tatty rucksack and was clearly going to be paying so much rent for this tiny unprepossessing toilet cubicle of an apartment that dining out every night was not going to be an option.

'Where do you live?' asked Betty.

'In Pinner,' Marni replied brightly, in a tone that suggested this 'Pinner' to be a most desirable locale. 'It's in Middlesex,' she continued, 'commuter belt. Metropolitan line. I live with my mum and dad.'

Betty nodded knowingly. This girl knew as much about glamorous Soho lifestyles as she did.

She showed Betty the sleeping area, a mezzanine in the living area, accessed via a wooden stepladder, with a curtained area underneath housing a free-standing clothes rail and cheap chest of drawers.

The bathroom was, in fact, the nicest room in the flat,

apparently the recipient of the majority of the redecorating budget, nicely tiled and very modern.

'Well,' said Marni, half an hour later, after some form-filling and tea-drinking and the handing over of a cheque for two months' rent, 'I'll leave you to settle in. And remember, anything you need, just shout. My boss has a mobile phone so you should be able to get hold of him twenty-four/seven. Here's his number, and, well, *enjoy*!'

Betty watched her leave a moment later, her dark head disappearing into the crowds below. She had a bounce in her step, the bounce of a carefree person, of a girl who had not yet asked herself any meaningful questions about her existence.

Betty watched her from the window until she'd disappeared from view and then her gaze fell upon the market trader, still packing up his stall, hefting the last of the boxes into a small white van. He was chatting to another man. She could hear him laughing, see him smiling. She examined him more closely now that he was at a distance: mid-brown hair, cut shaggy around his face in that style beloved of modern pop stars. He wore combats, an oversized sweatshirt, a leather jacket. He looked about twenty-eight, she reckoned, with an athletic physique and a strong profile.

Suddenly he looked up at the window and his gaze met hers, and Betty gasped and fell to her knees.

'Oh *shit*,' she whispered angrily to herself, 'shit.'

She let herself slide slowly to the floor, her back against

the wall, shame and embarrassment coursing through her veins. She sighed loudly.

And then, for the first time since she'd rung the doorbell downstairs and realised that there was no one there to let her in, she felt a small wave of excitement building within her. This place was not what she'd imagined it would be, it was not the shadowy high-ceilinged flat in which she would pace around smoking Gauloises and being moody and interesting. But it was clean and it was warm and, more than that, it was in Soho. Right in the middle of Soho. She got to her feet and turned once more to the window. She gazed out at the now-black sky, not a star to be seen in it, and she felt reality hit her, head-on.

She was here.

She was here.

Her real life had finally begun.

8

1919

Arlette De La Mare adjusted her hat, a grey tweed cloche, ordered in from Paris, especially for her trip, worn at a jaunty angle and down low upon her forehead. She pressed the porcelain doorbell and cleared her throat. A moment later the large red door was opened by a nervous-looking housemaid in a frilled white cap.

'Good evening, miss, can I help you?'

'Yes, I am Miss De La Mare. I'm here to visit Mrs Miller.'

'Oh, yes, of course. They're expecting you. Do come in.'

She pulled open the door and led Arlette into a large hallway from which arose two ornately carved mahogany staircases and in the centre of which stood a vast marble jardinière holding a vase of oversized Stargazer lilies and red-hot pokers. She followed the housemaid into a small room at the back of the house, which was furnished with two bergère armchairs upholstered in sage velvet, and a large japanned standard lamp. The room looked out onto a long lawned garden, which ended in a small wooded area and a tall wall, curtained in rusty-red Virginia creeper. The housemaid offered Arlette tea and cordial, and left the room.

Arlette's toes were sore, squeezed for too long inside velvet T-bar slippers, with a small heel. She should not have travelled in heels – her mother had said as much when she saw her off at the port that morning – but the suit she was wearing, a grey linen affair with a lean, almost angular silhouette, had demanded something feminine to soften it. She had not, after all, wanted to appear butch for her first visit to London, especially not to the home of her mother's best friend, Mrs Leticia Miller.

After a moment she heard a small burst of laughter in the hallway and there was Leticia, all daffodil-coloured curls and ostentatiously blue eyes.

'Lovely, lovely Arlette, in London at last. First, the blasted war then the blasted 'flu, keeping you from us for so long. So nice to finally have everything back to normal and to finally get you here.'

She clasped Arlette's hands in hers and stared fondly into her eyes for long enough to make her feel self-conscious. 'Last time I saw you, you were just a child. What were you, twelve, thirteen years old? Goodness, and now look at you. A woman, a lovely, remarkable woman. Now, tell me, did you have a good trip? How was the crossing? Have you asked for some tea? You must be quite worn out.'

Arlette placed her hands upon her lap and smiled politely. 'I am, rather, yes. I was awake at four a.m. to make the ferry.'

'Well, you have made it to your destination, still looking so pretty, and now all you have to do is make yourself at home and do as you wish until you get your energy back. Can I get you something to lift your spirits? A little Americano?'

Arlette smiled. She did not know what an Americano was but assumed it was a cocktail of some description. 'Why not?' she said. 'Yes, please.'

Leticia got to her feet and opened a cabinet behind her. Arlette admired her silhouette, the way her exquisite clothes fell from her slender, boyish body, not the body of a forty-year-old woman, not the body of her own rather solid and round-shouldered mother; not, in fact, the body of most women Arlette had yet encountered. Her yellow hair fell from a loose bun at the nape of her neck in soft baby-hair curls and her feet were bare. Arlette had never before seen a person in their own home standing without their shoes. She stared at the narrow ridge of bone that ran from Leticia's slender foot to the back of her ankle. It sent a shiver of pleasure through her, that hint of something new and brave.

She listened to the clinking of bottles, the fizz of bubbles, the chink of ice and Leticia's plummy chatter, all talk of people she'd never heard of, and plays she really must go and see, and swanky restaurants she'd love to take her to. Arlette nodded and hmmed and mmmed, and tried her hardest to be the sophisticated young lady that Leticia had already decided she must be.

Leticia passed her the Americano and, through sheer

thirst – the inside of her mouth was as dry as a desert – she drank it rather too fast and found herself drunk almost immediately. As the tight corners of her mind slackened and billowed, she felt herself strangely cocooned. It was as though this was a place where nothing bad had ever happened, and Leticia was a woman to whom nothing bad had ever happened, and while she was here, in this room, with this woman, all would be well for evermore. She heard footsteps against the tiles in the hallway and more laughter.

'Lilian!' Leticia called around the half-open door. 'Is that you?'

'Yes, Mother, what is it?' The voice sounded sulky but affectionate.

'Come into the snug. I want you to meet someone.'

Arlette heard a small sigh, and then more footsteps.

'Lilian, darling, this is Arlette De La Mare. Dolly's girl.'

A tiny slip of a thing sidled through the door, big blue eyes like her mother, soft blond hair hanging long down her back in a plait. She was unthinkably pretty and wearing a dress that immediately made Arlette feel like a large ungainly man: lace and chiffon, in a shade of faded rose, low-waisted and demure with little pearls and rosettes of lace stitched all across it.

'Good evening,' she said, smiling and striding confidently across the room to shake Arlette by the hand, although she was, according to Arlette's mother, only seventeen years old. 'How lovely to meet you. Mother has told me all about your mother and her, and their strange childhood in the middle of the English Channel. I believe you are staying with us for a while?'

'Yes,' said Arlette, cursing herself for the almost perceptible slur of her words and for allowing herself to feel intimidated by a seventeen-year-old girl. 'I'm here until I can find appropriate lodgings. I'm hoping to get a job of some description.'

'Well, don't feel you need to get a job and lodgings on my account. I'm delighted to have another girl in the house; too many boys as it is.'

Leticia had three boys, apparently. They were aged between sixteen and five. Two of them were at boarding school. The smallest one, Arlette assumed, was in bed.

'I do hope you'll be coming to my birthday party. It's on Saturday night. It's to be a masked ball.'

'Oh,' said Arlette. 'When is your birthday?'

'It's tomorrow, in fact. I shall be eighteen.'

'Well, what a coincidence. It's my birthday on Saturday. And I shall be twenty-one.'

'Oh, well, then, you have completely stolen my thunder.' She held a delicate hand to her face, dramatically, in a gesture that Arlette could see had been entirely stolen from her mother's repertoire. 'Twenty-one,' she sighed, 'a grown-up. How utterly glorious. We shall have to make it a joint celebration.'

'Oh, no need,' said Arlette. 'My mother has already thrown me a party. Last weekend.'

'Well, we shall raise a glass in your direction then, at least. Now, if you'll excuse me, I have somebody else's birthday party to rush off to. Mother, can I take the paste drop earrings from your stand, the new ones? Please . . .?'

Leticia wrinkled her pretty nose at her pretty daughter and then smiled. 'You may,' she said, 'but do not under any circumstances lose them. Your father will be very cross.'

Lilian smiled and winked at Arlette. 'I have my mother wrapped round my little finger,' she said in a faux whisper. And then she exited.

'She's right,' sighed Leticia. 'Seventeen going on twenty-seven. She's almost out of control. When I was her age it would have been unthinkable – a party, unescorted. But that's the way things are these days. Apparently, as a parent I'm to take a step back and let her go.' She sighed again. 'Ah well, I suppose I must trust that I've raised her well and that she won't do anything to shame me and her father. Now,' she clapped her hands together, 'some supper. You must be ravenous. I think Susan has made her famous lamb and mint cutlets. I'll show you to your room, and then when you've had a chance to freshen up, I'll meet you in the dining hall. Say, in half an hour?'

Arlette's room was small but very pretty, overlooking the garden square and the street. She rested her bag at her feet and stared for a while through the heavy curtains. She was in Kensington. Near Holland Park. The house was a stucco villa and Leticia was Arlette's mother's best friend from home, who'd married an incomer and left the island *tout de suite* when her husband's firm had offered him a promotion to their London office. 'She's a true one-off,' her mother had said, with a light in her eye that Arlette only ever saw when her mother talked about people whom she perceived to be somehow 'better' than herself. 'She will show you the world through beautiful eyes.'

Arlette had never been away from home before. But life was different on the island now. The war had ripped the heart out of the place. A thousand men, dead and gone. Including her own father. Before the war the island had been prosperous and growing more prosperous. Now it was a place of tragedy and open wounds. Arlette had felt restless and out of place for months. Then, one afternoon, watching her daughter staring restlessly out to sea, her mother had taken her hands in hers and said, 'Now. Go now. I don't need you any more.'

And so she had. On a soft September day, with no idea what on earth she was going to do once she got here. So, she would take it one step at a time. First a wash. Then some lamb and mint. And then, she supposed, somehow or other, the rest of her life would begin to unfurl, as mysterious and unknown as a well-kept secret.

9

1995

'It's *beautiful*,' Betty told her mother in a voice full of forced enthusiasm. 'Really gorgeous. Lovely modern bathroom.'

Her mother sounded unconvinced. 'I should hope so,' she said, 'for that money. And what's the security like.'

'The . . .?'

'You know. Locks on the doors? That kind of thing?'

'It's fine. Locks and chains and everything.' She had no idea if there were locks and chains and everything, she hadn't really been paying any attention.

'And what are the neighbours like?'

Neighbours? 'You don't *have* neighbours in Soho, Mum.'

'Well, the area, then, what's it like? Is it safe?'

She thought of the group of leering long-haired men outside the pub opposite, who'd just shouted, 'Hello, blondie,' to her as she left her flat, and the thumping bass of heavy metal emanating from its open door, and she smiled and said, 'It feels safe, yes. Safe enough.'

Her mother emitted a long, meaningful sigh.

'Mum!' snapped Betty.

'I'm sorry,' she said, 'it's just, *Soho*. Of all the places.

You could at least have eased yourself in with a few weeks at Grandma's. Got a feel for the place.'

'I've just spent the past twelve years of my life living with an old woman. I love my grandma but I do not want to live with her. Not even for a day.'

Her mother sighed again. 'Fair enough,' she said. 'But I can't help worrying.'

'Mum, I'm twenty-two years old! All my friends have been living away from home since they were teenagers!'

'Exactly!' said her mother. 'Exactly. They've had time to find their feet. Student life is not the same as real life.'

'I actually think I'm safer here than at Arlette's house. Out there, on that cliff, all alone. Anything could have happened. At least here I'm insulated.'

'Yes, but you're also anonymous. Everyone knew you here. Everyone had an eye open for you. There's no one there to keep an eye on you.'

'Well, that's not true actually . . .' She paused to drop another twenty-pence piece into the coin slot. 'That's not true. I've already made friends with the man who runs the market stall outside my flat. He'll keep an eye on me. And the girl from the agency, she knows I'm here. That's two people, and I've only been here a couple of hours.'

'Hmm, well . . .' Her mother sounded tired. 'Just be careful, that's all. Just be careful. You're my special girl. I couldn't bear it if something happened to you. I love you so much . . .'

'I know, I know.' Betty swallowed down her distaste for the words. She didn't want to be loved by her mother, not right now. 'Look, I've run out of coins. I've got to go. I'll call you tomorrow,' she said, 'or maybe the day after.'

'Tomorrow,' said her mother. 'Call me tomorrow.'

'I'll try,' she said. 'Love to Jolyon. Love to everyone. Bye.'

She hung up as the pips signalled the end of her money.

She exhaled and let herself lean heavily against the wall of the booth. The phone call had been an ordeal. She was not in the mood for having a mother. She wanted to spend a few days, maybe even longer, pretending she didn't have one, pretending to be rootless and unconnected. She had just left an island and now she wanted to be one.

She pushed her way out of the booth and put her hands into the pockets of the lightweight coat she'd packed into her rucksack in the early hours of that morning. She had ten pounds in her purse and was on a mission for basic provisions: milk, a microwave meal, some cereal and some tea.

The world came towards her like a computer game as she attempted to stroll nonchalantly through the streets. She had not taken a map with her. A map would have marked her out as a day-tripper. She would learn the streets of Soho using her instincts and her internal compass. Yes, she would.

She pushed her chest out and she put her hand into her handbag, feeling for the softness of her tobacco pouch, cursing internally when she realised she had left it in the flat. She needed a cigarette now, she needed a prop, she was walking funny, she could feel it, too much to the left, her right foot was dragging a bit. She cursed as she came off the edge of a kerb, her ankle twisting awkwardly. She had to break her fall with a hand on the pavement and she felt the skin come away from the heel of her hand as she did so. 'Fuck,' she muttered under her breath. 'Bollocks.' She pulled herself upright and rubbed away at the scuffed skin, not daring to look around her to see who might have seen her inelegant tumble. She carried on her way, turning left, turning right, wishing for a cigarette, wishing for a friend, wishing for . . . *a bowl of Chinese noodles in a tiny scruffy café with scuffed Formica tabletops and a dreamy-looking waiter standing with arms crossed, staring through the window into the middle distance.*

She hurled herself through the door of the café. It was called, somewhat unimaginatively, Noodle Bar.

Here, she thought, I'll start here.

The skies opened above her as she felt her way cautiously homewards an hour later, using her as yet untested internal compass. The rain fell hard as knitting needles, bouncing off the pavements and all over her cherry-red shoes. She had no umbrella. She had not even packed an umbrella. She would have to buy an umbrella. She could not begin to imagine where in Soho she might be able to buy herself an umbrella. Arlette's house had had an elephant's foot in the hallway, trimmed with brass and filled with umbrellas of various sizes. Betty had very much taken umbrellas for granted for the whole of her life until this exact moment.

Her internal compass took her to most of the streets of Soho over the course of the next hour. The rain obfuscated the world, turned it into one indistinguishable mass of tarmac, brick and glass, and when finally she found herself standing opposite what she now thought of as 'her' phone booth, she almost laughed out loud with joyful relief. She'd made it. Against all the odds and without asking anyone for directions, she had found her way back.

The flat felt unexpectedly welcoming as she turned the key in the lock and let herself in.

Home, she thought, I'm home.

She ran herself a deep bath and lay in it for an hour, feeling the water warming her bones. The bathwater sent rippling shadows across the ceiling, and the steam ran down the windows in rivers, and there it was: peace, solitude, Betty Dean, having a bath, in Soho, as though it was the most normal thing in the world.

Afterwards she poured herself a glass of cider and took three roll-ups and a box of matches onto the fire escape that led off the landing outside her front door. By now the sky was inky dark, but the rain had stopped. The fire escape looked out over the scruffy backs of other buildings. Below her she saw two restaurant workers sitting with their backs to the wall, smoking cigarettes and talking to each other in a language she could not name. She could hear the clank of pots and pans through another open window and smell curry spices toasting. The men below laughed out loud and then made their way back inside. And there, in the diagonal corner, Betty noticed what looked like a proper house: clean brickwork, three storeys, six windows, including one full-length window in the middle, which gave her a view of a funky chandelier and a piece of anarchic art. It warmed her, strangely, to think that among all these pubs and market stalls, restaurants and fabric shops, there lived a human being with nice taste in interiors.

That night Betty slept fitfully and uncomfortably. The street below was loud and unsleeping. When she woke the following morning she felt haggard and ill. But as she pulled open the curtains she smiled.

She had not, after all, come to Soho to sleep.

That morning she decided to find a library. There was no telephone directory in her flat and she wanted to look up Clara Pickle. It was a slim chance, and she was sure that Arlette must have tried directory enquiries over the years, but still, it was worth a bash. As she walked out onto the street she saw the record-seller was putting out his pitch opposite her front door. He was wearing a hat today, a kind of fisherman's affair, black felt with a small metal badge on the front. Two curls of hair flicked out from either side like dancers' legs. The silly bits of hair softened his appearance, put Betty at her ease. That and the fact that she suspected that with her hair up, and without Arlette's incongruous fur, he probably wouldn't notice her anyway. So she picked up her pace, kept her eyes to the pavement and marched determinedly onwards although she had not a clue where she was supposed to be heading.

'Morning,' he said.

She stopped mid-step. Then she turned. 'Oh,' she said, 'hello.'

'How are you settling in?'

Betty couldn't speak for a moment, so taken aback was she by his friendly interaction.

'Fine,' she said, after a moment. 'Just, er, popping out.'

He nodded at her and looked as though he were about to end the conversation, but then: 'I know someone you could sell the fur to,' he said almost nervously, 'if you're interested?'

'Sell it?'

'Yeah. The fur coat. I assume you want to sell it. It being a bit of an obsolescence and all.'

'Oh,' Betty said. 'Yes. I hadn't really thought. But, yes. Maybe I should.'

'It's my sister. She runs a clothing agency. For TV and film and stuff. She's always looking for furs. Hard to find these days, apparently.'

'Wow,' she said, 'what a brilliant job to have.'

'Well, yeah, our dad's an antiques dealer, our mum's an auctioneer – old stuff kind of runs in our blood.' He smiled and Betty noticed that when he smiled his crow's-feet fanned out like peacocks' tails and the groove between his eyebrows completely disappeared. 'Anyway,' he continued, his smile straightening out, the crow's-feet regrouping, the groove resetting, 'think about it. She's only up the road. Let me know.'

'I will, thank you. Yes.' She turned away first, slightly flushed by the encounter. She was about to head on her way when it occurred to her that this man might be a good source of local knowledge. 'I'm looking for a library,' she said. 'Do you know if there's one round here?'

He raised a curious eyebrow. 'No idea,' he said. 'Not much of a reader. Toff,' he called to the man on the next stall, 'is there a library round here?'

'Yeah,' Toff said, 'of course there is.' And he gave Betty directions.

The route to the library took her past the front of the house she'd seen from behind the night before, facing out onto Peter Street. She stopped for a moment and appraised it. Its windows were taped over with opaque film and the front door was painted shocking pink, with the number 9 nailed to it. Betty extinguished a roll-up beneath the heel of her trainer and put her hands into her pockets. She studied the building for a moment or two, trying to gauge its significance. It meant something to her, in some odd way, either from her past – had she seen it when she was in Soho with her mother all those years ago? – or in her future. She was sure she'd seen that door before, seen that oversized '9', those obscured windows.

She shook her head slightly and carried on her way. In the library she thumbed her way through twelve London telephone directories. In a small notepad she wrote down the numbers of seventeen people called C Pickle. She didn't even bother with the C Joneses. Then she bought chocolate bars, tobacco and chewing gum in three separate shops, paid for with notes, breaking them up for change.

When she got home, she came upon a man in a logoed polo shirt and a matching fleece doing something to the telephone in the hallway.

'Oh,' she said, 'hello.'

The man did not return her greeting, just looked up at her and then back again to the wires trailing from the innards of the phone unit.

'Are you fixing it?' she asked.

'No,' he said dully, 'I'm vandalising it.'

She peered at him through squinted eyes for a second, silently measuring his tone.

'Ha ha,' she said, 'but seriously? Are you?'

'Yes,' he said. 'I am attempting to fix your telephone. In fact,' he plucked a red wire and then plucked a yellow wire and then leaned back and appraised the situation, 'I'm pretty sure I have just fixed your telephone.' He pulled a mobile phone from his bag and pressed in a number. The phone in the hallway rang. He smiled. Then he pulled a twenty-pence piece from his pocket, punched a number into the payphone and the phone in his other hand rang.

'Sorted,' he said. 'All yours.'

Betty stared at the phone in some surprise for a moment or two after the engineer had left. She had a phone. And seventeen phone calls to make. What a piece of luck.

Betty dialled all seventeen numbers for C Pickle that morning. Of the thirteen people who answered not one had ever heard of Clara. The other four numbers were either disconnected or had not replied. But Betty had suspected as much. There was no way it could have been that easy. If it had been that easy, she mused, then Arlette would have tracked Clara Pickle down years ago. Betty appraised the five twenty-pence pieces left in her hand and called Bella.

'Guess who's calling you, live, from their Soho penthouse?'

'What?'

'Berwick Street. Top floor. Just around the corner from the Raymond Revuebar.'

'Seriously?'

'Yes! I just moved in! Yesterday!'

'Wow! I don't believe it. Finally!'

'I know, at the ripe old age of twenty-two.'

'So, how is it?'

'It's . . . fine, it's . . .' Betty was about to say, 'it's amazing' but as she started to form the words in her mouth she felt tears suddenly overwhelm her.

'Oh, Betty, sweetheart, are you OK?'

'Yes!' said Betty, trying to pull the tears back down inside. 'Yes! I'm fine. It's just all a bit, you know . . . Arlette dying, the funeral, coming here, everything's changed so quickly, after being the same for so long.'

'Oh, Bets, of course you're feeling weird. Are you alone?'

'Yes, just little old me.'

'No flatmate?'

'No,' she sighed, 'no. It's a studio.'

'Wow,' said Bella, 'that must be costing you a fortune.'

'Kind of,' said Betty. 'I guess. Arlette left me a thousand pounds. This place is four hundred a month. I've paid for two months up front . . .'

'So you'll have blown the lot on rent by the summer? And then what?'

'Oh God, I don't know. I'm going to get a job. And . . .' She paused. She'd been about to say, *if I can't find the woman in Arlette's will I'll be getting ten thousand pounds, so I don't need to worry too much about money*, but kept the thought to herself. She *would* find the woman in the will. She was determined to. 'I'll get a job,' she said.

'No! Betty Dean, getting a job. No way!'

'Well, it's about time.'

'Good grief, what sort of job?'

'No idea. Maybe an art gallery? A boutique? An auction house? Somewhere I can start at the bottom and work my way up.'

'Excellent,' Bella said. 'Have you even got a CV?'

'Ha,' Betty laughed, 'and what would it say if I did? "1990–1995: Squeezed an unexceptional B.Tech Diploma in General Art and Design in around caring for crazed old lady. The End."' She sighed. 'I don't think I'm really a CV type of a person. I think people will just have to take me as they find me.'

'Hmm.'

Betty groaned. She hated it when people said 'hmm'. 'Hmm, what?'

'Nothing. Just, you're in London now. As amazing as you are, I'm not sure just being "you" is going to be enough to get you the job of your dreams.'

'Urgh, God,' Betty groaned. 'You sound just like my mother.'

'I *am* just like your mother. That's why you love me so much. And she's right.' Bella paused. 'Well, maybe we're both wrong and you're right. But either way I agree with her. It wouldn't hurt to put something in writing. Talk yourself up a bit. Maybe you could say you were, God, I don't know, Arlette's personal assistant?'

Betty laughed. 'Not too far from the truth, I suppose.'

'Exactly!'

'I know what you're saying. But I think I'll try it my way first.' Betty smiled.

'Yes,' said Bella, 'of course you will. You always, always do.' They fell quiet for a moment. 'So,' said Bella. 'When are you coming to visit?'

'Was just about to ask you the same thing. Have you got any holiday coming up?'

'Not until next month. Why don't you come down here?'

Betty paused and pondered the suggestion. She envisaged Bella's bleak lodgings in a tumbledown cottage in a remote village just outside the zoo. She thought of cold fingers wrapped around chipped mugs of tea and condensation-covered windows looking out over tangled gardens and cool, flagstoned kitchens and early morning birdsong. She shuddered. She'd only just arrived in the kingdom of sirens and neon and filth and chaos, and double yellow lines as far as the eye could see. She could not yet countenance the prospect of a return to the countryside, even if it was to see her oldest, most-loved friend.

'Yes,' she said, 'maybe.'

10

The stallholder was outside when Betty left the house the next morning.

She glanced at him awkwardly, and was taken aback when he smiled at her. 'Morning, neighbour,' he said.

'Oh. Hi.'

'Any more thoughts about the coat?'

'Oh. Yes, definitely. Yes. I want to sell it.'

'I mentioned it to my sister. She said to take it round to her studio. Any time.'

'Any time, now?'

He shrugged. 'Yeah, now would be OK.'

Betty hurtled back upstairs to retrieve the coat.

'Here . . .' He was feeling his pockets rather randomly. She watched him as he did so, noticing that his fingers were long and slender, that he had a tattoo on the inside of his wrist and that his eyes were so brown they were almost black. 'Here.' He pulled a small card from the inside pocket of his jacket, and handed it to her.

She glanced at it.

Alexandra Brightly.

Betty smiled. 'Is that your name, too?' she asked. 'Brightly?'

'Yeah,' he smirked. 'John Brightly. I know. Not exactly fitting. Or maybe,' he continued, deadpan, 'I've deliberately played against type all my life.'

Betty laughed. 'It's nice,' she said. 'I like it.'

He smirked again and then turned, almost abruptly, away from her.

'Thank you,' she said to his back. 'Thank you very much.'

'No problem,' he said.

And that appeared to be the end of their exchange.

She stood, for a moment, suspended in an air pocket of uncertainty, wondering what she should do next. A propos of nothing she turned left, and then left again. She found herself outside the nice house on Peter Street. As she passed by, she noticed across the street a man with a large camera in one hand and a mug of coffee in the other. He was wearing a baseball cap and sunglasses, although the sky was far from blue. As she watched, another man joined him, also carrying a camera and a cup of coffee. They seemed to know each other, and made a few words of low-key conversation. Then they both turned and faced the house on Peter Street, as though waiting for something to happen. She watched them both for a moment or two, before realising that she now looked as strange as they did and hurrying on her way.

Alexandra Brightly's studio was called 20th Century Box

and was next to the Oasis Sports Centre in Covent Garden. It was up two flights of scruffy stairs in a soulless building shared with a tailor and a photographer.

'Yes?'

'Hi, my name's Betty, your brother, John, gave me your card. I've got a fur to sell.'

'Oh. Cool. OK. Come in! Second floor!'

The woman greeting Betty at the top of the stairs was tall and painfully thin, with long white-blond hair and a rather beaky nose. She was so pale, the blue of her eyes so watered down, that she almost gave the impression of albinism. She was dressed in a black chiffon shirt, a large crucifix on an overlong chain resting in the wide valley between her small breasts, and baggy jeans held together at her waist with an old leather belt. She held a fake cigarette in her right hand.

'Wow, wow, wow,' she said as her gaze fell upon the fur held like a slaughtered animal in Betty's arms. 'Wow,' she said again, resting the fake cigarette on a pattern-cutting table and putting an arm out towards the coat, running fingers as long as chopsticks through the fur. 'This looks fucking awesome. Fuck. I fucking *love* fur.'

Her voice was husky and smoky and her accent was half public school, half East End. She smiled at Betty, revealing smoker's teeth. 'Sorry,' she said, 'I get a bit carried away sometimes. Especially by the fur. It's so wrong, yet it's mm,' she caressed the fur again, 'sooo right. Let's have a look then.' She pulled half-moon glasses from the pattern-cutting table and rested them halfway down her aquiline nose. 'Oh, yes,' she said, now that the fur was unfolded on the table, 'oh, yes. This is amazingly good. Where did you say you got it from?'

'It was my grandmother's.'

'Class act,' she said, opening it up and feeling the lining. 'Oh yes, it's a Gloria Maurice. I thought it would be. They always put an extra couple of animals in, just for the hell of it, you know.' She peered at Betty over the top of her glasses and smiled. 'Yeah,' she said, turning back to the fur. 'I could definitely buy this from you. Definitely. I'm working with a production company right now, as it happens, on a period drama – nineteen forties – they'll love this. Let's have a proper look at it.' She swivelled an Anglepoise lamp over the coat and began to examine it in minute detail.

Betty glanced around the studio as she did so. It was jammed full of free-standing clothes rails, each one packed with plastic-wrapped clothes, divided into themes by laminated signs: '30s dresses', 'Flapper dresses', '50s Cocktail', '70s/Hippy beachwear'. There were cabinets full of sunglasses and silk scarves, and mannequins in silk ball gowns and bondage punk. There were clutch bags and corsages, stilettos and bovver boots. The walls were hung with framed stills from films and TV series, and there was Alexandra snuggled up against Colin Firth and with her arm around the shoulder of Emilia Fox.

'So,' said Alexandra, turning the coat over, 'how do you know my brother?'

'Oh. No. I don't know him. Not in that way. I live in

the flat next to his stall. On the market. He just mentioned you, said you might be interested in the fur. I think it was fairly obvious to him that I'm not really a fur kind of girl.'

'Aw,' said Alexandra, facetiously, 'bless.'

Betty recognised the dynamic; it was the same as the one between Bella and her younger brother, the grudging affection, the condescending praise.

'Is he younger than you?' she asked knowingly.

'Yeah. He is my baby brother by a matter of eighteen months. And one day. And, yes, I know, we look nothing alike. He is a carbon copy of our father and I am a carbon copy of our mother. And our older sister sneakily managed to take the best of both of them and is about the most beautiful person I know.' She raised her eyebrows sardonically.

Alexandra pulled the coat closed and fiddled with the hook-and-eye fastenings. Then, rather dramatically, she plunged her hands into the pockets of the coat, with a facial expression reminiscent of that of a country vet examining a pregnant ewe. 'Lovely deep pockets,' she said. And then: 'Oh, this must be yours.' Alexandra pulled out a piece of folded paper.

'Oh,' Betty said, taking the paper from Alexandra's hand. 'Wow. Let me see . . .'

She opened the paper to see Arlette's handwriting. It was her pre-stroke writing, neat and controlled, spelling out a name and address:

Peter Lawler
22a Rodney Gardens
London
SW5 3DF

Her heart leaped with excitement. 'Any idea where that is?' she asked, showing the paper to Alexandra.

'Ah,' Alexandra said knowingly, 'South Ken. Very smart. Friend of your grandmother's?'

Betty shrugged. 'Not that I know of. But then I think there are a few things we didn't know about my grandmother.'

'Ooh,' said Alexandra, 'a mystery, then. I do love a good mystery. You'll have to go and check it out. Might be a long-lost love. God, might be a long-lost *relative*.' She winked over her glasses and then removed them, rubbing gently at the bridge of her nose. 'Anyway. Lovely coat. Lovely condition. I can give you two hundred and fifty pounds for it.'

'Oh.' Betty felt her heart plummet with disappointment.

Alexandra looked at her kindly. 'Not much of a market for fur these days, sweetheart. I mean, you could hold on to it for a few years, see if they come back into fashion, but even then,' she shrugged, 'it's a good offer. I'd take it, if I were you. Well, if money's the issue?'

Betty paused and considered the suggestion. She pictured Arlette, standing in the doorway of the house on the cliff, all those years ago, in her remarkable red shoes, looking at her with that inscrutable gaze, making Betty feel like she could be anything she wanted. She thought of the smell in Arlette's boudoir, of the dull, exotic light cast through half-drawn chintz, the sense of another time, another place, another world. The coat summed it all up: obsolete, out of fashion, but still alive with glamour. She would never wear it again. No one in their right mind would ever wear it again. Maybe she would keep it for ever, keep it for an imaginary unborn daughter, keep it for posterity. But then she closed her eyes and imagined the coat on the back of a famous actress, lights, music, action, clapperboards, make-up artists and dry ice.

'No,' she shook her head, 'money's not the issue. But I'd like to sell it, anyway. If that's OK.'

'That is OK, yes. Cash OK?'

'Cash would be great. Thank you.'

Betty's arms felt oddly empty as she left Alexandra's studio a moment later, as though she'd just handed over a child or a pet. Her shoulder bag, however, felt ripe and heavy with the twenty-pound notes that Alexandra had just counted into her hands. And there, nestled against the palm of the hand in the pocket of her coat was the paper with the mysterious address on it.

Rodney Gardens was, as Alexandra had suggested, very smart indeed. Twin terraces of oversized red-brick houses with stucco pillars and tiled steps, each house immaculate.

Number 22a was in a house in keeping with the rest of the street. Doorbells were housed in a recently-polished brass plate, steps were trimmed with potted palms, the door was painted mirror-shiny black.

Betty pressed the button.

Peter Lawler.

He sounded like he might be a financial advisor. Or a solicitor.

The intercom crackled and the sound of an elderly lady's voice emerged.

'Yes?'

'Oh, hello. I'm looking for a Peter Lawler.'

'Who?'

'Peter Lawler.'

'Peter Morler?'

'No, Lawler. Peter Lawler.'

'Hold on, dear.'

She waited a moment and then a male voice boomed through the metal box, 'Who is this?'

'My name is Betty. My grandmother was called Arlette. I found this address in her coat pocket. Along with the name Peter Lawler. Does he live here?'

'Never heard of him. Lawler?'

'Yes. Peter Lawler.'

'Rodney Gardens?'

'Yes, 22a Rodney Gardens.'

'Well, that's us all right. But I've never heard of this other chap. Could be someone who used to live here, I suppose, though we've been here for more than ten years.'

'Oh, well, never mind. I'm sure it's nothing important.'

'Tell you what. Try Flat D. Mr Mubarak. He's the landlord. He's lived here since the house was converted. He'll know.'

'Oh, OK. Great, thank you. I will do.'

Mr Mubarak answered his intercom so fast it was as though he had been sitting next to it praying for someone to buzz.

'Hello.'

'Oh, hello. The gentleman at Flat A said you might be able to help me. Do you know if someone called Peter Lawler used to live here?'

'Peter Lawler?'

She sighed. She was growing tired of repeating the name. 'Yes,' she said, 'him.'

'Yes,' he said, 'I remember Peter. He moved out a long time ago. Who is it who's looking for him?'

'Well, it's me. I think.'

'You think?' He sounded partly amused.

'Well, yes.' She explained once more about the address in the coat pocket and finally Mr Mubarak sighed and said, 'I'm coming to the door. Wait there.'

Mr Mubarak was attired in a dressing gown and smoking a pipe. His hair was waxed away from his face and he had deep acne scarring. He looked simultaneously suave and decrepit. His face went from stern to lascivious when he saw Betty standing on his front step.

'Good morning,' he chirped, pulling his pipe from between his lips. 'I apologise for my appearance. I am trying to save on laundry bills.' He beamed at her. His teeth were yellow and misshapen. 'Now, yes, Peter Lawler. He moved out about ten years ago.'

'And do you know where he went?'

Mr Mubarak smiled, as though Betty had just asked him a suggestive question. And then he stopped smiling and looked a bit sad. 'Ah, well, yes. Poor old Peter. Such a nice man. Always used to stop and talk with me. A loner, but a friendly loner, if you see what I mean. But then, well, he was plagued by demons.'

'Oh.' Peter Lawler was beginning to sound a little more interesting than his rather serious name might have suggested.

'He was a drinker. A big drinker. He was in hospital for weeks. His liver. Had to let the flat go in the end, and I never found out where he went after that. I think he might have gone to live with his mother. Or I suppose it's also possible that he may have passed away.' Mr Mubarak sighed melodramatically and puffed thoughtfully on his pipe.

'What did he do?' asked Betty. 'I mean, as a job?'

Mr Mubarak pulled the pipe from his mouth again and narrowed his eyes at Betty. 'That is a good question. I do not know. He did not appear to do anything.'

'How old was he?'

'Hard to say. The drink had probably aged him. But I'd say he was anywhere between thirty and forty. Possibly a little older. He was a good-looking fellow, I'd say. Quite blond. Very English. But, you know, not *kind* to himself, if you see what I mean. A bit ragged. Around the edges.'

'Did he ever say anything to you, about a family. Or anything like that?'

Mr Mubarak shook his head. 'No. Most definitely not. No family. No lady friends. No nobody. A true loner.'

Betty nodded. There it was. The end of the line. She sighed. 'OK,' she said, 'thank you, anyway.'

'You're most welcome. And please,' he pulled, with some panache, a business card from the top pocket of his dressing gown, 'if you need anything else, anything at all, please do not hesitate to call me here. I hope you find what you are looking for.'

'Yes,' said Betty, taking the card and sliding it into her shoulder bag, 'yes, thank you. So do I.'

11

1919

Exeat.

Leticia's house filled suddenly with the turbulence of young men, with boots and bikes and balls and shouting. Arthur and Henry were fair, like their sister, and, so far as Arlette could tell, every bit as badly behaved as their small brother, James, who seemed to spend entire days hitting walls with sticks and screaming at his mother. Neither of them listened to anything their mother said. It was as though she did not exist, or spoke in a voice only audible to women. Arlette watched in shocked silence as the older one – Henry, she thought he was – took a newspaper from in front of his mother, who had been reading it at the time, and although she asked him immediately to return it, refused to do so, ruffled its pages horribly and then threw it in the air, leaving it to fall to the ground in separate pieces. Then he turned and left the room, his mother all the while calling, 'Henry, come back this instant. *Henry*.' He did not return and a moment later Arlette saw Leticia sigh and collect the sheets of the paper herself.

And such rudeness. She had heard Arthur refer to his

mother as both 'stupid' and 'old'. Arlette really had no idea how Leticia could prevent herself from slapping her insolent children and locking them in their rooms.

Leticia's husband had been promoted again, after the war, to the Brussels office, but this time he had left his family behind and returned, apparently, only once a month. Arlette had not yet met him, but she had seen his photograph: a somewhat hamster-cheeked man with a pencil moustache and thinning black hair. She could not imagine how a rose as delicate as Leticia could have allowed herself to be plucked by such an average-looking fellow, but Leticia did always talk very fondly and with great respect of her husband, and clearly, if the trappings of his fine Kensington home were any signifier, he was an immensely wealthy man. But still, it struck Arlette most emphatically that this house was in dire need of a man's presence to rein it back under control.

The older one, Henry, glanced at her now, across the hallway. He had the haughtiness of a man twice his age. 'Why are you wearing that peculiar jacket?' he asked.

Arlette looked down at it, unsure why he should be asking her such a question. It was just a jacket. Possibly a little old-fashioned, certainly not as chic and bohemian as the clothes that his sister wore, but certainly no different from something his own mother might wear.

'What do you mean?' she asked.

'I mean, it's peculiar. How old are you?'

'I'm twenty-one.' She said this with some incredulity as he had been at his sister's party only two weeks earlier, where a toast had been raised in her honour and she had been given twenty-one bumps by a group of people that included Henry himself.

'Oh, yes, yes, of course. I forgot. I suppose it's just the way you dress. It makes me think you must be older.'

She looked down at herself once more. A bottle-green jacket belted upon the hip, a long skirt in Black Watch tartan, dark stockings, green velvet sandals and a chiffon scarf at her neck in midnight blue. Smart, she thought, elegant, fashionable – the silhouette was absolutely spot on; she'd seen it in one of Leticia's many fashion magazines piled up around the house. She could think of nothing to say so instead pursed her lips and turned to walk away from him.

'Sorry,' he said, in a careless tone of voice, 'I didn't mean to upset you.'

'I'm not upset,' she hissed, and continued on her way. She felt tears stabbing painfully behind her eyes. The boy was sixteen. She could not allow a sixteen-year-old boy to reduce her to tears, she who had managed to make her way through the whole of her father's funeral without shedding even one. Her father who had lain in his coffin, his constituent parts reconstructed into some semblance of his living form, minus a foot, two fingers and half his face. No, she would not cry. But she would despise him, with every atom of her own self. For ever. She would also, she knew without any shadow of doubt, make sure that from this point forward he would never be able to look upon her with anything other than speechless admiration. For on Monday she started her new job. A sales assistant at a department store on Regent Street, called Liberty. A most magical place, like a demented fairy palace, with turrets and balustrades, panelling and a thousand twinkling leaded windows. A smiling lady called Mrs Stamper had talked to her sweetly and kindly in a tiny room behind the scenes and told her that she was a charming young lady and just the sort she was looking for, and said she could start the following week and be paid five shillings and sixpence, with only one Saturday a month.

Arlette had been walking on air ever since. Her first interview, and the job had fallen into her lap with absolutely no special effort. And not just any old job, but a magical job in a magical place working in a lavender-scented, wood-panelled room full of exquisite clothes with a clientele of the most gracious and tasteful ladies in London. Tomorrow night these nasty boys would be taken to the train station and sent back to their prison in the countryside and she would not have to look upon their smug, tiresome faces again until the end of October.

The thought brought a smile to her face and she continued on her way. Her life had been in stasis for so long, she had felt sometimes like she might go mad on that little island in the middle of nowhere, through the swirling years of war and then in the deathly lull afterwards. But now, at last, she had taken hold of this thing called life, had it held tightly by the reins and was ready to ride it into the distance. Finally her life had begun.

12

1995

Betty took her tobacco pouch and a glass of water out onto the fire escape. The evening was mild and muggy. It was spring but it felt more like September. The air in the vacuum between the buildings was damp with condensation and rich with soupy odours rising from the kitchens below. She made herself a roll-up and smoked it thoughtfully, staring at the house across the way, at the black windows, at the faint glimmer of the chandelier twinkling beyond. The house was dark and empty. The men with the cameras must just have been tourists. Strange tourists with a penchant for photographing unexceptional Soho architecture.

It was nearly eight o'clock.

It was Friday.

It was Betty's third night in Soho.

She had two hundred and fifty pounds in her bag.

She heard the sounds of the Soho night starting up below, saw the sky darkening, the streetlights coming on, felt it all building inside her like a burst of energy.

She did not want to be here in this tiny flat all alone, but then, she did not want to venture out by herself, sit alone in a bar like a character in a *film noir*, being offered drinks by morose men with broken hearts. She thought of Peter Lawler, this mysterious man kept tucked away in her grandmother's coat pocket for years and years, and she thought of the potential length of a journey that appeared to have no starting point.

Then she pulled on her coat, picked up her door keys and smiled grimly with resolve. She had no more idea of how to find a job than she had of how to find Clara Pickle, but she had to start somewhere and she may as well start right now.

Betty got home three hours later.

Her feet were rubbed raw from the seams on the insides of her wedges. Her face was stiff from smiling. And her ego was the size of one of the greasy peanuts she'd stuffed down her throat sitting at the bar of a restaurant on Greek Street waiting to hear yet another stressed-out manager tell her there was no work available and then ask her for a CV. She'd planned to take some of her fur money and spend it in a nice restaurant somewhere on a bowl of pasta and a glass of beer, but with each establishment she walked away from without even a hint or a suggestion of a job, she felt more and more attached to the cash and less and less disposed towards spending it.

She'd saved the Groucho for last.

The Groucho.

From magazines spread open across the kitchen table in the cold house on the cliff it had sounded to her as mystical as Narnia, as gloriously unlikely as unicorns. She had looked at the photos, pored over the grizzled rock stars, the sozzled artists emerging into the early hours, startled as wild deer, chippy as football hooligans and thought: imagine being in there. Inside there. With all those people. Surely this was where the raw red heart of Soho beat its rhythm; surely this, more than the sex shops and the Chinese lanterns and the tattoo parlours, was what Soho boiled down to: a glowing hub of celebrity, excess and notoriety, a magnet for people who created the colour of the world in which we all lived. And so she had pushed open the door and stepped into the brown murkiness of the reception area and asked to speak to the manager and been told, in charming but no uncertain terms that there was no manager available to speak to her but yes, of course, please leave your CV and we'll pass it on. Betty had barely been listening to the sweet, smiley girl, her gaze cast half behind her at the heavy doors swinging back and forth, open and shut, people passing through, inwards and outwards, wondering if any of them might actually be somebody, somebody worth gazing upon.

Before she'd had even a moment to really absorb her surroundings a smiling man in a suit jacket was holding the door ajar for her and wishing her gently upon her way and there she was, once again, back on the pavement, surrounded by babbling cab drivers and Friday night hordes. Without a job.

That was half an hour ago.

Now Betty was home, tiptoeing quietly up the stairs, her wedges in her hand, her heart full of disappointment.

The flat was dark and silent when she let herself in.

For a moment she missed her big empty bedroom in the big empty house, the metres of corridors, the never-used rooms, all the space and the oxygen and the silence. But she breathed it back inside, the sense of loss and nostalgia, and reminded herself instead of all the nights in that big silent bedroom, in that huge sprawling house, wishing herself to be exactly here.

She changed into pyjamas, wiped off the grime of her disappointing Soho night with a baby wipe and then fell into bed with the sound of people outside having a much, much better time than she had, ringing in her ears.

There were three more paps outside the house on Peter Street on Monday morning. This time there was no mistaking them. They wore capacious jackets, multiple pockets bulging with packets of film and spare lens caps, paper coffee cups clutched in gloved hands, eyes slanted against the piquant morning light, grumbling to each other quietly like bystanders at a stranger's funeral.

Betty stopped for a while to watch, but absolutely nothing appeared to be happening. She strolled back around the corner and waited for John Brightly to finish parking his van. He appeared a moment later, carrying a cardboard box with a coffee cup balanced on the top of it. He smiled grimly when he spotted Betty standing on his pitch.

'Morning,' he said.

'Morning,' replied Betty, taking the cup off the box and holding it for him while he found somewhere to rest the box. 'How are you?'

'Not bad,' he said, 'not bad at all.'

'Met your sister on Friday,' she continued. 'She bought my coat.'

He raised one eyebrow at her and said, 'Oh, yeah? Give you a good price for it?'

Betty nodded and passed him his coffee. 'Not bad,' she said. 'Amazing place, she works.'

He shrugged, pulled some LPs from the box. 'Yeah,' he said, as though the appearance of his sister's workplace had never before occurred to him. 'It's quite cool, I guess.'

'And she's really nice.'

'You reckon?'

Betty paused, unsure how to take what he'd just said. He was either being negative or he was being facetious. She decided not to venture down that grenade-littered path and smiled blankly. 'So, over there?' She pointed towards Peter Street. 'Load of paparazzi hanging around outside someone's house. Any idea who lives there?'

'What, on Peter Street?' He looked at her with a touch more interest now.

'Yeah.'

'That's Dom Jones's place.'

'Dom Jones?'

'Yeah, you know the singer with –'

'Yes! I *know*. Of course I know. Wall. And that's his

house? Over there?' Betty's mind boggled with the gloriousness of this fact. Wall were not her favourite band. Dom Jones was not her favourite singer. But he was the biggest singer with the biggest band in the UK right now. And it was *his* chandelier and anarchic artwork she'd admired through the window on her first night in Soho. Dom Jones was *her neighbour*.

'Yeah, that's his place. He used to live there until a couple of years ago. Moved out, you know, when he married —'

'Amy Metz. Yes, yes, of course.' Remembered facts from crappy magazines swirled around her mind, nuggets of regurgitated gossip, half-baked facts, how Dom Jones had left Cheryl Glass, the much-loved, elfin-beautiful lead singer of girl band Blossom, for Amy Metz, the hard-nosed, scary-beautiful lead singer of girl band Mighty. Two years later they were married with three children under three and living in a massive pink house in Primrose Hill amid a constantly raging storm of rumours and scandal. And then it hit her, the reason why that front door had looked so familiar the other day. She must have seen it dozens of times in paparazzi shots of Dom Jones taken outside his house.

'Yeah, he moved out then, but I don't think he ever sold it. It's just sat there. Empty.' John threw a glance towards Peter Street and shrugged. 'Maybe he's moving back. Have you checked the headlines today?'

Betty wrinkled her nose and then went immediately to the newsagent across the road, where the very first headline to hit her from the front of the *Mirror* screamed: 'DOM DUMPED', illustrated by a blurred photograph of Dom Jones looking very rough around the edges and leaving the Groucho Club 'in the early hours of last night'.

Betty grabbed the paper and started to read. Apparently Dom had been caught in a backstage toilet after a gig being gifted a blow job by a nineteen-year-old called Carly Ann. The only reason why this sordid yet unsurprising interlude had made it to the attention of Amy Metz was that Carly Ann's boyfriend had secretly filmed the encounter and then attempted to blackmail Dom Jones with it. Dom had failed to take the threat seriously and a copy of the tape had then been posted through the letterboxes of both Dom and Amy's distinctive pink house and the *Mirror*'s head office in Canary Wharf.

Beneath the article were three blurred stills taken from the tape. And there it was, at the very end of the article, a simple sentence that would mean very little to most people but sent shivers of excitement down Betty's spine:

Dom Jones is now believed to be returning to his bachelor pad, a three-storey town house in London's Soho, where the singer previously lived with former lover, Cheryl Glass.

Betty paid for the paper, suppressing an ecstatic smile. While those hapless men with cameras stood about pathetically hoping for a glimpse of their prey, Betty had a front-row view all to herself. She tucked the paper under her arm and dashed back to the flat, flashing the headline at John Brightly as she passed him. His response was just to raise one heavy eyebrow as if to say, 'Fairly interesting, I suppose.'

Betty bundled up the stairs, two at a time, to the fire escape at the top of the house where she made a roll-up with fluttering fingers. She lit it and looked across and into the windows of Dom Jones's house.

The light fell well at this time of day, not casting the glass impenetrably black but allowing a blurred glimpse of wall and furnishings. Her eyes roamed around the interior, searching for a sign of movement, and then suddenly, there it was, after all these days of stillness and silence, a shadow moving up a wall and then, too fast for Betty to really fix on any defining characteristics, a person walked past the window, turned, once, and then ascended the next flight. It was a man, of that she was certain, a smallish man with a lightweight build and narrow hips. She would not be able to say with one hundred per cent certainty that it was definitely Dom Jones, but she was fairly certain that it was. Another shiver ran through her. She was sitting here, at the very heart of a front-page controversy. Right here. In Soho. Watching Dom Jones walk up his stairs.

She rolled and smoked another three cigarettes, her gaze fixed upon Dom Jones's windows, but there was no more to be seen. She packed up her tobacco pouch and headed back indoors. She had wasted enough of her new life staring at the back of a stranger's house. She had more important things to worry about. If the bars and restaurants and clubs of night-time Soho didn't have a job for her, maybe the shops and galleries of daytime Soho would.

The interior of the fast-food restaurant was shockingly bright after the dimness of the street outside. It was filled with tourists and losers, and smelled cloyingly of congealed meat and stale oil. In the smoking section half a dozen single men pulled nervously on cigarettes in between handfuls of chips. Another corner appeared to have been put aside for emaciated alcoholics and tattooed junkies, who all sat snarling to themselves under their breath, nursing single cups of cold coffee. On the other side of the restaurant a group of high-octane language students shouted at each other with much hilarity in broken English.

Betty queued up behind a small group of bemused Japanese, true to stereotype, with large expensive cameras and oversized baseball caps. Muzak played in the background, Betty thought it might be a synthesiser version of 'Copacabana' by Barry Manilow, but it was hard to be sure.

She got to the front of the queue and an awkward boy with a hairnet on smiled at her and said, 'Hello! Welcome to Wendy's! What can I get for you today?'

She ordered herself a Crispy Chicken Sandwich, a portion of fries and a Pepsi, and as she waited for her order to be prepared, she glanced at a wall to her left.

'Wendy's are recruiting now!' said a small poster. 'Wendy's are looking for enthusiastic people to work as customer service professionals. Free uniform + generous rates . . .' blah blah blah . . . 'Please ask for an application form.'

Betty twitched.

A voice in her head said, *Get one. Get a form.*

Another voice said, *Don't be ridiculous. I can't work here.*

The first voice said, *Why not? It's local. It's well paid. It's something to put on your CV. It's money in the bank. It's the* rent paid. *And you have spent the whole day looking for jobs in nice places and nobody wanted you.*

'Can I have one?' she asked bluntly, pointing at the poster. 'An application form?'

The boy looked at her strangely and then smiled. 'Sure,' he said.

She snatched the application form from the young boy's hands and shoved it into her shoulder bag, her cheeks hot with embarrassment and shame. She thought of Arlette, imagined what she would say if she could see Betty now, her precious girl, her beautiful girl standing in a bleak burger shop in the middle of the afternoon, with an application form for a job here in her handbag. Arlette would snatch it from her and shred it into a hundred pieces without uttering so much as a solitary word. Arlette would take her from here, firmly by the hand, and treat her to a plate of oysters in St James's. But then, Arlette had never been in Soho, young and penniless and desperate not to have to go home. If Arlette wanted Betty to find Clara Pickle – and Betty knew she did – then Betty would have to earn some money, because here, in the city, a thousand pounds was not going to go very far.

13

Before she went to bed that night, Betty returned to the fire escape for a final cigarette. It was nearly midnight and the lights in Dom Jones's house were dimmed. The clank of crockery and the clutter of cutlery were a familiar soundtrack now to her moments out here. Comforting, almost. She lit her roll-up and as she inhaled something caught her eye, a movement across the yard. She looked up and saw a man in the window. He was pushing against the sash, trying to lift it open, struggling with unyielding mechanisms, his face screwed up with the effort. Betty stopped breathing and stared in awe at the scene unfolding. She couldn't tell if it was *him*. The view through the glass was obscured. As she watched she heard the sash come free and the window loop open and then there he was. Without a shadow of doubt it was him, Dom Jones, in a white vest, tattooed forearms, cupping his hands around a cigarette buried between his lips as he lit it with a Zippo. She watched his face contort with angry relief as the tobacco made its way down his throat and then she saw his eyes moving slowly across the backyard, tired and vaguely furious until they found Betty's gaze and froze.

Betty quickly looked away, horrified to have been caught staring. Then she looked back, feeling that pretending that she hadn't been staring at him wasn't going to fool anyone and would make her look even more stupid. He was still looking at her, with an expression of vague bemusement. He raised one hand to her and she returned the gesture, her heart racing with excitement. She wondered if he would say anything to her, but the thrum of air-conditioning units, the clatter of the kitchen, the yelling of the kitchen staff below, would have meant he'd have to shout to be heard. Instead he stared thoughtfully into the middle distance, sucking from his cigarette rhythmically before rubbing it out against the brickwork and letting it fall to the ground.

He threw Betty one more look before pulling himself back into his house. It was a strange look: half suspicion, half approval. Then he was gone, the sashes rattling back into place, his face a mere shadow behind the glass again. Betty quickly finished her own cigarette and then glanced at her watch. Ten past midnight. Too late to call Bella, the only person she knew who would care about what had just happened. About the most exciting thing that had ever happened to her in her life. But she had no one to share it with.

Betty did not open her eyes until ten o'clock the following morning. When she did she was painfully aware of the fact that from two thirty to four forty-five the previous night she had lain wide awake listening to the woman downstairs having sex. She had seen the woman downstairs only once or twice since she'd moved in, a small Asian woman who wore a lot of denim and looked rather pinched and anxious. She had not smiled or said hello as they'd passed on the stairs, and Betty had followed her instincts not to force a greeting upon her. She had not looked like a person who would have sex for two and a half hours in the middle of the night. She had not looked the type to scream at the top of her voice or to experience several multiple orgasms in quick succession and to bang the walls with her fists every single time she did so. Whoever she had been fucking (and there really seemed to Betty to be no other word for it) had left the building around three minutes after the woman's last orgasm, stamping noisily down the stairs and banging the front door very loudly in their wake.

Shortly after this the bin men had arrived.

Nobody had warned Betty about bin men before she'd decided to rent a flat in Soho. Nobody told her that in Soho the bin men came every single morning. And that they came early. That they whistled and they hollered and they bantered with each other in sonorous East End accents. That they slammed doors and banged lids and threw entire pieces of furniture into the back end of their growling truck without even a hint of restraint.

At five thirty Betty had finally fallen asleep, only to be awoken an hour later by the first of the market traders arriving in their vans. More banging of doors, more cockney hollering and inconsiderate moving about of furniture and crates.

She had considered getting up at this point, heading for the fire escape and an early morning cigarette, starting the day, but had somehow found her way back to sleep before a police car, pulling up very loudly, with much screeching of siren and squealing of tyres, had brought her abruptly back to awakeness. She pulled back her curtains and watched as two policemen left the doors of their car wide open and slowly sauntered around the corner into Peter Street, watched by a dozen pairs of curious eyes.

Betty threw on a cardigan and her trainers and dashed downstairs. John Brightly was talking to some hip-looking dude about a John Otway twelve-inch disc. He glanced up curiously as Betty appeared in the doorway exuding urgency and vague panic. Betty forgot her usual tendency to play it cool and calm in front of John Brightly and looked at him desperately.

'What's going on?' she asked, looking at the blue light still flashing on and off on top of the empty police car.

John Brightly gazed at her with confusion. 'What?' he said, with a furrowed brow.

'There?' she said. 'Dom Jones's place. The police?'

John looked again and scratched the back of his neck. 'No idea,' he said, before turning back to his customer and addressing him in a kind of compensatory way as though saying: 'I do apologise for the mad woman with the blond hair . . . now where were we?'

Betty sighed impatiently and headed around the corner where she found the two policemen giving a member of the attendant paparazzi a warning. She listened for a while, keen to discover what had been happening, and as she stood and watched she saw one of the policemen knock on the front door of Dom Jones's house. She rooted herself to the spot. The intercom crackled to life. She heard the vague outline of a male voice and then heard the door buzz open. The policeman pushed open the door and as she stared she caught a tiny glimpse of him, in jeans and a checked shirt. She saw he looked anxious and tired. And then the policeman was pulled inside and the door was closed again.

As the door closed, Betty felt something strange happening to her. It was an ache. It started in her heart, and ended in her stomach. It was an ache of pity and sadness, but more than that, it was an ache of longing and desire. He looked so beaten up. His marriage in shreds. His children in another house. Trapped in an empty house by a sentry of rabid photographers. His world burst open like a bag of garbage for everyone to see the sordid contents.

She wanted to take him home and care for him and make him smile. She wanted to make everything better.

She thought for a brief moment of the sleazy stills in the *Mirror*, the back of the girl's head buried between his legs. But then she thought, God, he was married to Amy Metz. She'd been pregnant for about three years, non-stop. She had awful friends. She looked like a cow. And she had terrible, terrible taste in clothes.

No, thought Betty, absolutely not. She was a woman

and Amy Metz was a woman, and no woman should ever find an excuse for a man to have cheated. Ever.

She set her jaw as she thought this, cementing it into her psyche, and then she headed home.

14

1919

Arlette felt the snow beneath the thin soles of her boots. It was soft and slippery as butter, and she held onto the wall with an outstretched hand to prevent herself from falling over. She wore a cloak with a fur trim and a hat made of grosgrain velvet. The Christmas lights of Carnaby Street gleamed in the creamy slush and the windows of public houses glowed like embers. She had completed her last day at Liberty before the Christmas holiday, a busy day of last-minute adjustments to party dresses and cocktail gowns, of harried husbands looking for gifts, and acres of tissue paper and garlands of ribbon, echoing carols and the coiling aromas of cinnamon and aniseed. Arlette could not imagine a more enchanted place to spend the day before Christmas Eve than the Liberty department store. More carol singers rejoined her once again to deck the halls with boughs of holly as she turned the corner on to Regent Street: a small group of men and women, rosy-cheeked and clutching lanterns, conducted by a man in a top hat upon which lay a thin layer of frozen snow. There was something odd about the energy being exuded by this group of people, something strangely frenetic and unnatural. They seemed as though they might be drunk, yet did not look at all like the kind of people one would expect to be drunk in public. They were well-dressed, fashionable, cocksure. The man in the top hat spun round ostentatiously as he coaxed the last rousing note from his band of bright-eyed carollers and the crust of frozen snow from atop his head spun away from him, like a clay pigeon. It landed as a pile of glitter at Arlette's toes and she smiled.

'Merry Christmas!' said the top-hatted man, and he removed the hat from his head with a theatrical flourish. Beneath his hat he had a head of dense dark curls. He ran the fingers of a gloved hand through the curls, and looked at Arlette curiously.

'Merry Christmas,' Arlette returned the greeting. She smiled again, a tight, modest smile, and then continued on her way. But as she walked she was aware of the man's eyes still upon her.

She heard one of the lady carollers call out to the man, 'What next, Gideon? "Silent Night", "We Three Kings" . . .?'

'Yes,' she heard him reply absent-mindedly.

'Well, which one is it to be? Your choristers await . . .'

'One minute,' he said. 'Just one minute. Wait!'

Arlette turned. As she'd suspected, the man in the top hat, Gideon, was walking urgently towards her. 'I want to paint you,' he said, his eyes taking in every contour of her face.

'I beg your pardon?'

'I'm an artist. My name is Gideon Worsley. I want to paint you. You have the most remarkable face. The bones . . . just so delicate . . . like the bones of a tiny bird.'

She blinked at him.

'It would require very, very tiny brushes, one or two hairs at most. My goodness. How do you not break? How do you not shatter into a hundred tiny pieces?'

Arlette couldn't help herself; she put a hand to her cheek, trying for herself to imagine what he saw. And then she looked up at him and saw again what had unnerved her before: the fire in the eyes, not normal, not quite sane. He was not drunk, she could see that much. He was not slurred or unfocused quite the opposite: he was electrified, possessed.

'Excuse me, if you would, Mr Worsley, I'm in rather a hurry.'

'Oh, no,' he said, 'you mustn't hurry, not in these treacherous conditions. You might fall, and if you fell you might break. You must walk very, very slowly, taking great care.' He offered her the crook of his arm and she heard a caroller from behind calling, 'Oh *God*, Gideon, please leave the poor girl alone.'

He turned to the heckler and said, 'I shall *not* leave the poor girl alone. Can't you see that she is made of fine bone china, that she is delicate? She cannot be expected to walk unaccompanied. Come, we shall sing and walk at the same time. Where are you going?'

'I'm going to get on a bus,' Arlette replied hesitantly, 'towards Kensington.'

'Well, we shall escort you to your bus stand. Please,' he offered her his arm again and this time Arlette took it. She felt that her behaviour was altogether acceptable. She was being escorted not just by a single gentleman, but by a whole band of ladies and gentlemen. And she had been concerned about her footing on these slimy paving stones.

'Thank you,' she said.

'What is your name?' asked Gideon.

'Arlette,' she said. 'Arlette De La Mare.'

'*Arlette De La Mare*! Did you hear that, everyone, this delicate young lady is called Arlette De La Mare? Arlette of the sea. Probably the most romantic name I have ever heard. And what do you do, Arlette of the sea? Do you have a job? Or are you, in fact, a mermaid?' He glanced down at her water-stained boots and sighed. 'No. Not a mermaid. But still, a divine creature, none the less. So let me guess, a teacher? No, not a teacher – your clothes are too fine. So possibly . . . *fashion*? Am I close?'

She smiled inscrutably.

'I am, I'm close. Are you a seamstress?' He picked up her hands and studied them under a streetlight. 'No,' he said, 'wrong again, your hands are as soft as kittens' ears. I think you are a shop-girl, in a smart department store. Possibly . . . Dickins and Jones?'

'No,' she laughed.

'Lillywhites?'

'No!'

'Then . . . Liberty! Must be!'

Arlette laughed and Gideon Worsley punched the air

victoriously. 'You see,' he said, 'as an artist, I have to understand people, to read them, to work them out. I am the Sherlock Holmes of the art world. I can probably tell you where you're from.'

'Right then,' she challenged.

'Well, no, not right away, not immediately. But if you were to allow me an opportunity to paint you, if I could study you, in a favourable light, at my leisure, I could certainly hazard some very good guesses.'

They had arrived at Arlette's bus stand.

'Come on, Gideon. More songs!' called one of his male friends.

'Yes, yes!' he snapped. 'One minute! Please,' he turned back to Arlette, 'this is a genuine request. I have never seen anyone with bone structure like yours. If I can't paint you I shall spend the rest of my life in a state of miserable dissatisfaction. Please.'

Arlette looked at Gideon. He was, beyond the madness in his eyes and his air of troubled desperation, an attractive-looking man, probably around her age, possibly one or two years older. His eyes were dark and small, set in broad features. His nose was Roman and his mouth was full and wide. She could imagine that he had been handsome all his life, never an awkward moment in his development from child to man. She knew she must say no to his request. Of course she could not let a strange man paint her portrait, if, indeed, a simple portrait was all that he had in mind.

But still, a portrait. An artist. She pictured his studio, a paint-splattered garret, a jam jar full of wild flowers, dusty windows overlooking rooftops, a cat maybe, thin and slightly anxious. She imagined sitting with her face tilted towards the light, while Gideon examined her through the frame of his own fingers, finding ever thinner and thinner paintbrushes to describe the delicate lines of her face. She imagined him looking calmer than he did right now, softer, asking her gentle questions, and she imagined answering them lightly and breezily with just a hint of mysterious restraint. And then one day, he would turn the canvas to face her and she would see her own likeness played out in tiny strokes of watercolour, or maybe oils, and she would sigh and clap her hands together and say, 'Gideon, it's beautiful.'

Her bus approached, although not in actuality a bus proper, rather a lorry with some seats on the roof, all London had to offer to its commuters in these rather ramshackle post-war days. 'That is a very kind offer and I am flattered, Mr Worsley, but I fear that I'm going to be too busy to accept.'

She stepped towards the bus and Gideon pulled a small leather wallet from his breast pocket. 'Please,' he said, 'take a card. Should you change your mind.'

She took it from his gloved fingers and allowed him to help her up onto the bus. 'Thank you,' she said. And then she found herself a seat and watched from a snow-splattered window as Gideon and his band of wild-eyed carollers rejoined themselves into a circle and launched into a full-throated rendition of 'Good King Wenceslas'.

She saw Gideon's gaze follow the bus as it passed by and then latch onto hers as she came into view. For a moment she saw someone else deep inside him. Not the fiery-eyed leonine man, but a small boy, with a look of vulnerability and sadness in his eyes. She smiled and raised her hand at him. He raised his back at hers, and then he was gone.

She looked at the card in her hand, but it was too dark to read in the early evening gloom. She would read it tomorrow. She would think about Gideon and his garret and his soulful eyes tomorrow.

15

1995

A bookshop, a comic store, two boutiques, a small gallery, a lingerie store, a brasserie and a cake shop all told Betty that they could not give her a job over the course of the next two days. One of the agencies she signed up with had offered her a three-day stint sewing on buttons in a tailor's shop in Bloomsbury for £2.85 an hour, which she had accepted wearily. But within two minutes of entering the shop, a festering lint-filled tomb owned by three ageing Portuguese brothers with skin like parchment and hair blackened with boot polish, who looked at her as though she had just burst out of a birthday cake, she had made her excuses (something about sore fingers) and fled.

The other agency were waiting to hear from a zip factory in Islington about two days' zip-sorting, and there'd been talk of a few days on reception at a photographer's studio in Kentish Town but Betty didn't hold out much hope for that, given her performance on the typing test they'd given her. She feared there were a dozen pretty girls with winning smiles out there who could type faster than thirty words a minute.

Betty was nearing the end of her first week in Soho and

she still did not have a job. She felt a small wave of panic rise up through her. Then she did something that chilled her to her core, something that made her want to cry and be sick, both at the same time.

She rummaged through the clutter at the bottom of her shoulder bag until she found a biro. Then she rummaged through the clutter by the side of her bed until she found the application form for Wendy's. She filled it in, very slowly, wanting to delay for as long as possible the moment at which she would pass it into the oily, miserable hands of a person who claimed to be in a position to decide whether or not she was worthy of a place within their oily, miserable company. She deliberately misspelled some words, trying to diminish her chances before she'd even left the house. She did not apply lipstick or put a comb to her hair. She threw on a baggy zip-up cardigan and a pair of trainers, and she made herself look as unappealing as was humanly possible.

As she slouched down the road towards Shaftesbury Avenue, she took on the demeanour of a loser. She did not want this job. She did not want this life.

The manager at Wendy's was a very small Spanish man by the name of Rodrigo. He had a moustache that was black and hair that was white, and a very pronounced lisp. He took the form from Betty and sighed when he saw the tea ring stain and the ink smudges. He glanced up at her unhappily, through thickly lashed eyes and looked so incredibly sad that Betty almost wanted to hug him.

'Thank you,' he said. 'What nationality are you?'

'I'm British,' she said brightly, trying to atone for her dismally presented application.

He looked at her in surprise, glossy black eyebrows shooting towards his silver hairline.

'British,' he repeated.

'Yes.'

'Oh,' he said, 'how great!' His sadness seemed to turn then to sheer joy, and Betty felt her own heart fill with something good and pure. Finally, someone was pleased to see her. Finally someone thought she was a good thing, by simple virtue of her existence, beyond anything she had said or done, or said she would do or could do. She had merely stated her nationality, a pure accident of her birth, and this small man with a nice face had wanted her.

'I can have you in for an interview,' he consulted a huge chunky plastic watch on his hairy wrist, 'well. Now. Ith good for you? You have time?' He looked at her keenly through those soulful eyes again and she nodded, very quickly, before she could change her mind. She could not have said no. It would have broken his heart.

His office was a small cubicle at the very end of a long breeze-blocked tunnel beneath the restaurant. The walls were painted gloss white and covered in motivational posters. Bits of paper covered every surface. He asked her some standard questions, but it was clear from the outset that he would offer her the job. And he did.

'Could I have a trial run?' she suggested. 'Just a few days. See if, you know, well . . .'

'Thee if you can bear it?' he asked with a broad smile.

'Well, no, not that. Just, I've never worked in a restaurant before. I may not be very good at it.'

'Oh.' He smiled, his fur-covered hands gently holding the edge of his desk. 'You will be good at it. I can promith you that. Thtart tomorrow? Nine a.m.? If you don't hate it, we can fill in the paperwork and get you on board. Officially.' He beamed at her again and offered her one of his furry hands. She squeezed it. It was soft and warm and reminiscent of a spaniel's ear.

She beamed back at him and said, 'Yeah. OK. Why not?'

Moments later she was being led back down the long grey tunnel, staring subconsciously at Rodrigo's generous bottom squashed inside nylon trousers, and then she was shaking his hand again and wandering through the greasy mayhem of the restaurant, past the tables of junkies and drunks and back out onto the fresh, bright normality of Shaftesbury Avenue. She stood for a moment like a tree trunk in a rapid and let the crowds surge past her on both sides.

And then she slowly made her way back to the flat, her head suffused and subsumed with total and utter weirdness.

'Wendy's?' her mother cried in horror. 'You mean the burger place?'

'Yes,' sighed Betty, 'that's right.'

'But – *why*?'

'Because it's good money. And regular work. Because

the boss is really nice. Because it's free dinners and free lunches. Because the people are . . . interesting. Because it's local and I can walk there. And because . . .' she sighed, 'because there's a bloody recession and no one else would give me a job.'

Her mother sighed too, a sigh weighed down with unspoken well-I-did-warn-yous.

'It's *fine*,' Betty interjected before her mother could say anything annoying. 'It's absolutely fine. It'll do for now. Stop worrying.'

'I'm not worrying,' her mother said. 'Like you said, you're twenty-two. Why would I be worrying?'

'Because I'm your baby girl.'

'Well, yes, obviously you're my baby girl. But I trust you. You lived virtually alone in that big house with that crazy woman . . .'

'She was not crazy.'

'Well, that sick old woman. You cared for her by yourself. I think you can cope with a bit of real life.'

'No you don't.'

'Yes,' her mother laughed, 'I honestly do! As long as you're happy, that's all that matters. Have you made any more friends?'

Betty shrugged. 'Sort of,' she said. 'There's a guy at Wendy's. A gay guy. Called Joe Joe.'

'Oh,' said her mother in delight. Her mother was nuts about gays, had got the ferry all the way to Portsmouth last year to see Julian Clary live at the New Royal. 'What's he like?'

Betty thought back to their first conversation the previous day. 'Hi,' he'd said, 'I'm Joe Joe. Nice to meet you.' His accent put him somewhere in the southern reaches of the Americas.

Betty had smiled. 'Likewise.'

'You are very pretty.'

'Oh. Thank you.'

'I like your hair.'

'Thank you!'

'And you have beautiful eyes. Like a cat. You know. Or a fish.'

'A fish?'

'Yeah. A beautiful fish.'

'Oh.'

'I love your accent.'

'Thank you.'

'I love the British accent.'

'Uh-huh.'

'I love your smile.'

'Thank you.'

'You have nice teeth.'

'Oh, thank you.'

'I'm from Argentina.'

'Oh, right. Buenos Aires?'

'Yes!' he'd cried with delight. 'Yes! Buenos Aires! How did you know? You must be, like, psychic or something!'

She smiled at the memory and said, 'Mad. He's mad. But lovely.'

At these words the front door opened and Betty found

herself face to face with the Asian woman from down-stairs. She averted her gaze at once in embarrassment and shuffled her bum across the step to allow the woman to pass her. The woman glared at her, through narrowed eyes. Betty looked at her askance and lost her thread for a moment.

'And I've been getting to know the guy outside, you know, the record-stall guy. So I'm getting there, you know . . .' she petered off as she became aware of the fact that her downstairs neighbour had stopped halfway up the stairs and was now staring at her expectantly. 'Erm, hold on, Mum, just a sec.' She put her hand over the receiver and looked at the woman. 'Yes?' she asked pleasantly.

'You,' said the woman. 'You live upstairs, yes?'

'Yes,' said Betty, uncertainly.

'You smoke, yes?'

'Er, yes.'

'I smell it,' she chastised, wrinkling her face distaste-fully. 'I smell it. It come through my window, into my home.'

'Erm, sorry,' said Betty, her heart racing slightly with the stress of confrontation. 'I can't see . . . I mean, I smoke up there, right up there. On the fire escape. It's not even on the same level as you.'

'No,' snapped the woman. 'It come down. It come down the stairs. It come through my window. It come everywhere. I smell it. Everywhere on my clothes,' she plucked at her sweater and pulled it to her nose. 'Hmm? And in my hair,' she held a lock aloft.

Betty gazed at her, nonplussed. 'God, I, er, I don't know what to say. I mean. It's outside. I don't really see where else you expect me to smoke.'

'You stop smoking! Yes! You stop! Then no more problem!' The woman smiled then, almost encouragingly. 'Another thing,' she continued. 'You in bed over my bed. Your bed squeak. Every time you turn over, I hear *squeak squeak. Squeak squeak.*'

Betty stared at the woman, trying and failing to find a response that wouldn't end in a bitch fight. Eventually she smiled and said, 'Sorry. I had no idea. What would you like me to do about it?'

'You stop moving so much. You move all the time.'

Betty blinked at her. 'So,' she said, 'you want me to stop smoking. And stop moving in my sleep?'

'Yes!' she smiled again, as though delighted to find that she had somehow just solved all her problems in one fell swoop. 'Yes! Thank you!' She turned to leave. Betty watched her disappear up the stairs and round the corner. She waited until she heard the woman's front door click closed behind her and then took her hand away from the receiver.

'What was that?' her mother asked curiously.

'Nothing,' Betty exhaled. 'Nothing. Just a neighbour.'

'Oh,' said her mother in a tone of voice that suggested she liked the idea of a neighbour.

Betty brought the phone call to an end, her whole body so suffused with rage and indignation that she could no longer form a proper thought.

As she walked into her flat she felt the emptiness of it really hit her, for the first time since she'd moved in. She wished for a flatmate now, for someone to cry out to: 'Oh my God! I cannot believe what just happened! You know that woman? The one downstairs. The one who *fucks so loud that it makes my ears bleed*? She just told me that my cigarette smoke gets into her flat. And that my bed squeaks. When I move. Can you believe it!'

Betty took a bottle of cider and her tobacco pouch out on to the fire escape, where she deliberately blew her cigarette smoke through the gaps in the steps so that it would find its way into the woman's flat. Afterwards she sat on the sofa, her head spinning with too much cider and too many cigarettes, her hair pungent with the scum of chip oil and Soho smog, the flat dark and empty around her.

The light faded beyond the windows outside and the Soho engine started revving up for the night: streetlights warming up, pubs unlocking their doors, the market dismantling and the drinkers arriving. Still Betty sat motionless, alone, letting the solitude filter through her system. Her job at Wendy's would pay her two hundred pounds a week. Now she had a job she could finally focus on her search for Clara Pickle. But she still had absolutely no idea where to begin.

16

1920

Lilian seemed to think little of the notion of being painted by a man you'd met just once in the street. She turned the card over between her delicate fingers and said, 'Well, why not? It's a nice address. And he's a Worsley. They're a good set.'

'You know his family?'

'Well, I know their cousins. Or is that the Horsleys? Hmm, well, it is a good address. And just think, your portrait. How nice to have a portrait. In the year of your twenty-first. When you are the loveliest you will ever be.'

'But alone?' said Arlette, who needed no convincing of the benefits of having her portrait painted for free. 'Surely that can't be wise?'

'Well, I shall come with you, if you're feeling that silly about it.'

Silly, thought Arlette, *silly*? Surely the person who would walk into the home of a strange man unaccompanied was the silly one. 'Would you really?' she asked.

'Of course,' Lilian replied flippantly. 'Why ever not?'

Two days later she and Lilian took a hackney carriage to a

street of tall white houses by the river in Chelsea. The street number took them to the door of a small cottage painted powder blue. Arlette breathed in deeply, touching the fabric of her favourite dress, a drop-waisted chiffon affair in dark plum, which she wore under a matching coat.

'Good afternoon, ladies,' said Gideon, greeting them himself at his door. He wore a white shirt, unbuttoned to a quarter of the way down his chest, and tight brown trousers, held up by elastic braces. He looked as though he were either halfway through getting dressed or halfway through getting undressed. Either way, it was a rather informal fashion in which to meet two ladies, Arlette could not help but feel, almost risqué, and she was glad for the bristling, effervescent presence of Lilian at her side.

'Good afternoon,' said Lilian, 'you must be Mr Worsley. I am Lilian Miller. It's very nice to meet you.'

'Gideon,' he replied expansively, 'call me Gideon. And Miss De La Mare, how charming to see you again. As beautiful as I recall. Do come in. Please.'

He held the door open for Lilian and Arlette, and ushered them into a small hallway piled high with coats and boots and packing crates and tea chests. 'I would like to say that I have only just moved in, but no, sadly, I have been in the cottage for over a year and still have not found the time or the inclination to unpack my possessions. And of course, the more time that passes the more convinced I become that whatever lies within those boxes is clearly not needed and maybe I should just dump them in the river and let the dead folk pick them over.'

Arlette noted that the house was also dirty and wondered if maybe Gideon Worsley lived without help. It seemed unlikely, but not impossible.

'I am terribly excited,' he continued, leading them through to a small sitting room furnished with three ancient armchairs, a brass-topped table, a credenza full of books and a statue of a naked woman carved out of old stone. The naked woman was dressed in silk lingerie and a hat. And there was indeed a cat, a Persian, extravagantly, dreadfully furry and in dire need of grooming, who sat on a cushion in the window watching them suspiciously. 'I've been brooding over the memory of your face for ten long days. And now, finally, you are here! Now,' said Gideon. 'Tea. Stay here and I'll bring it through.'

Arlette nodded uncomfortably. She had never before been brought tea by a host. She could not imagine how he would possibly be capable of doing such a thing.

'*Bohemian*,' whispered Lilian when he'd left the room.

'Well, yes, I did warn you.'

'Strange, though, he has no housemaid, or so it seems. He is clearly a man of substance and this house is in a very desirable area.'

Arlette surveyed the room again. On the brass-topped table sat a tray full of half-smoked cigars and cigarillos, and on a silver tray sat three cut-glass tumblers, sticky with the residue of Calvados poured from the bottle next to them. The air smelled sour and rancid, like the air that blew from the public houses that Arlette passed on her way to and from work. It did not smell like a home should smell, of wood-smoke and beeswax and dust. It had no order, no method. It both appalled and excited Arlette in equal measure.

Lilian was agog. 'Well,' she continued in her stage whisper, 'it is entirely what one would imagine the home of a reckless artist to be, I suppose. And do you think he covered over the lady purposely, to spare our blushes?' She nodded at the scantily clad statue and giggled. 'As though we haven't seen a naked woman before,' she laughed breezily.

Arlette laughed breezily, too, although she had never in her life seen a naked woman. Not once. The only possible notion she had of how a woman appeared underneath her clothes was the one she saw reflected in her bedroom mirror. She assumed that she was not unique in her arrangement of dips and peaks. She had spent a week in hospital two years earlier when she'd been struck down with the Spanish 'flu, and had been examined in most every respect from ankle to neck, and no one had at any point ventured the suggestion that there was anything unconventional about her physiology. She wondered for a moment how Lilian, a girl of just eighteen, had had the opportunity to see a naked woman, but assumed it was just another example of the yawning gulf between their upbringings.

'Here,' said Gideon, returning with a paint-splattered wooden butler's tray bearing a pot and three cups and a small jar of sugar cubes. 'I'm afraid there was no milk. Or at least what milk there was seems to have given itself over to a terrible attack of the lumps. So I hope you will forgive me and drink it black?'

'Oh, I prefer it black,' Lilian offered overfervently. 'Thank you.' She took a cup from his outstretched hand and perched herself on the edge of an armchair.

'So, you're here to ensure that nothing unseemly happens to your friend, is that correct?' he asked Lilian.

'Yes, indeed.' Lilian smiled and smoothed down the skirt of her dress. 'She is three years older than me but has had a rather sheltered upbringing. On an island.'

'Ssh,' Gideon put his finger to his lips dramatically. 'I have promised Miss De La Mare that I will be able to divine her provenance using instinct alone. So no clues, please,' he smiled. His teeth were not good, not for a man of his standing, but this did not detract from his general air of raffish handsomeness, and, despite the near-squalor of his home, Arlette couldn't help but notice how nice he smelled, of a scent, rather than of himself, of something to do with cloves and peppermint.

Lilian and Gideon chattered for a while, trying to find some common ground, and failing. The closest they got was a girl called Millie who'd possibly gone to the same school as his sister, but for only two terms. Arlette sipped her tea, clearly an expensive blend, served in cups that were also of a very good quality. She looked for clues as to the direction this experience might take.

'Well,' said Gideon, after a few more moments, placing his empty cup onto the brass-topped table, 'I think, if it's agreeable with you, Miss Miller, I would like to take Miss De La Mare up to my studio now.'

Arlette felt her stomach wobble. She wanted, she suddenly knew without a doubt, to do this alone, yet she could not judge the wisdom of this idea. She looked at Lilian for reassurance, trusting, for some reason, that this headstrong eighteen-year-old girl would know better than her whether this man with his half unbuttoned shirt had good intentions or bad.

'Well,' Arlette said, 'shall I stay on, alone?'

'Oh, yes!' said Lilian, springing to her feet, 'I absolutely don't want to hang around here, disturbing your artistic juices, not to mention your attempts to work out where the mysterious Miss De La Mare might have sprung from. I will leave you both to your afternoon and, Arlette, I will see you at home. If you're not back by six o'clock, I will send out a search party.' She laughed and pulled on her coat. Gideon saw her to the door and then he reappeared, looking, now that Lilian was gone, suddenly threatening and rather obscene.

'Come,' he said, cupping his large hands together, 'come up. Let's get started.'

Arlette placed her cup carefully upon the table, smiled the best smile she could find, and followed this strange man up uncarpeted stairs towards who knew where.

17

1995

The new dawn brought the dreadful realisation that Betty had slept through until 9.05 a.m. Her shift at Wendy's was due to begin at 9.00 a.m. and, to save time, Betty jumped, unwashed, straight into her uniform, brushed her teeth perfunctorily, glanced in the mirror and wished she had washed her hair the previous night, thought about applying some make-up, looked at the time and decided against it, forced down a mouthful of dry cornflakes, leaped out of the front door onto the street and straight into the path of Dom Jones.

'Whoa,' he said, putting out his hands to protect himself from her.

Betty gazed at him in shock and awe. 'Shit,' she said, 'sorry.'

He looked at her, half amused, half appalled, taking in the crumpled polo shirt and the nylon trousers and the baseball cap in her hand.

He said nothing for a moment, looked as though he were about to walk away. Then he looked back at her briefly. 'You're the girl,' he said, in his pop star voice, 'the one from over there.' He pointed behind him. 'On the fire escape.'

She nodded, not wanting to say anything, aware of cornflakes between her teeth and the fact that she had not brushed her teeth for long enough to take away the staleness of sleep.

He appraised her again. Even from here, at such close range, on this muted May morning, dressed down in a nondescript T-shirt, unshaven and puffy-eyed, it was clear that this man was a somebody.

Dom Jones nodded at her and then walked away, a slight smile playing around his lips.

Betty rocked back on to her heels, as though he had created a small hurricane in his wake. She gulped. And then she smiled.

Dom Jones.

He'd seen her.

He'd talked to her.

He'd recognised her.

She was on his radar.

And then, very suddenly, she stopped smiling.

She was wearing her Wendy's uniform.

She thought of every single time she had stepped onto this street from her flat in nice clothes. She thought of the cool T-shirts and the denim minis, she thought of the days her hair had gleamed in the sunlight and smelled like dewdrops, the slicks of red lipstick and the flourishes of liquid liner that had rendered her hard to resist. She thought of every single time that Dom Jones could have bumped into her outside her flat and threw down curses upon the gods of chance and timing.

Not that she wanted Dom Jones to fancy her. Particularly. He was a cheating scumbag and far from being the best-looking member of Wall.

But still.

Dom Jones.

She shivered away the memory of their encounter and walked very, very quickly to work.

Betty saw John Brightly, as she turned the corner a couple of days later. He was leaning against the wall of her house, smoking a cigarette. She wanted to talk to him. But she had no idea whether or not the wall John Brightly built around himself could be dissembled at all by the use of charm and familiarity, or if she was in fact putting up an even bigger barrier every time she tried to engage with him.

'How's your sister?' she asked, rather desperately.

He turned and grimaced at her. 'No idea,' he said.

She smiled tightly as another row of metaphorical bricks landed on the wall between them.

'Seen anything of Dom Jones lately?' she offered, as a last-ditch effort.

He shook his head. 'Not really.'

Not really? Not really? What did 'not really' mean? He either had, or he hadn't. She sighed, and was about to head back into the flat when he turned again and smiled and said, 'He was asking after you.'

She spun round and stared at him. 'What?'

'Dom Jones. A couple of days back. He was at my stall,

looking at my stuff. He said, "Who's the blond in the Wendy's uniform?"'

'Oh my God! What did you say?'

'Nothing much,' he shrugged. 'I said you'd just moved in. That you lived on the second floor.' He shrugged again.

'Oh my God! Did you tell him my name?'

He grimaced at her again. 'Well, I'm not sure how I could have told him your name when I don't know what it is myself.'

'Betty!' she almost shrieked. 'My name is Betty.'

He nodded knowingly.

'Oh God. What else did he say?'

'Nothing much. Just that. Who's the blond.'

Betty blinked and tried to stop a huge stupid smile take over her face. 'Wow,' she said. 'I can't believe it!'

John Brightly looked at her then as though she had just plummeted to even lower depths of stupidity.

'Did he buy anything?' she asked.

'What?'

'From you? Did he buy anything?'

'Nah. He was looking at a rare Dylan, but he didn't buy it.'

She nodded encouragingly, paused for a moment wishing she could think of something salient to say on the subject of rare Dylans and then she went indoors.

Ten days into her career at Wendy's Betty had already gained enough weight to subtly change the contours of her face: her cheekbones were less pronounced, her jaw less defined. The hours spent on her feet had done nothing to counterbalance the deleterious effects of two free Wendy's meals a day, and she could feel the waistband of her size eight denim skirt beginning to dig into her flesh. Her complexion, too, was starting to suffer. It had lost its petal-like gloss and she even had a few spots here and there. And then, two nights ago, unable to justify a visit to the hairdresser's on financial grounds, and with roots so grown out that they were now longer than the bleached bits of her hair, she had smeared a tube of something by Wella described as 'Deep Caramel' through her hair and turned herself inadvertently into a kind of low-rent, two-tone, washed-out brunette. She hadn't realised it until that very moment, but the colour, really, virulently, did not suit her in the slightest. In an attempt to get rid of the colour she had now shampooed her hair five times. The only effect that this had had was to turn her hair a kind of mouldy shade of green.

She thought of 'the blond', the elfin, fresh-faced girl that Dom Jones had bumped into ten days ago outside the flat and wondered if he would even recognise her any more. She applied some eyeliner and some pinkish blusher from a tube. Then she scraped her cheap greeny-brown hair back into a stubby ponytail and sucked in her stomach.

She had invited Joe Joe back to her flat after work, after he'd pleaded with her to let him see it, and he was now standing at her kitchen window saying, 'Wow, I can't believe you live here. This is the best flat *ever!*'

'I'm going outside for a smoke,' she said, waving her roll-up at him.

'Can I come, too?'

She shrugged. 'Sure.'

'Maybe I should start to smoke,' he said a moment later, dangling his feet over the edge of the fire escape. 'I always feel so left out when everyone else is smoking. All those little gangs, puffing away together, puff puff, chat chat.'

'*Don't* start smoking,' said Betty. 'That would be a really stupid thing to do at . . . how old are you?'

'Twenty-four.'

She threw him a look of surprise.

'You thought I was younger than this? Yes, I know. I look very young. Everyone always says this about me. I think it is my freckles. And my cheeky, cheeky smile.' He demonstrated his cheeky, cheeky smile and she laughed.

'So where does it come from, your colouring, your hair?'

'Ha,' he laughed. 'I am like a stray dog, you know, with many, many genes. I have some Mexican, some Jamaican, some Argentinian, of course, and also, going back, like, a hundred years, so far back that no-one really knows, there was an Irishman. And his genes, they are like the genes of a *god*. Just in my generation, of thirty cousins, there are seven of us with this red hair and this white skin. Seven, in thirty. It is *amazing*.'

Betty stared at the wild amber afro and nodded her agreement.

'What about you, what is on your genes?'

She smiled. 'Nothing much,' she replied. 'Bit of English. Bit of Welsh. Some German.'

'Ah, then you are pure-bred Aryan . . .'

They both turned then at the sound of a sash window being raised across the courtyard. Betty stiffened and grabbed Joe Joe's arm. 'It's Dom Jones!' she hissed.

'Who?'

'You know, Wall?'

'What?'

'Wall, the band. You know?'

He shuddered daintily. 'I hate the Wall. I hate all that Britpop shit.'

The sash window came rattling up and there he was, pulling a cigarette out of a soft packet, clamping it between his lips, searching his jeans for his Zippo. He didn't notice them at first, not until he'd finally located the lighter and taken his first drag. His eyes narrowed at them over his exhaled smoke.

Betty gasped. 'See,' she said to Joe Joe through clenched lips. 'It's really him.'

'Urgh, he is disgusting.'

Betty glanced surreptitiously over her shoulder at the open window. Dom Jones sat perched on the window-ledge, one skinny buttock overhanging, staring into the half-distance. He saw Betty looking at him and threw her a half-smile.

'All right?' he called out.

Betty blanched, every drop of blood in her body

rushing violently to her head. 'All right,' she replied in her best approximation of a cool mockney hipster's response. She turned away then, as nonchalantly as she could.

'He is *so* ugly,' said Joe Joe.

'Ssh . . . !'

'Why? Why ssh? He is ugly. I can't say this?' He put his hand against his heart and looked at her beseechingly.

'Well, no, not that loud. And anyway, he's not ugly, he's . . .' she threw another surreptitious glance in his direction and took in the mop of thick dark hair, heavily lashed eyes, petulant mouth, designer cashmere V-neck in baby blue '. . . he's cute.'

'Yes,' said Joe Joe disdainfully, 'cute like a baby monkey.' And then he started making baby monkey noises, very loud baby monkey noises. Betty hit him on his arm. 'Stop it,' she hissed, and Joe Joe laughed.

He stopped as the sound of ringing cut through the air. It was the distinctive tone of a mobile phone. Across the echoing courtyard they heard Dom Jones answering the call.

'No,' they heard him mutter. 'No, I know. I fucking know that. But she's left me with the baby. Yeah. I know. She's doing a shoot. In Kentish Town. Yeah. Yeah, she sacked the nanny. I don't fucking know. Probably just to fuck me off. Yeah. They were supposed to be sending someone over. No, I don't know, just some girl from the PR department, Clare something. Never heard of her. No, she's not here yet. They sent her on the fucking tube. Yeah, I mean, for fuck's sake. She's probably stuck in a tunnel. Yeah. No, of course I can't bring the baby. What the fuck would I do with a fucking baby in the middle of a fucking radio interview? No. She's ill. I don't know, a cold or something. She told me she's got to stay indoors. Yeah. I know. Anyway, I'll call you when the PR gets here. OK? Oh, fuck, that's the baby crying. I've got to go. Yeah. Later . . .'

He turned off his phone, extinguished his cigarette and headed back into the house. He left the window open and Betty could hear the plaintive mewling of a small baby.

Six months old, according to the reports in the newspapers.

After a moment the mewling stopped. And then, a minute later she saw him, Dom Jones, infamous philanderer, excessive drug-taker, extreme boozer, habitual frequenter of every members' club in London W1, friend to every debauched artist, musician and journalist in Soho, cockney/mockney art school dropout and darkly gleaming rock-and-roll supernova, clutching a small bundle of pink baby against his shoulder, rocking slowly from foot to foot and whispering tenderly into her ear.

Betty dropped any pretence at surreptitiousness and simply stared. Her stomach folded up against itself and she gulped. The man in the blurred photographs receiving sexual favours in a toilet cubicle and the man shouting aggressively into a mobile phone only five minutes ago faded away into the furthest reaches of her subconscious, and all she could see was a beautiful man soothing a tiny baby.

'Oh, look!' said Joe Joe, clasping his hands together gleefully. 'So cute! The baby monkey has a baby monkey all of his own!'

'Joe Joe,' Betty chastised, 'don't be mean!'

Joe Joe shrugged and snatched the roll-up from Betty's hand.

'Here,' he said, 'let me learn how to do this.'

He put it between his full lips and he sucked in deeply, his cheeky cheeks disappearing into hollows. He held the smoke for a count of three and then he expelled it loudly and dramatically, his eyes pouring tears, his face red raw, coughing so loud that Dom Jones across the way grimaced and pulled down the sash with his free hand, giving Betty and Joe Joe a slightly withering look, tinged, Betty couldn't help but feel, with a hint of melancholy. And then he was gone.

She grabbed the roll-up back from Joe Joe and rubbed it out. 'You silly bugger,' she teased. 'What did you do that for?'

He smiled through his tears. 'I don't know,' he wheezed. 'But I have burned my lips, look.' He turned the skin of his lip outwards and showed her a roll-up-shaped burn running down the centre of both of them.

'Ow,' said Betty, 'and good. Now hopefully you won't do it again.'

He smiled at her sheepishly, with his burned lips. 'So,' he said, 'I have a special request. I want you to have a party.'

'A party?'

'Yes! We must have a party! In your dinky little flat. Maybe tomorrow night!'

Betty balked. 'It's Wednesday tomorrow.'

'I know! And you are not working. And I am not working. And I think, Betty Boo, it is time for you to have a house-warming.' He looked at her beseechingly.

Betty frowned at him.

'Pleeease.'

'But, Joe Joe, my flat's not big enough. It's –'

He interrupted her with his hand. 'Have you not seen *Breakfast at Tiffany's*?'

She frowned again.

'Holly Golightly. She lives in a tiny teeny weeny flat, just like yours. She has the best party *ever*! Small is good! More sweat. More, how you say, *proximity*. Please please please, Betty, can we have a party? *Please*!'

Betty narrowed her eyes and considered the proposal. How could she resist a comparison with Holly Golightly? 'OK,' she said, 'but don't invite too many people. Please.'

18

Betty's tiny flat was bulging at the seams with what looked like a casting queue for a Benetton advert, packed tightly wall to wall with young, attractive, interestingly attired people from all corners of the globe, people that Joe Joe had collected on his journey through London's language schools and fast-food purveyors and nightclubs. By eleven o'clock Betty had drunk so much that her vision was beginning to separate and her words were starting to bleed into each other. She was having an unnecessarily animated conversation with a Japanese American girl called Akiko, who spoke with a very strange Trans-Asian accent and kept calling Betty 'Mandy' because she looked like an old friend of hers called Mandy.

'And you know what, Mandy, that's, like, the really weird thing about, like, *life*, you know. The way it, like, just keeps changing, you know, every time you think you know where you are, it just totally *changes* again . . .'

Betty smiled tightly. She knew without any shadow of doubt that she was about to be sick. She could feel it rising ominously through her like bad weather, sour and suffocating.

She felt her skin prickle and a flush of sweat blossom from her upper lip. She said, 'Excuse me, I need to go to the toilet,' and the girl called Akiko looked at her curiously and said, 'I beg your pardon?' and Betty realised that she had actually just said, 'Squeeze me, needa godo toily.' She pushed her way through a mass of backs, through banks of densely packed humans, each glancing at her in turn as she passed, brown eyes full of curiosity, blue eyes full of alarm, black eyes filled with amusement.

'Out of her way!' she heard someone shout with hilarity. 'She's going to spew!'

She pushed against the bathroom door and it gave way against her, suddenly, as though someone had been holding it closed from behind and had let it go at the last moment. She stumbled through the door and landed with a thud against the edge of the bath, feeling the faint sensation of a bruise forming across her thigh, her silver beret falling half across her face, and became aware of John Brightly standing behind the door, looking at her with his usual expression of bland amusement.

'Oh my God,' said Betty. 'It's John Brightly. It's John Brightly. In my bathroom. Why are you in my bathroom?' She pulled the hat from her head dramatically and put out a hand to balance herself against the bath. And then, before he had a chance to answer, she was on her knees with her head arched over the toilet, dimly aware that it was blocked up with wads of pink toilet paper and urine, that there were fag ends buried in the mass and that as much as all this appalled her, she absolutely was going to have to be sick on top of all of it.

'It's blocked,' she heard John Brightly mutter from somewhere behind her. 'I tried to flush it. It's fucked.'

She sat on her knees in dim, ringing silence while she waited for the tidal wave of nausea finally to engulf her. She groaned, she groaned again and then it came, loud and violent and everywhere. Upon the pink toilet paper, on top of the accumulated piss of a hundred party guests, the old fag butts, the toilet seat, the wall, the floor, the pipes, a hand towel, a spare toilet roll and the edge of the bath.

'Jesus Christ,' said John Brightly.

Betty groaned again, wiped away a drool of vomit from her lower lip and ran her hands through her hair.

'Is that it?' asked John.

Betty nodded and groaned again. That was it. She was done. She got slowly to her feet and turned to face the mirror. As she'd expected, she looked too horrible for words.

'Here.' John Brightly offered her a piece of chewing gum.

'Thank you,' she said. She turned back to the mirror. If she was a man now she would splash her face with icy cold water straight from the tap. As a woman, however, if she were to do that, the already dreadful reality of her clammy complexion, green hair and red eyes would be compounded even further by melted mascara and streaked eyeliner. Instead she dabbed at her cheeks with wet hands and ran her fingers through her hair, chewing the gum urgently to rid her mouth of the sour juices of regurgitated vodka and cider.

'I'll get you some water,' said John Brightly.

Betty locked the door behind him and stood for a moment, staring at her face and listening to the strange noises of the party still, inexplicably, going on around her.

There was a soft knock at the door and she opened it a crack. John Brightly peered through the gap at her and Betty looked at him then, properly, for the first time since she'd come hurtling through the bathroom door. He was more handsome than she'd anticipated him being. She let him in and took the plastic cup of water from him.

'How long have you been here?' she asked.

He shrugged. 'An hour or so.'

'An hour or so? How come I didn't see you?'

He shrugged again. 'No idea,' he said. 'I wasn't hiding.'

'But, why are you *here*?'

He laughed. 'Because I was invited. Your friend with the ginger afro invited me.'

'Ah.' She picked her beret off the floor, and sat down on the side of the bath. 'But still. You didn't have to come just because you were invited. Why are you really here?'

'I have no idea,' he said, joining her on the edge of the bath. 'I think, if I'm going to be totally honest with you, I came because I was curious.'

'Curious?'

'Yeah, about what lies on the other side of that door.' He gestured beneath his feet. 'You know, I'm out there six days a week, I see people come and go. I wondered what it was like in here. And I suppose . . .' he paused '. . . I suppose I was curious about you, a bit.'

She laughed. 'Why would you be curious about *me*?'

'I don't know. The mysterious blond girl, with the fur coat and the big eyes, suddenly morphing into this brown-haired girl in a Wendy's uniform. The changes you're going through. Fresh in town. Wide-eyed and innocent. All that. It's interesting. You're interesting.' He paused again, clearly re-evaluating the wisdom of his last comment. 'Kind of,' he added.

She nudged him with her elbow and said, 'Huh.'

'Well, you asked . . .'

She smiled at him, feeling the euphoria of a recently emptied stomach, the sense of never having felt better in her life. 'I've been curious about you, too,' she said.

He raised an eyebrow at her and she thought that he looked very cool when he did that.

'Yes, curious about why you're so offish with me.'

'Offish?'

'Yes, ever since that first day, when I was wearing the fur. You've always been a bit, I don't know, a bit like you don't like me.'

He laughed wryly. 'I don't even know you. How could I not like you?'

She shrugged. 'No idea,' she said. 'Everyone likes me. But you've just acted like you didn't.'

He looked at her with a dry smile. 'I think,' he said softly, 'that that's just my personality. I don't really do effusive, you know. I don't really do all that fake stuff.'

'Why does it have to be fake? Why can't it just be, you know, *friendly*?'

'Where are you from?' he asked unexpectedly.

'Guernsey,' she replied. 'Why?'

He smiled. 'No reason.'

'What?'

'Nothing! Just I guessed it might be somewhere like that. Somewhere small. Somewhere where people are, you know, *friendly* to each other.'

Betty felt her defences pop up. 'Not *everyone* in small places is friendly, you know. We're not all these big cheesy, gurning stereotypes. Some of us are actually quite standoffish. And actually, I'm not even *from* Guernsey. I'm from Surrey. I just ended up in Guernsey. Through no fault of my own.'

He put a hand up to her, a signal to calm down. 'Wow,' he said, 'it wasn't meant to be an insult. It's just, you can usually tell, with new people you can see the thinness of their skin.'

'Have I got visibly thin skin?' she asked, slanting her eyes at him.

He appraised her. 'No,' he said, 'there's something there. Something more than just a small-town girl.'

She smiled at him triumphantly, basking strangely in his approval. Those last few months in that house on the cliff, tending to the demands of a dying woman, had left an indelible mark on her and she was glad. She would have hated it to be as though it had never happened, all that time, all that youth, all that love.

Someone knocked at the door then and Betty jumped. She'd almost forgotten where they were. She tipped back the rest of the cup of water and said, 'I'd better clean this place up a bit. Will you still be here when I've finished?'

'Let me help,' John Brightly said, getting to his feet.

'What? No! God, no. I can do it. You go and tell whoever's waiting outside that they'd better come back later.'

'Are you sure?'

'Christ! Of course I'm sure. There's no way I'm having you cleaning up my puke. That would just be totally gross. Get out of here!' She pushed him away playfully towards the door, and as her hand touched his arm she felt a flicker of energy pass between them, something warm and vital, something real and human, a connection.

He looked at her with some genuine softness in his eyes for the first time since she'd known him. 'Well, at least let me try and fix the toilet,' he said.

'I can do it!' she said. 'I used to live in a falling-down mansion. I'm an expert at fixing toilets. I promise you.'

'Falling-down mansion? Wow. I can't wait to hear all about it.'

'Meet me outside,' she said, 'on the fire escape. I'll tell you all about it.'

She closed the door behind him, opened up the cupboard beneath the basin, pulled out some spray bleach and a stiff J-cloth and applied herself to the thoroughly disgusting job of cleaning up her mess.

The first person she bumped into when she finally

emerged almost ten minutes later was Candy Lee, the angry woman from downstairs. She had a bottle of rum in one hand and a bottle of beer in the other. She was wearing a flowery blouse with a denim miniskirt and a denim jacket, and her shoes were denim mules with cork heels. Her hair was adorned with silk flowers and she had a big lipstick stain on her right cheek.

Her eyes widened at the sight of Betty.

'What you been *doing* in there?' she demanded.

Betty looked at her curiously. 'Fixing the *toilet*,' she said haughtily.

Candy Lee threw her a haughty look. 'Why it take you so long?'

'Because it *did*.'

'Come in with me.' She dragged Betty by the hand into the bathroom and locked the door behind them. Candy had clearly been carrying a heavy bladder for quite some time. Her urine was audible hitting the water in the bowl and she sighed with pleasure as she peed. Betty stared at her in horror.

'Can I go now?' she asked.

'No! No. You stay. I like you. I want to talk to you.'

'Someone's waiting for me,' Betty said, 'outside. Maybe we can talk later?'

'No,' Candy leaned towards Betty and grabbed her wrist, '*now*. I want to talk *now*. Why it stink so bad in here? Someone been sick. So disgusting.' She waved her hand in front of her nose and then pulled a canister of Impulse body spray out of a small bag slung diagonally across her chest, which she sprayed liberally around herself. 'Here,' she said, 'you too. You smell of sick.' Before Betty had a chance to argue, she had been aggressively perfumed with something that smelled like old ladies and toilet freshener.

'Listen, you, you are a beautiful girl.'

Betty stared at her mutely.

'You are prettiest girl I ever seen.'

'Er . . .'

'Well, nearly prettiest girl I ever seen. Meg Ryan prettiest girl I ever seen. But you are close. I like girls.'

'Oh . . .'

'I like girls like you. Pretty girls, with big eyes and skinny bodies. You are my dream girl,' she smiled. 'You ever been with a girl before?'

Betty shook her head. 'No,' she said, feeling that there should be no grey areas whatsoever in her response. 'Never.'

'You should go with a girl. You should go with me. I am the best girl. The best one in Soho. The best one in London.' She got to her feet, wiped herself and pulled up her lime-green pants. Then she pulled down her denim skirt and stared meaningfully at Betty for a moment. 'See this,' she said, stepping closer to Betty, 'look.' She stuck out her tongue and flashed a silver stud at her. 'This is for pretty girls, missy. Pretty girls like you.'

Betty smiled. 'Oh,' she said, 'didn't that hurt?'

Candy's face fell. 'No!' she barked. 'It did not *hurt*. It is for the pleasure of my girls. It is sweet feeling. I can make you come for ten minutes with this. Maybe some time fifteen.'

Betty tried not to flinch at these words. 'It's not really . . . I'm not quite . . . I like boys.'

'Ha!' snapped Candy. 'We *all* like boys. Everyone likes boys! Boys are *nice*! But girls are nicer.' She was standing very close to Betty now, close enough for the rum fumes on her breath to form a cloud around her head, close enough to feel her body heat, close enough to notice a small scar above her right eyebrow and a scattering of dandruff on the shoulders of her denim jacket.

Betty took a step back from her and smiled tightly. 'No, really, honestly, it's not my thing. It's not . . . I've never wanted to.'

'I was twenty-eight first time I slept with a girl. All those years before I thought I didn't want to. I was wrong.' She threw her a bright smile, all small white teeth and glinting silver. 'Come on,' she put her hand to Betty's hair and stroked it. 'Come downstairs. Come to me. Come with me. Come . . .' She licked her lips with her studded tongue.

'No!' said Betty. 'Thank you! Really. My friend is waiting, I really need to go . . .'

Candy sighed and let her hand drop from Betty's hair. 'Well, lucky for you,' she said, 'I am only down there.' She pointed beneath their feet. 'Lucky for you, any time you want me, you can come and have me. Just knock on my door.' She leaned across Betty's body so that they were touching almost from neck to crotch and banged against the bathroom door with her knuckles, *rat-tatatat*. 'Like this. Then I will know is you. What your name?'

'Betty,' she replied breathlessly.

Candy's eyes widened. She trailed her fingertips dramatically across Betty's cheek and then opened the bathroom door to leave, her beer in one hand, the rum bottle gripped beneath her arm. But before she went she turned one more time and looked at Betty sharply. 'And stop smoking outside my window. So rude.'

She tutted loudly and pulled the door sharply closed behind her, and Betty let herself fall onto the side of the bath. She touched her cheek where Candy's finger had just been and shuddered. Then she found her way to the kitchen and poured herself another tumbler of vodka. She noticed briefly that the party had thinned out, that the DJ was asleep on the sofa, that the music was quieter, that Candy was nowhere to be seen, that the Japanese American called Akiko was pensively writing something in a journal and that Joe Joe was rammed up in the corner kissing a man with a blond buzz cut and a vintage bowling shirt, his hands tucked casually in the man's back pockets.

She absorbed all this numbly and slowly, as though on a two-second time delay. Then she took the tumbler of vodka and her tobacco pouch out of the flat and up towards the fire escape. She felt curiously excited, a swell of anticipation in her chest as she ascended the three steps to the fire-escape door. She could see where most of the party guests had gone as she pulled open the door. The escape was rammed with bodies, the air was thick with the smell of tobacco and marijuana, there was a low-level buzz of muted conversation, someone was playing a guitar. The only light out here came from the bulb on the landing downstairs.

Betty squeezed her way through the mass of people, searching for the reassuring shape of John Brightly, dying to tell him about her encounter with Candy Lee, dying to carry on their conversation, find out more about him, tell him more about her. She stepped over legs and climbed over couples, but it was soon obvious to her that he wasn't there. Maybe he'd come out here, taken one look at this messy sprawl of stupefied youth and decided that he was too old and wise to hang around here.

She sighed and fell to her haunches.

She was tired now.

It was late and she was tired and she wanted to go to bed.

But she couldn't because there was a party in her house. A party, probably, in her bed.

She rolled herself a cigarette and smoked it slowly and unhappily, surrounded by strangers, and she wished for a moment that she had never left Guernsey.

19

1920

'Isle of Man?'

'No.'

'Isle of Wight?'

'No.'

'Jersey, then?'

'No,' said Arlette, 'but close.'

'Guernsey? Yes! Guernsey!'

'Well, yes, Mr Worsley, but if you don't mind me saying, you have reached that conclusion only through a process of painstaking elimination. I think you left out only Lundy and the Scillies.'

'Well, your accent, it's not one I've heard before. But really, the clue should have been in your name, I suppose. De La Mare.'

'Yes. I think my name was probably a giveaway.'

'Hmm.' Gideon smiled into his fist sheepishly. 'Yes. I think maybe I need to sharpen up my regional knowledge. Not quite as perceptive as I thought I was. So, an island with a French flavour. And you with your French name. And, now I think of it, of course, such fine, French features. Have you been to France?'

'No,' Arlette replied. 'Before I arrived in Portsmouth in September I had never before left the island.'

He looked at her with surprise. 'Well, well,' he said. 'And you're twenty-one? That is a long time to have spent on a rock in the middle of the Channel.'

'Yes,' she replied, 'quite.'

'And now you are here. Free. Unfettered. *Alive.*' He chuckled and sharpened his pencil, leaving the curl of shavings to fall to the floor.

'And having my portrait painted by a man I barely know.'

'You are clearly not as timid as your appearance might suggest.'

'Oh, no,' she teased, 'I am. This is entirely out of character.'

She gazed through the bowed windows of his studio. She had been here for almost an hour now and was feeling braver and braver by the minute. From the moment she had walked into this room and seen the portraits stacked up around the room, exquisite renderings in pencil and watercolour of a dozen beautiful women, all fully clothed and serene, she had felt reassured that Gideon Worsley was, as he said, a professional artist with an interest in her face.

'So, Mr Worsley . . .'

'Please, call me Gideon. Please.'

'Gideon. Tell me. Have you always lived in London?'

'Oh, no, not remotely. I lived in my family's house in Chipping Norton, until I was twenty-one.'

'Chipping Norton?'

'Oxfordshire. And then I came down, after university, stayed, like yourself, with a friend of my parents, and then I wandered past this cottage one watery November morning over a year ago and saw that it was for rent, and enquired with the landlord's agent and suddenly, here I was, in a blue house by the river, which I can barely afford, alone and without help, a single man fending for himself. And not particularly well, it must be said.'

'You need a wife.'

'Yes, indeed I do. Can you suggest anyone who might be interested in taking up the position?'

Arlette laughed. 'What would be the benefit? For the prospective wife?'

'A blue cottage by the river? An artistic man with love in his heart? Weekends at a charming house in five acres of wild meadows with my spectacular mama and papa? Eclectic friends? A wild social life?'

'Wild, you say?'

He smiled and examined the top of his pencil in the light of the window. 'Yes,' he said circumspectly.

'Wild in what way?'

'Oh, gosh, in that normal, ordinary way of wildness. When I am not working, I am playing. And playing very hard indeed.'

'Were those your friends?' she ventured. 'The ones you were singing carols with when I first met you?'

'They were some of my friends, yes. I have a lot of friends. And they are all wild.'

'Lots of friends, but no wife?'

'Precisely. But I am twenty-four. It is time, hopefully, to combine the two.'

'So where does it happen, all this wildness?'

'Here. As you could probably guess from the state of my sitting room. And there are clubs, in Mayfair, in Soho.'

'Soho?'

'Yes. Soho. Colourful, colourful places. I'd like to ask you to join us one night but I fear your faint Jersey heart –'

'*Guernsey*!'

'Of course . . . your *Guernsey* heart may not be quite up to the challenge.'

Arlette flushed.

'Have I made you cross?' asked Gideon, peering at her playfully from behind his canvas.

'No, Mr Worsley. You have not made me cross. Why ever would you think you had?'

'So,' he said, 'would you? Would you come out to play, one evening, in the dark corners of Soho?'

'That depends,' she said, 'on what exactly you *do* in the dark corners of Soho.'

'We drink, we sing, we talk, we think, we dance, we love, we *live*, Miss De La Mare. And then, eventually, quite often when the sun is above the roofs and the whey-faced commuters have sprung out of their miserable little holes, we come home and sleep.'

Arlette pursed her lips. She was sure there was something she wanted to say, about Gideon and his dirty house and his slovenly way of life and his disregard for the people who got out of bed every morning and made his precious city run, but she could not find the words.

'I, of course, do *not* include you in that number. No, no, no. Beautiful shop-girls selling dresses at Liberty. No, you are a separate breed entirely. A cut above . . .' He smiled and his face retreated once more behind his canvas.

Silence fell upon them. They had reached a tiny but perceptible impasse. For now, Arlette felt, it would be better not to talk.

20

1995

Betty slept on the sofa that night, snuggled up next to Joe Joe and his conquest of the previous evening whose name, it transpired, was Rolf and who hailed from Munich. She had sacrificed her mezzanine to three girls from Poland who had missed the last tube home to Rayners Lane, and when she tried to stand up she couldn't because her whole body had seized up. She eventually managed to shake out the knots in her muscles and stumbled towards the bathroom. The door was locked from the inside. She sighed. She did not want to know what was on the other side of that door. She wanted coffee. She wanted water. She wanted a cigarette. She'd finished her tobacco last night. Or, at least, the three girls from Poland had finished her tobacco, using it in numerous attempts to construct a Camberwell Carrot in order to impress an English man called Joshua, who was, apparently, their TEFL teacher. She glanced at the time on the microwave: 7.12 a.m. She'd been asleep for approximately three hours.

She ran her hands through her weird green hair, pulled on her silver beret, located her shoulder bag, checked for her purse and her front door keys, then left the flat. She tiptoed nimbly past Candy's front door, a sudden overwhelming memory of lime-green stretch-lace knickers and a studded tongue puncturing her consciousness unpleasantly, and then she pushed open the front door and tumbled out onto the street.

It was a chilly morning for the beginning of June, the air was damp and it felt more like dawn than seven thirty. She had not yet seen her reflection, and if she had she would have observed that she was wearing only one of a pair of diamanté earrings, that a tuft of green hair was sticking out from beneath the silver hat, and curling upwards like a frond of greenery. She would also have observed that all the eyeliner on one eye had rubbed off on the sofa while she was sleep, yet the eyeliner on the other eye was fully intact. She would have seen that there were creases in her cheek from the cushion she'd slept against, that a small rash of zits had broken out on her jawline and that the seam around the waistline of her dress had split slightly in the night, revealing an inch of pale white flesh.

She would have seen all this and she would probably have decided to stay at home and not wander the early morning streets of Soho in plain sight of the world.

But she hadn't seen any of these things. She imagined herself to look glamorously careworn, sweetly rumpled. She sat in an Italian coffee shop on Wardour Street nursing an extra large cappuccino and smoking a roll-up, feeling like a character in a novel. She'd felt lonely last night. Now she felt alive again. Early morning Soho, in her party clothes, surrounded by chattering Italians in stained white shirts, the hiss and clatter of espresso machines, the smell of bacon, the vague edges of a hangover. She smiled to herself and thought that if the sixteen-year-old version of herself had walked past this window and seen her sitting there, she'd have wished to be her.

And as she thought that, the door of the café swung open and a small man walked in. A small man in a short-sleeved T-shirt, in spite of the chill, one hand holding a lit cigarette, his other hand in his jeans pocket, dark hair tousled and hanging around his face, a cloud of stardust glittering in his aura.

Betty froze.

It was him.

It was Dom Jones.

She put a hand to her cheek, a cheek that had suddenly, inexplicably, flushed red. She watched him from the corner of her eye, standing at the counter, ordering a full breakfast, with extra bacon and strong tea. She saw him take a seat at a table in the corner, pull a phone out of his pocket and tap something into it, scratch his scalp through his thick hair, put out his cigarette in a small metal ashtray, identical to the one on Betty's table, and pull open a newspaper.

She saw his right leg, jigging up and down beneath the table, one hand nonchalantly scratching at his crotch through the denim of his jeans. She saw that he had a two-day stubble on his chin and that his eyes looked puffy and blank.

Unwritten rules said she should leave him be, like a free-roaming animal in a zoo. Look, don't touch. But there was too much connecting them this damp June morning, and before she could censor herself or ask herself what she was hoping to achieve she had turned fully towards him, waited a beat for him to acknowledge her gaze and then said, 'Hi.'

He looked annoyed for a moment. He threw her a tight smile, nodded tersely. But then she saw it, in his eyes, a tiny glint of recognition.

'Do I know you?' he asked.

'No,' she said, 'well, not properly. I live in the building opposite you. You know? Across the courtyard.'

He looked at her blankly, his tired eyes taking in the detail of her, still failing to make the connection, until his eyes alighted upon the packet of Golden Virginia on the table in front of her and he nodded slowly and said, 'Ah, yeah, the girl on the fire escape. Yeah. I know you.'

That should have been the end of the conversation. What else was there to say? But Betty still felt it, this sense that she and this man had something to talk about, that she was allowed to engage with him.

'Sorry about the noise last night,' she said. 'Hope we didn't disturb you.'

He moved his paper away from himself, a gesture that Betty took as an acceptance of her attempt at social intercourse. 'You fuckers,' he said, with a wry smile. He leaned back into his chair and gazed at her impenetrably. 'You absolute fuckers. I went to bed early last night, too. First time I've been to bed early in about six months.'

Betty clapped her hand over her mouth. 'Oh God,' she said, 'I'm really sorry.'

She could see from the curl of his mouth that he wasn't really cross.

'It's all right. I moved to a bedroom on the street, took a temazepam. Feel like shit now; that stuff really knocks you out.'

She smiled at him encouragingly, amazed by how normal it felt to be chatting to Dom Jones in a café.

He picked his cigarettes from the table and offered the pack to Betty. Her instinct was to say no. She hated cigarettes. All that gunk and poison. But she absolutely had to smoke one of his cigarettes. She would regret it when she was ninety if she didn't. She took one and let him light it for her.

'Good party?' he asked, blowing some smoke out of the corner of his mouth.

She nodded. 'Yeah, well, it wasn't really *my* party. It was supposed to be a housewarming. But in reality I think it was just an excuse for my friend to invite everyone in London with a foreign accent.'

'And you were just trapped there with nowhere to go?' he smiled at her knowingly.

'That kind of thing.'

'Yeah,' he said, 'I remember those kinds of parties. I used to lock my bedroom door and pee in a bottle until it was over.'

A short silence followed, during which time Dom's

breakfast was delivered to his table. It looked amazing, particularly the eggs, two glistening white and yellow discs, shiny as glass. She wanted eggs. But she could not afford eggs. Eggs on toast, according to the illuminated price list above the counter, were £2.50 and she had only £3.50 left in her purse to last her until her next pay cheque. She stared at the eggs lustfully, while Dom Jones folded away his newspaper and poured sugar into his tea from a glass canister.

She was about to move back to her table, aware that the conversational window had just closed up, when Dom picked up his knife and fork and said, 'So, how long have you been living over there?'

She picked up her cappuccino and took a sip from it. 'Three weeks and five days,' she said.

'Oh,' he said, 'right. So not much longer than me then.'

She feigned ignorance of his current domestic situation and looked at him quizzically.

'Yeah, I've had the place for three years but only lived there for a month or two before I moved out again. And now I'm back.'

'Oh,' she said cautiously, 'right.'

'And where were you before you were in a flat in Soho?'

'I was in Guernsey,' she said.

'Oh, right. That's an island, yeah?'

She laughed. 'Yes. A very small one.'

'Yeah,' he said, sawing through a piece of toast and egg, 'I think I've got some offshore accounts over there.' He paused and shrugged. 'Or maybe Jersey. One or other.' He put the egg and toast in his mouth and Betty experienced a surreal moment of thinking, I am watching Dom Jones eat an egg. She put it to the back of her mind and continued her approximation of a cool chick who could not care less about celebrities eating eggs.

'And you're working at Wendy's, yeah?'

She looked at him with surprise. 'How did you know that?'

'I saw you,' he said, 'remember, in your uniform? You had blond hair then . . .' He looked disconsolately at her head as though her current lack of blond hair was a great personal sadness to him.

'Hair situation's gone a bit pear-shaped,' she said. 'I really need to get it coloured professionally, but I can't afford to. So until then I'm stuck in a hat.'

He sliced through a thick sausage, heartily and crudely, attacking it like a lumberjack. 'And what's it like,' he continued, talking with his mouth full, 'working at Wendy's?'

She shrugged. 'Not as bad as you might think. Nice people. Nice boss. Free dinners.'

'I love Wendy's,' he said. 'Always used to go in there after a gig, before . . . you know . . . before I couldn't any more.'

She left his allusion to his supernova fame hanging uncommented upon.

'Do you still do those chicken sandwiches,' he asked, his body wriggling with boyish excitement, 'you know, with the spicy sauce?'

'Yes. They're a bestseller, actually.'

'God, I used to love those. That takes me back.' His eyes filled with a nostalgic mist. 'Yeah,' he sighed. 'Wendy's, Shaftesbury Avenue, *youth*.'

'You're still young!'

'Yeah, I'm young, but I'm not *youthful*. Once you've crossed over from twenty-five, that's it,' he clicked his fingers, 'youth takes a ride. Then you get to be young for as long as you like. I'm going to be young until I'm about forty, I reckon. Maybe even forty-five.' He winked and chuckled to himself. 'How old are you?' he asked.

'Twenty-two. Twenty-three next month.'

'Ah,' he said, 'youth. Yeah. There it is. Twenty-two. Man. I would give a lot to be twenty-two again.'

'No,' she said. 'Seriously. You wouldn't. It's shit. I live in a cupboard. Or actually, a cupboard *within* a cupboard. My downstairs neighbour is a crazy Asian dyke. I've got literally *no money*. And because no one in this whole city would give me a job I like, I flip burgers all day. It *sucks* being twenty-two, seriously.'

Dom laughed and wiped the corners of his mouth with a paper napkin.

'Yeah, right, I get it. And I do remember being twenty-two, and I did live in a squat, and I did have crappy jobs, but I suppose I'm looking at it through this, like, bottle bottom. It's distorted; seems so long ago I've forgotten what it felt like. And what sort of jobs were you looking for? Before you ended up at Wendy's?'

She told him about the art galleries and the boutiques

and the temping appointments at button factories. 'My problem is, I've got no work experience,' she said, 'and because I've got no work experience, I can't get a job. And it's just a vicious cycle.'

'What did you do in Guernsey? I mean, you're nearly twenty-three, you must have been doing *something*, right?'

'I was looking after my grandmother,' Betty said. 'She had Alzheimer's and brain damage from a stroke. No one else wanted to live with her, so I did.'

She saw a flash of something across his features, something bright and dazzling. She couldn't decipher it for a moment and then realised with a swell of pride that it was respect. He had thought she was an amusing young girl, some kind of diverting reflection of his own shabby, youthful existence. And now he thought she was something more than that.

'Wow,' he said, after a moment. 'That's, er . . .'

'It was nothing,' she shrugged. 'I loved her.'

'So what, you did everything? Bum-wiping, the lot?'

'Yes. The lot.'

'On your own?'

'Well, yes, most of the time. There was a carer, but only eight to five. I was there twenty-four-seven.'

He nodded knowingly. 'Amazing,' he said, 'what you'll do for someone you love.' He glanced at his wristwatch and tucked his cutlery together on his plate. 'I've got to run,' he said. 'The wife's dropping the kids off.'

'You've got kids?' she asked, amazing herself with her fine acting skills.

'Yes, three. Tiny ones.' He raised his eyebrows exasperatedly. 'And no nanny. Should be an interesting day.'

'I can help,' she said, the words propelled from her mouth by the force of some kind of latent insanity.

He looked at her questioningly. 'What?'

'I'm not working today. Well, not till later. I could come and help you. With your kids.' She smiled a panicky, I'm-not-crazy-I-swear kind of smile.

He stopped completely in his tracks, then. She watched him, watched a thousand different and conflicting thoughts hurtling through his mind. He put a hand to his chin and rubbed it gently. Then he put his other hand to the back of his neck and squeezed it. He gazed at the floor and then at the ceiling. And then he stared straight into Betty's eyes and said, 'Yeah. Shit. Why not? I mean, if you're sure. I can pay you. Obviously. Tell me how much you want.'

She shrugged and smiled. 'Nothing. I don't want anything. I just like kids and my flat is full of people with hangovers and I've got nothing better to do.' This wasn't strictly true. She planned to go to St Anne's Court today, to see the building where Clara Pickle had once lived, see if there was anything new she could dredge up from that. But really, she suspected that was another dead end. And what was happening here now, in this steamed-up café, was too remarkable to ignore. She shrugged again and then Dom smiled at her.

'I don't know what it is . . .' he said vaguely, as though

he were thinking out loud, 'what it is, about you . . .?' And then in a louder voice, he said, 'Cool. Excellent. Well, you want to come now?'

She fingered the rip in the seam of her dress absent-mindedly and shook her head. 'I might pop home, first,' she said, 'have a shower, brush my teeth, that kind of thing.'

He looked at her, half smiling, half dazed, as though trying to ignore a persistent voice in his head telling him not to let her in his home whilst at the same time not quite believing his luck.

'Cool,' he said again. 'Great. Well, you know where I am. Peter Street. Number nine. I'll see you there in, what, half an hour?'

She nodded and tried to exude an overwhelming aura of trustworthiness and sanity. 'Roughly,' she said.

'Good,' he said. Then he scratched his head, again, put his hands into his pockets and turned to leave. He stopped at the door of the café and turned back towards her. 'Don't tell anyone, though, will you? Don't tell them where you're going?'

She gave him her best Guide's honour fingers-up and waited until he'd disappeared from view before exhaling and collapsing bodily and dramatically onto the slightly greasy tabletop.

21

When Betty got home five minutes later and finally made it to the bathroom, she saw the full horror of the reality of her appearance. She stared into the bathroom mirror for so long and with such distress that all the features on her face seemed to start moving around, wriggling like fish.

She attacked her face in the shower with a bar of soap and a facial scrub. While she scrubbed she told herself it was good that she hadn't known how bad she'd looked. If she'd known how bad she'd looked she would never have left the flat, let alone have had the gall to start a conversation with a pop star. If she'd known how bad she'd looked she would not be on her way into the pop star's house to help him look after his children for a day.

She put on a black and white striped Lycra dress with the sleeves pushed up, knee-high boots and a denim jacket. She tucked all her hair inside the silver beret, reapplied her make-up, sprayed on some perfume, ignored every attempt by Joe Joe to find out where she was going all dressed up like that, and left the house feeling sick with nerves and excitement.

Dom Jones did a double take when he saw Betty

standing on his doorstep a moment later. He had a small baby in his arms and another small child attached to his ankle. His eyes took in the full length of Betty from her crown to her toes.

'Fresh,' he said eventually. 'Come in.'

He held the door open for her, his eyes scanning the street outside his house in both directions before closing it quietly behind them.

'Come in,' he said again, 'excuse the chaos. This house was never meant to have kids in it.' He smiled drily and led her through a tiny hallway painted matt black, then through a tiny, half-panelled sitting room painted aubergine. The living room beyond was furnished with two oversized, vintage tan leather sofas, art deco in appearance, a huge chrome and crystal chandelier, a wide-screen TV, distressed wooden floorboards, brown shag-pile rugs and two rectangular fish tanks embedded into a wood-panelled wall at the far end. The walls were hung with outrageous pieces of art, one of which, at least, Betty recognised immediately as a Damien Hirst. The coffee table was glass and covered in Lego and plastic beakers and plates of half-eaten toast. Betty saw the table as it had been intended, as a place for drug-fuelled sex with nubile strangers, a place for cutting up lines of top-quality cocaine, for late night card games and for displaying interesting books about artists and film-makers and dead rock stars. It had not been intended as a resting place for children's plastic ephemera.

'Right,' said Dom, leaning down to pick up the small

child who was still attached to his lower leg, so he was now holding two of his children, 'let's do some introductions. This is Acacia,' he nodded towards the toddler, 'this is Astrid,' he nodded at a ringleted baby who looked like an actual doll. 'And somewhere over there,' he looked over his shoulder, 'is my big boy. Where are you, Donny?' A small boy appeared in the doorway, holding aloft a large plastic gun, with a war stripe painted across his nose and a belt of bullets thrown across his chest. 'This is Donovan. Donovan, this is . . .?' He looked at her, aghast. 'Jesus. I'm really sorry. I didn't even ask you your name?'

'Betty,' she said, smiling from bemused child to bemused child. 'Betty Dean.'

'Cool name,' he said, 'excellent. Yeah. Kids, this is Betty. Betty lives just around the corner and she's going to help me look after you all today until Mummy gets back. OK? So I want you all – especially you, Donny – to be really, really super-extra good today, OK?'

Donny narrowed his eyes at his father and then sat down heavily on the sofa behind him. 'I want Mummy,' he said.

Dom raised his eyebrows and turned to address him. 'I know you do, mate, but Mummy's busy today, Mummy's working.'

'Then I want Moira.'

Dom sighed and sat down next to him, a baby balanced on each knee. 'Sorry, mate, but Moira had to go home, didn't she? Moira had to go back to New Zealand.'

'I wish there was no Noo Zeeling,' he said, jutting out his lower lip and staring forlornly at the shag-pile rug.

Dom rubbed his hand across Donny's thick blond shag cut and smiled. 'Me too, buddy,' he said. 'Me too.'

'So,' said Betty, 'how old are they all?'

'Well, Astrid here is . . . shit, I dunno – how old is the baby, Donny?'

Donny shrugged.

'It was just before I went to Hong Kong, so must have been December, so she's about six months. Yeah, that's right. December the sixth. Of course. And Acacia is a year older, she was December the twelfth, so she's eighteen months, and big boy Donny here, he turned three in . . .' he squinted, trying to conjure up the birth month of his first-born child. 'September,' he said triumphantly. 'Yeah, he was three in September.'

'Wow,' said Betty. 'You packed them in.'

Dom tucked the toddler, Acacia, between himself and Donny on the sofa and passed a beaker into her outstretched hands. 'Well, yeah, not exactly planned that way. Cashie was supposed to be our last – well, *I* was happy for her to be our last – but it didn't quite work out that way. Did it, little one?' He looked down at the baby in his arms and smiled at her adoringly. 'But still, you know, once they're here, they're here, and then there's no going back. Forwards all the way, isn't that right, troops?'

Donny put his hand to his head in a salute and Dom rubbed his hair again.

Betty stood, her hands in the pockets of her denim jacket, staring down at this family of three beautiful children and a handsome young father, and wondered for a moment what she was doing here. He didn't need her here, surely. She was just an interloper, intruding into their beautiful world.

But as she thought this, the baby began to cry and the toddler dropped her beaker, spilling water onto the shag-pile rug, and Donny lifted his gun to his shoulder, and marched from the room. Then Dom looked up at Betty with his big brown eyes and said, 'Thank God you're here.'

'Well,' she said, 'what can I do first?'

He got to his feet and handed her the baby. 'You hold her,' he said, 'I'll make us some tea.'

She took the baby from his arms. She was warm and solid and a little damp. 'Does she . . .' Betty began, hesitantly, 'does she need a change?'

Dom looked at her blankly, and then with realisation. 'Oh God, yeah, she probably does. Sorry, yeah, um, there's some changing stuff in the bathroom,' he said, going to switch on a light on the staircase and pointing her in the direction of upstairs. 'First door on the left. Light comes on automatically.'

She nodded and looked again at the baby. The baby looked back at her with a look that said, 'I don't know who you are, and I don't care, just do what you have to do.'

'Er, OK.'

Dom poked his head back into the hallway and said,

'Are you OK doing this? I mean, have you changed a nappy before?'

She nodded. 'Yeah,' she said, 'no problem.' She thought it only polite not to mention that it had been an incontinence nappy on a doolally old lady.

'Just shout if you need anything.'

'I'll be fine,' she said, lacing her words with cool, calm and collection.

The stairs were dark, bare floorboards with a thin piece of black and cream striped carpet running up the middle. At the top of the stairs, steps went off in two directions. The steps on the right led to what looked like it must be Dom's bedroom. Through a gap in the door she could see black bedding, a low-slung chrome ceiling light, a fan of discarded newspapers, a huge art deco mirror, a sculpture of some description that looked like it had been built out of motorbike parts, and another fish tank, this one built into a unit that also contained a flat-screen television.

She stood for a while and watched the bubbles rise up through the water, silent and nubile, mesmerising and calming.

In Dom Jones's bedroom.

She shook the thought from her head and turned left.

The bathroom was tiled in floor-to-ceiling gold mosaic. A bejewelled bronze Moroccan lamp hung overhead, and in the middle of the room was a free-standing bath made of copper with an enormous rectangular copper shower head hung above it. Free-floating glass shelves housed piles of fresh white towels; there was a row of three white orchids in gold-leafed pots on the window sill. And there, in the corner, a tatty, plastic-covered changing mat, a packet of Huggies, three packets of Johnson's wipes, a basket full of plastic bath toys, and three small towelling robes with chocolate stains on them.

Why had one of the most famous people in the whole country let a total stranger into his home? Only three weeks ago this man's house had been staked out by paparazzi. Only three weeks ago, Betty had been awoken by a police car sent to keep people away from Dom Jones's house. He had seen her twice from his back window. He had bumped into her once outside her flat. And now, after just their fourth meeting he had invited her into his home. He had let her take his precious baby girl out of sight. How did he know she wasn't a journalist? A stalker? How did he know she wasn't up here poisoning his baby or drowning his baby because she was, in fact, a psychopath? Why did he trust her?

But she knew why he trusted her. He trusted her because they'd made a connection. Not just now, in the café, but weeks ago, across the courtyard. He'd seen her and she'd seen him and they had seen that they were equals. He'd seen a girl he could be friends with, a girl he might know in his real life, a girl he might once, possibly, have fallen in love with, but certainly a girl he could trust.

She placed the baby on her lap and then put everything back exactly where she'd found it, then she carried her down the stairs and into the kitchen at the back of the house, a dry, smiling baby in one arm and a balled-up nappy in the other.

'Where does this go?' she asked Dom, who was slicing up carrots into batons at a rough-hewn wooden surface next to a butler's sink.

He glanced at the balled-up nappy and then at Betty and the baby, and said, 'Well done, excellent! Bung it in here.' He held open the lid of a large chrome bin and she dropped it in, on top of carrot peelings, beer cans, takeaway containers, old pizza and the contents of an ash tray.

Dom Jones's rubbish.

Stop it, she told herself sternly, just stop it.

Donny was sitting on a very tall barstool, at a zinc-topped counter in the middle of the room, cutting paper into strips with a pair of blunt-ended scissors. He looked up at Betty with his big sad eyes and then turned back to his paper.

'What are you making?' she asked, balancing the baby on her hip.

He said nothing.

'Don,' said Dom, a carrot in his hand, 'Betty asked you something . . .'

Donny shrugged. 'I just want Moira,' he said.

Dom sighed and put down the carrot. He put a hand on Donny's shoulder and squeezed it. 'Guess where Betty works?' he said into his ear.

Donny shrugged.

'Betty works at a burger restaurant.'

Donny turned and glanced at her. 'McDonald's?' he asked, with even bigger eyes.

'No,' she said. 'It's a bit like McDonald's but it's called Wendy's.'

His face fell. He shrugged again.

Dom looked at Betty and smiled. 'Oh, well,' he said, 'one day, when you're big, you'll know what Wendy's is and you'll be really impressed.'

Betty took the baby and sat down on a big leather armchair in the corner with her on her lap. The toddler, whose name she had already forgotten (although she suspected it was tree-related), was sitting on the counter next to Dom, picking up carrot batons and putting them in her mouth. Unlike her baby sister and her big brother, this child had fine blond hair and a less exuberant-looking physiology. This child, in fact, looked nothing at all like Dom or Amy, but like a slightly consumptive orphan with eczema. But still, she was not without her own appeal, not the least of which were her enormous blue eyes and ladylike posture. She was dressed in a smock top and leggings, both black, which struck Betty as a strange way to dress a tiny child until she remembered that this was not any child.

This child was rock royalty.

'I love your house,' said Betty.

'Thanks,' said Dom. 'It was always the big dream, the place in Soho. Ever since I was young.'

'Yeah, me too.'

Dom looked at her with interest. 'Oh, yeah?'

'Yes. My mum brought me to London when I was fifteen. We ended up getting kind of lost in the backstreets. And I remember just feeling all this kind of *electricity* fizzing up through me, just wanting to get more and more lost, to never find my way out again . . .'

'Yeah,' Dom nodded. 'Yeah, that's exactly it. Same here. Probably when I was about twelve. I remember walking past this basement, just this shabby set of stairs leading down into this kind of manky pit. The windows were all dirty and there was this little blue neon light pinned to the wall, saying "Members Only". Christ, I wanted to know what was down those steps *so badly*, wanted to be a member. Didn't care what it was, could have been anything. And when we got our first advance, when we signed our first contract, I knew what I wanted to spend it on.' He looked around the kitchen. 'My own little slice of Soho.' He smiled.

'Wow,' said Betty. 'And you did.'

'Yup. And whatever happens, I'll never sell this place. Not ever.'

'No,' said Betty, with wide eyes. 'No, you mustn't. Never.'

She smiled, feeling the loose strands of their connection growing stronger and stronger.

Dom pulled a spoon out of a drawer, took the lid off a huge brown teapot and stirred the contents. 'Milk?' he said. 'Sugar?'

'Both, please,' she replied. 'Three sugars.'

He raised an eyebrow at her. 'Girl after my own heart,'

he said. 'I used to have five. Cut it down to two and a half. How's your hangover?'

She considered her hangover. She'd completely forgotten she had one from the moment she'd said 'hi' to Dom in the café two hours ago.

'Fine,' she said. 'I was, er, I was sick last night. Big time. Think it saved me from the worst of it.'

He smiled at her and passed her a large white mug full of tea. She put it down on a small table to the side of the armchair. The baby on her lap sat still and compliant, playing with the plastic bangle on Betty's wrist. A small radio was broadcasting Xfm. They were playing the new single by Supergrass; the lyrics were all about smoking fags and being young. Dom turned it up.

'Have you heard this?' he said.

She shook her head.

'This is going to be massive,' he said. He put a finger to his chin and listened intently. 'Seriously,' he continued. 'These guys are good. Look like a bunch of chimps, but they're good. Did you like "Caught by the Fuzz"?'

She shrugged and tried to look like she may or may not have liked it but really couldn't say.

'Absolute *gem*, that song. Total gem. Wish I'd written it. Do you like this song, Don?' he asked his small son.

Donny looked up from his pile of slivered paper and said, 'Hmm, yes, it's like a holiday.'

Dom laughed. '*Exactly*!' he cried. 'Spot on, mate. That's exactly what it's like. It's like listening to a holiday. A holiday from being old.'

'Or from being little,' suggested Donny.

Dom laughed again.

'What's a fag?' Donny asked.

'It's another word for a cigarette. Another word for those disgusting things that Mummy and Daddy always have hanging out of their mouths.'

Donny's face wrinkled up. 'Euw,' he said. 'I'm not ever going to smoke a fag.'

'Good,' said Dom. 'Good.'

'Disgusting habit,' Betty agreed.

'So, Betty,' Dom began, 'what time do you have to be off?'

'My shift starts at five, so about four?'

'Cool,' he said. 'Amy's PA's coming to collect the kids at three, so that's perfect. I've got some stuff I need to sort out in my office. Are you going to be OK if I leave you alone down here for a couple of hours?'

'Er, yeah. Yes! Of course. Sure.'

'I'll just be in my office, top of the house, if you need anything. Erm, they've all had some snacks, you've done Astrid's nappy. Donny knows how to switch on the telly. Don't you, mate?'

Donny nodded seriously.

'Help yourself to anything you want; got loads of nice cheese in the fridge.' He opened the door of a pale mint-green double American fridge. 'Tea.' He pointed to the kettle. 'Coffee.' He opened a cupboard door. '*Activities*.' He opened another door revealing shelves of paper and pens, jigsaws and dolls. 'Only rules,' he began to count them off on his fingers, 'no felt tips around the house, only at the table, no sugar, no dairy for Acacia – there's soya milk in the fridge – no slamming doors – no doors at all, in fact – and *no touching the music system*. Apart from that, anything goes. And, I don't care what you say, I *am* going to be paying you for this, OK?' He threw her a fond, almost paternal look and Betty smiled.

'OK,' she said. 'I'll allow that.'

'Cool,' he said, one hand holding the back of his neck. He looked as though he were about to say something else to her, but he didn't. Instead he addressed his children, warning them of the swift and harsh consequences of any mutinous behaviour and then she heard him leaping up the stairs, two at a time, to a mysterious room of business at the top of his house.

She got to her feet and looked around her. The toddler sat on the kitchen counter, eyeing her suspiciously through a mouthful of chewed-up carrot. Donny went *snip snip snip* with his childproof scissors and the baby sat in her arms, a heavier weight than Betty had at first suspected, but still and mellow. Betty thought, how bad can this be? These children are *angels*. And as this foolish thought passed through her mind, the toddler's eyes began to fill with tears and her face turned puce. At first Betty thought she was about to scream a tantrum but then she realised that the child was unable to breathe, that the child was in fact choking.

'Oh my God,' she said, wishing that she could remember the child's name. 'Oh my God, sweetie. Are you OK?'

The child's face went from puce to magenta and towards violet. 'Shit,' said Betty. 'Shit.' She put the baby down on the armchair and grabbed the toddler in her arms. The baby began to wail hysterically. The toddler still had not made a sound. 'Open your mouth, sweetie, let me have a look, that's it, that's it, oh God.' She forced her fingers into the child's mouth and inserted them into the back of her throat. There she felt the outline of a hard lump. She tried to prise it out with a hooked finger, but she seemed instead to be pushing it further down. And then she remembered an incident a few years earlier. Arlette had choked on a piece of chicken and Betty had watched the carer drag Arlette from her chair, turn her back to front, lock her arms around Arlette's frail chest and force the piece of chicken out with a hard and fast squeeze. The Heimlich manoeuvre. Or something.

She put the toddler back on the kitchen surface, turned her to face the wall, and then crunched her firmly inside the circle of her arms. The baby had fallen onto its side and was wedged, screaming, halfway down the side of the armchair. Donny said, 'What are you doing? Stop it! Stop it!' and then just as Betty was about to yell out for help, she felt the toddler's body go soft inside her arms and she heard a small thud as a large piece of carrot exited her throat and hit the tiled wall in front of her.

Donny had climbed down from the bar stool and was running out into the hallway, calling, 'Daddy! Daddy!' The baby was now flat on her front with her arms and legs splayed out around her. But Betty and the toddler stood still, both breathing in and out in terrible, awed relief. Betty held the toddler close to her and turned her round to face her. 'Are you OK, sweetie? Are you OK?'

The toddler cried and nodded, and buried her face into Betty's shoulder. Betty picked up the piece of carrot and showed it to the little girl.

'Look!' she said brightly. 'Look! Naughty carrot! Look at that naughty carrot! Shall we smack that naughty carrot?'

The toddler pulled her face out of Betty's shoulder and appraised the piece of carrot fearfully. She nodded once, and Betty hit the carrot. 'There,' she said. 'Bad carrot. He won't do that again . . .'

'What's going on?' Dom asked breathlessly in the doorway.

'Daddy!' said Donny. 'That lady hurt Cashie. She did *squeeze* her, very hard.'

Dom waded across the room and collected the screaming baby from the armchair. Then he threw Betty a quizzical look, tinted with anger.

'She was choking,' Betty said calmly, stroking the toddler's pale silky hair. 'She had a piece of carrot wedged in her throat. I had to squeeze it out.'

Dom blinked at her. He gulped. 'Shit,' he said, after a moment. 'Shit. Cashie. Baby girl. Are you OK?' He touched her cheek with his fingers and stared desperately into her eyes. Acacia nodded and shuddered as the last of her tears left her body.

Betty held up the offending piece of carrot.

'Oh my God.' Dom glanced at it in horror. 'Christ.' He slapped himself on the forehead. 'I should have thought,' he began, 'I should have said. I shouldn't have –'

'It's fine,' said Betty. 'It's fine. We're all fine. Aren't we, sweetheart?' The little girl held her arms out to her father and Dom and Betty swapped Acacia for the baby.

'Shit,' he said again, 'how did you know . . .? I mean, how did you . . .?'

She shrugged. 'I saw someone doing it to someone before. To my grandmother. It's called the Heimlich manoeuvre.'

'Christ,' he said, into Acacia's hair, rocking her back and forth against his chest. 'Christ. Thank God. Thank God you were here. Thank God you knew what to do. Thank you.' He looked up at her, over Acacia's crown, with big, fearful eyes. 'Thank you, Betty.' He looked down at Donny, who was standing at his side, watching everything suspiciously. 'Betty saved Acacia's life, Don,' he said to the boy. 'Betty saved her life. Do you understand?'

Donny shook his head.

'Cashie had some carrot in her throat. She couldn't breathe. She might have died. Betty squeezed Cashie to get the carrot out. Betty saved her life. Betty is a *hero*, Donny. Like a real-life *hero*.'

Donny looked at Betty uncertainly, and then away again. He shrugged, as though heroes without capes and swords and guns could not possibly be of any interest to him, and then he climbed back onto the barstool.

Dom looked at Betty. 'You must think I'm really . . . *crap*,' he said sheepishly.

Betty shook her head. 'Why would I think that?' she asked.

'I don't know,' he continued. 'Leaving my kids with some stranger, leaving you alone, not making sure everyone was, you know, safe.'

'But you did,' said Betty, 'you knew they'd be safe. With me. I'm a safe pair of hands. You knew that. You trusted me.' She smiled at him, his baby in her arms.

He gazed at her for a moment, absorbing her words. His face softened. He smiled. 'I suppose so,' he said. 'I suppose, if you put it like that . . .'

'It's true,' she said. 'You knew what you were doing. Now go back to your study,' she said. 'Go and work. We'll be fine. Won't we?'

She asked this of Donny, who said nothing, just snipped and snipped at his shards of paper, silently.

Dom inhaled, thoughtfully. He looked from Donny to Astrid to Acacia and then to Betty. 'No,' he said. 'No. I'm staying here. And not because I don't trust you. Because you're right, I do trust you. But because I'm supposed to be spending time with my kids. And the stuff up there,' he glanced upwards, 'that can wait. That can wait until later. Can't it, Don?'

Donny nodded.

'You know,' Dom continued, addressing Betty, 'I just had this feeling about you, when I first saw you. I just had this feeling. You know when you look at a person and you think there's a reason for them being there, that they're going to be, you know, *significant*. Weird . . .' He shook his head dismissively as though he'd said too much. 'Weird,' he said again. And then he looked at Betty once more and he smiled sincerely and mouthed, 'Thank you.'

And Betty smiled and mouthed back, 'You're welcome.'

22

1920

Arlette recognised one or two of the faces that were currently staring at her. She recognised both a girl whose name was Anna and a man whose name was Charles as members of the band of carollers from that night before Christmas Eve. The rest of the group swirled overwhelmingly before her eyes, all young, loud, bright-eyed with names like Virginia and Magenta, Claude and Francis, an amorphous mass of glamour and chatter. She had come with Gideon and met 'the rest of the gang' at a club in Windmill Street called the White Oleander. She could never before have imagined herself in such a place. First of all, the general environs of Soho, a shabby, dirty place, urchins running through the night-time shadows, muck-strewn pavements, a deep stench of rotting vegetation and unwashed flesh and general putrefaction. The buildings were small and packed tightly together, like the grimiest, most secret corners of Old St Peter Port, where sailors flashed their tattoos and breathed out fumes of old brown rum and chewing tobacco. And here there were prostitutes; blatantly, unashamedly, showing themselves to the street, in gaudy clothes and with faces smeared with make-up, and a lady with breasts so large they seemed almost to be swallowing her whole.

The door into this club had seemed at first to be not so much an entrance as a trap door, located in a basement and with rickety wooden steps leading down to a dark cave of a room, lit around the walls with flickering gas fittings. But now, through a gold curtain and into the main body of the club, Arlette felt thrilled by the place, by its walls hung with gold, its tables set around a small stage draped with red velvet, lamps on every table and waitresses dressed as Greek goddesses. Upon the stage a smiling man with brown skin and shorn afro hair strummed at a double bass, held to his side like a dancing partner, and a woman with bright blond hair and a bugle-beaded evening gown ran her fingers up and down the keys of an upright piano.

The party had been shown to a small booth, all red velvet and gilt. Arlette was squeezed between Gideon and the girl called Anna, and one of the toga-wearing waitresses was unloading a tray of cocktails onto the table. Arlette had ordered an Americano, Leticia's drink of choice and still the only cocktail she could name. It arrived with a shiny red cherry on a stick and a small bowl of dark-skinned olives.

She had by now spent three afternoons in Gideon Worsley's studio and felt quite comfortable in his company. She felt, in fact, that he was not nearly as interesting or mysterious as her first encounter with him might have suggested and that he was, despite his top-hat-wearing ways and his eccentric cottage by the river, really a rather conventional young man, the type one's mother would approve of.

His circle of friends, though, appeared to be anything but conventional.

Anna, who sat to her right, was wearing a silk kimono and talking very loudly of her job as a life model.

'A life model? What is that exactly?' Arlette asked her.

'It is a person who removes every last stitch of their clothing and stands stark-hooter naked in a room full of artists for hours on end.'

Arlette widened her eyes and Anna laughed. 'Well,' she said, 'how else is an artist meant to learn how to draw the naked form? Imagine the world if no one had ever removed their clothes for an artist before. No Rubens. No Renoir. No Alma-Tadema. These people did not paint from their imaginations, you know.'

'And are you paid? For your, er, work?'

'But of course! Well, I am hardly going to put myself through such physical hardship for nothing, am I? And it is hard work, you know. Cold, cold rooms, not moving for an hour or more, sometimes in the most extraordinary poses. Once, with my legs wrapped around my neck, like a necklace,' she laughed. 'A human pretzel, no less!'

Arlette did not know what a pretzel was, but smiled and laughed appropriately.

'I could barely walk normally for a week after that! Although I was indeed paid extra. And you, Arlette – tell me about you.'

'Oh, well, there is really nothing to tell.'

'Oh, poppycock. If there's one thing my twenty-four years on this earth have taught me it's that there is *always* something to tell. Where are you from?'

'Guernsey,' she replied. 'In the Channel Islands.'

'Oh, yes, I know Guernsey. I went there once, as a child for my summer holidays. A glorious place.'

Arlette felt a bubble of warm feeling rise up through herself. 'Oh,' she said, 'how lovely. It's rare to meet anyone who knows of the island.'

'And how long have you been in London?'

'Well, only a few months. I arrived in September. And I'm staying with my mother's best friend in Kensington.'

'What's her name? The fricnd?'

'Leticia Miller. The Millers.'

'Yes. Of course. I know the Millers. Abingdon Villas?'

'Yes!'

'A wild family! By all accounts.'

'Well, yes, they are, rather. How do you know them?'

'My mother was at Oxford with Mr Miller. Back in the days when women at Oxford were rather a novelty. Back in the days when my *mother* was rather a novelty. And Leticia was the loveliest thing, apparently. When Anthony Miller brought her around, jaws hit the floor, fights ensued, but he stuck to his guns and he got her. And now they have a heap of wild children and a huge ungainly house, and Mr Miller is nowhere to be seen.' She rolled her eyes. 'That would not happen to me, let me assure you. I never want to have children. No. I shall spend the rest of my life being fêted and adored by a dozen different men. I shall keep myself in small rooms, neat and tidy – no need of teams of staff just to keep it from falling into squalor – independent and reckless. That is how it will be for me. I will not be like my mother with her tired body and her faded eyes, and her house full of things that need to be cleaned, and furniture needing to be rotated, and a husband who looks upon her much as one would look upon a particularly hard-wearing and reasonably attractive chiffonier.'

'I will wager a week's wages on you being married and pregnant before your twenty-seventh birthday,' Gideon interrupted.

'Firstly, Gideon Worsley, you do not *earn* a week's wages. You do not, in fact, earn anything, as far as I can tell. And secondly, no, it is *you* who will be married and tied down to a hundred screaming brats, gasping for air in some gigantic mausoleum in the countryside, forced to work for a living and easing your woes with a large whisky for your breakfast!'

Gideon laughed. 'That may well be true, Anna, my beautiful friend, but we will all, each and every one of us, revert to type as the reality of middle-age begins to dawn upon us. It is all well and good to live this way now. We are young. We are free. But as the spectre of thirty begins to loom, which of us would want to find ourselves with all our friends lost to another way of living, alone in some hovel with no one to care if we have aches or pains, to bring us a hot toddy when we have a head cold, to tell us of being young and being modern? Which of us would want to set ourselves in aspic, in one glorious golden moment, and never ever experience the other golden moments of life, beyond mere youth, of family and growth and love and –'

'Nonsense,' retorted Anna. 'Who said anything about aspic? I am talking of absolutely anything but aspic. I am talking of the freedom that childlessness would bring. To travel the world. Experiences we cannot even begin to imagine at our young age. We came so very close to losing our freedom. Our liberty. It was nearly snatched away from us. Who in their right mind would tie themselves down with matrimony and a household to run? Who would not want to take our freedom, the freedom that our boys and men laid down their lives for – my cousin, *your brother*, Gideon, darling sweet Edwin, all those men, all that blood, all that war – so that we can do as we please? No, I shall not use that expensively bought freedom to do as my mother and her mother and her mother before her have done. It is the greatest gift and I intend to use it well.'

Gideon shrugged. His smile had dropped at the mention of his brother. He said, 'Well then, if the ultimate freedom is in doing as we please, it will please me to marry well and to have at least four children.'

Anna smiled and clutched Gideon's hand inside hers. 'You are the sweetest man. And the woman you marry will have married well also. But look after her. And no running away to Belgium. Keep her on a pedestal.'

'But of course,' said Gideon. 'It is my job to put women on pedestals. That could never change.'

'And what about you, Arlette?' Anna turned to her. 'Are you the marrying kind?'

Arlette laughed. It felt like only five minutes ago she had been a child, and then there had been four years of war and she had come out of the other side of that with no firm ideas about what sort of adult she might like to be. But as she looked at Anna, her handsome face, her vermilion lips, her upright posture and the glint in her eye of fierce intelligence, it struck her that she would like to be like her, just like her. She smiled and said, 'No. I'm not sure that I am.'

Anna looked at her with surprise and smiled. 'Good,' she said simply, 'good.'

And Arlette's heart sang.

23

1995

The book antiquarian had approximately three strands of hair, one the colour of rancid butter, one a dark Jamaican ginger and the last one pure white. All three strands had been lovingly pasted across a bald, age-spotted pate. His face hung from his skull in folds and his mouth was loose and overly wet-looking. He spoke with a nasal twang and used a pince-nez to examine the book he held in his hands.

'Amazing,' he said, 'totally incredible. Where did you find this?'

He said this accusatorily as though he suspected she had stolen it from the bed-stand of a wealthy dowager that very morning.

'It was left to me,' Betty said, 'by my grandmother.'

He nodded and put the pince-nez back to the bridge of his wizardly nose.

'It's a second edition. Nowhere near as valuable as a first edition, of course. But still, not inconsiderable, except . . . oh dear . . .' He turned the frontispiece over and stared disconsolately at Arlette's handwritten inscription. 'Was your grandmother famous?' he asked.

'No.'

'Shame. Inscriptions from people of note can actually add to the value of a book. But this,' he ran a finger sadly across Arlette's immaculate handwriting, 'this rather detracts, I'm afraid. But still, beautiful, beautiful book. I could sell it for you in a flash.'

Betty gulped and looked at him curiously yet innocently, as though the value of her grandmother's heirloom could not be of less interest to her.

'Yes, I could put this out for you; ask about forty, forty-five pounds for it?'

Betty gulped again. The exact price of the hairdressing appointment she so badly required. But she had not come here to sell it, she had come to see if it held any clues.

'Little Miss Pickle,' said the man, closing the book gently and running a finger down the spine. 'Who's that? Is that you, then?'

Betty shook her head. 'No. It's a bit of a mystery. There's someone called Clara Pickle mentioned in her will, but nobody in the family knows who she is.'

'Sounds almost wistful, don't you think?' The man held his pince-nez at an angle and eyed Betty almost fondly. 'Almost like she's writing to someone she hasn't seen for a long time. Or maybe someone she never saw at all. When did she die?'

'About two months ago,' she said, somewhat vaguely, thoughts crowding her head.

'Interesting,' he said. 'Fascinating. I do love the inscriptions. They always tell a story. *Pickle*,' he smiled. 'I wonder who she was . . .'

'I was hoping there might be a clue. In the book,' she asked hopefully.

He turned it over, back to front, looked at it again and said, 'Sadly no. It could have come from anywhere.'

Betty took the book away with her, clutched tightly to her chest inside her shoulder bag. It held no clues to the identity of Arlette's benefactor, but she was one hundred per cent sure that Arlette had fully believed that Betty was one day going to put it into the hands of its rightful owner. Whoever the hell she was.

The fur, the book, the name and address of a man in South Kensington.

Betty had assumed these were all random: a hastily assembled group of things that bore no relationship to one another. But now she was not so sure. Now she was remembering the Arlette of yesteryear, the sharp-as-a-pin Arlette, the woman who did not bear fools gladly, who cut a swathe and made a fuss and always got exactly what she wanted. The essence of that woman had still been there in September 1988 so it stood to some kind of reason that these items all bore some relationship to one another. That she had put them there for a reason. Without the folded piece of paper and the inscription they were just a coat and book. But with them, they were clues. She had spent too long finding her place here in Soho, and she knew now, without a shadow of doubt, that it was time to get serious, time to find Clara Pickle.

She forced the twenty-pence piece into the slot at the

sound of the man's voice. 'Hello, is that Mr Mubarak?'

'Yes, this is. Who is this please?'

'My name's Betty Dean. I came to see you a few weeks ago. I was asking about a man called Peter Lawler.'

'Oh, yes, of course. I have not forgotten you! What can I do to help you?'

'I was wondering . . . you said that Peter Lawler had gone to hospital when he left his flat. Can you remember which hospital he was at? And, if possible, when this was?'

'Oh, yes, that is simple. I remember because I went to visit him. And it was a terrible journey. Out in Fulham somewhere. Two buses and it was the coldest day since records began, and on the way home I had to wait nearly fifty minutes for my return journey and it was one of those miserable days that stamps itself in your head, permanently.'

'Fulham?' she asked, trying to curb her impatience.

'Yes, it is the big hospital there. The Charing Cross Hospital.'

'In Fulham?'

'Yes. I do not know why it is called this, but it is. And it was January. I remember that. The Arctic freeze. The whole world was cold. January 1985.'

'And what ward was he on?'

'Well, it was his liver. It was the drink. So, now, what would that be called . . . I used to work in a hospital, I should be able to remember this . . . Oh, yes, *hepatology*. He was on the hepatology ward.'

Betty smiled and popped another twenty-pence piece into the phone. 'That's totally brilliant. Thank you.'

'You are still trying to track him down then? This mystery man?'

'Yes,' she said. 'I'm really hoping he'll be able to help me with another mystery. If he's, you know . . .'

'Still alive, yes, that is not at all certain. But listen, I am so glad you called. I had been hoping that you might because after you went the other day, I found his original rental agreement. I can tell you two more things about him. Do you have a pen?'

Betty caught her breath. Why hadn't she called earlier? 'Yes. Yes, I do.'

'I can tell you that his old address was Flat 2, 23 Battersea Park Road, London, SW11 2GH. I can also tell you that his middle name was John. Peter John Lawler. Did you get that? Peter. John. Lawler. Is that useful?'

'Yes!' said Betty. 'Yes. That's brilliant. That's absolutely fantastic! Thank you so much.'

'And remember, Miss Dean, I am here at your disposal should you have any more questions or needs or problems. At your disposal.'

'Thank you, Mr Mubarak. Thank you. That's really kind of you.'

'Not at all, my dear. Not at all.'

Number 23 Battersea Park Road was a dry cleaners called Smart's, and the entrance to the flats above was up an alley that ran behind the parade of shops. Betty felt rather nervous as she turned off the main road and into this dead end of overflowing paladins and grimy back windows. She rang the doorbell and glanced warily around her while she waited. Eventually a voice came to the intercom. 'Hello.'

'Hello, I'm looking for someone who might know someone who used to live at this address? A Peter Lawler?'

The voice on the intercom went silent, but Betty could hear them breathing.

'Hello?'

'Yes. Hello. Sorry. Who is this?'

'My name's Betty. I found Peter's name and address in my grandmother's possessions. I think he might be able to help me find someone. I was wondering –'

'Wait,' said the voice, 'wait there. I'm coming down.'

Betty turned away from the door and faced the alleyway. A black cat appeared from behind an upturned milk crate and scurried past her nervously. Then the door behind her was unlocked and she found herself face to face with a middle-aged woman with fiercely dyed black hair and a baby in her arms. 'Hi,' she said, 'I'm Liz, I used to be married to Peter.'

'Oh,' said Betty, 'I'm Liz too – well, sort of. I used to be. I'm Betty now. Nice to meet you.'

The woman's face softened. 'I think I might be able to help you,' she said. 'Do you want to come in?'

She followed the woman called Liz up a scruffy flight of stairs and into a claustrophobic living room overlooking Battersea Park Road. The woman put the baby down on a play mat and offered Betty a drink. She left the room and returned a minute later with a cardboard box in her arms.

'That's my grandson,' she said, sitting down with the box on her lap and nodding at the baby. 'Zac, the love of my life.' She smiled fondly at the baby and the baby kicked its legs at her with excitement. 'I have him every Tuesday and every Thursday. *Don't I, my lovely boy*?' The baby kicked his legs again and Liz sighed happily and then turned to the contents of the box in front of her. 'So, I've been waiting for this moment,' she said, 'half-expecting it. This was basically all I got after Peter died . . .' She stroked the cardboard box absent-mindedly.

'Oh,' said Betty. 'Peter's dead?'

'You didn't know?'

'Well, I thought he might be. I got this address from his old landlord. He told me he'd been very ill.'

'Yeah. Very ill. We were already divorced then, been divorced for ten years, but he never met anyone else and this was the last place he lived before he moved out. I was still his next of kin. It was me who they called when he passed away.'

'What was it, in the end?'

'Emphysema. Of course. Stupid bastard. Had so much. Chucked it all away. When I met him he was the most handsome man I'd ever seen in my life. Couldn't believe he wanted to be with me. But then soon realised the looks were just a frame, the picture was a mess . . .'

'So, what's in the box?'

Liz snapped herself from her sad reverie and looked

down. 'Oh, yes, this is all the paperwork from his last unsolved cases, the ones we couldn't send back, the ones without addresses.'

'Unsolved cases?'

'Yes. Peter was a private detective.'

'Oh! Wow! Really!'

'Yes, I assumed you'd have known.'

'No. Had no idea. I found his name and address in my grandmother's coat pocket. After she died.'

'Your grandmother. I see. What was her name?'

'Arlette Lafolley.'

Liz flicked through the green cardboard folders in the box. 'Lafolley, Lafolley . . .' she muttered to herself. 'Ah, here.' She pulled a folder free. 'I remember this well, another one with no address.'

She passed it to Betty.

'What was he doing for her?' said Betty. 'Do you know?'

'Well, trying to find someone, I'd imagine,' Liz replied. 'That was what Peter did. He tracked down missing people. Usually for legacies.'

Betty squeezed the bulging file and then peered inside it. A photograph wallet from Boots, photocopied listings from Yellow Pages, a vintage photo album smelling of old paper and mildew, and a programme for a jazz concert featuring a trio called Sandy Beach and the Love Brothers. She pulled it out and read it. They were three handsome black men, with gelled-back hair and tuxedos, one holding a double bass, one brandishing a fiddle and the other with a clarinet. They had played a concert at a club called the White Oleander in Windmill Street on Thursday 8 January 1920. Betty could feel the glamour bristling from within this record of a long-dead moment. She opened the programme and read the copy.

Sandy Beach and his Love Brothers, Bert and Buster, are all members of the world-famous Southern Syncopated Orchestra. Tonight, we welcome them in a rare arrangement as a trio to the White Oleander. So, for one night only, sit back, sup up, relax and let Sandy and his Love Brothers take you on to the dance floor for a night you'll never forget!

'Wow,' she said softly.

'Anything interesting?' asked Liz, snapping Betty back into real life.

She shrugged. 'I'm not sure. Can I take these? Take them away and look at them at home?'

'Oh God, yes, absolutely. Please. I just wish everyone would come and take their files. I hate having them here. All those unfinished stories, all those incomplete lives.'

The baby began to grumble and Liz got to her knees to pick him up from his play mat and brought him to the sofa.

'So,' she said, 'your grandmother. Any idea who she was trying to find?'

Betty glanced down at the programme on her lap, at that luscious suggestion of post-war decadence, of mink stoles and hackney carriages, of cigarettes in holders and feathered headdresses. She sighed. 'Someone called Clara Pickle,' she said. 'That's all we know. Clara Pickle. Used to live in Soho. A total mystery. Arlette never even came to London.'

'Oh,' said Liz, kissing the top of her grandson's head and smiling drily, 'you never really know a person until after they're dead. That's when it all comes out. All the stuff they locked up in boxes. All the secrets, all the lies. That's when you really know the truth.'

Betty smiled and gripped the folder to her chest. She wondered how true that might be.

24

1920

Arlette could not entirely tell if she was drunk or not. The night had been so extraordinary, the atmosphere so other, the company so eclectic and the music so stimulating, so unlike anything she'd ever heard before, that she could barely remember what her life had felt like before she'd walked into the White Oleander three hours earlier. She had been drinking Americanos, slowly, sip by sip, not downing them like some of Gideon's friends, but still, she'd had at least three, maybe even four.

'Come on,' said Gideon after the band had finished their musical set. 'Let us go and congratulate the musicians. Come with me!'

'We can't do that!' cried Arlette.

'Why ever not?'

'Well, because they must be so tired after their performance. Surely.'

'No! Of course they won't be! They'll be full of energy long into the night, I'm sure. Come along!'

She picked up her glass and followed him from their booth and towards a curtained area to the side of the stage. Gideon peered through and then beckoned Arlette.

She ran her hand down her hair and paused for a moment. It had been remarkable to her to see these men, even from a distance, with their skin as dark as the night and their teeth as large and as white as sugar lumps. She had never before, beyond the occasional fleeting glimpse of a brown-skinned sailor, by the light of a gas lamp in a St Peter Port alleyway, been at such close quarters to a negro. And not just a negro, but three negros, all from the Caribbean. She felt breathless with nerves as she followed Gideon behind the curtain and into a small lounge where the three musicians sat with their ties loosened and cold beers in their hands.

'Gentlemen,' Gideon began, 'congratulations. Really, that was quite, quite tremendous.'

'Why, thank you, sir, we're glad you enjoyed it.'

The accent! Arlette could barely breathe. It was an accent laced with palm trees and calm blue seas; it was the most exotic thing ever to have passed through her ears.

'Allow me to introduce myself. My name is Gideon Worsley, an artist. And this is my very good friend, and my current *muse*, Miss Arlette De La Mare.'

'Good evening. My name, as you probably know, is Sandy Beach,' the singer said, getting to his feet and shaking Gideon's hand. 'This here is Bert, and this here is his brother, Buster. It is nice to make your acquaintance. And yours, Miss De La Mare.' He bowed slightly and Arlette blushed violently. She had no idea how to respond. She was overwhelmed by this man and his skin and his accent, and the smell in this room of freshly boiled sweat and sickly pomade. She had been left mute with exhilaration. She wanted to touch him, see what his skin felt like against hers. She wanted to say something impressive and unforgettable. She wanted him to talk for ever, in that soft voice, tell them things about coconuts and flying fish, coral reefs and hummingbirds. Instead she stood and stared, not at him, but at some indistinct point behind him, looking, she was sure, as if he was of no interest to her whatsoever. She felt the atmosphere turn and knew immediately it was because of her, but still she could find no words inside her head or persuade her eyes to look upon his. Instead it was left to Gideon to fill the air.

'You've had quite a year, by all accounts,' he opened. 'The Royal Albert Hall and the King himself, no less. How I wish I had been invited to attend that performance. A friend of my parents was there and said it was quite the most exciting thing they had ever seen. Unforgettable.'

'Yes, I must say, London has taken us to its heart. I'm not sure any of us anticipated such a warm reception.'

'Well, it's a tonic, isn't it? Just what we all need after these long dark years of war. And your sound is really quite remarkable. So new. So fresh. So . . . so . . . *thrilling*.'

'That's so very nice to hear,' said Sandy Beach. 'We do aim to please.' Sandy Beach smiled and there were those teeth again, teeth that bore little resemblance to the mean off-white pegs that sat unhappily inside the mouths of English people. His teeth looked happy. His whole demeanour spoke of contentment and good health.

'Mr Beach, you'll have to excuse my candour, I have

had more than one or two gin-and-its tonight, and am probably speaking more freely than I would do under normal circumstances, but my eye has been taken irresistibly by your bone structure. So strong, so fierce. I paint faces. I have, I am proud to say, painted the exquisite face of Miss De La Mare amongst many, many others, and I wonder – and of course I presume the answer to be no – but I wonder if you would consider sitting for me, some time, at my studio in Chelsea?'

Sandy Beach smiled and laughed. 'Oh, Mr Worsley, it embarrasses me somewhat to say, but you are not the first painter to ask me to sit for him. I have been asked, what, brothers . . . ?' He laughed and turned to Bert and Buster, who laughed in response.

Bert sighed and said, 'Oh, this must be the twelfth time that Sandy has been asked to sit. But why not? I mean, *look at him*. He is such a very, very beautiful man.'

All three musicians broke into a laughter then that sounded to Arlette's unaccustomed ears like music rolling across warm white sands.

Gideon laughed too, but Arlette could tell he had been thrown off course by the unoriginality of his request.

'Listen, though,' said Sandy Beach, 'I will make you a deal, young man, because I can see that you are a good soul and I like your hair. And also, I have the next three days off and nothing else to do. So I will come and sit for you, if I can ask for the privilege of sitting with this beautiful young lady at the same time.'

Arlette gasped and finally managed to pull her gaze

from the wall behind Sandy Beach and directly into his eyes. They were dark, dark brown with a faint phosphoric wash of yellow, framed with lashes like chenille, and bulging slightly from his skull as though, independently of his body, wanting to suck in the world. She looked away again and he laughed.

'Miss De La Mare, I am sorry, I did not mean to embarrass you. It's just, you are a rare beauty, that is plain to the eye, and if I am to give up one of my only three free days this month then I need something more inspiring to look at than your good-natured friend here. And can't you just see it?' He made a frame from his hands. 'Black and white, ebony and ivory, my full features against your fine bones. What a joyous, miraculous contrast that would be. What do you think, Mr Worsley. Am I right? Or am I right?' He laughed again and Gideon laughed, but Arlette saw his uncertainty.

Suddenly she felt overcome with a strong sense of conviction. As she had imagined herself when Gideon had asked her to model for him, in his garret with the wilted wild flowers and the emaciated cat, she could see herself once more, entwined with this man, this famous musician, his black skin against hers, the sound of barges passing down the Thames, the scratch of Gideon mixing his watercolours, the exotic smell of Sandy Beach in her nostrils, the thrill of doing something so far from anything she'd imagined she might once do when she was just a young girl on an island she thought she'd never leave.

'Oh, no, Mr Beach, I'm not embarrassed,' she said as

lightly as her excitement would allow. 'I think it's a marvellous idea. And it would be an honour to pose with you. Truly.'

Gideon looked at Arlette, surprise playing along his full lips, and then immediately he turned back to Sandy Beach and clapped his hands together. 'Wonderful!' he cried. 'That really is quite wonderful. Miss De La Mare, when would you be free to come to my studio?'

'Saturday,' she replied breathlessly. 'I have no commitments on Saturday.'

'Well, then,' said Gideon, his hands still clasped together, 'Saturday it is. Here is my card, Mr Beach. Come at twelve.'

'Two,' said Sandy Beach, 'I'll come at two.'

'Yes,' said Gideon, 'of course.'

They left then, back through the velvet curtain and into the last red-hot embers of the nightclub.

25

1995

Who was this woman, thought Betty, peeling through the black-and-white photographs on her lap? It was Arlette, of that she was sure. But which unknown, unfamiliar version was this? In all the photos she'd pored over in Arlette's boudoir – of sailing regattas and picnics on clifftops, of terriers in open-topped cars and building sandcastles with the infant Jolyon – Arlette had always been immaculate in tailored dresses and court shoes, always a hint of a smile through painted lips, always cool, always covered, always slightly removed from the centre of the photograph. And now here she was in these new photos, a slight gleam of sweat on her forehead, feathers in her hair, smoking! Smoking a cigarette, through a holder! Laughing, showing her teeth, leaning into the embrace of a variety of young men, in nightclubs, in lounges, one showed her *sitting on the floor*. Sitting on the floor. With her legs stretched out and crossed at the ankles. On the settee behind her were the disembodied legs of men, one of them dangling a cigar casually between ringed fingers on a black-skinned hand. And then there was one that was so extraordinary that every time Betty looked at it her head swam. It showed

Arlette standing, one slim leg pointed ahead of her, in a sequined flapper dress, her arms around the waists of two black guys in dinner jackets and waistcoats. She blinked. She stared again. The black guys were still there. Handsome black guys. With their arms around Arlette.

Betty grabbed some coins from her purse and ran down to the payphone in the hallway.

'Mum! It's me! Is Jolyon there?'

'Yes, why?'

'I need to talk to him! Now!'

She heard her mother pass the phone across to Jolyon and she heard Jolyon clear his throat; she pictured him straightening his tie or his collar or his cuffs.

'Good evening, Lizzy. What can I do for you?'

'Arlette,' she began abruptly. 'Did she ever say anything to you about being in London?'

'No. She never went to London. She always said she hated the place.'

'Listen. She'd hired a private detective. To find this Clara woman. He's dead now, but his ex-wife gave me all his files on her and there are these photos, Jolyon, of Arlette, in London.'

'Hmm.'

'Hmm what? I've got them in my hands. Evidence. Actual photos. She was here. And not just here but, like, partying. Big time.'

The line fell silent and Betty could hear Jolyon's big, soft brain trying to rearrange the facts he'd just been presented with into something he could agree with.

'It sounds a bit . . . well, unlikely.'

'Well, of course it does. That doesn't mean it isn't true.'

The line fell silent again and then Jolyon sighed and said, 'What else was there? What else did he have, this private dick?'

'Nothing really: the photos, a programme for a jazz concert at a nightclub, some sketches on paper of Arlette, unsigned, matchbooks from lounges and bars, and some printed notepaper with a London address on it, no writing. And some photocopied correspondence with that address on St Anne's Court – you know, the one where Clara Pickle was supposed to have been living. Nothing new there, just saying sorry, we're non-residential. And another one from the landlord of the house on the headed paper, saying it was split up into flats in 1961. And that's it.'

'What was the London address?'

'Erm, hold on, let me see . . .' She pulled the paper from the green folder. 'It's twenty-one Abingdon Villas, W.'

'The Millers,' said Jolyon. 'Of course.'

'Who are the Millers?'

'They were this crazy family. My mother was always talking about them, Leticia was the mother. She was an old school friend of my grandmother's and she had these four wild children. Mummy would get letters from the daughter sometimes – Lilian, I think she was called. Drank herself to death in the end, I think. Or killed herself. Either way, very young. Very sad.'

Lilian, thought Betty. *Leticia.* Arlette had called her those names sometimes, in the night, when she didn't know who Betty was. She'd read nothing into it at the time. Arlette had been so full of strange words and confused memories. She bit her lip, wondering now about all those hours Arlette had talked and talked of things that made no sense, all those hours that Betty had tuned out of, comments she had responded to with half-hearted, distracted *oh reallys* and *gosh, is that trues*. But maybe within all that flabby blabber there was some reality, some proper memories. And she hadn't even been listening.

She wished now she'd recorded everything, wished she'd wired the house up, caught every utterance on tape. But no, all she had was some photos, some sketches and the name of a woman who even a private detective had been unable to find.

But still, she thought, maybe this Peter Lawler had been too sick to do his job properly. Maybe there were more leads at these two addresses, the St Anne's Court address, the Holland Park address. Maybe she should prod them with a stick and see what she could scare out of them.

'What do you think happened to those letters?' she asked. 'The ones from the family in London?'

'No idea,' said Jolyon. 'We've totally emptied Mummy's rooms now, found some love letters from Daddy. Found my letters from boarding school. Some official bits and bobs. But that was it. Nothing from London. Nothing to do with London. Nothing at all.'

'I'm going to chase it all up,' Betty said to Jolyon. 'Leave it with me.'

'God,' said Jolyon, 'I feel a bit sick.'

She laughed. 'Why?'

'Because . . . I don't know. Because I had Mummy all decided in my head. And now she's gone, I'm not sure I can face having her undecided again. Not now. Not when it's too late to do anything about it.'

Betty dropped another coin in the slot and sighed. 'It's not too late,' she said sternly. 'It's not too late at all. Leave it with me. Next time I call, I'll have something amazing to tell you. I promise.'

26

The doorbell rang and Betty groaned. She'd only just climbed into the bath. She waited a beat, hoping that it was a mistake, a drunk. The doorbell rang again and she sighed and climbed out of the bath, pulled a towel around herself and stomped to the front door, leaving a trail of wet footprints in her wake.

'Hello!' she shouted into the intercom, water dripping from her elbows and onto the floor.

Silence.

'Hello!' she shouted even louder.

She heard the crackle of the street outside and then she heard a voice: 'Who's that?'

'What do you mean, *who's that*?' she demanded. 'You're the one who rang my doorbell.'

'Is that Betty?'

'Yes! Who's this?'

'It's me. John.'

'Oh.'

'You missed him.'

'Who?'

'Dom Jones. He was just at your door. He's gone now.'

'What! Shit! Can you still see him?'

'He's headed back down Peter Street.'

'Fuck.'

'He's probably just gone home.'

'Yes. I know. But . . . urgh, never mind . . .'

'You all right?'

'Yeah. I'm fine.'

There was a brief silence.

'Don't suppose I could come and use your toilet, could I?'

'I'm naked,' she said.

John Brightly laughed. 'I don't mind if you don't mind.'

Betty laughed too. 'Give me five minutes. I'll give you a shout.'

She glanced through the window. It was sunny. She pulled through her clothes on the rail beneath her mezzanine until she found her favourite summer dress, then she smoothed her hair back with an Alice band, put on some red lipstick and buzzed John Brightly in. It was the first time she'd seen him since the party two days earlier. Their schedules had kept them apart. Now she breathed in deeply, sucked in her stomach and listened to his footsteps up the stairs, wondering how she would feel when his face came into view.

She pulled open the door at the sound of his knuckles on the other side and decided that she felt excited. John looked fresh and cool in a white polo shirt and jeans, a hint of a tan, and sunglasses on his head. His arms were heavy and toned. He smelled of sunshine. 'Yeah,' he began, 'cheeky. I know. But I figured after our little bathroom interlude on Wednesday . . .' He raised an eyebrow at her and she smiled.

'Of course,' she said. 'I always wondered where you went to pee.'

'Well, usually I use the pub over the road, but then so does every other sod on the market. And it looks like it.'

'Well, you're welcome to use mine whenever you like.'

'Cheers,' said John Brightly, and headed towards the bathroom.

Betty filled the kettle.

'So,' said John, a moment later, emerging from the bathroom and rubbing his hands against the back of his jeans, 'how've you been? Haven't seen you for a while.'

'Good,' she said, 'I've been great. Working hard. Hanging out with Dom Jones, that kind of thing.' She smiled.

John's eyes widened. 'Really? And how . . . ?'

She smiled again and said, 'Nothing like that. Just helping out with his kids. He has too many of them. That's probably why he was ringing at my door just now.'

John raised an eyebrow. 'I hope he's paying you well,' he said. 'He can afford to.'

'He is. At least, he did. I've only done it once.' She glanced out of the window, as though Dom himself might be sitting on her windowsill. 'Tea?' she suggested. 'Coffee?'

'Yeah,' said John. 'I'd love one. I'll have to take it down with me, though. I've left some twelve-year-old in charge of my stall; he's probably just wandered off somewhere.'

Betty made him a milky coffee and passed it to him.

'Well,' said John, taking the mug, 'thank you for that. I'll bring the mug back later.'

'No rush,' she said lightly. 'Actually, give me two seconds, I'll come down with you.' She picked up her sunglasses and her bag and together they left the flat.

She stared at the broad set of his shoulders as she walked behind him down the stairs. His hair was so thick, even at his crown, the kind of hair that looked like it would still be there when he was an old man.

'What happened to you, anyway?' he said suddenly, without turning round.

'What?'

'At the party? You were going to come out and find me. You didn't.'

He sounded diffident, curious.

Betty thought about her proximity to the front door of Candy Lee's flat and said, 'Ah, yes, sorry about that. It's a very long story. And one best saved for another time.'

He turned then and said, 'Tonight?'

'Tonight . . . ?'

'Yeah. Tell me the story tonight. I'll buy you a drink.'

'I'm working tonight,' she said, too fast and too carelessly. 'Sorry.' She immediately cringed at the sorry. Sorry implied that she was letting him down, implied that she had taken his power away in some way when all he'd done was suggest a quick drink. 'I mean –'

'No problem,' he said. 'You'll just have to save it for me for another day.'

'Yes,' she said. 'I will.' She inhaled and then said, 'Tomorrow? I'm free mid-evening?'

He shook his head. 'I'm DJing. Most nights, in fact. I don't get much free time.'

Now he was reclaiming his power. He was too busy for her. It was tonight or never. She smiled tightly and said, 'Ah well, never mind.' They left the building and John slid his sunglasses down onto his face and smiled at her nervously.

'Yeah,' he said. 'Although . . .'

'Yes?'

His body slackened again. 'No,' he said. 'Nothing. I'll see you around.'

'Yes,' she said, 'yes. You probably will.'

'Oh, thank God. Thank God. Come in.' Dom Jones ran his hands through his unruly hair and pulled the front door closed behind him. In the background Betty could hear a baby screaming and someone else having a tantrum.

'Listen. What are you doing today?'

She opened her mouth to reply but he talked over her as he led her into the kitchen. 'I'll give you two hundred quid,' he said, scooping the baby from a bouncy chair and stepping over a prostrate Donny on the floor. 'For the day,' he continued. 'I've got to go out, like, *now*. I mean, like an hour ago. I'll be out all day. Don't know what time I'll be back. Will you do it? Please?' He looked at her with angel eyes. 'Please say you can do it?'

Betty looked from Dom to the screaming baby, to Donny on the floor, to Acacia sitting on the kitchen table eating an overripe mango, sticky juice running down her face and onto her white cotton T-shirt. Then she thought about two hundred pounds. A week's rent. A new hair colour.

'I'm supposed to be working tonight,' she said, 'but I suppose I could call in sick. What time, roughly . . . ?'

'No idea,' he said snappily. 'Could be late.'

'So you want me to put them to bed?'

He shrugged and moved the convulsing baby onto his other shoulder. 'Yeah. I don't know. Probably.'

She smiled and nodded. 'OK,' she said, 'sure.'

'You little star,' he said. 'You perfect little star.' He looked at the clock again, looked at her, handed her the wailing baby and said, 'I'm going to have a shower. Help yourself to anything. And yeah, thanks. Really. You're the best.' He smiled cheekily, the stress leaving his demeanour almost immediately.

Betty smiled back. 'You're welcome,' she said.

She waited until he'd left the room and then she finally exhaled.

The baby quietened in her calm embrace, Donny had stopped yelling and was looking at her curiously through a gap under his arm. Another stream of mango juice dripped down Acacia's chin. It was silent.

Dom poked his head round the door a few minutes later.

'Wow,' he said, surveying the scene. 'You really do

222

have the magic touch. Here,' he passed her a piece of paper. 'My mobile number, if you need to call me. I'll ring when I'm on my way back. And, you guys,' he addressed his children, 'be good, otherwise Betty won't come back and look after you again. OK?'

He threw Betty a smile and said, 'Got everything you need? All cool?'

'Yes,' she said. 'All cool.'

He glanced at Betty. 'You look lovely today, by the way.'

Betty blushed and buried her face in the baby's hair, but couldn't think of anything to say in reply.

27

1920

Arlette could not think what to wear for such a meeting. Lilian lay upon her bed, still in her nightdress at almost eleven o'clock, watching as she pulled items from her wardrobe. She had a cup and saucer balanced on her stomach and was tickling the cat with her big toe.

'No,' she said, 'absolutely not. Mr Beach will think you are a nun. A nun with very poor colour sense. Don't you have something, I don't know, something *green*?'

Arlette shook her head. Her mother's friend had once told her in a very disdainful tone of voice that no one with even a hint of red to their colouring should ever wear green. *Red and green should never be seen.*

'But, you aren't red,' cried Lilian when Arlette repeated this aphorism. 'Where are you red? You are brown! Brown hair, brown eyes, brown brown brown! *Brown and green, looks like a dream.*' She laughed gently at her little joke and pulled herself up to a sitting position. 'I have the loveliest green jacket. And a matching hat. I'll get them for you.' She put the teacup and saucer onto Arlette's nightstand and collected the cat to her chest.

Arlette grimaced at her reflection in the mirror. She'd

learned how to dress herself very well during these weeks in London. She knew exactly what was à la mode and precisely how to wear it. But this event was so unaccounted for, so beyond the realms of any fashion mores or rules of etiquette that she was lost entirely. How did one present oneself to have one's portrait painted with a famous negro?

Lilian returned, clutching both the cat and a bundle of clothes.

'Here,' she said, throwing cat and clothes upon Arlette's bed. 'This is perfect.' She held up the jacket. Not the drab bottle green that Arlette had been expecting, but a soft sage, and not the harsh tailored shape that Arlette favoured, but a floppy angora affair with a huge pearl button at the front and a velveteen collar.

She slipped it on and knew that Lilian was right. She looked soft and fresh and young and vulnerable. The matching hat was a beret shape with a velveteen bobble and a pearl stitched to the rim.

'You look so lovely,' said Lilian, curling herself into a ball around the cat and stroking her cheek against the fur on its face. 'You should keep them. I've never worn them. Keep them. Oh, Arlette, I'm so jealous of you, so jealous I could almost *vomit*.' She sighed and lay down her head, staring mournfully and theatrically at the ceiling. 'Imagine,' she said, 'having your portrait painted with a world-famous musician. And not just that, but a *negro*. I mean, how utterly, utterly, *utterly* glorious . . .'

*

'Miss De La Mare, how lovely to see you.' Gideon held her hand in his and kissed the back of it. Arlette removed her hat and her gloves and passed them into Gideon's waiting hands.

'Lovely to see you, too, Gideon.'

She looked to either side of Gideon and across his shoulder but could see no sign of his other sitter. According to her wristwatch it was already ten minutes past two – she had planned her journey meticulously to ensure that she arrived later than Sandy Beach.

'I'm afraid Mr Beach is not here yet,' said Gideon, placing Arlette's things upon the sideboard. 'I do hope he hasn't got lost. These Chelsea backstreets can be terribly confusing, especially for a tourist.'

He made her some tea and she took it in his sitting room, a small and familiar ritual by now, but one that did nothing to quell her rising anticipation. She watched the hands on her wristwatch move from two sixteen to two seventeen and breathed deeply to slow her heart. Two outcomes were now likely. The first was that at any moment there would be a knock at the door and then Sandy Beach would be here in this room, with his smell and his eyes and his teeth, and she would have to find a way to feel normal in his presence for the remainder of the day. The second was that there would be no knock at the door and that Sandy Beach might have found something more pressing, something more appealing to do with his precious day off, and that she and Gideon would sit here in an uncomfortable state of limbo until they had both accepted that he wasn't going to come. Either way, Arlette felt vaguely nauseous.

She was about to start making small talk with Gideon when it happened.

Knock knock knockity-knock.

Arlette and Gideon smiled nervously at each other and Gideon went to his front door. Arlette listened to their greeting, to the incongruous honey tones of Mr Beach's voice in Gideon's hallway.

'Come in, come in,' she heard Gideon implore.

And then there he was, smart in a starched white shirt, white waistcoat and dove-grey double-breasted suit, his shoes polished to a dazzling gleam and a single yellow gerbera daisy in his hand.

'Miss De La Mare,' he said, greeting her with a slight incline of his head, his left hand flat upon his stomach. '*Enchanté.*'

He handed her the gerbera and Arlette blushed, as she'd known she would, and smiled. 'Likewise, Mr Beach.'

'And, please,' he said, 'now that we are outside the realms of my professional persona, call me Godfrey.'

'Godfrey?'

'Yes, miss, for that is my real name, the name my mother chose for me twenty-eight years ago. Godfrey Michael Pickle.'

Arlette attempted to stifle a smile. *Godfrey Pickle.* It was no less unlikely than his stage name.

'What a wonderful name, Mr Beach,' said Gideon,

entirely missing the point. 'Now, let me pour you some tea.'

'So, Miss De La Mare, you too have an interesting name. *Lady of the sea*. What is the provenance of such a name?'

'I'm from the Channel Islands, Mr Pickle. A small cluster of rocks between the south coast of England and the north coast of France. It is a melting point of both English and French cultures.'

'Ah,' his yellow-tinted eyes lit up, 'so you understand the island life. Like myself. The limitations and the joys of being hemmed in on all sides by the sea.'

'Oh, yes, I certainly do. Although I should imagine there are more joys involved being hemmed in by the Caribbean Sea, than there are by the cold dark waters of the English Channel.'

Godfrey smiled. 'Indeed,' he said, 'indeed.'

'Do you get back at all?' she asked.

Godfrey Pickle shook his head and said, 'I have not been back to my island for eighteen *looong looong* months. And neither do I have any plans to return. The orchestra is booked up for the next year ahead. It's possible that I may never return.' He shrugged. 'And what about you, Miss De La Mare . . . will you be returning to your rock in the English sea?'

'I honestly do not know, Mr Pickle. I've been here for only four months. I'm certainly not ready to return yet, but maybe one day. If my mother needs me.'

Godfrey's eyes clouded over. 'Ah, yes, the poor

mothers. My mother sits in my heart like a piece of grit every day of my life. She feels I am punishing her by leaving her without me. All the money in the world doesn't appear to be compensating for my absence . . .' he sighed.

The three of them fell silent for a moment, until Gideon slapped his hands down upon his thighs and said, 'Well, I suggest we crack on. The light will begin to fade away soon; better move fast.'

In his studio upstairs, Gideon had arranged a striking tableau: a daybed draped with red chiffon and ivy, three church candles on towering sticks behind, and parlour palms in copper pots to either side. He asked Godfrey to remove his jacket and unbutton his waistcoat, and then Arlette to take off her angora jacket, under which she was wearing a cream blouse with a ruffled collar.

'Would you mind, Miss De La Mare, just to pull open the top two buttons? Just to give me more skin to . . . to make a feature of. And yourself, Mr Beach. Mr Pickle. I think we do need to see just a fraction more of your . . . complexion.'

Godfrey and Arlette glanced at each other and Godfrey laughed. 'You have a certain way with words, Mr Worsley. But let me first check with Miss De La Mare before I put any more of my *complexion* on display. Miss De La Mare,' he turned back to Arlette, 'if you are comfortable with the opening of extra buttons, then so am I. But I will not undo a single fastening if it any way offends you.'

Arlette smiled. And then she put her fingers to her top buttons. 'It is only buttons, Mr Pickle, and it is only skin – how could I find it offensive?'

Godfrey looked at her through his velvet lashes, and his full lips turned up into a sensual smile. 'Indeed, Miss De La Mare,' he said, his eyes still upon hers, his fingers now on the buttons of his own shirt. 'It is only skin . . .'

Arlette felt herself redden under his gaze, felt the erotic suggestion of what they were both doing, the unbuttoning of clothes, the beginning of the process of getting undressed, an act normally carried out in the privacy of their own sleeping quarters. She smiled and looked away.

'Now,' said Gideon, 'if it is agreeable with both of you, I would like you, Mr Beach – Mr Pickle – to sit upon the daybed, at this end,' he patted the mattress at the left end. 'And you, Miss De La Mare, to sit in the middle here, facing this wall,' he indicated the right, 'with your back leaning against Mr Pickle's shoulder.'

Arlette looked from the bed to the wall and then back to Gideon. 'So,' she said, 'where are my legs to be?'

'I thought,' he said, walking to the bed and demon-strating the pose himself, 'that maybe you could hang them over the side, crossed, like so, and if we could have your hair untied, Miss De La Mare – would that be all right? So that it hangs down Mr Pickle's shoulder, here, and Mr Pickle will be looking, like this, directly at me – if that is agreeable with you, Mr Pickle? And you, Miss De La Mare, will be staring at this point, just beyond my easel, see, at that damp patch just there.' He clambered from the bed and let Arlette copy his pose. 'Yes, like that, but possibly if you could just press yourself a little closer to Mr Beach. Mr Pickle. As if you were, well, I suppose as if you were a romantically entwined couple, possibly pondering the future of your relationship, possibly wondering if your love could ever be realised. Do you see?'

Godfrey laughed. 'Yes, I see, Mr Worsley. The Love That Shall Not Speak Its Name.'

'Well, yes, something like that. Something illicit, dangerous, yet also something beautiful, something . . . *grand*. A grand, grand love, one that has brought both joy and heartache. Yes?'

Godfrey looked at Arlette and Arlette looked at Godfrey. 'Is there to be a suggestion that myself and Miss De La Mare have . . . ?'

'Hmm?' Gideon looked up at him sharply, a finger held thoughtfully to his lips.

'I mean, is an observer to draw the conclusion that there has been something . . . carnal between us, between this couple.'

'Oh, oh, I see. Well, yes, I mean, I suppose, *possibly*. Although –'

Godfrey cut him off and turned to Arlette. 'Does this make you feel uncomfortable in any way?'

Arlette considered the question. She was still a virgin. She had not yet experienced any of the emotions that Gideon was asking her to portray. Yet, sitting here in this room, with this man, her blouse unbuttoned to her collarbone, her hair falling down around her face, she could grasp the tips of those feelings, she could imagine it, and so she smiled at Godfrey and whispered, 'No, it does not make me feel uncomfortable in any way.'

She saw Godfrey's eyes widen in surprise at her acceptance of this scenario and she felt her heart swell with anticipation. In opening her buttons she had opened a door into a part of herself she had not known was there.

Gideon moved from behind his easel towards the pair of them and teased the long tendrils of Arlette's hair into a more pleasing form, his eyes narrowed with concentration. Behind his easel again he peered at his tableau and then he smiled. 'Yes,' he said, 'yes. I think that's just right. Maybe an inch further back, Mr Pickle. Yes. And your head, Miss De La Mare, a fraction to the right. Yes. Now. That is truly perfect. Truly something to behold . . .'

The three of them fell silent, while Gideon put down his first marks. Outside Arlette could hear, just as she'd imagined before, the bleating of a passing barge, the metallic rattle of a carriage on the street below. But not just that. She could also hear the sound of Godfrey Pickle, breathing in, breathing out, his heart pattering lightly beneath his ribs. She could feel the solid mass of his body underneath his crisp white shirt and feel the first flush of warm sweat against the cotton. And there, across the room, she saw Gideon, his soft handsome face aglow with excitement, clearly seeing something remarkable before him. Her eye caught his for a brief moment and she smiled, encouragingly.

'Are you comfortable, Miss De La Mare?' he enquired gently.

'Yes,' she said assuredly, 'I am most comfortable. Most comfortable indeed.'

28

1995

Betty was asleep on the sofa, pinned beneath Astrid, who was slumbering on her chest when Dom Jones finally came home at twelve forty-five.

She opened her eyes and stared at him blearily. Her neck sang out in pain when she straightened it. She clutched it with her hand and grimaced.

Dom smiled at her fondly, and then at Astrid.

'Couldn't settle her then?' he asked.

'Mmm,' she said, through a yawn. 'No. Miss Astrid did *not* want to go in her cot. So she watched TV with me instead.'

'Sorry I'm so late,' Dom said.

Betty shrugged. 'No problem. You told me you probably would be.'

'How was it?' He leaned down to take the baby from her and the smell of tobacco on his breath reminded her that she had not had a cigarette in over eight hours and hadn't even noticed.

'Fine,' she said, through another yawn. 'Good. Well, once I'd worked out how to put that double buggy up.' She gestured towards the hallway. 'That took nearly an hour.'

'You took the kids out?' He looked surprised.

'God, yes,' she said, stretching out her arms. 'Would have gone crazy stuck in here all day. We walked down to St James's Park. Fed ducks. Went on swings. That kind of thing.'

'Wow,' said Dom, looking pleasantly surprised. 'Cool.'

'Yeah,' she said, 'it was fun. We had fun.'

He looked at her in awe. 'Well,' he said after a moment, 'you're either lying, or you are, genuinely, Mary Poppins. Either way is fine with me. As long as you promise you'll come back.'

He smiled at her. His eyes creased at the corners and he looked tired and sad.

'Of course I will,' she said, getting to her feet. 'When do you need me?'

'They're with Amy tomorrow, but she's dropping them back early evening. Could you do a late one? Possibly, like, early hours?'

She would have to phone in sick again, break Rodrigo's little heart, but it was worth it. Dom was paying her more than three times her Wendy's hourly rate. 'Sure,' she said, 'yes. What time?'

'Come at five,' he said, 'if that's OK?'

He saw her to the door, the baby sleeping across his shoulder, and as she left he said, 'Oh, wait, hang on,' and pulled a roll of notes from his back pocket. 'For you,' he said, 'and well worth every penny. Will you be all right walking home?'

'Er, yes,' she said, rolling her eyes. She tucked the roll of notes into her shoulder bag without looking at them. It felt strangely unseemly to accept such a large sum of money from someone for a day's work. But then she thought of supermodels and decided that it was fine. And supermodels did not, after all, have to clean anyone's bum.

'Thank you, Betty,' Dom said. 'I'm glad we met. I feel good about this. I really do.'

He closed the door quietly behind her, and she headed back towards Berwick Street.

It had not been an easy day. The logistics of getting three small, uncooperative people from place to place had been challenging and exhausting, and there had been a moment after the tenth time she'd come back into Astrid's room to attempt to settle her, when she'd had to keep herself from crying with frustration. But really, she'd enjoyed it. They were nice children. And it was all worth it to see Dom's face soften with gratitude, to hear him say he appreciated her. Because Betty liked being appreciated and she missed looking after someone.

She rolled a cigarette as she walked, quickly and clumsily, and was about to head straight up to the fire escape and smoke it when she noticed a card in the wire basket beneath the letterbox in the front door with her name scrawled on it. She picked it out and stared at it for a second. It was a flyer for a club night in Windmill Street. The club was called the Matrix and the night was called Lovecats. With DJ J.B. on the decks.

J.B.

John Brightly.

She turned the flyer over and read: 'I'm here 10 p.m. to 1 a.m. Come and sit with me if you're not too whacked, John.'

Betty looked up at her window. She looked down at her clothes. Her summer dress, creased and vaguely stained after her day with Dom's children, battered Converse, pale legs. She imagined her face: make-up long crumbled away, mascara long picked off. She thought of her breath, stale from the hour's sleep she'd had on Dom's sofa, her hair unbrushed and flat at the back.

And then she thought of John Brightly, alone at his decks, his strong toned arms gleaming under the disco lights. DJ J.B. It was nearly one o'clock. She was just in time. She lit the cigarette and smoked it urgently as she turned back to the front door, opened it and headed back out into the night, towards Windmill Street.

The Matrix was in a basement, the only outward signifier of its existence being a piece of paper taped to the wall imploring patrons to respect the residents of the area by leaving the building quietly, and a dusty blue light above the door with the letter M painted on it in black.

Beyond the grubby entrance, however, the Matrix was a gloomily glamorous place clad with tatty red velvet, scuffed gilt and chandeliers. She followed the sound of 10,000 Maniacs into a small room at the back, where around fifty people danced beneath a disco ball and another thirty or so stood around the edges drinking beer from bottles, smoking and looking quite serious. She saw

John at the back, squashed into a small corner behind his decks, pulling a vinyl album from its sleeve and examining the surface of it under the dull lights.

She queued for a minute at the bar and bought two beers, which she carried over to the DJ booth.

'Hi!' she said, holding a bottle aloft.

John looked up at her and she saw his face turn from steely concentration to something suggestive of pleasure. 'You came,' he said, pulling his headphones from his ears and accepting the beer. He looked at his watch. 'You just finished work?'

She nodded.

'Wow, that was a long day.'

'Babies, not burgers. Dom Jones gave me two hundred quid for it.'

John's eyebrows jumped towards his hairline. 'Seriously?'

She pulled the roll of notes from her shoulder bag and showed them to him.

'Christ,' he said, 'you should be careful with that.'

'I know,' she said, putting them back in her bag and holding it close to her stomach, 'I'm being very careful. And straight to the bank first thing. But in the meantime,' she smiled, 'beers are on me.' She knocked the bottle against his and he held open the door of his booth so that she could squeeze in next to him.

'Bit of a squash,' he said, offering her his stool.

'No problem,' she said, feeling the heat radiating from his body. 'It's cosy.'

He smiled at her and said, 'Stick with me. I won't be able to chat much, but I'll be off in a minute and then we can find a quiet corner. Unless, of course, you want to dance?'

She looked at him in horror. 'No!' she said. 'No thank you.'

He smiled down at her as if to say, 'Good,' and then he put his headphones back on and lifted the needle from Tom Tom Club, while on the other turntable the needle came down on the opening bar of 'Papa's Got a Brand New Pigbag' and every thirtysomething ligger at the back of the club let go of the wall and headed for the dancefloor, eyes shining with nostalgia.

Betty glanced up at John, watching him work. She saw sweaty clubbers walk across to the booth to shout in John's ear, asking for requests. She saw a pretty girl in a négligée and thick black eyeliner pass him a beer with a smile. She saw him examine each disc of vinyl as if it were a rare diamond, searching it for flaws, before placing it gently as a baby onto the felt-covered turntable. She felt his body move in time to the music, smelled his sweat, damp and musky, through his thin T-shirt, watched his strong brow furrow with concentration every time he faded one song into another. She noticed that he never smiled, not at the pretty girls, not at the euphoric, sweat-drenched dancers. Every few minutes he would lean down and shout something in her ear. She only heard half of what he said, but she noticed that every time he looked at her, he allowed himself a half-formed smile.

At one fifteen John finished his set with 'Born Slippy' and took her to a small bar two doors down. He came back from the bar with two pints of lager and two whisky chasers, which he placed on the table in front of them alongside his packet of Lambert and Butler and Betty's tobacco pouch. Betty had watched him at the bar. The barmaid knew him, had smiled warmly and flirtatiously as she'd served him. He'd nodded and winked at people sitting at a couple of tables on his way back and she'd heard someone call out, 'All right, J.B.?'

'This is your local, then?' she enquired.

'Yeah. Kind of. It's my club.'

'Your club?'

'Yeah. My club. Mostly market people. Some sex workers. Dom Jones's got the Groucho. I've got the Windmill. Cheers.'

She raised her pint glass towards his and appraised him under the slightly liverish lights. She barely knew the man, yet he was growing layers day by day. A man of twenty-seven, brought up by an antiques dealer, obsessive about music, obsessive about vinyl, a smoker, a drinker, a man who liked hats. He was fit and he was a night owl. He worked fourteen-hour days, did not blanch in the face of a bucket-load of someone else's vomit, but did not smile at pretty girls in négligées who gave him beer to drink.

'Where do you live?' she opened, wanting to flesh out the picture with yet more layers.

'Paddington,' he said. 'Harrow Road.'

She nodded. It meant nothing to her. 'Is it nice?'

He laughed and shook his head. 'I live in a shithole,' he said. 'Rising damp. Subsidence. Dry rot. Water comes down the wall when it's raining. The place should be condemned. If I had the time I'd find somewhere decent to live. But I haven't got the time, so I'm stuck there.' He flexed his knuckles on the tabletop, and winced. 'It's affecting my joints, you know, the damp. That's why I have to go so easy with the vinyl when I'm DJing, have to really move slowly otherwise I'd drop stuff or miss the beat. And then of course I spend all day outside, which doesn't help . . .'

'What about your sister?'

'What about my sister?'

'Couldn't you live with her?'

He looked at her aghast. 'No,' he said. 'Eighteen years living with her was plenty long enough, thank you all the same. I'd rather put up with the dry rot.'

Betty nodded, as if she knew what he meant. But she had no idea. She was an only child. 'And your mum and dad?'

'Mum lives in Hastings. Dad lives in Bedford. It's fine,' he said. 'I only sleep there. You know, most nights, when I'm DJing, I crash out like a light, one, two a.m., then I'm up and out again at five thirty.' He shrugged.

'Why don't I ask Marni?' Betty said, filled with horror at the thought of this fine man living in squalor, his strong hands growing weak with the damp. 'You know, the girl who found my place for me. I bet she's got loads of places round Paddington. Loads of places you could see.'

He smiled and nodded. 'Yeah,' he said, 'you're right. Maybe I should. It's just like a vicious cycle. I don't want to go home so I make sure I'm busy and then I'm too busy to find somewhere decent to live.' He sketched a circle on the tabletop with a square fingertip, before drawing his hand back into a fist.

'I'll call her,' said Betty, 'tomorrow. If you want.'

John looked down at her. His dark eyes crinkled at the corners. 'Thank you,' he said. 'That's really kind of you.'

'That's OK,' she said. And she patted the hard ridges of his knuckles, fondly.

He looked at her in surprise and Betty put her hand back in her lap.

'You know,' he said, after a short pause, 'when I first saw you . . .'

'You thought I was a stupid bint,' she finished for him.

He laughed gently. 'Well, no, not quite. I just thought, I don't know, you seemed like one of those Trustafarian types, playing at being grown up, Mummy and Daddy paying for you to live life on the edge, that kind of thing. And then I've watched you these last few weeks and I can see how wrong I was. You're the real deal, you know. A real, proper person.'

Betty gulped. 'Oh,' she said. 'Thank you. And since we're being honest, when I first met you I thought you were a total wanker.'

John threw her a look of injured surprise, and then he laughed. 'Yeah,' he said, 'most people think that when they first meet me. It's why I haven't made any new friends since I was eight years old. So,' he turned to face her, 'have I done anything to disavow you of your first impressions?'

She gave him a stern smile. 'Yes,' she said. 'You have.'

'So you don't think I'm a wanker any more?'

'No,' she said, 'I think you're . . .' She paused. She had no idea what she thought he was. 'I haven't made my mind up yet,' she finished.

He laughed. 'Fair enough. I can't say I've really made my mind up about myself yet, so no reason why you should have.'

Betty turned down John's offer of a cigarette and made herself a roll-up. For a moment they sat in silence. But it wasn't an awkward silence, it was more a moment of reflection between two people who'd had a long, hard day, sitting late at night in a scruffy members' bar in Soho.

'So,' said John, inhaling on his cigarette and resting it in a glass ashtray, 'tell me about Dom Jones. What's the deal there?'

Betty shrugged. 'Well, Amy Metz has sacked the nanny and keeps leaving the kids with him at short notice. So I'm saving his bacon, basically.'

'And what's it like,' he continued, 'you know, behind the doors?'

Betty threw him a patronising smile and said, 'Oh, come on now, John, surely you don't have the slightest interest in the domestic minutiae of some boring megastar pop singer. Surely you're *far* too cool to give a shit.'

John smirked. 'Yeah, well,' he said, 'I'm not really

interested, just, you know, making conversation. Taking a polite interest in your job.'

Betty laughed. 'Right,' she said. 'Sure. But unfortunately I am not at liberty to divulge any personal details about Dom Jones's private or domestic life.'

'What, he's made you sign something, has he?'

'No! Right now we're just working on a gentleman's agreement. He trusts me. And I don't want to abuse that trust.' She pursed her lips piously and lit her roll-up.

John nodded at her approvingly and said, 'Good on you. I respect that. But seriously, what's he like? Is he a total nob?'

'No,' she said, 'he's a bit vague, a bit scatty. But from what little I've seen of him, I think he's quite decent. Loves his kids. Keeps a nice house. Eats well . . .'

'A lot of cheese, yeah?'

'A lot of cheese,' she laughed. 'Tons of fruit. *No crisps.* And believe me, I *looked* for crisps.' She stopped and put her finger to her lips. 'But that,' she said, 'is more than enough. No more Dom talk. Let's talk about you.'

'Oh God, no way. Number one: I hate talking about myself, mainly because, number two: there is nothing to say. And anyway, what I really dragged you out tonight for was to find out the long story. The night of the party. Why you disappeared, left me sitting on a fire escape for half an hour with ten Polish language students.'

'Ah,' she said, 'yes. Of course. Candy Lee.'

'Candy Lee?'

'Mad Chinese lesbian. From the flat downstairs.

Cornered me in the bathroom. Tried to seduce me. Wouldn't take no for an answer.'

'Oh my God, she didn't assault you, did she?'

Betty laughed. 'Er, no, not quite. But she made it quite clear she would like to. With her *studded tongue*.'

'So what happened?'

'Well, I said thank you but no thank you, and then she left. With an open offer to visit her downstairs if I ever change my mind.'

John looked at her mock-seriously. 'Do you think you will?'

'Well, you know . . .' She winked and laughed and smoked her roll-up.

'That wasn't a long story.'

'No. You're right.' She exhaled. 'It was pretty short, really. Felt like for ever at the time, mind you. Maybe I just pretended it was going to be a long story to subliminally persuade you to invite me out for a drink.' She stopped and flushed red. John raised an eyebrow at her sardonically. She had not meant to say that. 'I mean, not because I wanted to, to . . . you know, like a date or anything. Just because you're down there and I'm up there and we keep passing, and it was time, you know, time to get to know each other.'

'I agree,' he said, and he raised his whisky shot to hers. 'Cheers. And while I reserve the right not to tell you anything about myself, I do still insist, if we are getting to know each other, that you tell me everything about yourself. All of it. Starting with the crumbling mansion. If you don't mind.' He flashed her a cheeky smile, one of his rare 'full' smiles, one that involved both his eyes and his lips. She flushed again. His face in repose was calm and slightly forbidding – not a mask as such, but certainly a net curtain. When he smiled like that it was like pulling open the net curtains and discovering that it was the first day of summer. It made her glad that he didn't smile very much, otherwise she might get used to it and stop seeing it as the beautiful thing it was.

She drew in her breath. There were feelings stirring within her, feelings she was not ready to acknowledge. She made her face look wry and cool and said, 'The crumbling mansion *on a cliff-top*, you mean?'

'Oh, yes,' he smiled again, 'yes. On a cliff-top. Windswept, I hope?'

'Very windswept, battered daily by the elements.'

'And please, please tell me it was haunted?'

'No, not haunted. But a very, very old lady lived there. A very old lady with red satin shoes.'

'Red satin shoes?' said John, rubbing his hands together. 'I'm hooked. Tell me everything. The whole story of you.'

Betty smiled. 'It's quite boring.'

'I don't care,' said John. 'It's about you. And you're not boring.'

'Aren't I?'

'No,' said John. 'You're not.'

Betty smiled again, and told him everything.

29

1920

'Good morning, ma'am. My name is Mr Pickle and I am looking for Miss Arlette De La Mare. I wonder if you would be so good as to tell her that I am here? I thank you.'

Mrs Stamper, the manager of the ladies' apparel department, glanced up at Arlette's gentleman visitor and her arched eyebrows shot towards her hairline. She put a hand to her chest and appraised the man in front of her from the tips of his shiny black shoes to the top of his expensive mohair bowler hat. She took in the coffee-and-cream-striped satin waistcoat, the gold fob watch hanging from a chain across his stomach, and the large bunch of white gladioli clutched inside his dark-skinned hands, and said, in a voice set midway between shock and delight, 'I'm not entirely sure. Let me just check for you.'

Arlette peered from behind the curtain at the back of the store and caught her breath. She let the curtain drop and leaned heavily against the wall behind her.

Godfrey Pickle.

At Liberty.

Bearing flowers.

She pulled herself up straight and patted her hair. She had only this minute seen her face in the mirror – she had come to the back of the floor to check her appearance after Mrs Stamper had commented on a loose hairclip – but she felt that she now needed to check her appearance once more. Just to be sure.

Mrs Stamper pulled open the curtain and addressed Arlette's reflection in the mirror.

'Miss De La Mare,' she said breathlessly, 'there is a gentleman on the shop floor. A Mr Pickle. He says that he has come to see you.' She moved closer to Arlette and lowered the tone of her voice to a serious whisper. '*He has flowers,*' she hissed.

'Oh,' said Arlette, lightly. 'Yes. Mr Pickle. He is an acquaintance of mine. We are having our portraits painted by my friend Mr Worsley, the portraitist I have told you about.' Her hand was at her throat, which was flushing an angry red.

'Well,' said Mrs Stamper, 'I must say, I have never before encountered such a handsome negro. And so well-dressed.' She smiled a half-smile and Arlette saw the skin of her neck, too, take on a mottled red hue.

'Yes, Mr Pickle is a world-renowned musician. He plays as part of the Southern Syncopated Orchestra. You may have heard of them?'

'No, I have not heard of them.'

'They perform *jazz* music, Mrs Stamper.'

'I have heard of that,' she replied, looking rather pleased with herself, for although she was only thirty-two, she did like to act out the role of a much older woman.

'They have played before the King of England,' Arlette said with a rush of pride, 'and are currently taking a break from a long tour of the British Isles, where they have performed at all the biggest music halls. I have been very fortunate to meet him at this point in his career, where he has a little time to contemplate other projects.'

'Such as you, you mean?'

Arlette blushed again and giggled. 'Oh, no,' she said. 'Mr Pickle and I are nothing more than acquaintances, I can assure you.'

'Well,' said Mrs Stamper, 'I would go out there and witness for yourself the spectacle of the voluminous bouquet of flowers he has brought for you today before you assume yourself to be sure of anything, Miss De La Mare.' Her eyes shone with something that Arlette took to be vicarious delight at the path of someone else's life taking a strange and hitherto unimagined direction. Arlette returned the smile, patted her hair once more and headed through the curtain towards Mr Godfrey Pickle.

'Mr Pickle,' she said, approaching him from behind.

He spun round at the sound of her voice and smiled at her, removing his hat with his spare hand.

'Miss De La Mare,' he said. '*Enchanté*. Once more.' He bowed slightly and returned his hat to his head.

'What a lovely surprise, Mr Pickle. And what brings you to Liberty's this morning?'

'Scent,' he replied, his smile still firmly in place. 'I was told that this is the place to come for scent. Have I been advised correctly, Miss De La Mare?'

'Yes,' she said brightly, 'yes. We have a splendid perfumery. World renowned.'

'Good,' he said. 'And a very fine flower shop also. Here,' he passed her the flowers, as heavy as a small child in her arms. 'I could not resist them. And then I remembered that you'd told me you worked here, in the ladies' apparel department, and well, to be honest with you, Miss De La Mare, I had an urge to see you again. A violent urge.' His smile faltered a fraction as these words left his lips, betraying a note of uncertainty.

Arlette tried to hold her own smile in place but also felt a jolt of uncertainty.

'Well,' she said quietly, 'how lovely.'

'Yes,' he said. 'How lovely.'

There passed between them a small moment of awkwardness, which Godfrey Pickle broke with the words, 'Well, my dear, if you are permitted a break in your labours here, I wondered if you might accompany me in the perfumery, maybe help me with my selection?'

Arlette glanced at the wall clock behind Godfrey's head. 'In fifteen minutes,' she said, 'I will be free for half an hour.'

'Well, now, that's just perfect,' he said, his smile now fully restored. 'And if it is agreeable with you, I will sit right here,' he gestured at a large silk-dupion pouffe in the middle of the floor, 'and wait for you?' He looked at her questioningly and she nodded, just once, in reply.

'Yes,' she said, 'that would be agreeable.'

He beamed at her and then sauntered, slow as a snail, towards the pouffe where he arranged himself in such a way that he looked for all the world as if he were waiting to have his portrait painted. He spread the tails of his fine worsted overcoat behind him, tugged at the legs of his trousers so that his black silk socks and half an inch of smooth brown flesh showed beneath, and then from the inside pocket of his overcoat he pulled out a folded edition of the *London News*, which he leafed through absent-mindedly.

Customers entering the ladies' apparel department reacted in different ways to the sight of a tall, handsome negro sitting slap-bang in the middle of the shop, upright and nonchalant. Some stared in awe, some pretended that they had not seen him, one lady left him with her hat and gloves and said, 'If I'd known you were going to be here I'd have brought some shoes in to polish.'

Godfrey had just smiled at her and said, 'Well, ma'am, that is a pity.'

But the reaction of London shoppers to a negro sitting in the ladies' apparel department was as nothing compared to the reaction of London shoppers to a negro shopping for scent with a white lady. As Godfrey and Arlette circled the perfumery together, they were greeted with jaws slung open like oven doors, loud whispers, hushed silences, some loud tutting, and, from a lady too old to know that it was impolite to pass audible comment, the words, 'Well, I never thought I would live to see such a thing. I think I shall go back to shopping at Lilley and Skinner.'

Arlette had never known such attention before. She felt simultaneously appalled, embarrassed and thrilled. She attempted to ignore the fuss and to focus instead on the matter in hand: the choosing of a suitable scent for Mr Pickle.

'This one, Mr Pickle, says that it contains notes of sandalwood and vanilla. Shall we try it?'

The shop-girl dabbed a drop upon the flesh of Mr Pickle's outstretched wrist and smiled at him shyly from beneath fine lashes. 'I've sold this before,' she offered helpfully, 'to a negro gentleman. Like yourself.'

'Oh,' Godfrey laughed, 'then contrary to all available indications, I am not the first negro to shop in this store.'

'No, sir,' said the shop-girl, 'not at all. I think there have probably been at least three or four others, before you.' She nodded and smiled encouragingly, and then looked at him enquiringly. 'What do you think?'

He sniffed his wrist again and then offered it to Arlette.

Arlette paused for a moment. He had fine bones for a man so tall and broad. His wrists were very delicate. She brought her nose down to his skin and she inhaled. She blinked and smiled. The scent was so evocative. It smelled of another world, another hemisphere, another climate. It smelled of Godfrey.

'It's very good,' she said circumspectly. 'I think it suits you very well.'

'Yes.' He looked at her warmly and smiled. 'Indeed. It

reminds me of home. It smells like my father.' He turned his smile to the shop-girl. 'Miss,' he said, 'I thank you for all your assistance. I think you have made yourself à sale.'

The girl smiled coquettishly at Godfrey, decanted the scent into a small ribbed glass bottle and wrapped it for him in purple paper.

'And now, Miss De La Mare, since you still have another ten minutes until your return to work, maybe you would allow me to help you choose a scent, for yourself?'

'Oh, no, thank you. I can't really afford the scents here . . .'

'My treat, miss, my treat.'

'But, Mr Pickle, you have already treated me to flowers today. That is more than sufficient. I could not in all good conscience accept another thing from you.' She smiled tightly, feeling a slight wash of discomfort pass through her. 'Besides,' she finished, 'I have always worn the same scent, since I was a very young girl.'

'Really?' he said. 'And are you wearing this scent today?'

'I am indeed.'

And then, before she could decide whether or not it was what she wanted, Mr Pickle had brought his face towards her neck, put his nose an inch from her skin and breathed in deeply. He pulled away from her slowly and smiled.

'Jasmine,' he said. 'And lily of the valley.'

She blinked at him and smiled nervously. 'Not quite,' she said. 'You are right about the jasmine, but I believe it also contains notes of lavender.'

'Yes!' he said. 'Lavender. Of course. All the English ladies smell of lavender. I thought it was just your natural scent.'

Arlette glanced at her wristwatch. It was five to one.

'I'm afraid, Mr Pickle, that I really must get back to work now. But it has been a pleasure to see you today.'

Godfrey Pickle removed his hat and tipped his head towards her. 'Miss De La Mare, I had a violent urge to see you and I am afraid that that urge has not been sated today. I believe we have another sitting with Mr Worsley on Saturday. Maybe you might consider the possibility of accompanying me afterwards to a club? I have the night off.'

'Oh,' said Arlette.

'Oh,' repeated Godfrey Pickle, with an amused look.

'Well, yes. I suppose. And maybe we could ask Gideon to come with us?'

He looked at her strangely and was silent for a moment. 'Absolutely,' he eventually concurred. 'Mr Worsley must come with us too. Indeed. Thank you so much for spending your time off with me today, Miss De La Mare, and I shall look forward tremendously to seeing you on Saturday at the studio of Mr Worsley. *Au revoir, Mam'zelle.*'

He bowed his head again and then returned his hat to his head, adjusted his worsted overcoat, tucked his purple parcel under his arm and sauntered through the shop towards the street, every single pair of eyes on him as he did so.

Arlette stood for a moment, like a sapling in a river,

letting the shoppers pass by her on either side. She waited a while, for the colour to pass from her chest and face, letting the oddness and the exhilaration of the last thirty minutes settle within her. And then, before returning to the second floor, she headed towards the shop-girl who'd sold Mr Pickle his scent.

'Excuse me, please,' she began. 'Would it be possible, at all, to take a drop of that scent on a muslin?'

'The one I just sold to your gentleman friend?' she asked.

'Yes, that's the one.'

'Of course, miss.'

She pulled the large glass bottle from a shelf behind her and let three large drops fall from the glass dropper onto a small square of muslin. She handed the square to Arlette with a knowing smile. 'Lovely-looking fellow,' she said, 'your gentleman friend.'

Arlette did not correct her. Instead she tucked the square of muslin under the sleeve of her jacket and headed back to work, the scent of Mr Pickle a heady secret hidden within the folds of her clothes.

30

1995

'Sweetie, come up!' The buzzer went on the door to Alexandra Brightly's studio and Betty pushed her way in. It was strange being back here again after all these weeks. The girl who'd come here clutching a fur coat back in early May seemed like a figment of Betty's imagination, a silly skinny wisp of nothingness. No wonder no one had wanted to give her a job.

Alexandra stood at the top of the stairs, a plastic cigarette in one hand, a cup of coffee in the other, her wispy blond hair twisted on top of her head and held in place with a bulldog clip. She wore layers of black chiffon with leather trousers and leather flip-flops, and her reading glasses on a chain around her neck.

'So timely,' she said, holding the door open for Betty and pointing at a vintage railway clock on the wall. 'Dead on ten.'

Betty had called her an hour ago, asking if she could pop round to see her, to talk about the Soho Historical Society. She'd been talking to John last night at the Windmill about Arlette, and Clara Pickle, and Peter Lawler and the jazz club, and John had said, 'You should talk to my sister. She's a complete jazz nut, and she's a member of the Soho Historical Society. I bet she'd be able to help you.'

Alexandra had sounded thrilled on the phone when Betty had said she wanted to talk to her about Soho jazz clubs in the 1920s, and was fizzing with excitement now as she buzzed around making Betty coffee and pulling out information leaflets from a reclaimed plan chest.

'So,' Alexandra said, putting the coffee and a pile of papers on the pattern-cutting table between them and pulling up two stools, 'what is it you need to know?'

'Well,' said Betty, pulling her own papers from her shoulder bag and spreading them out in front of her, 'remember that address on that piece of paper you found in my grandmother's fur?'

'Ooh, yes, I do indeed. The start of a grand mystery, I seem to recall . . .'

'Yes, well, kind of. Actually it was the name and address of a private detective. My grandmother was paying him to find a woman called Clara Pickle, the woman in her will.'

'Oh, wow,' said Alexandra, her pale blue eyes bright with exhilaration. 'Wow. Go on . . .'

'Yes, and I tracked him down, but unfortunately he'd died. Leaving the case unsolved. But I've got all his research, all the stuff my grandmother must have given him to work with. It's not much . . .' She fanned it out. 'Nothing concrete. Just some memorabilia, some photos, and this.' She pulled out the programme for the jazz trio at the White Oleander. 'See,' she said, 'Great Windmill

Street, just round the corner from my flat. I was there last night with your brother, some club called the Matrix. I asked the manager if he knew anything about the history of the place but he had no idea, said it had been a sex dungeon before he took over the lease.'

Alexandra grabbed the programme greedily. 'Wow,' she said, 'look at this.' She turned it over and smiled dreamily, and then she held it to her nose and breathed in deeply. 'Mmm,' she said. 'Seventy-five years old. Such good condition. Sandy Beach and the Love Brothers. Wow, look at them. They're so handsome.' She turned it over and read the back copy. 'Hmm,' she said, gazing at it through her half-moon glasses, 'Southern Syncopated Orchestra. Yes. I think I've heard of them; sound familiar.'

'I'm guessing it's, you know, relevant in some way. She obviously kept this programme for many, many years; there must be a reason.'

Alexandra lowered her half-moon glasses and held them at her chest. 'Absolutely,' she agreed. 'Maybe she met the love of her life here? Maybe something seismic happened that night? Gosh, it's just so tantalising, isn't it? I love this kind of thing. What else have you got?' She put her glasses back on and took some photos from Betty. 'So this is . . . ?'

'That's Arlette. Yes, my grandmother.'

'The owner of the amazing fur. Incredible.' She pored over the photo in minute detail. 'What a beauty,' she said. 'What an exquisite beauty.' She ran a thin finger across

Arlette's image and took a drag on her plastic cigarette. 'She looks like you,' she said, turning to Betty.

Betty laughed. 'That's a lovely thing to say, but it couldn't possibly be true. She wasn't my real grand-mother. I mean, not in terms of blood. She was my stepfather's mother.'

Alexandra squinted at her over her glasses and said, 'Well, then, your stepfather must subconsciously have chosen your mother because she looked like his mother. The resemblance between you both is quite startling, especially in this one.' She pushed towards Betty the photo of Arlette sitting on the floor in front of the black men on the sofa. 'Here,' she tapped the photo with her plastic cigarette, 'around the eyes.'

Betty looked at the photo and tried to see what Alexandra could see, but failed. She had always felt not quite pretty enough to be considered in the same league as Arlette.

'So,' said Alexandra, coming to the end of the pile of photos, 'looks like your grandmother had a whale of a time in the twenties, and I do recognise some of the locations. This, here,' she pulled out a photograph; 'that's the Royal Albert Hall. Good seats, too – front row. This here is Kingsway Hall, Holborn; used to be a famous recording venue. I think some famous jazz acts performed there in the twenties. Turned it into a hotel now, I think. Might be worth popping up there, see if anyone can help with the history? And this,' she pulled out another one; 'this is Chelsea Embankment. I recognise this little row of cottages. It's about halfway down. I wonder who these other people are?' She pointed at a tall leggy man with a dark moustache and wearing a rather scruffy overcoat, and a pretty young girl with her hair braided on top of her head and a delicate chiffon dress on. 'They all look so happy, don't you think?'

Betty nodded. That was the most overwhelming thing about the photographs: the sense of *joie de vivre* that emanated from them, the sparkle in Arlette's eye that Betty had rarely seen in all her years living with her.

'You know, if I could go back to any period in time,' said Alexandra, 'it would be then. The twenties. Bright Young People, jazz. Everything new and fresh and semi-illicit. I mean, the fact that your grandmother was socialising with black men – it would have been unthinkable before, and for a long time after, too – but the twenties were this little window of optimism and broad-mindedness. And the clothes, sweetie,' she raised her eyes blissfully towards the ceiling, 'the clothes. To die for . . .'

Betty smiled. 'Arlette always did like clothes,' she said. 'She left me her wardrobe, but the stuff she wore when I knew her, well, it was all very formal, you know, very stiff. Lots of starch and boning and tailoring. And in such tiny sizes. I took a few things,' she said, 'some négligées, some knitwear, but most of the rest of it, well, we sold it as a job lot.'

Alexandra gasped and put her hands to her mouth. 'Don't tell me,' she said. 'Please don't tell me. I shall cry.'

'Sorry,' said Betty.

'No. It's fine. If it was that small it probably wouldn't have fitted many actresses. Even the tiny ones often aren't as tiny as women from earlier generations. It's the waists, usually. Even skinny women today don't have those hand-span waists they used to have in the old days. Anyway, anyway, what else have you got . . .?'

'Erm, some matchbooks.' Betty passed them over.

'Can I keep these?' Alexandra said. 'I know a guy at the Society who is like a walking encyclopaedia of jazz clubs; he might be able to shed some light on these.' She shrugged. 'So exciting.'

She beamed at Betty and Betty smiled back, feeling herself filling up with optimism. Not only did Alexandra have a ton of enthusiasm about the era when Arlette was in London, but she also had access to other people with enthusiasm and knowledge. Betty felt suddenly that solving the mystery was within her grasp, that she had taken a giant leap forward from the back leg of the journey to somewhere near the front.

'When do you think . . .?'

'Oh, tonight!' Alexandra replied. 'I'm seeing him tonight. I mean, actually, if you wanted to meet him, ask him some questions for yourself . . .?'

Betty sighed. 'Can't tonight,' she said. 'I'm baby-sitting.'

'Oh, shame. But never mind. Leave it with me. I'll find out everything I can. Come and see me tomorrow, lunchtime. I'll let you know what he says.'

'That would be fantastic,' said Betty. 'Thank you so much. If you're sure you don't mind?'

'Mind!' cried Alexandra. 'Why would I mind? Jesus, no, this is my idea of total and utter heaven.' A phone rang and she threw Betty an apologetic look before answering it. Betty waited while she conducted a fascinating and rather heated conversation about a pair of mouldy patchwork flares and an afghan coat that smelled of piss. 'They were immaculate when they left here,' she was saying. 'I can only assume that they haven't been stored properly on the set.'

'Sorry about that,' she said a moment later. 'Pissy afghans. Mouldy jeans. Sublime to the bloody ridiculous. I sometimes feel like my life is being written by a team of stoned students in the sky.' She smiled. 'Anyway, give my love to that ugly brother of mine. And we'll talk tomorrow, OK. And hopefully I'll have loads of exciting things to tell you.'

She kissed Betty properly on both cheeks, holding on to her arms slightly too tightly. And then she smiled warmly and closed the door, leaving Betty on the landing with a renewed sense of urgency and enthusiasm. She would take over where Peter Lawler had left off. She would be Betty Dean, private eye.

She left the building and headed towards Tottenham Court Road underground station where she took the tube to Holland Park, her heart racing slightly with excitement. This was it, she thought, this was it. Finally the search was properly under way.

31

Number 21 Abingdon Villas appeared to be the best house on a remarkable street. The sky was perfectly clear and blue, and the trees on either side of the street were heavy with cherry blossom. The houses were ice-white stucco and it all looked improbably perfect, like a film set. Betty stood outside the house and stared at it for a while. It was fully detached and double-fronted, three floors high and taller than it was wide. The front garden had been given over to parking spaces, four of them. Betty had bought a disposable camera from WH Smith, which she now pulled from her bag. She photographed the house from across the street, furtively, and then slipped the camera quickly back into her bag. She wondered if Arlette had ever been here. Maybe she'd even stayed here. That would probably have been the way things were done, back then. A young girl coming to London would have stayed with a family friend, not rented herself a tiny flat in the red-light district. And this was, according to Jolyon, the home of Arlette's mother's best friend from childhood.

Betty crossed the street and approached the house. As Peter Lawler had confirmed, it had been divided into flats, four buttons on a panel by the double front door labelled A, B, C and D. She cupped her hands to the glass panels in the door and peered inside. She could see a large hallway, a front door on either side and two staircases in front of her that grew from the centre of the hall and rose in curves towards a landing. In the middle of the hallway was a plinth on which stood a large vase full of silk flowers.

She stepped back onto the driveway. The windows on the ground floor were full height. On the right they were obscured by net curtains, on the left the window was uncovered and Betty could see a glamorous interior, a gold standard lamp in the window and the end of an ivory chaise longue with curled wood trimmings.

Betty sighed.

There was nothing here, nothing to allude to anything about Arlette's friends, her history. An anonymous building on a beautiful street, all ties to the past categorically severed the minute the house was cut up into apartments. She was about to turn and head back to the tube station when she noticed that the wooden door to the side of the house that led to the back garden was ajar. She glanced round her. The street was quiet and still. She looked up at the house and into the window at the plush apartment but could see no signs of life. She knew that it was bordering on pointless, that a back garden could not possibly hold any clues to the history of someone who had been here seventy-five years ago, and may never have been here at all, but still, she thought, she had come all the way here, she might as well try.

She pushed open the wooden door and tiptoed past another window, through an alleyway full of bins and out onto a long sweep of manicured grass. She kept to the sides of the lawn, not wanting anyone looking from their back windows to see a strange girl tiptoeing across their garden. At the end of the garden was a cluster of trees and rose bushes. If she could get down there, she decided, then she'd be able to obscure herself and have a proper look at the back of the house. She hid herself behind a tree, her shoes sinking into soft soil, and then turned to face the house. The ground floor opened up into two sets of double doors, onto a wrought-iron veranda, which ran the width of the house. There was no furniture in the garden, just a lawn and flowerbeds. The back of the house was as bland and uninformative as the front. She crouched down and took a photograph anyway and was about to head back to the street when she saw something carved into the trunk of the tree that she was holding on to for support. She traced her fingertip over it, rubbing off a film of reddish summer dust. Then she scraped away some moss and stared at what lay underneath:

Her pulse quickened and she quickly pulled her camera back out of her bag and took another photograph.

G&A. *Someone and Arlette*. Maybe? Proof, possibly, that Arlette had been here, with someone whose name began with the letter G? At first she assumed the two Xs to be representations of kisses, but then it occurred to her that maybe they were Roman numerals. Maybe it was the number 20: 1920.

She ran then, no longer caring either way, across the lawn and back towards the street. It was still early. She wasn't due at Dom's until 5 p.m. Buoyed up and desperate now to build up her body of evidence, she set off for Chelsea Embankment.

32

1920

'If you let me come with you,' said Lilian, fingering a string of silver and pearl beads at her neck, 'I will love you for ever and ever and ever.'

Arlette peered at her over the top of Leticia's sewing machine and frowned.

'And that is supposed to be an irresistible enticement, is it?' she said drily.

'All right then, I will give you something. A gift. Some jewels, a dress. Anything you desire. There must be something of mine you've always secretly hankered after?'

Arlette laughed. 'No,' she said, 'not really. Anything I do like, I know I am free to borrow.'

'Well, then,' Lilian pursed her pretty lips together, 'if you don't let me come with you tonight, then I shall never let you borrow anything of mine ever again!' Her dark eyes flashed confrontationally at Arlette.

Arlette laughed again, wetted the end of the reel of blue cotton against her tongue and rethreaded the needle on the machine. 'Lilian,' she said, 'it is not up to me. It is up to your mother.'

Lilian rolled her eyes. 'As if my mother would be able to stop me,' she said.

'It is one thing,' Arlette replied cautiously, 'for you to disobey your mother's wishes when it is to socialise with people I don't know, but when it comes to socialising with my own friends, well, I would feel responsible for you. What if something were to happen? How would I explain it to your mother?'

'Nothing is going to *happen*!' Lilian exclaimed.

'Something *may* happen,' said Arlette, lining up the hem of her new dress against the machine. 'If you can persuade your mother to agree to it then, yes, of course, it would be wonderful.'

'Fine!' Lilian stared at her angrily for a moment before getting to her feet and flouncing from the room. 'Fine,' she muttered again as she stamped off.

Arlette watched her leave with a look of wry amusement. A moment later she was back. 'Mother says yes,' she announced triumphantly.

'Are you certain?'

'Of course I am certain,' she said haughtily. Leticia appeared in the doorway then, in a silk robe, holding a small china teacup that Arlette knew would have not a drop of tea in it, but a large measure of gin and a lemon slice instead.

'I have told her,' she said, 'that I trust you, Arlette, and that so long as she does everything you tell her to do, and so long as she does not once leave your side, then yes, she can go to the club with you tonight. But home by midnight. And no more than a small drink or two. Here . . .'

She passed Lilian a pair of coins, which Lilian glanced at disdainfully.

'Home by midnight,' Leticia said again. 'Is that clear?'

'Yes, Mother,' said Lilian, throwing herself into an armchair. 'Whatever you say, Mother.'

Leticia smiled, giving the impression that she somehow felt that she had done what was required of her as a mother and could now return to her own world of gin and romance novels and tea parties without a backward glance. Even as a young girl of twenty-one, Arlette could see that when it came to raising her children, Leticia set herself very low standards.

Lilian and Arlette arrived at Gideon's cottage at 2 p.m. Although this was the fourth sitting and Arlette now knew exactly what to expect each time, after Mr Pickle's impromptu visit to Liberty the previous week she felt a wave of nervous energy pass through her. She remembered his words: his *violent urge*, his needs not being *sated*. She thought of the large phallic flowers, the patch of scented muslin she'd tucked beneath her sleeve, the way she felt every time she brought it to her nose to remind herself of his aroma. She'd thought of his slender wrists, his silk socks, his air of total and utter entitlement to everything that London had to offer. She was pulled halfway between desire and sheer terror. She was an innocent, in every sense of the word. She knew nothing of the world. She knew nothing of men. It felt, in some ways, as if all of this – eccentric artists, jazz clubs and slightly flirtatious visits from handsome, worldly negroes – was happening to the wrong girl. There was another girl in London right now who would be better suited to all this attention, to all this excitement, she was certain of it.

'Arlette,' said Gideon, greeting her with the customary kiss on the back of her hand. 'And Miss Miller,' he beamed at Lilian. 'How enchanting to see you again. I believe you will be joining us all tonight after the sitting?'

'I shall indeed, Mr Worsley,' she smiled coquettishly.

'Please,' he said, 'call me Gideon.'

Lilian beamed at him graciously and they all shared tea. Arlette sat knitting her fingers together nervously, trying to imagine how she would feel when the knock came on the door, when Mr Pickle was in the room. How it would feel to act out the role of thwarted lovers upstairs in Gideon's studio when Mr Pickle had now implied that he had some kind of feelings for her, that he had *violent urges*. She swallowed down a wave of nausea and watched the hands on her watch as they marched towards two fifteen and there it was, the knock on the door. *Knock knock knockity-knock.* His customary tattoo.

But then her heart both slowed with relief and crumpled with disappointment when he showed no particular joy at seeing her perched on the edge of Gideon's sofa, when his eyes did not rest upon her for any longer than it took to intone: 'Miss De La Mare, *enchanté.*' And then to see him fuss over his greeting with Lilian. To see him hold her gaze and say, 'No, I do not believe we have met before, Miss Miller. Yours would be a face that

I should remember, Mam'zelle.' To watch Lilian blush and fumble under Mr Pickle's attentions.

When they sat arranged once more upon Gideon's chaise longue in a fabricated approximation of illicit love, she felt no ardour glowing from his warm body, no awkwardness in their physical connection.

Afterwards, when they left the cottage in high spirits after drinking two tumblers each of cognac, they waited upon the pavement outside for a hackney carriage to take them into the West End. Mr Pickle asked Gideon if he would be so kind as to take a photograph of him with Lilian and Arlette. When Gideon had taken the photograph he suggested that he might take one of Gideon and the ladies, one he could keep, to take home to show his mother and his father, the friends he had made in London. 'The famous artist,' he said, 'and the beautiful ladies.'

So Arlette stood between Gideon and Lilian, outside the cottage, his words echoing in her thoughts. *Beautiful ladies*. Just one of many, she realised, her heart again reeling between disappointment and relief. Just one of many.

Godfrey counted to five while they stood poised, waiting for the shutter to click shut, and then the camera was returned to the cottage and a carriage was located. Before Arlette was even aware of it, Lilian had taken the seat opposite Mr Pickle, making herself the object of his charm and attention.

'So, Miss Miller, if I may be so bold, could I ask how old

you are? I ask only because I am finding it very hard to match your fresh face with your worldly demeanour.'

'I am just eighteen,' she answered breathily.

Godfrey's eyebrows arched and he said, 'So very young. Yet so poised and elegant. When I was eighteen I was a big lanky buffoon with straw in my hair!'

'Oh, I cannot imagine that could be true for a moment, Mr Pickle.'

'Well, maybe I exaggerate.' He beamed at her, and it was as if, for all the world, there was no one else in the carriage but the two of them. 'And, Miss Miller, do you have a job of work?'

Lilian laughed. 'No!' she replied. 'I do not. I should hate to work. I help my mother,' she continued, as if this was somehow more worthy of respect, 'with my young brother and running the house. My mother is a little . . .' she smiled a knowing smile that was so false and so silly that it set Arlette's teeth on edge '. . . a little immature, shall we say.'

Godfrey threw her a curious look. 'And your father?'

'My father lives in Belgium,' she said in a tone of voice laden with the weight of unthinkable responsibility. 'He rarely gets home; once a month, sometimes less.'

'So it all falls to you, then, Miss Miller?'

She sighed dramatically and said, 'Yes, I'm rather afraid it does.'

Arlette pursed her lips and glowered out of the carriage window.

No mention of the housemaid, no mention of the junior

housemaid, no mention of the housekeeper or the cook, no mention of the nanny or the nurse. No mention of the hours Lilian spent curling her hair with rags or softening her feet with French lotions. No mention of the parties and the balls and the afternoons spending her mother's money in department stores on hats and collars and fripperies.

Lilian was trying to impress Godfrey. And it appeared to be working.

The carriage brought them to a Georgian building on a street off Piccadilly, and Gideon paid the driver. They entered the club, two by two, Lilian with Godfrey, Arlette with Gideon. It was Godfrey who helped Lilian with her gloves and cloak, and Godfrey who showed Lilian to a seat.

They sat in a booth, painted fiery gold and draped with folds of velvet. Their table was lit with a single lamp, and had Arlette been feeling a little less infuriated by Lilian's behaviour and the turn the evening seemed to be taking, she might have noticed that the club was peopled by extraordinary-looking men and women, ladies with feathers in their hair and cigarettes in extravagantly long holders, gentlemen with waxed moustaches and asymmetric fringes. There was a lady dressed as a man in a severe suit and with cropped hair. There was a man dressed in full dandy attire, including a powdered wig and a beauty spot. A woman in her late middle age sat with a Pekingese upon her lap while a young man of around twenty-five kissed the dip of her neck. Another man was dressed in a silk brocade dressing gown and fez, sitting upon the lap of a very thin woman wearing heavy, Cleopatra-style make-up, a skin-tight velvet dress and an elaborate paste-diamond headdress that was almost the same size as her head.

Arlette would have noticed that in the context of this bohemian mix of people, she and her companions appeared dull as daisies, even Lilian in her delicate drop-waisted chiffon dress and Godfrey in his sharply tailored, camel-coloured suit. Gideon, with his wild black curls and slightly scruffy clothes, looked almost as though he belonged here, but still, this place, the Cygnet Club, was absolutely not like anywhere else any of them had ever been before.

'Well,' said Godfrey, after ordering dry Martinis for the whole table, 'I feel a little as though I have fallen down Alice's hole and woken up in Wonderland.'

Lilian laughed over-loudly. 'I absolutely agree with you, Mr Pickle,' she said, in the silly new voice she appeared to have developed for his benefit. 'But isn't this just the most divine place in the world? All these beautiful people!'

'And some not so beautiful,' he replied, nodding in the direction of a woman with a heavily pencilled-in brow and a beak-like nose, dressed in head-to-toe black like a Spanish widow.

'But still, all so different, all so unique.'

'Well, yes, that they are.'

A young girl approached their table then. She was

small as a wood nymph and dressed in gold. Her black hair was bobbed to her jaw and her lips were painted into a red rosebud. 'Gideon!' she trilled, lowering her cigarette and blowing some smoke from the side of her mouth. 'My goodness, I haven't seen you for such a dreadfully long time! How are you?'

Gideon got to his feet and clasped the girl's hands between his. 'Miss McAteer!' he beamed. 'How wonderful to see you!'

'Oh, Gids, please don't call me Miss. That's just so old-fashioned.'

Gideon looked stung at the suggestion that he might be out of date and puffed out his chest. 'Of course,' he said, 'Minu. Lovely Minu McAteer.' He turned to his companions. 'Everyone, this is my dear friend Minu McAteer. Minu, this is Mr . . .' he stopped and smiled '. . . sorry, this is Godfrey, Lilian and Arlette.'

Minu McAteer blew kisses at all of them and Gideon pushed himself up the banquette so that she could sit down.

'So, *Mr Worsley*,' she teased, 'how are you? And what on *earth* are you doing here?'

'I am absolutely fine. And I am here at the suggestion of Mr . . . of Godfrey, whose portrait I am currently painting, at my studio.'

She eyed up Mr Pickle curiously. 'I feel I recognise you,' she said. 'Is it possible we have met before?'

'Well, yes, indeed. I am a musician; you may well have seen me performing with one of my bands.'

'One of your bands! Well, how impressive. And what bands might they be?'

'I play clarinet, Mam'zelle, with both the Southern Syncopated Orchestra and also my own ensemble, a three-piece called Sandy Beach and the Love Brothers.'

'Sandy Beach! Yes! Of course. We have met before. You played at another club I frequent. I asked you if you might be able to do some songs at my birthday party; you said you were too busy.' She pouted at him and he laughed.

'It has certainly been a busy year for me, Miss McAteer . . .'

'Call me Minu.'

'Minu.' He smiled at her broadly and Arlette felt her despondency grow again. 'I have been on the road constantly since last summer. The length and breadth of your country, an itinerary that would leave you quite breathless. I apologise for being unable to play at your party. And for not remembering your quite, quite lovely face.'

Arlette tensed at his words and resisted the *violent urge* to collect her hat and gloves and jump into the first carriage home.

Minu McAteer turned to Arlette then and smiled sweetly, and Arlette felt her heart lift at the thought that she might be about to bring her into her conversation with Mr Pickle. But instead she said, 'I wonder, would you mind awfully if I sat to the other side of you, so that Sandy and I may have a little chat?'

And then the winsome young thing climbed over Arlette's lap, squeezed herself in between them and turned her tiny, gold-clad back fully on Arlette and Gideon.

Gideon looked down at Arlette and smiled. 'Well,' he said, 'this place is rather a find, wouldn't you say?'

Arlette nodded wearily.

'All these people. Extraordinary.' He shook his head slowly and smiled. 'Everything all right, Arlette?' he asked gently. 'You haven't seemed quite yourself today.'

'I'm fine,' she said, through a stiff smile. 'Absolutely fine.'

'Your friend Lilian, she's quite a girl, isn't she?'

Arlette sighed. 'Ah, yes, that she is. As is your friend Minu.'

'Two girls, it seems, rather spellbound by our friend Mr Pickle.'

'You mean *Godfrey*,' she said archly.

'Ah, yes,' Gideon smiled. 'I must get with the modern way. The new etiquette. *Godfrey*.'

'I think it sounds rather vulgar,' said Arlette, primly. 'We barely know him.'

'Well, yes, that is true. But times are changing, Arlette. The world is a different place. It is impossible, I suppose, for the world to go through such upheaval and not come out of it rather changed. I rather like it. And you, well, I would call you the poster girl for the new world. A young woman of independent means, living off your own money, working at a job, finding your way in the big city almost single-handedly. You are the new modern woman. Why be scared of change?'

'It's not change I am scared of, Gideon, it is decline.'

'Oh, Arlette, Arlette, Arlette . . .' He smiled affectionately and patted the top of her hand. 'You are such a lovely little dichotomy. Such a puzzle. So unlike any girl I have met before.' He looked at her fondly and then covered her hand with his completely, wrapping his fingers under her palm.

Arlette stared down at her hand and stopped breathing for a moment. She had no idea what to make of it. In another context, a more formal context, that hand over hers would be a shocking approach, but here, in this peculiar, decadent place, full of bohemians and eccentrics and ladies whose stocking tops were clearly visible above the hemlines of their clothes, it seemed somehow sweet and reassuring. She heard Godfrey say something behind her and then the ear-splitting sound of Lilian and Minu both exploding with carefully orchestrated mirth. She curled her fingers carefully around Gideon's and squeezed.

'Well,' said Gideon, flushing slightly, 'I am glad to see that at least one woman in this party has not succumbed to the charms of Mr Pickle.'

Arlette smiled tightly and said nothing.

33

1995

Chelsea Embankment was far more beautiful than its name might have suggested. On one side sat the Thames, fringed with evenly spaced trees and lampposts shaped like dolphins. On the other side the houses ranged from blowsy mansion blocks to narrow town houses, and, as Betty walked westwards along the wide pavement, clutching Arlette's photograph in her hand, to clusters of pretty stucco cottages. She held the photograph before herself and slotted it into the panorama like a missing piece of a jigsaw puzzle. There, she thought, there it was. She found a pelican crossing and headed to the other side of the street. The cottages, which looked grey in the photograph, were actually painted in sugary tones of pink and blue, and the trees that had once been tiny saplings were now full-size chestnuts, but it was, undoubtedly, the same place.

She positioned herself in front of the cottages and realised she was standing in the exact spot that the photographer must have stood in to take the shot. And then she moved forward a few paces and put herself on the precise corner of the precise paving slab that Arlette was standing on looking slightly wistful next to her friends on some unspecified evening back in 1920-something. She felt an energy as she stood there, a jolt of something amazing and strange. Arlette had stood here, she thought to herself, a girl of her own age, alone in London, just like her.

She stared for a moment at the man in the photograph, a happy man with dark, straggly hair and a scruffy overcoat on. But he looked artfully unkempt; his features were refined, his stature proud and tall. Betty wondered if this man might be G. And as she wondered this she turned to appraise the row of pastel-coloured cottages behind her and saw that the smallest of the six, the one closest to the spot where the picture had been taken, had a blue plaque attached to the front wall. She moved closer and read it:

The painter and photographer
Gideon Worsley
lived and worked in this house
1918–1923

Betty blinked and looked from the plaque to the photo and from the photo to the plaque. *Gideon*. Gideon Worsley. He was G. The scruffy man with the beautiful nose must be G, she thought. He looked like an artist. He had a camera. And he was in a photograph directly outside a house that now bore his name. And if he was G, then Arlette was A, which meant that it must have been Arlette and Gideon who had scratched their initials into the tree at the bottom of the garden in Abingdon Villas, which meant that Arlette must have lived there. But if Gideon Worsley had been Arlette's lover, then how did he fit into the rest of the story? What did he have to do with Clara Pickle and Soho jazz clubs?

She found a bench and sat down. Then she pulled out the rest of the photographs and flicked through them urgently, looking for any more images of this man, this artist and photographer. But she found none. This was the only picture Arlette appeared to have of him.

She took her disposable camera from her bag and took some photos of her own, of the cottage, of the plaque. And then, pulled along by an overwhelming wave of momentum, she opened the garden gate, walked up the lupin-lined path and knocked on the door of the cottage with the plaque. She knocked once, then again, but nobody came to the door. She looked up at the windows on the second floor but saw no signs of life. She sighed. Her day as a private eye had brought itself to a natural close. And anyway, it was nearly four o'clock; it was time to go to work.

Amy Metz got to her feet and fixed Betty with a terrible shark-like stare.

'Betty, I presume,' she said in a mockney/California drawl.

Betty gulped and looked at Dom. 'Oh,' she said, 'hello. Er, yes.'

Amy narrowed her eyes and offered Betty a limp-wristed hand to shake.

'I'm Amy,' she said, somewhat unnecessarily. She was wearing a short leopard-print tunic with sheer black tights, and her violently red hair was pinned on top of her head with a big diamanté butterfly. On her feet she wore red platform boots and she smelled, overwhelmingly, of Opium. Her pretty face was gaunt and pale, and her thin arms were covered in scratch marks and patches of eczema. She looked, Betty thought, nothing like she did in photos; she had none of the glitter and the mystery.

'Well,' she said, 'first off, I gotta tell you, I am *not happy* that Dom has been leaving my kids with a fricking stranger. OK? And I'm not saying that is your fault. It is *obviously not* your fault. OK? But this is not a situation that I am happy about. *In the least.*'

Betty gulped and let her gaze fall to the floor. Amy Metz was only about five foot tall but had the fearsome aura of a giant.

'But,' she said, letting her features soften by an iota, 'Dom tells me you're great with the kids and Donny tells me you're the bee's fricking knees.' She smiled sardonically. 'So listen, *Betty*,' she spat out her name as if she doubted its veracity, 'what we're gonna do here is make this official, OK? I've got some agency girls coming over the next day or two so I'm gonna get you in for an interview. OK? At my house. I want you to bring a CV, some references. OK? We're gonna do this *properly*.' She threw Dom a withering look, then turned back to address Betty. 'OK?'

'Er, yes,' Betty said, adjusting the strap of her shoulder

bag, which she had not yet had a chance to put down. 'When?'

'Tomorrow, eleven a.m. Dom'll give you the address. Meantimes, I'm happy for you to sit with the kids tonight. Yeah? I've got an idea of you now. Well, half an idea, at least.' She threw Dom another rancid look. 'If you need *anything* tonight,' she said, 'anything at all, you call *me*, OK. Not Dom. *Me.*' She passed Betty a small business card and then, after some hurried but intense kisses and cuddles with her three children, she was gone, into a waiting car and towards a gig in Guildford.

The house was silent for a moment after her departure. The three children sat in a row on the sofa looking slightly dazed and Dom sat quietly on the arm of the sofa, chewing the inside of his cheek. After a moment he pulled himself straight, dragged his fingers through his unkempt hair and raised his eyes towards Betty's.

'Er, yeah. Sorry about that. I didn't have a chance to warn you. Donny was full of Betty this, Betty that, all day apparently. Amy asked who Betty was . . .' He shrugged, rubbed his hair again. 'I suppose I should have known it would happen.'

'So . . .?' Betty tried to form a question she knew needed asking, but couldn't quite find the words.

'I think she'll give you the job, I really do. I mean, getting the kids to like you is most of the battle, and they already do. And Amy is a big fan of cutting corners financially so if she can get someone without having to pay out an agency whack, she will see that as a huge bonus.

And if you get the job then, well, we're talking *big salary*. Travel. Some extra benefits. A car . . .'

'A car?'

'Yeah, our nannies get a car. A little runaround. Paid taxes. Health care.'

Betty sat down heavily on the armchair, her shoulder bag buried in her lap. Her dreams were coming real and the reality was only now hitting her. 'Wow,' she said. 'But hard work, yeah?'

He nodded. 'Really hard work. Long hours. But fun.' He glanced at Betty and then down at his fingernails. 'I'd've thought. Anyway, even if you don't get the job, I'll still need a baby-sitter. I am out, quite a lot.'

'Yes,' said Betty, 'I know.'

He looked up at her and smiled. 'Do you think I'm a bad father?' he asked, his eyes cast down towards his feet.

'What? God, no! Why would I think that?'

'Well, you know, what Amy just said, leaving my kids with a stranger, going out when I should be hanging out with them, all that, you know . . .'

'It's your job,' she said. 'You're a pop star.' She shrugged. 'It's part of the job description. And as for leaving your kids with me, well, you and I both know the truth about that. You and I both know that I'm a safe pair of hands.'

He looked up and smiled at her gratefully. 'I haven't always been the best judge of character,' he said, alluding silently but heavily to the mother of his children. 'But I guess that's one of those things that you get better at, the older you get. Anyway,' he pulled himself up straight and moved Acacia from his lap onto the sofa, 'I need to get ready. And these guys,' he rubbed Acacia's curls, 'need some tea. There's a bolognese on the hob.'

'Yummy. Home-made?'

'Er, yeah, but not by me, Amy brought it with her.' He smiled apologetically. 'See. Bad father.' He stood up and surveyed his children. 'Right,' he said, 'hands up who's hungry?'

'Me!' shouted Donny, waving both short arms in the air. 'I'm completely and totally *starving.*'

'Come on then,' said Betty, getting to her feet and offering Donny her hand. 'Why don't you come and help me get tea ready?'

'Can I eat raw spaghetti?' he asked, hopefully.

'Do you *like* raw spaghetti?'

Donny nodded.

'Well, then, of course you can.'

'Yes!' Donny punched the air. 'Yes!'

After the children were in bed (and this time she managed to settle Astrid on just the third visit to her bedroom), Betty rolled herself a cigarette and took it to the window on the first-floor landing. She felt the same sense of strangeness she'd experienced earlier, standing on the pavement outside Gideon Worsley's cottage, that sense of echoes and reflections, of being in someone's shadow. As she pulled open the sash, felt it stick, pushed it again, heard the sound as it reeled itself loose and the window lifted in its frame, she felt like she'd slipped through a mirror to the other side of her life.

She lit the roll-up and perched herself on the ledge, in the same place that she'd first seen Dom, and she looked across the courtyard, through a haze of steam and smoke, to the other side of the mirror, to the fire escape outside her flat. For a moment she saw a ghostly vision of herself: blond and fresh, full of silly dreams. The fresh blond version of herself smiled at her across the courtyard and Betty smiled back. She wasn't that person any more. She was fatter and darker and older and wiser. It struck her that the changes she could see in herself mirrored the changes she'd seen in Arlette between the photograph outside Gideon Worsley's cottage and the photograph of her sitting on the floor between the legs of black men. The same face, two completely different women.

And then she thought of this job. A full-time nanny. In Primrose Hill. It would be round the clock, unsociable hours, it would be total responsibility for three small children, it would mean obeying orders and following routines. It would give her absolutely no freedom at all. And after today, after her meeting with Alexandra, her visits to the houses in Holland Park and Chelsea, she knew that what she needed more than anything right now was time.

She lit her roll-up and inhaled, and then she remembered that there was one thing she needed more than time. She needed money.

She sighed.

She would go to the interview. If nothing else it would be fascinating to see inside Amy Metz's Primrose Hill mansion. But as to what happened after that, if Amy offered her the job, she had absolutely no idea, none whatsoever.

34

1920

One Monday morning in early May, Mrs Stamper invited Arlette into her office behind the curtain at the back of the shop floor. She seemed twitchy and uncomfortable, and had a slightly oily, grey pallor.

'Miss De La Mare,' she said, grimacing slightly, 'please, sit down.'

Arlette smoothed her skirt behind her and sat before Mrs Stamper, rather apprehensively.

'I have a small announcement to share with you and I would be obliged if you didn't share this with other members of staff, but I discovered yesterday that I am to be a mother.'

Arlette stared at her in surprise. She had often wondered at Mrs Stamper's lack of children and had not liked to mention it in case it were to upset her.

'Yes,' she said, registering Arlette's surprise. 'It was unexpected. After ten years of marriage myself and Mr Stamper had rather thought that it wasn't to be. But now, well, I am terribly happy to say that it is. I have offered my resignation to the directors and they have accepted, and asked me to work out a four-week notice period.' She paused and appeared to swallow down a wave of nausea inside a large cotton lawn handkerchief that bore her own initials. 'They have also asked me to put forward a suitable person to take over my position. And I have put you forward, Miss De La Mare.'

'Oh,' said Arlette, her eyes widening.

'Over these last six months I have found you to be both reliable and sensible. You are also bright and have a way with numbers that most of these other girls,' she gestured beyond the curtains, 'do not appear to possess. It is a harder job, slightly longer hours and fewer holidays, but you will be recompensed, I feel, more than satisfactorily. I will leave Mr Jones in the accounts office to tell you exactly what that will be. And, of course, a much increased responsibility. But I know you can take it on board. You are so very mature and have such a lovely way with the clientele. So . . .?' She stopped and looked at Arlette.

Arlette stared at the tabletop.

'Would you consider it?'

Arlette looked up at her and beamed, entirely uncontrollably. 'Oh, yes!' she said. 'Yes. I would like that very much. Very much indeed. And congratulations, Mrs Stamper. I'm delighted for you. I really am.'

Mrs Stamper smiled softly at Arlette and said, 'Thank you so much, Miss De La Mare. And, please, call me Emily . . .'

'Whatever happened to your lovely friend Godfrey?' asked Minu.

They were lying together on a silk-covered bed in the Mayfair apartment of a man called Badger. Badger was an absurdist who drew cartoons for *Punch* and wrote a rather strange column in the *Illustrated London News* about his social life, which had a cult following. Being referred to, however obliquely, in one of his columns was something of a badge of honour and all the socialites would pore over it religiously every Monday morning to see if they had merited a mention. As a result, Badger had become one of the most popular men in town, in spite of being overweight and a rather uncharming drunk, so when he invited everyone back after the Cygnet closed on this Friday night at the tail-end of May, everyone automatically said yes.

'I believe he is in Manchester,' Arlette replied, 'but I can't be sure.'

She was being disingenuous. She knew exactly where he was, but she did not wish to give the impression that she cared too much either way. Godfrey's tour of Great Britain had resumed itself shortly after their last sitting at Gideon's studio and Arlette had not seen him since. He'd taken Arlette's address and sent postcards every couple of weeks, addressed not to Arlette, but to Arlette and Lilian. The postcards were perfunctory and light-hearted: 'My dears, I am waving hello to you both from Liverpool. We play here for three more nights and then we take the train to Lancaster. Liverpool is wet and windy and I do not understand a word anyone says to me. I should be in London again in a few weeks. Please pass my regards to Mr Worsley. Your friend, Godfrey Pickle.'

Lilian would shriek with excitement every time one of these cards landed upon the doormat and read it and reread five, six times, as if the more she read it, the more it would reveal.

Arlette did not display her feelings. She would pluck the cards indifferently from Lilian's fingers and say, 'Hmm.' Or, 'How nice.' Or, 'Where on earth is Bradford?' Then she would pass them back to Lilian, who would store them somewhere, tied with ribbon, as if they were irreplaceable love letters or tear-soaked odes.

In Godfrey's absence, Gideon and Arlette had become something more than just friends, although it was hard for Arlette to know exactly what it was that they had become. He painted her still, apparently far from being tired of the lines of her face and the angles of her bone structure. And together they visited all the newest and most exciting clubs in London. They danced together at the Cygnet and they laughed together at the Criterion. And without Godfrey Pickle there to swallow up her attentions, Minu McAteer had become a friendlier proposition, drawing them into her own circle of friends: artists, poets, novelists and eccentrics, people with names like Bunny and Boy, people who Arlette liked but did not understand. People like Lilian, who came from backgrounds of wealth and advantage, tennis clubs and boarding schools. They welcomed Arlette into their sanctum, not because she was one of them, but because she was pretty, and because she knew Minu and Gideon; because they assumed that she was one of them.

'I wonder how it would feel,' said Minu, looking at Arlette mischievously.

'How what would feel?' she replied, half knowing in her heart the path her friend was leading the conversation towards.

'To be with a man like Godfrey. A coloured man.'

Arlette bristled slightly. 'What on earth do you mean?'

'I mean, to feel a mouth like that against yours,' she breathed. 'To touch that hair. I mean . . .' She rolled onto her side and propped her head against her hand, staring into Arlette's eyes. 'I think it would be rather dreamy, don't you?'

'I can't say I've ever thought about it,' Arlette replied drily.

'No,' sighed Minu, 'of course you haven't. You have eyes only for Gideon.'

'That is not true,' she huffed.

'It's nothing to be embarrassed about. Gideon is lovely. And he's also very eligible. And it is clear that he utterly adores you . . .'

'Oh, nonsense.'

'Not nonsense. He would marry you tomorrow.'

'I've only known him for six months, barely that.'

'Yes, but he is twenty-five and I have never known him to be close to a girl before. He needs to marry and it is clear to me that he would like to marry you.'

'Well, I am only twenty-one and I feel I hardly know him. Marriage is not on my mind.'

'And that, Miss De La Mare, is exactly what makes you

such an attractive proposition. Well, that and your lovely accent and your creamy complexion and your tiny waist and big blue eyes and your little feet that look like they're shod by fairies in the night . . .'

'Such silliness,' Arlette tutted playfully, and Minu laughed.

'You're the silly one,' she retaliated, 'having no idea how lovely you are, sitting around like a maiden aunt when you could be taking London by storm. I mean, Arlette, what do you really think of us all, with our crazy ways? You're here every night, you join in, but you always seem to be . . . I don't know . . . more of a spectator than a participant, like you are studying us, possibly for some sort of anthropological purpose. I mean, do you even like us?'

Arlette laughed. 'Of course I like you!'

'But do you . . . do you *approve* of us?'

Arlette paused. She was in a world that she would not have chosen for herself, but did that mean that she did not approve? She nodded and smiled and said, 'But of course I approve. We are all young, we have all lost people we love. I should be more disapproving of people who locked themselves away from a world of freedom that was so hard won.'

Minu smiled. 'Such wisdom. And there I was thinking that all I was doing was having lots of silly fun.' She paused and took a sip from a tumbler of something brown and ice-filled on Badger's bed-stand. 'So what do you think will happen to you, Arlette? Will you stay in

London? Or will you go back to your little French island and think wistfully of your wild days in London?'

'I think I shall stay,' she replied. 'Unless I am called upon to return. I have a good job and now I have a promotion and pay rise I can afford to rent a room of my own. I have friends and a social life . . .'

'And dear Gideon . . .'

'Yes. I have dear Gideon.'

'And you have me.'

Minu curled an arm around Arlette's shoulder and rested her head against the crook of her neck. Arlette smiled. 'Yes. I have you.' They lay like that for a moment until the bedroom door opened and two men burst in, both clutching champagne flutes and with their arms around each other's shoulders. One said, 'Well, well, well, beautiful Minu and beautiful Arlette, in an embrace . . .'

And the other said, 'Almost Sapphic, wouldn't you say?'

'Spellbindingly so,' replied the first. 'I don't suppose, ladies, that there is room on that bed for two more?'

Minu sat up straight and sighed dramatically. 'Foolish boys,' she said, 'Arlette and I clearly have eyes only for each other. Isn't that so, Arlette?'

'Oh, yes,' she rejoined. 'Absolutely.'

'Well, then. Perhaps we might just stay and watch?'

'Strictly no spectators, I'm afraid, boys.'

The men bumbled drunkenly against each other, giggled and then left the room, shouting, 'Sapphic Sex Show! Sapphic Sex Show!' in their wake.

'But listen,' said Minu, turning to Arlette brightly, as

though the preceding episode had not just happened, 'I just had the most super idea. Why don't you and I find a room together? Pool our incomes?'

'*Our* incomes?' questioned Arlette, because, as far as she was aware, Minu had been writing a novel for the past eighteen months and had no income.

'Well, yes, your income to start with, and of course my mother and father will be happy to pay my half. They despair of me ever getting married and leaving home. And of course, once my novel is published . . .'

Arlette smiled.

'Well, what do you think? I can cook, you know. And I'm relatively neat and tidy.'

Arlette doubted very much that Minu was neat and tidy, but she did quite like the idea of a roommate. She'd known Minu for only a few weeks, but apart from Gideon and Lilian, she was the closest friend she had made so far in London.

'Well, yes,' she said, 'that is a very good idea. I should like to share a room with you. Very much.'

Minu clapped her hands together and kissed Arlette on the cheek. 'Oh, how wonderful!' she exclaimed. 'Our own rooms! Can you imagine! They shall be the most popular rooms in town. People will be queuing outside our door to take tea with us! We will have so much fun, Arlette, so much fun!'

'Arlette! Look! Look!' Lilian scampered towards her clutching something in her hand.

Another postcard from Godfrey, she wagered. Arlette sighed and put down her knife and fork. It was a fine Saturday morning in June and she was halfway through a breakfast of scrambled eggs and toast. The newspaper sat open before her, and Leticia sat at the other end of the table with a cold pack clutched to her temples and her breakfast going cold on the plate in front of her. James, the youngest boy, sat upon the table, cross-legged in his shoes, with the cat on his lap, looking at his mother defiantly every now and then to see if she would admonish him. But she did not, just looked at him sadly and released another sigh.

'This weather,' she sighed, 'it fills my head with pressure until I feel fit to explode.'

'James!' said Lilian, the card still held in her outstretched hand, 'get down off that table immediately!'

'No,' said James, 'I shan't.'

'Well, then, I shall burn your insectarium and every last gruesome little creature in it.'

'No!' he screamed. 'Don't you *dare*!'

'Well, then do as you are told, young man, and get down from that table.'

James sighed and folded his arms across himself, his jaw set tight with annoyance. 'I hate you,' he said.

'Good,' said Lilian. 'I hate you, too.'

He flounced from the table and the cat escaped from his arms in a flurry of loose fur that fell upon the tabletop like snow.

Lilian took her seat at the table and looked at her mother. 'Go to bed,' she said coldly.

'Oh, how I wish I could,' Leticia sighed. 'But I have too much to do today, far too much to do.'

Lilian raised her eyebrows, turned to Arlette and smiled. 'Look,' she said. 'Look what the postman brought.' She slid the card across the table to Arlette, who read it nonchalantly.

My dear girls, here I am in Wales, which has no whales to speak of, but is a very jolly country none the less. On 5 July the Orchestra commences a ten-week spell at the Kingsway Hall in London, and myself and the Love Brothers will be taking some rooms in a house in south London for the duration. I hope that I will be able to meet up with all once again, and I will of course send you both some tickets once they have been released.

In the meantime, my best wishes to you both.

Your friend,

Godfrey Pickle.

Arlette swallowed some food and read the card again.

A ten-week spell.

Godfrey Pickle would be in London for ten weeks.

And she would have her own room.

She flushed red at her own boldness, as unspoken as it had been.

'Oh,' she said, circumspectly, 'how lovely. I should like very much to see the orchestra playing.'

'Yes!' said Lilian. 'So should I. But also, just to see Godfrey again . . .'

'Who,' sighed Leticia, 'is Godfrey?'

'Oh, Mother,' tutted Lilian, 'I told you about Godfrey. He is Arlette's coloured gentleman friend. The famous musician, from the Caribbean.'

'Oh, yes,' Leticia batted away the reply absent-mindedly, 'yes. I'm sure you did.'

'He is terribly handsome and very charming.'

'That's nice,' said Leticia dreamily. And then she winced and said, 'Actually, yes, I think I may go to bed. I really cannot bear this pain in my head for another moment. Will you tell Sally to take James to the park, and ask Susan to bring me some tea to my room? Thank you, darling.' She kissed the top of Lilian's head as she passed by and Arlette recoiled slightly at the overpowering aroma of old alcohol she emitted.

Lilian rolled her eyes at Arlette and sighed. 'Foolish woman,' she said. 'No wonder Daddy never wants to come home.'

Arlette said nothing. The unpeeling of the pretty façade that Leticia had presented her with when she first arrived in London nine months ago had been an unedifying process and not one that she felt able to comment upon.

Arlette turned to Lilian and smiled. 'I have some news,' she said. She spoke carefully because she was not sure how Lilian would react.

Lilian looked at her curiously.

'I have found myself some rooms. I will be moving out

next month.' She drew in her breath and held it, waiting for Lilian's reaction.

'Oh,' she said.

'Yes, they are in Bloomsbury. Two rooms and a bathroom. It is heavenly,' she smiled.

Lilian's demeanour brightened. 'Two rooms?' she said. 'Then you might have room for me?'

'Oh,' said Arlette, 'well, no. Minu McAteer is to take the other room.'

Lilian's face dropped and her eyes filled with tears. 'I see,' she said.

'I have upset you . . .'

'Yes,' said Lilian, staunchly, 'you have upset me. If I were to take rooms with someone you would have been the first person I should have asked.'

'Oh, Lilian. It's not that simple. You're only eighteen. Minu is twenty-five. And your mother needs you here.'

Lilian turned her tear-filled eyes onto Arlette and attempted to smile. 'My bloody mother,' she whispered. 'She is making me grow up before I am ready. She is making an old maid of me. I shall never leave home and I shall never be independent. I shall be stuck here with her for ever.' Her face crumpled then and she began to cry.

Arlette put her arm around her shoulder and said, 'Oh, Lilian, that is not true. Your brothers will be home from school soon. Then it can be their turn to look after everything.'

Lilian laughed scornfully. 'No,' she said, 'that won't happen. They will find a way to disappear, to college, to stay with friends. They will not stay here knowing the responsibilities it holds. But please,' she grasped Arlette's arm, 'promise me one thing. Promise me I can come and stay with you and Minu in your lovely rooms, just sometimes?'

'Of course you can,' said Arlette. 'Of course.'

'I will miss you very much. I was so glad when Mother said that a young girl was coming to stay with us, and at first I thought you seemed a little distant, but having got to know you, well, you are nothing of the sort. You are everything that I should like to be.'

Arlette patted her hand and smiled. 'You will be much more than I could ever be, Lilian, just you wait and see. Much, much more.'

35

1995

The front door was painted gleaming ebony and the stucco work was sugar pink. Over the past couple of years, Betty had seen so many photos of this house, of this door, she felt like she must have been here before. She stared into the lens of a security camera and said, 'My name is Betty. I'm here for an interview with Amy.'

The door buzzed and Betty pushed it open. The hallway was papered with a violently patterned paisley print in lime green and black. A black velvet chaise longue with elaborate gilt decorations stood beneath a silver-plated bust of a lion with bared teeth. The floor was stripped-back floorboards painted pink and the stairs were carpeted jet black. It was like finding oneself embedded inside an oversized Liquorice Allsort. Amy Metz stood before her in towering boots, skin-tight jeans and a black chiffon blouse. Donny appeared behind her and she tutted loudly as he banged up against the backs of her legs. 'Watch it, honey,' she said. Donny spotted Betty standing in the doorway and smiled shyly, burying his face in the back of his mother's legs.

'Betty,' said Amy, offering her a hand, 'come in, come

in. We are in total chaos. Total and utter chaos.' Acacia toddled into the hallway then and banged up against Donny, who banged up against Amy, who turned and lifted her arms in the air and shouted, 'Jeez, you guys, will you cut it out!'

She took Betty into her office, a room painted black and covered wall to wall in framed black-and-white prints of her and her band live on stage.

'Right, right, right . . .' She rustled haphazardly through a pile of paper on her desk. 'OK,' she turned to face Betty and crossed her pin-thin legs together. 'So, Betty, tell me a bit about yourself.' She had a pen in her hand and a pad on her lap and looked strangely like a journalist.

'Well,' said Betty, 'I'm twenty-two. I'm from Guernsey, in the Channel Islands. I studied art at my local college.'

'Oh!' said Amy, glancing up at her from her notepad, which Betty noticed she was writing on in shorthand. 'I studied art, too! Go on . . .'

'Yes, well. I was hoping to study in London but I was living with my grandmother, in her house, and then she got ill and my mum and stepfather couldn't cope with her – or rather, she couldn't cope with them – so they moved out and then it was just me and her, and we'd always had this special bond so it seemed only natural that I should take care of her.'

Amy narrowed her eyes at her. 'Right,' she said, 'and by "take care of", you mean, *everything*.'

'Yes,' said Betty. 'Apart from her medical care – she

had a nurse for that. But yes, I did everything. For three years.'

'And then she died?'

'Yes, she died. In April. And she left me a small amount of money so I came to London. To find my fortune. And instead I ended up working in Wendy's.'

'Oh Jesus. What a story!' Amy cried, looking at Betty with concern. 'Wendy's! You know, where I come from that is the bottom of the barrel. And from the bottom of the barrel, the only way is up and outta there. So well done to you.' She looked at Betty fondly for a moment, an unexpected change in demeanour, which Betty found rather unsettling. 'Anyway,' she pulled her face back to business and examined Betty's CV, 'so, no actual childcare to speak of?'

'No,' said Betty, realising that they had reached the sticking point and that if she wanted to move past it she would have to deploy the only fact that worked in her favour. 'The only children I've ever looked after are yours.'

Amy glanced up at her again and Betty saw something pass through her eyes, something sad and guilty.

'Yes,' she said busily, 'right. That is true. Dom tells me you took them all out. To the park. How did you find that?'

Betty shrugged. 'Once I'd worked out how to put the double buggy together, it was fine.'

'And tell me about your other skills. I mean, cooking, for example. As you probably know, Dom and I like our kids to eat super-healthy. What can you say about your abilities in that area?'

'Well, you know, if there's healthy stuff in your fridge, I'll give them healthy things to eat. I won't be sneaking them out to McDonald's behind your back. You tell me what to give them and I'll give it to them.'

'But can you cook?'

Betty nodded. 'I cooked for myself and my grand-mother. Never poisoned either of us.'

'Right . . .' Amy trained her gaze back onto Betty's CV, as if looking for something to trip her up with. 'And what kind of activities would you do with the children? Sometimes I'm out from early a.m. until last thing; that's a lot of hours to fill.'

'Well, I don't really know. I mean, drawing, obviously – we could do art things – there's the park over the road, playgroups, walks.'

'Hmm.' Amy looked unconvinced.

'What do you do with them?' Betty asked.

'I beg your pardon?'

'When you're at home, during the day. What kind of things do you do?'

Amy looked trapped suddenly, and uncomfortable. She wriggled in her seat and said, 'Well, yeah, like you say, art, crafts, walks. I meet up with other moms for coffee, the kids hang out together. Just, you know, simple stuff.'

'Great,' said Betty, 'then I'll just do what you do. Apart from hang out with your friends, of course.'

'Well, yeah, but you can hang out with my friend's

nannies. That's what the other girls have tended to do.'

'Great!' said Betty. 'Sounds like fun.'

'Yeah, it is.' Amy looked puzzled for a moment, before turning back to the CV. 'So, another important thing: discipline. Where do you stand on discipline.'

'Riding crop always does it. Ruler across knuckles. A wooden spoon . . .' She mimed whacking herself on the bum with a spoon and laughed.

Amy blinked at her and Betty smiled. She'd walked into this house feeling utterly terrified, but within two minutes of her encounter with Amy she had seen straight through her to a small-town girl with big ideas, just like herself.

'Right, I see, you're joking . . .'

'Yes, sorry. No, obviously I have no training in this area, but my mother brought me up as a single parent until the age of ten and I feel she had a lot to teach me about child-rearing. She gave me lots of positive attention. She gave me firm boundaries, there were lots of rules in my house and I knew never to breach them. Lots of cuddles and kisses. It's not rocket science.'

Amy narrowed her eyes at her. 'Only a person who has not had children would be able to say that. Right, moving on. Hours . . .'

Betty inhaled. This was the bit she was most concerned about.

'Flexibility is *key*. Every day is different. Ideally I should have a live-in nanny, but I've never been good sharing my house. So, it would work a little like this: probably two sleepovers a week, an eight a.m. start would be regular, but sometimes earlier if I'm catching a flight. If I'm away for more than one night, the kids go to Dom, and so do you. Regular finish time would be six o'clock. I like to be home for bedtime and baths, so I'm rarely later than that. I am super-organised and I will give you lots of notice about everything. I appreciate you have a life to live and it's not fair to keep you hanging around or have you cancelling your own plans, so we'll work out the schedule week by week. There shouldn't be any surprises. But, if there are surprises, I need to be able to rely on you. Sometimes you might have to cancel a plan, OK?'

Betty gulped and nodded.

'Conversely,' Amy continued, 'there may be days when I don't need you at all, like if I have family coming to stay, or if I take the kids away. I am not one of those moms who need help around the clock. I do actually like looking after my own kids. I do actually like just hanging out with them on my own.' She smiled at Betty defensively, as though Betty might not believe her. But actually, Betty did believe her. She was just a woman, after all, not, as it had appeared at first sight, an android.

'So, of course, the last thing we need to discuss – apart from money, which we can talk about later if I get you back for a second interview – is privacy. More than anything I need to be able to trust you, like, one million per cent. There are people out there who would pay you life-changing amounts of money to find out what happens in my house. As much as I would love for you to receive a life-changing amount of money, that is not going to happen at my and my children's expense. So you would have to sign a lot of stuff. OK?'

Betty shrugged. She was not sure she wanted this job. She was not sure she wanted to work for Amy Metz. She felt she had nothing to lose. 'Fine with me,' she said.

Amy paused then, and inhaled audibly. 'Listen,' she said, 'there is one more thing. Dom.'

'Dom?'

'Yeah. Don't go there. OK?'

Betty gazed at her blankly. 'I don't . . .?'

Amy raised her eyebrows impatiently. 'I mean, Dom would fuck a pig if it happened to be sitting in his house after a night out drinking. And you are far from a pig.'

'Oh!' said Betty, her own eyebrows shooting towards her hairline. 'Oh. No. I mean . . . no. Of course not.' She cast her gaze downwards, not wanting Amy to read her expression, which, she felt, might have given away some of the more carnal thoughts she had had about Dom in the past couple of weeks.

Amy smiled, clearly satisfied with her reaction. 'Good,' she said. 'Well, I think that's about as far as we can go now. I'm seeing two more girls today. If I want to see you again I'll let you know this time tomorrow. OK?'

'OK. And would you mind letting me know if you don't? Just so I can get on with finding something else.'

'Sure. Yeah. No problem. I'll give you a call either way.'

'When?'

Amy grimaced at her. 'Shit, I dunno, tomorrow. Some time.'

'Yeah, right, except I don't have a phone. Just a pay-phone. A communal one. I'd need to know you were calling to make sure I was –'

Amy stopped her and smiled. 'Yeah. Of course. I get it. I remember those days,' she laughed wryly. 'I will call you . . .' she looked at her wristwatch '. . . at two p.m. How's that?'

'That's great. Really great.'

'And yeah, if you do come and work for me, first thing we'll have to do, sort you out with a cellphone.'

Betty smiled. *A cellphone.* She could not imagine herself with a mobile phone. But she was sure she could get used to it.

Betty stood in the doorway to Alexandra's studio, watching while she collected things into plastic bags and hunted for her sunglasses, which were on top of her head.

'I got us a picnic,' Alexandra was saying, 'it's such a lovely day.'

They walked through the sunshine to Soho Square and Alexandra flapped out a vintage Black Watch rug and spread out sandwiches and dips and a half-bottle of wine.

'I sometimes forget it's summer at all, cooped up in that place from dawn to dusk. Cheers.' She handed Betty a plastic cup and held hers towards it. 'To summer. And to your amazing grandmother!'

Betty took a sip of wine and looked at Alexandra expectantly.

'Had *such* a fascinating chat with David. I really wish

you'd been there. He'd heard of most of those clubs and they were, literally, the first jazz clubs in London.' She dragged a breadstick through a pot of hummus and waved it around as she talked. 'I mean, your grandmother was trail-blazing. She was out there, in the thick of it, way before the Bloomsbury set, way before anyone had even heard of the Bright Young People.'

'Bright Young People?'

'Yes, they were a social set, back in the twenties. Crazy, wild hedonists. Written about in all the newspapers. They were like, I suppose, the equivalent of the Primrose Hill set today, you know, all leaping in and out of bed with each other, all thinking they were terribly fabulous and important. But, you know, this wasn't really established until well into the decade. At this point,' she pulled out the Sandy Beach and the Love Brothers programme, 'this was all brand new. All these clubs,' she pointed at the matchbooks, 'the first of their kind. And what's really interesting is that your grandmother doesn't seem to have frequented any of the clubs that came later, when the scene was really established. It's like she came and then she went.'

'Back to Guernsey.'

'Well, yes, probably. So she missed out on all the really juicy stuff. But in a way, far more thrilling to be there at the start. Breaking new ground.'

'Did you find out who any of these people are, all these black guys?'

'Well, I'm assuming they must be musicians. There was a big influx after the war. And this lot,' she pointed again at Sandy Beach, 'part of the Southern Syncopated Orchestra, and they were *massive*. I mean, they played for the King, played all the biggest venues. *Huge* deal. And there were dozens of them, from all over: the States, the Caribbean, Africa. It looks like your grandmother might have been a bit of a groupie.' She held out the photograph of Arlette sitting on the floor between the legs of the well-dressed black men.

Betty laughed. 'No way,' she said. 'Not Arlette.'

'Well, darling, a few weeks ago would you have thought it possible that Arlette might have been a jazz club habitué?'

'No, but I can believe it. As surprising as it is, I believe it. But being a groupie? No.'

Alexandra removed some slices of cucumber from a tuna sandwich and said, 'Well, sweetie, you knew her better than anyone. And maybe we'll never know the truth. But David's going to fish out some more stuff about this jazz orchestra, see if we can find out more about them. Between us all we'll stitch some kind of bigger picture together.' She bit off some sandwich and chewed it thoughtfully. 'Did you get anything?' she asked. 'On your mission yesterday?'

Betty beamed. 'Yes!' She told Alexandra about the tree in the back garden of the house in Kensington, the A and the G, the double X, and she told her about the cottage by the river, the blue plaque, Gideon Worsley. Alexandra's eyes sparkled with delight.

'A portraitist,' she said, folding up the packaging of her

mainly uneaten sandwich and putting it back into an empty carrier bag. 'Well, then,' she lit a cigarette, 'there's only one thing for it. The National Portrait Gallery. Let's go.'

'What, now?'

'Yes. Finish that up, and we can walk over there right now, see if anyone's ever heard of this Gideon Worsley character. You never know,' she said, 'they might even have some of his work on display.'

'But, don't you have to get back to work?'

'Yes, I most certainly do. And I most certainly have no intention of doing so. This is much, much too exciting.'

36

1920

Arlette, Lilian and Minu stood together before the Kingsway Hall, chattering excitedly. They were all dressed extravagantly in chiffon and bugle beads, with ornate hair decorations, velvet slippers, and lips painted carmine red. Lilian had her arms linked through Arlette and Minu's and was hopping from foot to foot.

'Do you think there might be anybody famous there?' she asked.

Minu smiled and said, 'Well, *we* shall be there.'

'We are not famous, Minu,' chided Arlette.

'No,' said Minu, 'we are *infamous*.'

'We are that neither.'

'We are *potentially* infamous.'

'Well, that's as maybe,' she conceded.

'Do you think we will even recognise him?' Lilian asked breathlessly. 'I mean, it has been a long time since we last saw him. Do you think he will recognise us?'

'Lilian,' said Arlette, tiring greatly of the fevered anticipation that she had been subjected to since the tickets had arrived in the post two days earlier, 'we are here to see a performance of jazz music by a world-renowned orchestra. We are not here to ogle the famous and make eyes at Mr Pickle.'

'Well,' said Lilian, 'you may not be, but I certainly am. Oh, oh, look! Is that Sarah Bernhardt over there?'

Arlette turned to see an elderly lady in a regal headdress. 'No, of course it isn't. Look, that lady has two complete legs.'

They all peered at the lady in question and agreed that yes, she did appear to have both her legs.

They ascended into the hall and fanned themselves with their programmes, for it was a steamy July night and they were half-crushed by a crowd of hundreds. Lilian's head darted around like that of a sparrow looking for worms, while Minu and Arlette took in their surroundings more circumspectly.

Arlette was rather more anxious than she wished to appear. There had been a covering note attached to the tickets, in Godfrey's now familiar neat handwriting, which had said: 'My dear ladies, please do come by and say hello when we have finished our performance. I will be looking out for you.'

Arlette had not known whether this meant that they would be allowed backstage, that they would be seated and entertained, subject to Godfrey Pickle's full-hearted attentions, or that they were to wait like everyone else at the stage door, like hopeful pigs around a trough, for a glimpse and an autograph. She almost thought she should not like to find out, and that it would be safer and less humiliating just to go straight home when the show ended.

A bell sounded the start of the show and they found their way up dark staircases to their fine seats in the front row of the stalls. The hall was filled with the sparkle of chatter and anticipation, the rustle of people finding their way to their seats, the flutter of a hundred hand-held fans flapping away at the intense heat.

'Look! There!' Lilian pointed rather crudely across the theatre to a box. 'That's Ivor Novello! Look!'

'Ssh,' said Arlette, throwing apologetic glances towards the people seated near them. She glanced across the hall and saw that it was indeed Ivor Novello, and the thought that a man of such standing in the world of popular music should be sitting in prime seats to watch her friend Godfrey Pickle perform on his clarinet brought shivers down her spine.

The lights went down, the curtains rose and Arlette straightened herself in her seat. And then the spots illuminated and there they were, the Southern Syncopated Orchestra, all smart in matching black suits and bow ties, some in bowler hats. Unlike a traditional orchestra there was no warming up, no creaking of bows on violins, no dull plunking of piano keys and ponderous thumps on bass drums. They smiled first at the audience and then at each other, and they launched straight into their first number.

Arlette strained to pick out Godfrey from amongst the abundance of musicians squashed together elbow to elbow upon the stage, until Lilian shoved her roughly with her own pointy elbow and said, 'There he is! Look! There, on the left, see, without a hat.'

Arlette's eyes found him and she felt her heart expand and contract, her stomach convulse. She pushed Lilian's elbow from the arm of her seat. 'He looks well,' she said.

'He is the most handsome man on the stage,' breathed Lilian.

'I would beg to differ,' whispered Minu. 'Do cast your eyes upon the gentleman playing the double bass . . .'

All three women turned their gaze upon the double bassist, and yes, he was handsome. He was lighter-skinned than Godfrey, his features were more even and his face more youthful, but he did not, to Arlette's eye, have the same air of intelligence and neither did he have – and it was not a phrase she could ever utter out loud or even admit to being aware of – the same animal magnetism.

She watched Ivor Novello in his seat across the hall. He was on his feet and his eyes were alight with joy.

All around them the audience pulsated with repressed dancing. The energy was extraordinary, and Arlette realised that for some people this was their first exposure to jazz music in a live setting. She allowed herself to rock gently in her seat, to nod her head in time to the rhythm, and for the next hour she lost herself in the sound of the music, in the world it suggested of bayous and crocs, of verandas and pineapples, mint juleps and muggy nights.

But as the show drew to a close she started to feel anxious again. For now she would discover whether or not she would see Godfrey, and whether or not he would show her even the slightest interest.

*

'Miss De La Mare!' he greeted her warmly, drying the sweat from his face and hands with a fluffy white towel. 'Miss Miller. And Mam'zelle,' he smiled at Minu, 'I do remember your face but your name escapes me.'

'Again,' teased Minu. 'That is the second time you have forgotten me, Mr Pickle. My name is Minu McAteer.'

'Of course,' he smiled, 'of course. I will not forget a third time, of that I assure you.'

The three ladies stood before Godfrey Pickle and he smiled at each of them in turn. 'Well, well, well,' he said, 'what a lucky man I am.'

He caught Arlette's eye and she blushed. She felt sure that his look had contained a grain of something more than he showed to the others, but she could not be sure, and besides, this entire situation now felt faintly ridiculous. The backstage area was tiny and crammed full of musicians in varying stages of undress. There were also many other ladies, not unlike themselves, gathered around the musicians, giggling and jostling and making themselves, in Arlette's opinion, look like nothing but desperate fools. There was not room for them in this place; it was hot and the smell of fresh sweat was almost overwhelming.

'Mr Pickle . . .' she began.

'Oh, now, please, I think it is time you were to call me Godfrey.'

'Of course,' she smiled. 'Godfrey. I just wanted to say that that was a truly marvellous performance. Really. Electrifying. And it was gratifying to see Mr Novello in his box seemingly unable to control the impulse to dance.'

Godfrey smiled and shook his head. 'Mr Novello?' he repeated, in wonder. 'Well, that is something, that really is.'

'So, I thank you so much for the kind gift of the tickets. But now, I think we really must get back, and to ensure that Miss Miller gets home safely.'

The other two women both turned and threw her looks of sheer horror.

'Well, Arlette,' said Minu, 'I must say that I have absolutely no intention of going home. And in fact I was going to see if perhaps Godfrey and some of his friends might like to join us at the Cygnet.'

Arlette looked at Minu aghast but had not managed to form a response before Godfrey smiled and said, 'Well, I must say, that idea holds great appeal. I have far too much energy left to end the night here. Thank you. That is a very kind invitation.'

'And I wondered, Godfrey,' Minu continued audaciously, 'your friend, over there, the gentleman who plays the double bass. Perhaps he could be persuaded to join us for the evening.'

Godfrey laughed. 'You mean Horace? Oh, yes, I am sure he could be persuaded.' He called Horace over and introduced him to the three of them. Arlette felt herself torn between two reactions. She would hate to imagine Minu and Lilian dancing the night away with Godfrey at the Cygnet Club without her, but equally, she had to get up for work the following morning and was feeling uncomfortable about the turn the evening was taking: this undignified hanging around backstage, the strange atmosphere around Minu and Lilian, this air of something beyond mere socialising. She had dreamed of seeing Godfrey once again for eight long weeks and this was not how she had hoped it to be. She thought of the quiet hours spent on Gideon's chaise longue, the delicacy of their interlude in the perfumery at Liberty. There was none of that present in this situation. She did not want to be a part of this situation. But neither did she want to rob herself of time with Godfrey.

She sighed and said, 'I'm afraid I do need to go to bed at a reasonable hour tonight, so I shall come along for a dance. But only one.'

Godfrey smiled at her. 'Well, if there is to be only one dance tonight, Miss De La Mare, then I really will have to insist that it is with me.'

She looked into his eyes and saw it there: that look she had not seen for so long, a look filled with violent urges. Something hot and immediate flowed through her at his gaze, something that almost scorched her from the inside out. And she knew then that one dance would not be enough. That she would want to dance all night, until her feet were rubbed raw.

37

1995

The National Portrait Gallery shone pale gold in the early afternoon sunshine. Betty and Alexandra strode in and towards the information desk, both filled with a sense of certainty that there was something within this building that would add a layer to their story.

'Excuse me,' Alexandra started in her throaty rasp. 'We're looking for work by a guy called Gideon Worsley. He was a portrait painter in the early twenties. Ever heard of him?'

The man behind the desk stared at Alexandra inscrutably for a moment and then nodded. 'Gallery five,' he said, and then pointed rather dramatically to the left, indicating a slight bend with a curve of his wrist.

Betty and Alexandra looked at each other and smiled. 'You have his work?' said Alexandra, disbelievingly. 'Here?'

'Gallery five,' the man repeated slowly. 'Follow the signs.'

They smiled at each other again and set off at a pace towards gallery five.

Betty almost laughed out loud as they chased each

other through the corridors. To think that a small piece of paper buried away deep inside the pocket of Arlette's fur coat could have brought her here. It suddenly seemed the stuff of children's adventures. They arrived at gallery five breathless and giggling quietly. It was a small gallery, and empty. They scanned the walls and immediately identified Gideon Worsley's work: two medium-sized paintings, one of a black man in a bowler hat holding a viola, and the other of a young woman who was incontrovertibly and unmistakably a young Arlette De La Mare.

Betty grabbed Alexandra's arm and inhaled loudly.

'That's her, isn't it?' Alexandra whispered.

Betty nodded and took two steps towards the painting.

Arlette was dressed in a chiffon and lace blouse with a small ribbon at the neck. She was turned away from the artist so that her face was almost in profile. Her hair was swept back in a small bun, with tendrils falling about her neck and face, and she was smiling softly. The painting was entitled, simply, *Arlette*.

Between the two paintings was a plaque. Betty read the description:

Gideon Worsley was a renowned portraitist of the early 1920s. He lived and painted in Chelsea, using as subjects musicians and socialites he met at the various jazz clubs and drinking establishments that sprang up in London in the wake of the Great War. Nothing much is known of the sitters in these works.

The musician depicted in the *Viola Player* is thought to be a member of the world-celebrated Southern Syncopated Orchestra, but has never been properly identified. And it is believed that the mysterious Arlette was a shop-girl with whom Worsley was conducting an affair.

Worsley developed carpal tunnel syndrome in his late twenties and turned to photography as his chosen art form for the last years of his life. He died at the age of thirty-four, on the eve of his wedding to his second cousin Antoinette Worsley, after breaking his neck falling from his horse.

*

Betty looked at her watch and sighed. It was two fifteen the following afternoon. Amy's phone call was now fifteen minutes late. She decided she would wait until two thirty and then she would give up. She made herself a roll-up and took it out onto the street. John Brightly was serving a customer to a soundtrack of the Pixies. He turned briefly at the sound of Betty's door opening and threw her one of his half-smiles. 'Hello, trouble,' he said.

'Hi,' she replied. She kept the front door open with her back and sank to her haunches. The sun was out and it shone on her in a narrow stripe through a small gap between the buildings opposite.

'What's happening?' said John, turning to join her after saying goodbye to his customer.

'I'm waiting for a phone call,' she said, inhaling.

'Oh, yeah, who from?' John took out a cigarette and lit

it, then sank to his own haunches against the wall of her building.

'Amy Metz,' she said, and then turned and smirked at him.

'Amy Metz?' he repeated.

'She interviewed me yesterday,' she said. 'For a full-time nanny.'

His eyes widened. 'Cool,' he said.

'You reckon?'

'Yeah, why not?'

She shrugged. 'I don't know,' she said. 'I suspect she'll be a nightmare to work for.'

'Yeah, but you like the kids, right?'

She nodded. 'The kids are great.'

'Well then,' he said, 'just focus on that.'

She sighed. 'Yes, but that's the thing. What if I take the job, and love the kids but then hate her so much that I have to leave? That's not fair on the kids, surely?'

John laughed. 'Having Dom Jones and Amy Metz as parents isn't fair on the kids.'

Betty laughed and then stopped when she heard the phone ringing in the hallway. She threw John a desperate look and ground her roll-up against the pavement. 'Wish me luck,' she said.

He looked at her and smiled. Then suddenly, softly, he put a hand against her face and said, 'You don't need any luck. You *are* luck.' His eyes held her gaze and slowly he pulled his hand from her cheek. He looked embarrassed, as though he'd taken himself by surprise. 'Go,' he said, the phone still ringing insistently. 'Your destiny awaits.'

Betty scrambled to her feet and grabbed the receiver, her face still smarting sweetly from John's touch. 'Yes?' she said, rather brusquely, which was not at all how she'd intended to begin the conversation.

'Betty?'

'Yes.'

'Amy Metz.'

'Hello,' she said, bluntly. It appeared that John Brightly had stolen her vocabulary.

'Listen. It was really good meeting you yesterday. And I've gotta say, you were by far the best of the bunch. By a mile. But still, I have these misgivings, you know? All these other girls have got qualifications and references jumping out of their asses. You, you've got nothing. Just a nice personality and a back story. So what I'm gonna do is this. A trial. Two weeks. If you like it and I like you, then after that we'll talk about a more permanent thing. I'll give you the going rate, six an hour, and we can discuss a salary if we get to that point. What do you think?'

Betty nodded. And then she found her voice and said, 'Oh. Yes. That sounds great.'

'Great! I'll need you to come in today, sign some legal stuff, nothing fancy, just some basic privacy stuff. Pretty standard for this kind of thing. Then we'll start you properly tomorrow at eight. Yeah?'

'Er, yeah.'

'Can you get here at five?'

'Sure.'

'Cool. I'll see you then.'

Betty put the phone down and sank onto the bottom step. She breathed away a rising sense of panic and then she opened the front door and smiled at John Brightly.

'I got the job,' she said quietly, too scared to hear the words out loud.

He smiled at her. 'Of course you did,' he said.

She felt waves of pleasure ripple through her belly at his words.

'Shit,' she said, biting her lip and relighting her half-smoked roll-up.

'It's great,' he said. 'A real kick-start for your CV.'

'You think?'

'Yeah. Of course it is. Listen,' he looked at his watch, 'I haven't had any lunch yet. If I can get someone to cover this for me,' he indicated his record stall, 'will you come and have a bite with me. By way of celebration, if you like?'

'A celebratory sandwich, you mean?'

'Yeah, and a lemonade, if you're up for it.'

She looked at John Brightly, let the essence of him wash over her for a second; his everyman demeanour, the smooth tanned arms, the face that gave nothing away, the thick head of hair that she sometimes found herself dreaming about running her fingers through, the tattoo on his wrist, the almost militaristic style of dressing. And then she thought about the more vulnerable side of John Brightly; the half-arthritic fingers and creaking joints, the slight tang of damp about his aroma, the hats he wore, hats he must have tried on in mirrors, turning his head this way and that to check the angles, caring about his image, caring about whether or not they suited him. And then that moment just now, the softest part of himself he'd yet shown her: the warm palm against her face, the words of gentle encouragement.

She had two hours before she needed to set off for Primrose Hill. She wanted to pop into Wendy's, tell Rodrigo that she wouldn't be coming into work for a couple of weeks (she wouldn't hand in her notice just yet, not until she'd been offered the job properly). And she'd wanted to spend some time in the library, researching jazz orchestras and Gideon Worsley, but as important as that was, she knew that it could wait. For now.

'A lemonade sounds good,' she said. 'But make it a strong one.'

38

1920

'Arlette!' Gideon leaped up from his seat at the back of the Cygnet Club where he'd been talking to a man wearing a pink cravat. 'I had no idea you were coming tonight. What a wonderful surprise!'

Arlette smiled at him, uncertainly. 'Well,' she said, 'Gideon, I wasn't expecting to see you here, either.' She accepted a kiss on her cheek and saw Gideon's face drop slightly at the sight of her entourage, coming in behind her.

'Oh,' he said. 'Mr Pickle. I didn't realise . . .'

'We've been to see Godfrey playing with his orchestra. At the Kingsway Hall.' She said this quickly, breathily, as though she were lying. 'It was absolutely marvellous,' she finished. She moved aside so that Minu and Lilian could be greeted by Gideon and then watched awkwardly as Godfrey and Horace moved in to say hello, to shake hands and exchange pleasantries.

Arlette felt her spirits deflate. Although she and Gideon were probably widely held to be courting, in reality they had gone no further in their private moments than to hold hands. Gideon had made it plain that he would like to kiss her on many occasions, and on every occasion Arlette had fondly told him that she did not think she wished to kiss anyone. She saw Gideon as a handsome older brother, someone whose company she enjoyed, someone she looked forward to seeing and someone she felt she could trust. But she did not feel sufficiently passionate towards him to want to kiss him on his lips. But she was also aware that in spending time alone with him, that in encouraging his friendship and allowing moments of hand-holding and gentle affection, she had unwittingly been pulling him along on a lead, like a small dog. It was perfectly reasonable of him to assume that theirs was a special friendship within which there should be no room for anyone else.

And now, here she was, torn between the man who kept her safe and the man who made her feel mad with wanting.

'So,' Gideon was saying, his voice slightly betraying his disappointment in finding himself forced to share Arlette's attentions, 'I hear the performance was incredible. I'm sorry I missed it.'

'Ah, Gideon, I will send you some tickets tomorrow, don't you worry.'

'And all these lovely ladies,' Gideon continued, sounding slightly melancholy, 'coming to see you. You must feel so flattered.'

'Oh, indeed I do,' Godfrey smiled. 'Indeed I do. And now, well, Mam'zelle Arlette has to rush home to get her beauty sleep and she promised me a dance before she has to turn into a pumpkin so, if you don't mind, I will whisk her away.' He smiled heartily at Gideon, and Gideon smiled bravely back at him.

'Of course,' he said magnanimously. 'Of course.' He threw Arlette a slightly injured smile and then brought Lilian, Minu and Horace onto his banquette and started loudly ordering drinks for everyone.

'I think our friend Gideon is worried that I am trying to steal you away from him,' said Godfrey, his hand gently pressed against the small of Arlette's back as they made their way towards the dance floor.

'Oh,' said Arlette. 'No. I'm sure he isn't. Because I do not belong to him.'

Godfrey stopped and looked at her. His face was a picture of charmed delight. 'Well, no,' he said. 'Of course you don't. A fine woman like you belongs to nobody.'

'Absolutely, Mr Pickle.'

'Godfrey.'

'Yes. Godfrey.' And then she smiled a smile she'd never known she was capable of producing. It was both innocent and worldly-wise. The smile of a woman who had experienced little, but felt a lot.

'I have much respect for your friend Gideon,' he continued.

'As do I.'

'He is a good man, with a good soul. I would wish him nothing but the best of everything.'

'Me too.'

'And I must say that I thought, from our last meeting, that he had laid a claim to your heart.'

'Not in that way, Godfrey.'

They turned to face each other on the dance floor. The band were playing a torch song. The light was faded red and marbled with cigarette smoke. Godfrey smiled at Arlette and said, 'Shall we?' He offered her a hand, which sent a jolt of electricity through her body when she touched it. The other hand he brought down upon her hip where it burned a hole through her flesh. On the stage a middle-aged woman in a tight velvet dress sang songs of loneliness and heartbreak. Arlette smiled at Godfrey and he smiled back at her. Then he brought his face down to hers and for one extraordinary moment Arlette thought he was going to kiss her, here, on the dance floor, in front of her friends, in front of Gideon, and she held her breath and thought, yes, let it be, let it be now. But he didn't kiss her. Instead he put his mouth to her ear and said, 'I would like to take you home, Miss De La Mare.'

She did not speak. Instead she simply nodded her head, just once, and then quickly, before anyone could stop them, before, indeed, she could stop herself, she took Godfrey's hand and led him through the club, past the enquiring gaze of Gideon and her friends, out onto the pavement and into a hackney carriage.

'Bloomsbury, please,' she instructed the driver, breathlessly. 'And quickly.'

They removed their shoes at the bottom of the stairs of the Bloomsbury town house and ascended the stairs on tiptoes. They heard the murmur of Arlette's landlady through the door of her upstairs sitting room and paused momentarily before continuing on towards the attic rooms.

Once inside her apartment, Arlette drew the bolt across the door and then stood, for just a moment, flushed with desire, her back against the door, her arms clasped behind her, her chest rising and falling, while Godfrey stood before her, a slight smile on his face.

'You are so beautiful,' he said, and then put a hand to her cheek. She fell against his hand, greedily, and brought it to her mouth where she kissed it and tasted it and knew without any doubt that tonight she would lose her virginity.

His hand moved from her face, down her neck and then stopped upon her breastbone. She grasped it and pulled it down, so that his hand cupped her entirely. They stared at each other and then all the things that Arlette had suspected but never known for sure made themselves plain to her. She felt his mouth against hers, soft and urgent, his hands on her, all over her, the smell of him in her nose, the smell of sandalwood and vanilla, the same scent that had faded to nothing on a square of muslin in her bed-stand drawer over the past ten weeks.

And then, as though possessed by a secondary soul, one that had resided within her for twenty-one years without her knowledge, she found herself removing Godfrey's trousers, then allowing him to remove her own clothes and within a few small, almost unthinking movements, they were upon her bed and he was on top of her, looking into her eyes and saying, 'Miss De La Mare, have you ever done this before?'

She shook her head.

He looked at her sweetly, pushed some hair from her face and said, 'Then I shall be gentle.'

And it was all she could do not to say, 'No! Don't be gentle!' But instead she smiled and brought his mouth back down upon hers and allowed him to take her away from her state of purity.

It took all of five minutes. But what came after took all night. For hours, until the sun shone through the small dormer windows, they talked and they held each other. Godfrey told Arlette about his family: his father, the chief of police, his mother, a former beauty queen, his house at the foot of the Pitons, his childhood spent practising music, studying, singing in the choir at his local church. He told her about his experiences of the war and his adventures travelling with the orchestra, the friends he'd made and lost, and his plans for the future.

At around two in the morning, Minu returned. 'Arlette,' they heard her whisper into the darkness, 'are you here?'

Arlette and Godfrey giggled into each other's necks and Godfrey called out, 'Indeed she is, Miss McAteer.'

Minu made a strange noise and said, 'Oh. Oh. Oh. I see. Well, good night then, Arlette, Godfrey. Sleep tight.'

'Night-night, Minu,' they replied in unison.

But they did not sleep. They talked more. Arlette told Godfrey about her own childhood, the windswept house on the top of a cliff, her stoic mother, the death of her father, her childhood spent staring out of windows and wondering what it would be like to be an adult. She told him about the Miller family, about poor Leticia and her teacups of gin, about the absent father and the naughty boys, and Lilian torn between wanting to grow her wings and needing to stay grounded for the sake of her little brother. And she told him about her job at Liberty, the eccentric ladies with their impossible requests, and the fact that she was the youngest department manager in the history of the store.

It was nearly the hour to get up for work by the time they finally fell asleep, and when Arlette opened her eyes and saw him there, long lashes resting against his high cheekbones, one long, sinewy arm draped across her stomach, her heart lurched and she instinctively brought her lips down against his forehead, and when he opened his eyes and smiled sleepily at her, then pulled her closer to him and nestled his head into the crook of her shoulder, Arlette thought again of that funny, serious girl, staring dreamily through the leaded windows of the house on the cliff, across the Channel, into a distance that held nothing but secrets and mysteries. She knew that that girl was gone, that she was now where she was meant to be, a modern woman, strong and certain, held safe in the embrace of a man called Godfrey Pickle.

39

1995

'I've been hanging out with your sister,' said Betty, stirring sugar into a cappuccino and bringing it to her mouth with both hands.

John tore the top from a packet of sugar and looked at her quizzically. 'She's helping you out then?' he asked. 'With all this mysterious jazz stuff?'

'Yeah. She's been brilliant. She even took some time off work with me yesterday. We went to a gallery, had a picnic.'

'This is my sister you're talking about?'

Betty smiled. 'Yes. I think you two should get together some time. I think you might actually like each other.'

John smiled sardonically. 'And where have you got to, with your quest?'

She told him about the blue plaque and the engraved tree, the jazz orchestra and the painting of Arlette in the National Portrait Gallery.

John's expression passed beyond his usual cut-off point of slight interest and towards wonder and surprise. 'Wow,' he said, when she'd finished. 'I mean, wow, that's extraordinary.'

'I know,' said Betty. 'And now, well, I've got this job, I

probably won't have much free time to look into it. I mean, all the libraries, Somerset House, all only open during working hours.'

'I can help,' he said suddenly.

Betty looked at him curiously. 'How? I mean, you work longer hours than anyone I know.'

He shrugged. 'I can take time off. An hour here or there. Everything's walking distance. Let me know what you're looking for and I'll find it.'

'Seriously?' she asked.

'Sure. Why not?'

'Er, because your name is John Brightly and you are an island.'

He laughed and stirred his coffee. 'What do you mean?' he said, although it was obvious from his tone of voice that he knew exactly what she meant and just wanted to hear her say it.

'I mean,' she said, 'that you live in a bubble. The Bubble of John. Record stall, club nights, damp flat . . .'

'Don't forget the record fairs, every weekend.'

'Record fairs every weekend,' she continued. 'You don't exactly put a lot of yourself out there, do you?'

He shrugged. 'I've got friends,' he said.

'Right. So you say. And when do you see them, these so-called friends?'

'I see them,' he said. 'Not that much. Most of them don't live in London. But I see them when I can.'

Betty smiled. 'You're not fooling me,' she said. 'You've got bars up all over the place.'

He laughed and put his hands up in front of him in a gesture of surrender. 'Yeah, right, OK. I hear you. I am kind of closed off. I always have been. But that doesn't mean I can't get close to people. That doesn't mean I'm not a nice bloke.'

'Oh, John, I don't think I was suggesting that you're not a nice bloke. You're just not the sort of bloke to get involved in other people's shit. So thank you. For the offer. I really appreciate it.'

John smiled and nodded.

'And actually,' Betty leaned down into her coffee, hiding her face from him, 'I think you're a really nice guy.'

He peered at her and said, 'Say that again, this time so that I can see you.'

She laughed. 'I like you. OK? I think you're really nice.'

He smiled again. 'So you've made your mind up then? You've decided?'

'Yes,' she nodded, 'I have decided. John Brightly is a nice bloke and I like him.'

They both laughed then, and John said, 'Good. Then it's mutual.'

She peered at him suspiciously. 'You like me too?'

'Yes. I like you. I think you're nice.'

'Very nice or quite nice?'

He pretended to mull over the question and then said, 'Very nice.'

'Good,' she said. 'That's good.'

They smiled at each other and Betty felt the air around them fill with something light and golden.

Then John said, 'Promise me one thing.'

She nodded.

'Promise me you won't fuck Dom Jones.'

'What?'

'Seriously. No good will come of it.'

'But – what on earth makes you think I'm going to sleep with him?'

He cocked an eyebrow at her.

'No. Seriously, Amy Metz said the same thing. I don't even fancy him!'

He cocked his eyebrow a little higher.

'Why do you think I fancy him?'

'I don't think you fancy him. I just think you could end up in bed with him.'

'Because he's a pop star?'

John shrugged.

'So you think I'm that shallow?'

'I don't think you're shallow. I just know how these things go.'

Betty narrowed her eyes at him and said, 'I might have to review my recently expressed opinion of you, John Brightly.'

He held his hands out, palms up. 'Sorry,' he said. 'I totally retract everything I just said. I know you wouldn't. You're better than that. You're *different*.'

'That's better,' she smiled. 'Much better. Thank you.'

But even as she said it, Betty suspected that John was just placating her, that deep down inside he did believe that she was capable of sleeping with Dom Jones because he was a pop star. And deep down inside, Betty thought that he was probably right.

The noise of the buzzer cut through a dream that Betty had been having about Arlette and John Brightly and Amy Metz, and she awoke, vaguely with the sense that she was still in Amy's house, making a ridiculously big strawberry cake for everyone in a ridiculously big pink Aga. She looked at the time. It was midnight. She had been asleep for only an hour, and she cursed the ringer at the bell for robbing her of the benefits of an early night.

'Yes,' she muttered into the intercom, feeling fairly certain that it would be just a drunken reveller, mistaking her front door for the front door of a drinking den or that of a young model.

'Betty, it's Dom.'

'Who?'

'Dom. Jones.'

Betty ran her hands down her hair and grimaced, no longer certain where her dream had ended and reality was beginning, and thinking that maybe this was just an example of the events of the day influencing the things you dream about; that she was imagining this because of the conversation she and John Brightly had had earlier in the café.

'Betty?' said the voice again, and Betty did then, literally, pinch her own flesh, before clearing her throat and saying, 'Yes.'

'I'm lonely,' he said.

'Sorry?'

'I'm lonely. I just got back from Berlin and I'm not tired and I'm missing my kids and I want to have a drink with someone.'

'I've got no booze,' she said.

'Come out with me, Betty. Please. Put on a nice dress and come out with me.'

She took her finger off the button and gazed at the floor for a moment, plucking the last remnants of sleep from her head and considering the proposal. She was starting work the next morning, had to be at Amy's house at eight o'clock. She had turned down John's offer to sit with him during another club night because she needed an early night, because she wanted to be fresh for work. And now Dom Jones was standing in the street outside her flat asking her out for a drink.

Dom Jones.

'Will you take me to the Groucho?' she said.

'You wanna go to the Groucho?'

'Yes,' she said.

'I'll take you to the Groucho, then.'

'Good, but just a quick one, OK? I'm starting work for Amy tomorrow.'

'You got the job!'

'Yeah. On a trial basis.'

'Well, then, get down here fast as you can. I can feel champagne in the air.'

Walking into the Groucho with Dom was an experience that Betty would never forget. Faces opened up like lotus blossoms at the mere sight of him, doors were held open, drinks were brought without being ordered. It was as though the club were a dark room and Dom was a light bulb. Betty wrapped her cardigan tight around herself and tried to pretend she didn't exist. It was clearly ridiculous that she was walking in here with Dom Jones, and everyone who looked at her would know it too.

People whose faces she vaguely recognised put out hands to Dom as he passed, which he clutched at and patted and then said things like, 'Yeah, man, good to see you. Hanging in there, mate. Hanging in there.' A man played a piano by the staircase, and another man behind the bar shook together a Martini in a silver shaker.

Dom walked Betty across the room and they sat together on a leather sofa. Betty felt dazed and bewildered, all the lines between dreams and reality entirely blurred. Champagne arrived and was poured, and she and Dom toasted each other and people swivelled their heads surreptitiously in their direction and then whispered to each other excitedly.

Betty smoothed down her bed hair and scraped a blob of something off the hem of her black Lycra dress and remembered a night that felt like months ago, but was in reality only a few weeks, when she had walked in here hoping for a job, and been charmingly ejected back onto the pavement without even a sniff at the interior. And now here she was, warm in the heart of the place, sharing a sofa with Dom Jones.

'So,' said Dom, turning to face her, his elbow on the back of the sofa. 'Welcome to the family then, I guess.'

'It's just a trial run,' Betty stressed.

'Yeah, but think about it. Unless something goes drastically wrong, why would Amy get rid of you, have to start looking all over again?'

Betty shrugged. 'We'll see,' she said.

'It's good,' he said. 'It's brilliant. I couldn't be happier. Seriously.'

Betty smiled and drank some champagne and hoped that it might take her away from this sense of being a joke. The scruffy young nanny, dragged from her bed by a drunk pop star and plied with champagne in a celebrity hangout.

'You know, I fucking hate living on my own,' Dom said, suddenly and unprompted.

Betty looked at him with concern.

'It fucking stinks. It's OK during the day, but at night . . .' He ran his hands down his face and sighed and suddenly looked tired and ten years older. 'I used to love getting back when I lived in Primrose Hill, even if it was really late, even if everyone was asleep. You know, I liked having to tiptoe about the place, seeing the kids' things here and there, you know, their little shoes, then going into their rooms, watching them sleep, all that shit.' He sighed again and smiled sadly at Betty.

'Is there any chance that you and Amy, might, you know . . .?'

He shook his head and laughed. 'No,' he said categorically. 'No. That ship has sailed. She hates my fucking guts. And yeah, you know, got no one to blame but myself. And, you know, my little fella.'

He glanced down at his jeans and Betty's eyes followed his until she too was staring at his jeans. 'Oh,' she said, pulling her gaze away hurriedly. 'I see.'

'Yeah. I think I've got a problem, you know. Maybe I need therapy. Or maybe I need a chemical castration.' He laughed hoarsely and Betty smiled nervously, wondering why Dom was being so open with her, why he was telling her so much. And then something occurred to her. Firstly, Dom was very drunk. But secondly, and more pertinently, she'd signed the privacy agreement that afternoon. At Amy's house. He must have known. And now he was using Betty for free talk therapy, because he knew that she could never tell anyone.

The thought emboldened her and she said, 'But surely if it meant that you got to live with your kids again, if it meant that you could get your old life back, surely you'd do anything?'

Dom downed his glass of champagne, poured himself another and topped up Betty's. 'Yeah, you'd think so, wouldn't you. You'd think it would be easy. But that's what I'm saying. I think I've got an addiction. And it's like, you know, if you're an alcoholic and someone offers you a drink, you'll say yeah, but most people with a sex addiction don't get offered sex all the time, but when you're in my position, well, you know . . .'

Betty nodded.

'It's hard to say no. It's impossible. It shouldn't be. But it is. Even if the girl's, like, ugly. You know.' He shook his head from side to side and then downed his fresh glass of champagne in three thirsty gulps. 'Everywhere I go, I swear, they're there, they want me to sign their tits, they want me to touch them just so that they can go home and tell their mates that I touched them. It's like I'm a talisman, you know, like they'll get something from me. And it's all just utter bullshit, because of course I've got fuck all to give. I'm just a bloke, with a dick. Who can sing. And write amazing songs. But I've got nothing to give. Nothing real. Unless it's a baby.' He laughed out loud, a sudden burst that made Betty jump slightly in her seat. 'Yeah. I'm pretty good at giving women babies.'

Betty held her breath. There had long been a rumour in the tabloids that there was a Dom Jones love child somewhere in north London, a child only two weeks younger than Donny. But nothing had ever been proved. The mother, an emaciated sculptress called Tiffany, who'd also had a baby with another rock star, had never said anything to either fuel or kill off the rumours. But there was a suggestion here – the use of the plural 'women' – that maybe he was the child's father. Betty looked into Dom's eyes. They were bloodshot and slightly dazed. He'd clearly spent the whole day drinking to some extent or another. He was drunk and tired and vulnerable. She didn't ask the question. Instead she smiled and said, 'Yes, and very nice babies you make, too.'

'Ah, yeah, my babies.' His face softened. 'My beautiful fucking babies. I miss them so much. So fucking much.' And then he started to cry. He dug the heels of his hands into his eye sockets and sobbed. 'I've fucked it all up, Betty,' he sniffed. 'Fucked the whole thing up. I wish I could be different. I wish I could be just like some normal guy, you know, off to work with my lunch in my bag, kiss the kids goodbye, home for bath-time, glass of wine, shag the wife. But you know, I never could have been that person. I've always had it in me, all this creativity, all this power, all these urges, these overwhelming urges. Even when I was at school. All I did was chase girls and make music and cause trouble. And now I'm like, thirty-two, you know, and maybe it's too late for me to change. Maybe this is it. Maybe this is all there is for me. Just all this arsing about. And sometimes that's enough, you know.' He sniffed again and wiped his nose against the sleeve of his denim jacket. 'And sometimes it just ain't. I mean, tell me, honestly, Betty.' He looked up at her through wet lashes. 'What do you think of me, truthfully? I mean, the real me, the one you've got to know against the me you used to read about in the papers?'

Betty took another sip of champagne, buying herself time to consider the question. 'I don't know,' she said eventually. 'I mean, obviously I read stuff about you, and obviously I had an opinion, but I don't think those opinions really count for much . . .' She paused and saw that he was staring at her intensely, like his whole future depended on her opinion of him. She took a breath and continued, 'And yeah, I suppose I thought you were a bit of a . . .'

His eyes widened, waiting for her pronouncement.

'. . . a bit of a rabble-rouser,' she finished diplomatically. 'And, you know, I'm not really a Wall fan so I haven't followed the stories religiously but I just saw you as being part of a select group of people all doing the same things, hanging out in the same places, drinking too much, sleeping around, putting two fingers up at everything, all being really, you know . . . *clever clever*.'

He winced at her words and then smiled encouragingly. 'But what about now?' he urged. 'Now you've got to know me a bit. Has your opinion of me changed at all?'

Betty looked at him again and felt a small surge of annoyance. He had moved beyond using her for therapy and was now using her for ego-maintenance. He didn't really want to know what she thought, not really. He just wanted reassurance that he was fabulous. She sighed and said, 'You know, when I see you with your kids I think you're nothing like the guy in the papers. I saw you once, across the courtyard, just after you moved back in, and you were holding Astrid in your arms, comforting her, and that was the very first time I really thought anything about you at all, to be honest. And I thought, oh look, he's a human being . . .'

His eyes widened and he nodded encouragingly.

'But then, I see you like this,' she said, 'you know, necking champagne, making it all about you. And, I don't know, it's like going back to the beginning again.'

His eyes narrowed and he looked at her questioningly. 'What do you mean?' he said in a slightly injured tone of voice.

She paused while she tried to find a tactful way to express herself and then she looked at Dom, at his soulful puppy-dog eyes full of hurt and hope, and then she thought of the blurred photos of the girl giving him fellatio in a toilet cubicle and she thought, he is just a child, I shall spare him. So she shook her head and smiled and said, 'Oh, nothing. Nothing. Just, you know, I suppose seeing you here, a bit the worse for wear, it fits with the media image. But really, I think, yes, you're a good guy.'

His face flooded with relief and he took her hand and squeezed it and said, 'Thank you, Betty, thank you. That means a lot to me because, you know, you're such a great girl, such a cool girl, and I really, really value your opinion.' He smiled at her cheesily and looked like he was about to say something else, but instead he picked up his champagne glass, drained it, picked up the bottle to top them both up again, stared at it with surprise and disappointment when it yielded nothing more than one small drop and then called over a waiter.

'Another one of these, please,' he slurred.

'No problem, Dom,' said the waiter.

'Actually,' Betty interrupted, 'you know, I really need to get back now. I've got to be up really early . . .'

'Yeah, yeah.' Dom pulled himself straight and ran his hands down his face. 'Of course. You're going to take care of my babies and so I will obviously not even attempt to persuade you to stay for another one. Even though I'd really like to.' He turned back to the waiter and said, 'Jack Daniel's, please, a big one.'

'Sure, Dom.' The waiter smiled and took away the champagne bucket and their empty glasses.

'I'll see you out,' Dom said, getting to his feet.

'No need.'

He considered this for a second and then he suddenly looked tired and wan, and as if simply getting up from the sofa would be a severe physical effort, and he said, 'Are you sure?'

Betty nodded. 'It's fine.'

'You'll be all right getting yourself home?'

'I think I can probably manage the walk home,' she smiled. 'How about you? Will you be all right getting back?'

He smiled. 'Yeah. I'll probably kip down here.'

'What, here?' She pointed at the sofa.

'No. Upstairs. There's rooms.'

'Oh. I see. But your house is so close.'

'Look at the state of me, Betty,' he said, his hand against his chest. 'There's paps out there. I don't wanna give them the *wasted Dom Jones* photo. And besides, they'll give me breakfast here. Bacon and all.' He smiled weakly and looked like he might be about to fall asleep.

A man with a huge head of unruly curls that sat atop

the body of a child approached Dom then and said, 'All right, mate?'

Dom said, 'Yeah, man, I'm great. Long time no see.'

And the man with the mop top said, 'Saw you last week, mate.'

Dom said, 'Yeah, yeah, course you did. I'm all over the place, mate. All over the place. Park yourself. Take a seat. I'm just saying goodbye to the nanny.'

The mop top man looked up at Betty and squinted at her through his curls. 'The nanny?' he repeated as though there was something inherently sexual about the concept of a person paid to look after children. 'Hello, nanny.'

'Hi.' Betty considered introducing herself by her given name, but decided she couldn't be bothered. 'And bye. I'll see you soon, Dom,' she said.

He stood and hugged her around her neck, and he smelled of sour wine, departure lounges and too much time in the same clothes.

'Next time,' he whispered boozily into her ear, 'we'll do it properly. Yeah? Next time I'll plan it, take you somewhere nice. Yeah?' As he said this she felt his hand snake from her hip to her buttocks, and give them a gentle squeeze.

She nodded, with confusion. He was drunk and had no idea what he was talking about, but it did sound to her that he was suggesting a date. She moved his hand from her buttocks and pulled herself away from his over-firm grasp, then smiled tightly. 'Night-night, Dom. Take care.' She turned to the mop top and said, 'Look after him, will you?'

Mop top simply smiled blankly and somewhat lasciviously.

Betty turned and left, moving slowly this time, her arms swinging by her sides, her eyes making contact, drinking it all in: 1 a.m. at the Groucho, the whole place imbued with a communal lack of focus, of hazy memories and forgotten conversations.

She left calmly and happily, the nanny, sober and wide awake. She would go to bed and sleep for five hours and then she would wake up tomorrow in her own bed remembering every last detail. But she would not, she was sure, have even the first idea what to make of any of it.

40

1920

As the companion of Godfrey Pickle, Arlette finally shed the last few layers of her former self and embraced the world in which she'd unwittingly found herself. It was as though she'd been reborn that first night in Godfrey's arms, or more, as if she'd been born for the first time, as if previously she had been nothing more than a wooden doll, waiting for the magician's gift of life. Now when she walked into a club, she would carry herself like an Egyptian goddess, tall and regal, although she was neither. She plundered the rails at work, no longer looking for an outfit that would mark her out as an upstanding and stylish citizen, but rather one that would elicit overblown compliments from her friends in the club, costumes instead of clothes. She formed herself an image, distinctive and her own.

Lilian called it 'The Arlette Look', and attempted to emulate it, but it never looked quite the same on her rounder, fuller frame, with her pale colouring and babyish face.

'I look like a child who's plundered the dressing-up box,' she sighed dramatically, ripping an ornate headdress from the top of her head and flouncing backwards into Arlette's settee.

'Oh, darling girl,' said Minu, 'you *are* a child who has plundered the dressing-up box. And you should be *glad* about that.'

'Well, I'm not,' she replied sulkily. 'I shall be nineteen years old next week. And I'm more or less running my mother's home single-handedly. I feel like I'm at *least* thirty, yet every time I look in the mirror, a child looks back at me. It's all very tedious . . .'

'I can absolutely promise you, one day you will dream about that child in the mirror and wish for her back.'

Lilian glared at Minu, looking as if she were about to say something, but she failed to find the words and fell back again into the settee.

'Did you see,' said Minu, 'in the *Illustrated London News* last night, another mention for Arlette in Badger's column?'

'No!' said Lilian. 'I did not. Did you keep a copy?'

Arlette passed her the paper from her dressing table and Lilian read it out loud, her voice tinged with pride and awe.

'And I arrive shortly after midnight at the Cygnet; my companion for the night, the Duchess, has mysteriously disappeared, leaving me high, dry and not a little damp after a sudden downpour on the northern stretches of Piccadilly. And so I attach myself, leech-like, to the side of the exquisite Lady

Cleopatra, resplendent and somewhat tickly in an ostrich-feather crown. Lady Cleopatra tells me that her beau, the equally exquisite ebony-skinned brass-blower who I shall call, simply, the Man from the Pitons, is not joining her tonight, for he is playing his clarinet in Brighton, and who can blame the girl for not wanting to join him on the windy south coast when she could be snug and cosy sitting with the Badger in sparkling W1?'

'Was he awfully smelly?' said Lilian, lifting her eyes from the paper.

'He smells like an old horse in high summer,' Arlette replied, and all three of them burst into laughter. 'And he was so drunk,' she continued, 'that I am surprised he remembers a thing about it.'

'Why does he call you Lady Cleopatra?' asked Lilian.

'I have no idea,' replied Arlette.

'It's the eyes,' said Minu. 'You have Egyptian eyes.'

'I absolutely do not have Egyptian eyes,' Arlette retorted. 'I have Guernsey eyes.'

'Whatever they may be,' Minu rolled her eyes.

'Guernsey eyes are the eyes of my mother and my grandmother. Neither of whom has ever been to Egypt.'

'Well, either way, Lady Cleopatra is a fine pseudonym,' said Minu. 'I should be more than happy with it.'

Lilian lay fully stretched out along the settee, rubbing her stomach in circular movements. 'You know,' she said,

'I may have to go home and take to my bed. I'm having an awful time with my monthly visitor.'

'I'll fill you a water bottle,' said Arlette. 'You can't possibly stay home tonight. It's Godfrey's last night at the Kingsway. The party will be absolutely the bee's knees.'

'I know,' Lilian grimaced. 'But I feel utterly awful. And look at my skin. I am literally covered in spots. I can't.'

'You can,' insisted Minu, 'and you will. This might be the last chance we get to see the orchestra in London. Put on some panstick.' She passed her a tube. 'And let your hair fall down. No one will notice.'

Arlette turned back to the mirror and finished off her make-up. She could barely believe that this was the last night of the London run. For ten weeks she had spent nearly all her free time with Godfrey. She would meet him most nights after his show and go for drinks and dancing, sometimes with his friends from the orchestra, sometimes just the two of them. Most nights, at around 1 a.m., they would go their separate ways, but on Fridays and Saturdays she would smuggle Godfrey up the stairs of her Bloomsbury lodgings, past her landlady's rooms, and Minu would stay out late, and they would spend the night making love and talking. The only night she didn't see Godfrey was on Sundays, when he and the orchestra would fill the gap in their schedules with extra shows in Brighton and Eastbourne. They had made themselves a routine and now that routine was coming to an end. The orchestra had a string of shows booked in Manchester and would not be back in London until 14 October. She would not see him for a month. He would miss her birthday. It was too painful to contemplate.

In some ways it would be a relief. She was growing tired of the late nights and the early starts. To go to her bed at a reasonable hour would be something of a treat. To find the time to sit and write to her mother would be wonderful. She had not written her mother more than a few lines since early July. To mend some clothes and write in her diary, to pull herself out of the whirl, just for a few weeks. But she would miss her Godfrey more than she could say.

The show was spectacular. In spite of two shows a day and regular trips to the coast, in spite of a schedule that had taken these musicians around the four corners of Great Britain not once but twice in the space of only a year, in spite of the late night parties and the sleepless nights in crowded lodging rooms in noisy corners of south London, and in spite of coming here fresh from the tribulations of a terrible world war, still the men sparkled and glowed on stage, still their music made it impossible not to move in rhythm and smile from start to finish.

Arlette swallowed away a lump in the back of her throat as the show came to an end and the audience got to its feet, and cheered and hollered and stamped and clapped.

'Darling,' she said, throwing herself into Godfrey's embrace as he walked towards her after the show, 'you were absolutely wonderful. Really, the best show yet.'

He held her close to his body and rested his face against her hair. He held her closer and tighter than he usually would, because he too knew that this time tomorrow he would be settling into a damp room in a small house under a railway bridge in the outskirts of Manchester, that this time tomorrow there would be no glitzy, gilded club waiting to welcome him into its womb-like interior, no beautiful, fine-boned woman sitting by his side, no smiles from strangers and fawning attention from puffed-up journalists and double-barrelled socialites. Tomorrow he would be a jobbing musician again, a mere brass-blower, and all of this would feel like a dream.

'Come on, my sweet Arlette,' he whispered into her ear, 'let's join the party later. First I want to walk for a while, through the city, just you and I.'

Arlette looked up at him and nodded. 'That would be wonderful,' she said.

They made their excuses and then headed out into the mild dark night. Summer still clung to the edges of the air, and Arlette tucked her arm through the crook of Godfrey's.

'To the river?' he suggested.

'Yes,' she said, 'why not?'

They headed in a straight line south, down towards the Aldwych. Arlette's feathered headdress shivered in the mild breeze and the heels of her shoes clipped the pavement like tiny hoofs. At the river they sat together on a stone bench. Godfrey brought an arm around Arlette's shoulders, ignoring the curious gaze of a passing couple.

'This has been the most remarkable ten weeks of my life, Arlette,' he said.

She looked up at him and smiled. 'I would have to echo that sentiment, Godfrey.'

'I would never have thought it possible that I could have been taken so deeply into the heart of a foreign city, that I would fall in love with a beautiful English girl, that I would have seen the things and been to the places and felt the things that I have felt. Whatever happens in my life, this will always be for me the best of all possible worlds.' He smiled and kissed her on the lips.

'And I too,' she concurred. 'I never thought that I could live a life like this, to be accepted and loved, to be at the very heart of things, to be with a man like you, a musical genius, a man with such a soul.'

Then she smiled too and kissed him on the lips.

'You know,' he said, after a moment, 'I would like to settle here.'

She looked at him with surprise. Godfrey had never before spoken about the future, only ever about the next show, the next city.

'I would,' he continued. 'I always knew I would not go home, but I never knew where I might be instead of home. And now I think I know. Here. London.' He opened his arms out towards the river, to the belching chimneys and the muted gaslight on the opposite side of the river, and then behind him to the sweeping stucco curve of Aldwych, the theatres and the hotels and the fine ladies passing by in horse-drawn carriages. 'Such a vibrant place. So accepting and open. And, of course, it is the place where you are, Arlette.'

'So, when . . .' she paused, not wanting to push too hard on the subject of future plans, but needing something to hold on to, however small '. . . when do you think you might stop touring? When do you think you might settle?'

Godfrey laughed. 'That is the greatest mystery of all, my sweetheart. As long as we are in demand then we will keep on. There is too much money being made. When the people stop coming to see us then we will all have to choose new paths.'

'But, Godfrey, you are such a fine musician, possibly the greatest clarinettist in the world. Do you need to keep travelling with the orchestra? Could you not, possibly, give them your notice, take a position at the clubs in London, maybe with the Love Brothers?'

Godfrey smiled wryly and brought Arlette closer to him. 'After Manchester,' he said, 'we will be back in London, possibly for a long time. Certainly for some weeks. I have promised Mr Cook another year. After that, well, yes, a London spot with the Love Brothers, a little house . . .'

Arlette's heart jumped.

'A little wife . . .'

Arlette turned then and stared at him sternly, for this was no matter for humour.

'A little family. A little dog.'

'*Godfrey!*' she chided. 'That is not remotely funny.'

'And neither was it intended to be, Arlette.'

She paused and stared first at him, then out towards the river and then again back at him. 'Mr Pickle,' she said, 'what on earth . . .?'

'Miss De La Mare,' he smiled affectionately, 'I am not in a position to make you a formal proposal of marriage, but you are the only woman I have ever met who I would want to be in a little house with, do you see? Other women make me want to get on boats and run away. You, you make me want to stay somewhere, so that I can see your face every day. So that I can hold you every day and watch you grow and change and get older. You make me want to be an adult man. You make me want to settle down.'

Arlette wrinkled her nose and said, 'Oh, my beautiful Godfrey. How simply frightful.'

He glanced at her with surprise.

'A girl like me does not want to make a man think about small houses and settling down. I want to make a man think about big houses. And big adventures. All the things we can do together.'

He widened his eyes and then he laughed. 'Oh, yes,' he agreed with a smile. 'A big house. Of course. And a big dog. And a big family. Can you imagine our babies, Arlette De La Mare? Can you see them?'

She smiled and nodded, for she had already passed many a quiet moment imagining the children that she and Godfrey could make together.

'I suppose what I am trying, very badly, to say is that I want you, Arlette. I want you for a long time. I want you to be mine and for me to be yours. In a little house. In a big house. On a ship running away together. Whatever it may be. Can you see that, Arlette? Can you feel it?'

Arlette closed her eyes, let the warm September breeze pass over her and through her, let the moment open up and swallow her, and she did feel it. She felt it in every nerve, every bone in her body.

'I am yours, Godfrey,' she said. 'For ever.'

He brought her close to his body and held her there. 'Good,' he said. 'Then let for ever begin tonight.'

41

1995

John Brightly had already packed away his stall and left by the time Betty got home from work the next day. She felt curiously deflated, having assumed that he would still be there, wanting to share her first day with someone. With anyone. She thought about calling Bella, or her mum, or even Joe Joe, although history had taught her that she could only understand about thirty per cent of what he said when they spoke on the phone. Then she checked her purse for twenty-pence pieces and sighed when she realised she didn't have enough to make a phone call.

But she needed desperately to talk to someone.

So many remarkable things had happened today.

Isabel O'Dell had popped over to pick up a serving dish!

She'd had tea with Ed and Sam Todd's nanny and their two horribly behaved children!

She'd seen a plaster cast of Amy Metz's vagina in the bathroom!

She'd played football in the park with Donny and his little friend Jackson, who just happened to be the son of the world-famous film star Jonny Clyde!

Then she remembered something. Her new phone. In her handbag. Amy had given it to her today, told her she could make private calls on it 'within reason'. She took the steps to her flat two at a time, made herself a roll-up and a cup of tea and went onto the fire escape.

There she stared for a moment at the device in her hand. Amy had given her a crash course in its use but she still struggled to remember where the on switch was. She finally figured it out, and typed in Bella's number.

'Guess where I'm calling you from?' she began.

'The Presidential Suite at the Ritz?'

'No.'

'Neptune?'

'No.'

'The bowels of the earth?'

'No. I'm calling you from *outside*.'

'What?'

'Yes, I am outdoors and calling you from my new mobile phone.'

'Cool! And how, pray, can you afford a mobile phone on Wendy's wages?'

'Oh, Bella, I have got *so much* to tell you. It is unbelievable!'

By the time Betty had finished telling Bella all her news, starting with, 'Well, first of all I was having a coffee in this greasy spoon, and me and Dom Jones got talking . . .' and ending on a final, triumphant '. . . and tomorrow I'm taking them all to play at Daisy Snow's house!' she had racked up almost thirty minutes of phone time to be paid for by Amy Metz.

'Shit,' she said, 'Bella, I'm going to have to go. This call's probably cost about a hundred pounds.' As she said these words she heard a loud cough from across the yard and jumped when she saw Dom sitting on his window ledge, watching her with a smile on his face.

'Keep talking!' he hollered through cupped hands. 'I'll pay for it!'

'Christ!' she shouted back. 'How long have you been sitting there?'

'Long enough.'

'I haven't said anything that breaks the terms of my contract,' she called.

'I believe you,' he teased, tucking his hands into the pockets of his jeans.

'Who are you talking to?' asked Bella.

'Him,' she hissed. 'Jones.'

'You're talking to Dom Jones? While you're on the phone to me?'

'Yes.'

'God. And I'm sitting here with goose shit under my fingernails wondering if the five-day-old shepherd's pie in the fridge is still OK to eat. You win.'

'It's not as glamorous as it sounds,' Betty replied unconvincingly.

'That's utter shit and you know it, Betty Dean.'

'Well, yeah, maybe a bit.' She glanced across again at Dom and saw him looking at her expectantly. 'Look,' she said to Bella, 'I really do need to go now.'

'Of course, of course,' said Bella. 'Do not let me keep you from Dom Jones.'

'Love you.'

'Love you, too.'

She turned off the phone and turned back to Dom. 'How are you?' she shouted across.

'Tired,' he said. 'Went on a bit late last night.'

'I thought it might,' she said.

'Was I being a wanker?'

She shrugged and smiled. 'Nah,' she said. 'Not really.'

'Listen,' he said. 'I've got a chicken in the oven. Wanna come over? I'm sober.' He smiled uncertainly and Betty felt her heart melt at the sight of him. He was a different person entirely from the idiot at the Groucho the night before. He was lonely and she was lonely, and not only that but she was absolutely starving and had not had anything as homely and nutritious as roast chicken for nearly three months.

'All right,' she said. 'When do you want me?'

'Now,' he said, 'come over now.'

Dom's house smelled good. Dom also smelled good when he leaned down to kiss her on the cheek. His hair was slightly damp at the ends, suggesting a recent shower. The TV was on, showing an old episode of *Prime Suspect*. Although it was high summer and still bright outside, it felt dark and autumnal in here, with curtains drawn and windows masked with milky film. For a moment it felt almost as if Betty could be anywhere, anywhere at all. It was impossible to believe that beyond the drawn curtains was the mayhem and hedonism of a summer's night in Soho.

'Wine? Beer? Elderflower cordial?'

'What are you having?'

'I was going to stick to the cordial tonight. After last night. But don't let that stop you.'

'Fine,' she said, 'I'll have a cordial.'

'Sure?'

She nodded. Her heart wanted a drink, her head told her that when her alarm went off at six o'clock tomorrow morning she'd be glad that she hadn't listened to her heart.

'Listen,' Dom began. 'I wanted to say sorry.'

'What for?'

'For being such a dick last night.'

'Honestly,' she said. 'You weren't. You were fine.'

'I wasn't. I'm just . . .' He paused and twisted the top off a bottle of cordial. 'When I drink it's like I revert to being a brainless teenage boy. And honestly, truly,' he put his hand to his heart, 'that's not what I am.'

'It's fine,' Betty said. 'We're all a bit different when we've had a drink.'

He shook his head. 'No,' he said. 'We're not. Some people become better versions of themselves when they drink. You know, funnier, happier, more affectionate, more honest. And then some people, like me, become lesser versions of themselves. Mawkish, immature and narcissistic, in my case.'

'Don't forget "lecherous",' she added.

'Oh, fuck, was I?'

'There was a buttock squeeze towards the end.'

His face crumpled. 'Oh God, Christ, how disgusting. I'm so sorry. I'm a dick. Really. Of the absolutely highest order.' He sighed and stared sadly at the floor for a moment. 'My apologies. So, anyway. Welcome back to me, the booze-free version. And tell me you like sweet potato, please!' He wrung his hands together and looked at her hopefully.

'Love sweet potato,' she said.

'Good girl,' he said. 'One good thing that I picked up from my years living with a crazy vegetarian Californian. The joy of the sweet potato. Fucking *love* them.'

He laid the table as they chatted and Betty sat in the armchair, sipped her cordial and ate the Kettle Chips he'd put in a bowl for her. She watched him pull a hefty candle down from a shelf, place it in the centre of the table and light it.

'What do you want to listen to?' he asked, flicking through a rack of CDs. 'And, yes, you don't need to tell me: not Wall. I may not remember squeezing your arse, but I do remember you telling me you weren't a fan.'

Betty laughed. 'Yes, sorry about that, but you were so gasping for compliments . . .'

'I don't blame you, honestly. I spend my whole life picking people out of my arse, it's good for me to get some honest feedback. Reggae?' He pulled out a CD and waved it at her and she nodded. The music softened the atmosphere and Betty felt herself begin to relax.

'So,' Dom said. 'How was your first day at work?'

She laughed. 'Surely you already know the answer to that after earwigging my phone call out there.'

He laughed. 'I was just winding you up. I didn't hear a word you were saying. Honest.' He flicked on the gas beneath a pan of water and pulled a bag of green beans out of the fridge.

'It was good,' she said. 'Full on. But good.'

He smiled knowingly. 'I'll ask you again in a week. The longest we've managed to keep a nanny is four months.'

'Now he tells me!' she cried indignantly.

'Nothing to do with my perfect children, I hasten to add.'

'Amy, you mean?'

'Bless her little heart,' he said, half under his breath.

'She was fine.'

'Give her a chance,' he muttered, trimming the tops off the beans.

Betty laughed. 'She was *fine*!' she reiterated. 'Perfectly nice.'

'I think it helps that you're not a real nanny.'

'What do you mean?'

'Well, you've got nothing to compare her to, no other children to compare ours with. You're a clean slate.' He looked at her and smiled. 'She'll be on strictly best behaviour for you.'

Betty shrugged. 'Well, it's only been one day. I'm going

to take it a day at a time. I didn't really come to London to be a nanny.'

Dom glanced at her again. 'What did you come to London for?'

'To see the Queen.'

He laughed. 'No. Really. I mean I know you had the big Soho dream and all that, but what did you want to do when you got here?'

Betty stared down into her cordial and shrugged. 'No idea, really,' she said. 'I was on a kind of mission. Trying to find someone.'

'Oh, yeah?' He looked at her with interest.

'Long story,' she said. 'But I think, really, I just thought I'd show up and everyone would be tripping over themselves to fit me into their lives. I thought I was just the right girl for everything, you know. The perfect fit. I even went into the Groucho, just after I arrived, looking for a job.'

'Oh, yeah?' he smiled. 'And what did they say?'

'They very charmingly told me to fuck off.'

He laughed. 'I could get you a job there, you know. Tomorrow, if that's what you wanted?'

'I don't think it is any more. All the jobs I went for I was convinced that this was it. This was my destiny. This was where I belonged. But now, I think I've realised that my destiny is still just a dot on the horizon. I'm nowhere near it yet. I studied art.' She shrugged. 'That could still lead somewhere. This nanny thing might turn into a career. Anything could happen. I'm so young . . .'

'That you are, Betty. That you are.'

'And you know, my grandmother . . .' She paused, as the thought had only just occurred to her and she hadn't worked out what it meant yet. 'Well, I thought she'd spent her life on Guernsey. I thought that had been her entire existence. Her husband. Her house. Her son. The Yacht Club. But now it turns out that she was here, too. That she came to London when she was my age. That she hung around with jazz musicians. And artists. You know, there's an actual portrait of her in the National Portrait Gallery.'

'What! Seriously? Your grandmother?'

'Yeah. My grandmother. And I just think, well, if she could have started her adult life like that, all those dreams and plans, all those ideas she must have had about how everything was going to turn out, yet she ended up back in her childhood home having a son she detested, then really, you've just got to go with the flow, haven't you? Because, really,' she shrugged again, 'anything can happen. Can't it?'

Dom nodded and smiled. 'Yeah,' he said, 'I guess so. Although, in my case, I've been pretty much on a one-track journey since I was a kid.'

'Well, yes, and you're still young . . .'

'Relatively.'

'Yes. Relatively. So this might not be your destiny. I mean, you might end up – I don't know – being a pig farmer or something. You might look back on all this and think: what the hell was all that pop-star stuff about? This is where I was always meant to be.'

Dom looked at her thoughtfully. 'Hmm,' he said, touching his chin, 'a pig farmer. I can see that. I can. And you could be the pig farmer's wife.' He laughed, lightly, leaching any awkwardness from his comment. 'Imagine that,' he said quietly. 'Imagine that.'

As he said it, Betty had a terrible overwhelming jolt of longing. Almost premonitory. She saw herself sitting at a long wooden table with Dom and his children, pouring milk into beakers. Beyond the windows she saw acres of rolling meadows and fields of fat, pink pigs. She smelled something wholesome roasting in the oven. Her. The farmer's wife. The ex-pop star's wife. The reformed hedonist's wife. She could see it and smell it. Then she shook it, quite violently, from her head.

She was doing it again. Seeing her destiny carved into every fleeting comment, every half-formed moment. Her destiny did not lie in Dom Jones's retirement plans; it lay here, in this very moment, drinking cordial, about to eat chicken and sweet potatoes. Because for all she knew, she too could end up back in Guernsey, seeing out her years alone in a big cold house on a cliff.

'Breast or leg?' asked Dom, carving knife poised above the golden chicken.

'Both,' said Betty, reeling herself back into the present. 'Thank you.'

The food was delicious. Betty ate as if she hadn't eaten for a month. They talked easily over the meal, about Arlette and her missing beneficiary, about Gideon Worsley and the Southern Syncopated Orchestra, about

Alexandra and her room of old clothes, about a woman called Clara Pickle.

Dom was dumbstruck.

'Amazing,' he said. 'Really amazing. You could write a book about it.'

'Well,' she said. 'Yeah. Maybe. But first of all I need to find out what the ending is going to be.'

'That's true,' agreed Dom. 'And how are you going to do that?'

'Don't know. Alexandra's friend is seeing what he can uncover. John from outside my house said he'd do some research for me, too.'

'That's the record, guy, yeah?'

'Yes.'

'Good bloke.'

'Yes. He is.'

'I reckon he's got the hots for you.'

'What!'

'Yeah.' Dom smiled mischievously. 'Whenever I go and ask after you, he kind of bristles a bit. You know.'

'Oh, I'm sure he doesn't. We're just friends.'

Dom raised an eyebrow at her. 'You never seen *When Harry Met Sally*?'

'Of course I have.'

'Well, then, there you go. No such thing as "just friends". Particularly not when the female friend looks like you.' He skewered her, then, with a long and deep-rooted look across the table.

Betty flushed and stared into her lap. 'No,' she said, 'he

definitely doesn't have the hots for me. I know he doesn't.'

Dom raised his eyebrow higher. 'Hmm,' he said.

'Really!'

'Maybe he just really *really* likes you then,' he said facetiously.

'Actually,' she said, 'he does.'

Dom leaned back into his chair, folded his arms across his chest and smiled. 'And reading between the lines I would suggest that it might be mutual.'

Betty laughed. 'Of course it is!' she said. 'I really like him. He's a really nice guy.'

Dom just stared at her with a smug smile on his face.

'What!'

'Oh, nothing,' he said, pulling himself straight and unfolding his arms. 'Just trying to work out if I've got competition.'

'Oh my God!' said Betty. 'What are you talking about!'

'Oh, nothing,' he said, 'nothing.'

She narrowed her eyes at him and he laughed.

'Nothing!' he said again. 'I just, well, God, you must know, Betty?'

'What!'

'You must know that I've got a massive crush on you?' He blinked, just once.

Betty blinked back.

'The first time I saw you I thought, you know: cute blond. But then that morning in the café. You looked like shit. That gross hat. Your make-up everywhere. You had a hole in your dress. And green hair. And I just thought:

that is the best-looking girl I have ever seen in my life. Seriously.'

'Oh,' she said.

'Yeah,' he said. 'Oh.'

Betty had no idea if she was supposed to respond to this declaration. The silence that had fallen since he'd made it felt strangely comforting, as though it was protecting her from something. She smiled nervously, and then, like the onset of an uncontrollable sneeze, she felt a wave of laughter building up inside her. She held it down for as long as she could, until it physically started to hurt, and then she let it rush to the surface and explode across the table.

Dom looked at her, half injured, half amused. He looked as though he was about to question her laughter, but then he too caught the joke and started to laugh.

Betty put her hands up to her face and made a show of trying to control her laughter, but still it rolled out of her, unstoppable, like the ocean. She brought her head down onto the tabletop, then up again to look at Dom and then they both started up again.

The laughter peeled on for the next five minutes and by the time it finally came to a still, gentle close her head was spinning and it was as if they'd been drinking, as if they were a bit tipsy, a touch stoned.

'Not sure where the fuck we go from there,' giggled Dom, drawing his hands down his face and sighing.

Betty smiled. 'Pretend it never happened?'

He glanced at her. 'Really?'

'Well, isn't that what you'd like to do?'

He stared at her for a moment, as if he were trying to work out a really complicated puzzle. 'No,' he said, his voice serious again. 'No. Not at all.'

Betty held his gaze and stopped breathing. 'Then . . .?'

'Well, then . . .' He looked for a moment as if he were about to kiss her, but at the last second his demeanour changed and he said, 'Fancy a spliff?'

She looked at the oversized clock on the kitchen wall. It was nearly eleven o'clock. She should head back, head for bed, get the early night she'd failed to get the night before. But she knew she wouldn't be able to sleep now, not with a stomach full of roast chicken and a head full of Dom saying he had a crush on her, and a drag or two on a spliff would definitely help her to sleep.

'Yes,' she said, 'why not?'

He brought a little box through to the kitchen and made one quickly and deftly, and then she followed him up the stairs to the window on the landing and she tried not to muse too much on the fact that his bedroom was just there, the door ajar, his bedding visible from where they sat. She tried not to think too much about the fact that they were sitting, knee to knee, facing each other at a negligible distance, their fingers brushing as they passed the spliff back and forth, the warm summer air vibrant against their skin, their lips taking it in turns to touch the same damp spot on the end of the spliff. She tried just to concentrate on the precise wording of her imminent announcement of her intention to leave, to go home, to her bed. She thought about Amy's words, she thought about John's warnings, she reminded herself that she had never looked at a picture of Dom Jones in a newspaper and thought that she might want to sleep with him. She thought about anything and everything apart from the sense of overwhelming desire building within her, the sense that the air between them was being sucked away in rhythm with the spliff, that every time their fingers touched it was bringing her closer and closer to some kind of ludicrous inevitability.

'I wish I'd met you first,' said Dom, staring at her thoughtfully.

'What do you mean?' She passed him back the last nub of spliff.

'I mean, before Cheryl. Before Amy. I wish I was sitting here with you ten years ago, a clean slate. I wish . . .' He turned and stared through the window, drew the last inhalation from the spliff, then hurled it, thoughtlessly, into the spiralling darkness below. And then, suddenly, almost stealthily, he was on his feet and tipping Betty's head upwards towards his, and then he was kissing her, as though she were overripe fruit and he was hungry.

Betty stopped thinking entirely.

John Brightly stared at Betty curiously as she dashed past his stall and towards her front door at seven o'clock the following morning.

'Morning,' she trilled, feeling his gaze taking in every tiny detail of her appearance: the faded make-up, bed-hair, possibly even the bulge of her balled up knickers in her shoulder bag.

He nodded but didn't reply, just carried on staring at her inscrutably.

'Just . . .' She stood before him, waiting nonsensically for a miraculous rush of words to pour from her mouth that might offer a more savoury explanation for her appearance and her demeanour. But of course none came, so she pulled her keys from her handbag, smiled awkwardly and a touch psychotically at him and disappeared inside her flat, slamming the door hard behind her in her wake.

And then, her back pressed up against the door, she took a moment just to breathe, to contemplate the implications of what had just happened.

She stood like that for thirty seconds, let the embarrassment wash through her like a foul-tasting tonic, and then quickly and mindlessly, she got ready for work.

42

1920

Like the other half of a Swiss weather clock couple, as Godfrey mounted a train headed for Manchester on a misty September morning and disappeared from Arlette's life, so Gideon reappeared, new and shiny, full of charm and romantic intentions.

He was on the pavement, outside Liberty's staff entrance on Tuesday evening, holding a bunch of roses the colour of flushed skin.

He removed his hat with his free hand when he saw her emerge, and smiled shyly.

'Good afternoon, Arlette,' he said, holding her hand in his and kissing the back of it with dry lips. 'I feel I have barely seen you. You look utterly radiant.'

Arlette looked at him quizzically, because she knew that she looked anything but. 'I have not slept in three nights, so doubt it very much. But thank you, anyhow. All compliments are welcome.'

He stared at her dreamily for a moment before gathering his senses and saying, 'Oh, yes, flowers. For you.'

He handed them to her with a flourish and she smiled and said, 'Thank you.' She did not want to ask what the flowers were intended to suggest, because she did not wish to know the answer.

There was a moment of awkwardness then. It was incumbent upon Gideon, Arlette felt, to make his intentions clear, but he seemed reluctant to do so.

'So,' he said, eventually, 'where are you headed to now?'

'I'm going home, Gideon,' she replied patiently.

'Yes,' he said, 'yes. Of course you are. Maybe I could walk you home?'

She smiled. 'That would be very nice. Thank you.'

He looked at her then with a mixture of awe and joy. 'Wonderful!' he said. 'Super.'

It was obvious to anyone with half a brain that Gideon was in love with Arlette. And Arlette had substantially more than half a brain. She had kept him at arm's length these past few weeks, ever since the night at the Cygnet when she had first taken Godfrey back to her lodgings and into her bed. Thereafter she had no longer automatically taken the seat next to him in clubs and bars and had taken instead to waving at him politely across rooms.

'Poor Gideon,' Godfrey would say, with feeling, 'I have never before seen a man look so lost. His heart has been pulverised.'

To avoid any further pulverisation of his vital organs, Arlette had severed all but the most basic ties with him, yet now she was allowing him to walk her home and accepting his gift of flowers. In answer to the unasked question 'Why?', she would have to reply that she had not a single clue. It was possible that she was lonely. It was also possible that she had missed him. After all, their friendship had been a close and intimate one, forged over hours spent in his studio alone together, his eyes engaged with every detail of her.

As they strode through the darkening streets of London that evening, the pavements glowing gold beneath their feet, funnels of crisp russet leaves twirling and dancing in their wake, she started remembering the way it had felt to have Gideon at her side, his height and his humour, his air of always being on the verge of doing something peculiar and wonderful. She remembered the first time she'd seen him, singing carols on Regent Street last Christmas, the wild look in his eye. He'd later told her it was absinthe. His one and only meeting with the green fairy. He'd been violently sick the next day and never touched the stuff again. But seeing him like that the first time had left him forever in Arlette's imagination as someone flighty and strange, someone almost magical.

'It has been a long time, hasn't it?' she said.

'I wanted to see you before,' he said. 'But I didn't like to *intrude*. You've seemed very much involved these past few weeks.'

'Yes,' she agreed. 'I feel I have been on a different planet. A completely different world.'

He looked at her curiously. 'Has it been a nice world?' he enquired.

She looked at him then with shining eyes. 'Oh, Gideon, it really has been the most unexpected and beautiful world. I . . .' She tried to say more but her words got caught up with her tears.

Gideon stopped and stood before her. They were outside the London Palladium on Argyll Street where a small queue was forming for a variety show. Arlette allowed Gideon to draw her head into his shoulder, not wanting strangers to witness her tears.

'Oh, sweet Arlette,' he soothed. 'He has your heart. Doesn't he?'

She nodded into the rough fabric of his overcoat.

He turned himself back towards the direction of their journey and kept her held close to him as he steered them east, towards Bloomsbury.

'When does he return?' he asked.

'Four weeks.'

'Oh, four weeks. That will speed by in a blur, my dear.'

She sniffed and shook her head. 'No,' she said. 'It absolutely won't. I can assure you of that.'

'Listen to me,' he said, mock-sternly. 'I am your friend and I will make *sure* that the next four weeks pass by in a blur. If you'll allow me, Miss De La Mare, I will keep your mind occupied and your heart warm. If you'll allow me I will do everything I possibly can to make sure there are no more tears.'

She smiled at him. 'And how do you propose to do that, Gideon?'

'Just say you'll allow me.' He squeezed her tight against him.

She considered the offer. She had intended to spend the

next four weeks sobbing and fretting and becoming worryingly thin. She had intended to spend it sitting by the front door waiting for the postman to come. But now she had been offered an alternative, and she had to say she found it rather appealing.

'Yes,' she said. 'I will allow you to *attempt* to distract me. But I reserve the right to be utterly miserable if I so desire.'

'But of course,' he smiled. 'That is your prerogative.'

'Good,' she said.

'Good,' he said. 'So, shall we begin?'

'Now?'

'Yes, why not?'

'Well, I had intended to write some letters tonight.'

'Letters to whom?' he demanded, aghast.

'My mother.'

He considered this for a moment with one fingertip against his bearded chin. 'Fine,' he said. 'Well, it is for you to decide, but I intend to head from here to a poetry salon in Russell Square where they have promised home-made ginger snaps and fine sherry. And possibly an appearance from Mr Siegfried Sassoon.'

Arlette raised her eyebrows and Gideon cleared his throat and continued, 'From there I am due to meet my eldest sister, Rebecca, for drinks at her apartment in Knightsbridge. She has just returned from a trip to *Hollywood*.' He paused and let his words sink in. 'Where she dined with *Lionel Barrymore*. Amongst others.'

Arlette's breath caught. She thought of her mother, alone in the big house on the cliff, waiting for a letter of a decent size. And then she thought of herself again, as a girl, staring out to sea, wondering what might become of her. She had arrived, somehow, dead centre of another social tornado. She could not turn her back on it.

'Fine,' she said, 'yes. I'll come with you. But I shall need to be home before midnight.'

Gideon beamed at her. 'Of course!' he said. 'Of course. I will guarantee it!'

'Well, then, we must hurry,' she said, taking his hand in hers, 'I must change into new clothes and do something with these flowers.'

Gideon smiled widely and mischievously at her, and together they ran, breathlessly and exuberantly, hand-in-hand, through the streets of London towards her Bloomsbury apartment.

Arlette's landlady popped her head out of her sitting room when she heard them thundering up the stairs together a few minutes later. Miss Chettling was a single woman of around fifty with a cloud of white curls and a twinkle in her eye. She loved having the two young women in her attic, always keen to talk to them about their lives and their adventures, always admiring their clothes, their hairstyles, borrowing the latest style magazines from them and sighing with delight when she handed them back. She was also mainly deaf, which was most beneficial in regard to spiriting boyfriends in and out of their rooms at ungodly hours.

She smiled at Gideon and said, 'Good evening, young man. Good evening, Miss De La Mare.'

'Good evening, Miss Chettling. May I introduce my friend, Mr Gideon Worsley.'

'A pleasure to make your acquaintance, Mr Horsley.'

Gideon tipped his hat and then removed it. 'Likewise, Miss Chettling.'

'I've heard you,' she hissed conspiratorially at him, still smiling brightly.

'I beg your pardon, Miss Chettling?' Gideon smiled down at her questioningly.

'Up and down the stairs. All times of the day and night. I hear you come and go. I know you think you're being very quiet, but you're not.' She let out a small peel of laughter then and covered her mouth with her fingertips, girlishly.

Gideon smiled at her uncertainly.

Arlette cleared her throat. 'Well,' she said, 'we'd better be on our way. We've got dozens of parties to go to and we mustn't be late.'

'No!' agreed Miss Chettling overbrightly. 'No, you must not be late. Off you go.' She patted Gideon's arm and, using the low conspiratorial voice again she said, 'I don't mind, you know. They're modern young women, you know. They pay their rent on time. I like my house to be busy.'

Gideon looked at her fondly and said, 'Yes, indeed. Indeed, indeed.' Arlette pulled him firmly by the arm, up towards her room. 'Must go. Lovely to meet you,' he called out to the landlady, before they both ran helter-skelter up the stairs, laughing so hard it hurt.

'She thinks I'm Godfrey,' Gideon said, once they were safely behind Arlette's door.

'It does appear that she does, yes.'

'So, clearly, she has not been introduced to Godfrey?'

Arlette smiled wryly. 'No, indeed not.'

'Hmm,' said Gideon, sinking into the settee.

Arlette looked at him crossly. 'And what is that supposed to mean?'

'What?'

'"Hmm"? What do you mean by "hmm"?'

'I mean nothing by "hmm" . . .' he countered.

'Well, I think you're lying. I think you do mean something by it.'

Gideon narrowed his eyes. 'I find it strange,' he started, carefully, 'that Godfrey has been visiting you in your rooms for ten weeks and not encountered your charming landlady, yet I have met her on my first visit.'

Arlette bridled gently. 'Well,' she said, 'it has always been at a much later hour. I have not wished to disturb her.'

He looked at her sceptically.

'Are you suggesting, Gideon, that I have not introduced my beau to my landlady because I am in some way *ashamed* of him?'

'Absolutely not.' He looked appalled at the suggestion. 'No. No, no, no. I just merely *wondered*, I suppose, how it has been taken beyond the narrow confines of our perfect little world. Your . . . *affiliation* with a gentleman of a different hue.'

Arlette drew her shoulders up and glared at him. 'What nonsense,' she cried. 'Godfrey is not a gentleman of a different hue! Godfrey is a world-famous musician, the best clarinettist of his generation. He is educated and well read, he is far far cleverer than me.'

Gideon put up a conciliatory hand and smiled patiently. 'Arlette,' he said, firmly but gently, 'you're not listening to me. I would not refute a word of what you have just said. I am as awed and impressed by Mr Pickle as you, my dear lady. He is clearly an impeccable gentleman and a man of great depth and talent. I merely wonder . . .' He paused, looking for words that would not enrage Arlette any further. 'Beyond this world,' he waved his arms around the room, 'beyond the liberal, colourful bubble in which we conduct our lives, how do you see a future with Godfrey? How would the rest of the world, the grey, the closed-minded, view your pairing? What, for example, would your mother think?'

Arlette felt a pain to her chest then, as though she had been slammed hard with the handle of a broom between her ribs. She put a hand to the spot and rubbed it absent-mindedly. 'My mother is neither grey nor closed-minded,' she murmured.

'No, of course not. Of course not. And it was discourteous of me to suggest that she was.'

Arlette sat then, next to Gideon, feeling the wind had been taken out of her entirely. Her mother was not grey or closed-minded. This was true. But then her mother had seen nothing of the world beyond the shores of her small island. What would she think of Godfrey? And what would she think of their babies? She thought of the dusky, lurking sailors in the backstreets of St Peter Port as foreign and other-worldly, as if they had come down from the moon. And as different from Godfrey as it was possible for two people to be. And then she thought of the whispers and the stares in the perfumery at Liberty, one of the few times she and Godfrey had walked together in daylight hours. She thought of the woman with her mouth knitted together with disapproval and her vow to shop at Lilley and Skinner.

'Gideon,' she said after a moment, 'I understand your concern. But love will be enough. Love will be enough.'

Gideon looked at her fondly, fraternally. 'Yes,' he said, squeezing her shoulder. 'Yes, I'm sure it will.'

43

1995

There was a note in the mail catcher on the back of Betty's door when she got home that night. It was in John's handwriting and for a split second Betty felt her heart race with anticipation. And then she remembered that last night she had had sex with Dom Jones and that this morning John Brightly had seen her coming home with her knickers in her handbag. She sighed and picked the note out.

'Betty,' it said, 'Alex wants you to call her. She's got news. J.'

She felt a curious wave of disappointment engulf her. Five days ago she and John had been bonding over pints in his scruffy members' club. Two days ago he had put his hand to her cheek and told her she was capable of anything. She'd been slowly pulling apart the bars he surrounded himself with and had been about to find a way in. But now he was pulling the bars closed again. Now he was leaving dry, impersonal notes in her mail catcher. And she had no one to blame but herself. She crunched the note into a ball and threw it angrily across the hallway.

On the fire escape she pressed in Alexandra's number

and listened to an answerphone message. She almost hung up, but then she heard Alexandra say, 'and if that's you, Betty, meet me Friday night at Jimmy's, Frith Street. I'll be there from eight. *So* much to tell you.'

Betty looked at the time on the display of her mobile phone. It was seven thirty. Then she looked across the courtyard towards the back of Dom's house. It lay in darkness. She sighed and brought her knees up to her chest. Dom had sent her a text message earlier. It had said: 'I'm off to a secret location with the band. Back on Friday. Take care. D x.'

She hadn't known quite how to take this. She was pleased, in a way, that he'd thought to let her in on his plans. But crushed that he hadn't alluded in any way to what had happened the previous night. But still, she thought, they both knew what had happened last night. What had happened last night had been good. But he was a rock star and she was his nanny, and really, whatever happened next was moot.

44

1920

'Arlette!' Leticia skipped across the drawing room, a tumbler clutched in her hand, and drew Arlette towards her in a quinine-scented embrace. 'Happy birthday, darling girl. And you must be Gideon.' She drew Gideon down from his lofty height to embrace him too. 'Joyful to meet you.'

She was dressed from head to toe in white lace, with a white lace headband, and strings of sparkling diamonds around her neck.

'Here, champagne,' she pulled a passing waitress towards her gently by the elbow and plucked flutes off her tray for them.

'Thank you, Mrs Miller,' said Arlette, taking the glass, 'and thank you so much for throwing me this wonderful party. It really is so generous of you.'

'Nonsense,' said Leticia, still smiling up at Gideon with a kind of girlish wonder. 'The least I can do for Dolly's girl. How she must be missing you. And besides, Lilian *insisted* on sharing her party with you. She adores you, you know. You're the big sister she never had.'

Arlette smiled and said, 'Well, it is mutual. I always

dreamed of my mother giving me a baby sister. And I love Lilian as my own.'

Leticia beamed and turned to greet another arriving guest.

The house had been decorated to look like a Japanese garden. The tables were dressed with branches of cherry blossom, lanterns hung from the ceilings and the waitresses were wearing kimonos and Geisha make-up. The dress code was White and Yellow. Most people had played it safe and dressed in white, but some guests had chosen the more challenging option and come dressed as various slightly grotesque characters from *The Mikado*. Arlette herself was dressed in a white satin bias-cut dress with a knife-pleat skirt that fell to her ankles, and silver sandals. Her hair had been set into waves in the salon at Liberty, using hot irons turned the wrong way round, and she looked, according to Gideon, 'like a creature from the silver screen'.

'Arlette!' screeched Lilian, from the other side of the room. 'You look spectacular!'

Lilian was dressed as Pierrette, and looked adorable in big-eyed clown make-up and a billowing white romper suit.

'Happy birthday, little one.' Arlette kissed her on her cheek, which smelled of greasepaint and rouge.

'And to you. I can hardly believe that it was a year ago that we first met. Do you remember? Mother had made you one of her terrible drinks and you were almost cross-eyed with it. And you were wearing some awful green suit, I recall,' she laughed.

'It does feel like an awfully long time ago,' said Arlette. 'And it was an awful suit.'

They both laughed and Lilian stood on her pointed toes to reach up to kiss Gideon. He held her fingertips inside his hands, looked down at her fondly and said, 'Lilian. You look a picture.'

'A picture of what, exactly?' she asked accusingly.

'Of fresh-faced innocence and beauty,' he replied.

Lilian smiled.

'And tell me,' he continued, 'are you expecting a visit from Pierrot this evening?'

She smiled again and laughed. 'That is entirely possible, Gideon,' she replied. 'And if you do happen to stumble upon one, please send him my way. Oh, in fact, never mind, here he is!' Her face bloomed open into a smile and she put an arm out towards a beautiful boy with sandy curls and a matching clown suit. 'This is Philip. Philip, this is Arlette and Gideon.'

Philip looked unbearably young, a million miles away from the characters Lilian had been socialising with in recent months in the jazz clubs and piano bars in Soho.

'Well, well, well,' said Arlette, appraising the young man in slight wonder, 'wherever did Lilian find you?'

The boy smiled and said, 'I live next door.'

Arlette smiled. 'So not too far from home, then?' Lilian and Philip looked at them and smiled, and then their hands found each other's and knitted together.

Arlette felt her stomach lurch slightly at the sight of them, almost identical with their blond curls and baby faces, perfect twins in their matching outfits. And their lives, of course, simply, elegantly entwined by neighbourly proximity. The absolute opposite of her own romantic pairing: black and white, British and West Indian, London and Manchester. She wondered who she might have found herself holding hands with if she'd never left Guernsey. In Guernsey there had been no 'next door', just a cluster of stone cottages in the dip below the house, peopled with elderly, leathery-skinned couples and distracted young families. No golden-haired boys to pair up with in perfect homogeny. No Pierrot to her Pierrette. Had she stayed on Guernsey, she pondered, she would probably have found herself irresistibly drawn to someone who would whisk her on the first boat away from the island, someone with an accent and a tan, someone utterly foreign in every way.

'Mother is delighted,' said Lilian, breathlessly. 'Philip's father is the richest man in the universe and Philip is an only child.' She laughed and Philip joined her.

'*Second* richest man in the universe,' he corrected.

'Oh, yes, sorry. But still, he needs to sell only one more motorcar and maybe he'll be the richest.'

They both laughed uproariously at their little joke, and Arlette pulled Gideon away by the hand.

'Come on,' she said, 'let's see who else is about.'

The party was spread across two rooms and out onto the wrought-iron veranda that led from the back sitting room. The air was scented with the tang of old bonfires and a warm wine toddy being ladled from a large vat by a girl in a green kimono. They mingled for an hour or so, taking every glass of champagne that was offered to them, until they were both quite merry. And then they came upon the two elder of Lilian's brothers sitting side by side on either arm of an armchair, one with his feet on the seat, the other with his legs crossed widely and somewhat obscenely, staring around the party and whispering the occasional sneering comment in the other's ear. The older one looked up when he saw Arlette heading in his direction and his eyes widened.

'Oh. It's you,' he said, 'whatshername.'

Gideon squeezed Arlette's elbow reassuringly.

'Arlette,' she said.

The boy clicked his fingers and said, 'Yes, that's right. Arlette.'

'Hello, Henry,' she opened pleasantly, no longer even a tad nervous in his presence. 'It is Henry, isn't it?'

He nodded.

'This is Gideon,' she said, 'my very good friend. I don't believe you've met.'

Henry shook his head and shrugged disinterestedly.

'Gideon, this is Henry, Lilian's little brother.' She emphasised the 'little' with a slight smile.

'Jolly nice to meet you,' said Gideon.

Henry put out a sulky hand and offered Gideon a limp handshake. 'The pleasure's all mine,' he replied sarcastically. On the other arm of the chair, they heard Arthur, the younger brother, let out a small snort of laughter.

Arlette and Gideon looked at each other and a mischievous spark flew between them.

'So, Henry,' Arlette began, 'I hear you have finished with school. I would imagine you must be about to head off to university somewhere?' She stifled a smile, well aware that Henry had failed all his examinations and was in fact due to start an unpaid apprenticeship at his father's firm, which would mainly involve sorting out the post in the mailroom.

Henry bridled and said, 'No. I decided against that. I'm to work with my father. His firm is looking for young blood.'

Arlette raised an eyebrow. 'Well, how marvellous. So you'll be bringing some money into the house? I'm sure your mother must be thrilled.'

He shuffled a little in his seat and shrugged. 'And you, Arlette, I hear you have been promoted to head of all the little shop-girls?'

'I am the department manager, yes,' she smiled graciously, 'the youngest in the store's history.'

He wriggled slightly again and said nothing.

'And of course, as manager I am on a fairly decent wage, enough to pay for a lovely room in Bloomsbury and all the trappings of a modern girl about town. You must be looking forward to having your own money to spend?'

He glowered at her and ground his heel into the fabric of the armchair. 'I do not need any money, Arlette. As you can see . . .' He waved his arms around the room proprietorially.

She smiled sweetly. 'Ah, well, Henry, so long as living off your father's hard-earned money is enough for you . . . But personally, I believe an individual should forge their own path in life. Wouldn't you agree, Gideon?'

Gideon nodded effusively. 'Oh, absolutely yes, Arlette. Because, as you know, my parents own half of Oxfordshire.'

Arlette pinioned Henry with a smile and nodded her agreement.

'If I'd wanted, I could have spent my entire life sitting at my mother's table waiting for handouts. But where is the manliness in that? All those men and boys, younger than me, gave up their lives, died in conditions of putrid torment, lost their legs, their arms, not, I believe, so that Gideon Worsley could sit and count his father's beans. No, no, no.' He shook his head slowly and sadly.

Henry glared at him and a silence landed upon the four of them like a collapsed ceiling.

'Anyway,' trilled Arlette, 'it has been lovely talking to you boys. Enjoy the party!'

'Yes,' said Gideon, stifling laughter, 'have a super, super night.'

And then he grabbed Arlette's hand and they moved briskly through the party crowds towards the open veranda doors, stopping briefly to accept mugs of mulled wine and then stumbling down the garden steps and out across the lawn where they let loose helpless peals of laughter that carried them into near madness.

'What ghastly, frightful children!' Gideon exclaimed, laid out on the grass on his back.

Arlette lay down next to him and laughed again. 'I know!' she said. 'If they were mine I would put them in the workhouse.'

Gideon laughed out loud again at that. 'If they were mine I would tie them down to railway tracks and let the next train deal with them.'

This struck Arlette as a little harsh and she let her laughter recede to a sigh.

A balmy breeze blew across them then, rustling the dead leaves scattered upon the lawn, making them rattle. The moon was out of sight, tucked behind the high trees at the bottom of the garden, and the sounds of the party inside billowed out across the garden in ethereal, indistinct bursts.

Gideon turned his head towards Arlette and smiled. Then he picked up her hand and held it in his, bringing it up to his mouth and kissing her knuckles gently.

Arlette smiled back and squeezed Gideon's hand. She was about to open her mouth and say something, something nice about how much she had enjoyed Gideon's company these past couple of weeks, how the period of Godfrey's absence was, as Gideon had promised, passing by in a whirl. She was going to thank him for taking her to salons, to soirées, to parties and to clubs, where she had met poets and writers and artists and actors, and for the fact that she had failed entirely to write her mother a letter longer than three or four lines.

Her heart was filled with warmth and affection for her friend, and so, when he brought himself up on one elbow and appraised her intently for a second before then bringing his mouth down upon hers and kissing her, quite hard, upon the lips, she did at first acquiesce, because it did, for a moment, feel the right thing to be doing, a mere heartbeat away from the hand-holding intimacy they'd been enjoying since they'd first met, not such a big leap and not so shocking. But when the kiss continued beyond the firm avuncular thing she'd been permitting and it became apparent that he was trying to part her lips with his she put a hand to his chest and pushed him back.

'Gideon,' she said, 'what on earth . . .?'

He looked at her quite strangely and said, 'Oh, now, come on, Arlette. It's not as though you've never been kissed.'

'Well, yes, but –'

'Well, but nothing,' he said, before bringing his mouth down firmly again against hers.

Again she pushed him back. She looked at him sternly and said, 'It is far from *nothing*, Gideon. I am spoken for. I can't –'

'Oh, Arlette, spoken for? Really? Do you really believe that? Do you really think your dear Godfrey is not, as we lie here, doing something rather similar?'

'I beg your pardon?' She blinked at him.

'Well, Arlette, my dear lovely girl, Godfrey is a West Indian. For goodness' sake, do you know nothing about the world? When it comes to affairs of the heart, they are not to be trusted.'

Arlette attempted to push Gideon away from her

entirely, but the force of her indignation was not enough to do so. 'Rubbish, Gideon,' she said, trying to get to her feet. 'Utter, utter rubbish. Godfrey is not a West Indian. Godfrey is a gentleman. Now, if you'll excuse me . . .'

She managed to scramble to her feet, and was about to storm back into the party when suddenly, and dreadfully, she found herself being dragged backwards, away from the house, down the lawn and towards the small wooded area at the end. She struggled against Gideon's pull, but it was impossible. 'Gideon!' she cried out. 'Will you let go of me!'

'No, Arlette, I will not let go of you.' He turned her to face him, her wrists still held tightly inside his hands. 'I will not let go of you, you silly woman, because I have been in love with you since the very first time I set eyes on you and I have had enough.' His eyes flashed angrily and Arlette felt something twist and spoil inside her gut.

'Enough of all this nonsense. Enough of you treating me like a fool. I want you . . .' He stared at her desperately and her wrists started to sting inside his rough grip. 'I need you to understand me. I need us to reach an *understanding*.' He tugged her backwards with every word, dragging her silver heels through the soil, her wrists feeling that they might come apart in his hands.

'Get off me, Gideon,' she hissed.

'No,' he hissed back. 'No! Absolutely not.'

They were in the wooded area now and Gideon was holding Arlette up against the trunk of a tree. He appraised her darkly for a moment and then he smiled, and for a moment Arlette thought he might be about to laugh and make the whole thing a joke, that she might walk away from here with everything the way it should be. But he did not laugh. Instead he brought his face down against hers once again, over-hard, roughly, forcing his tongue into her mouth. Arlette thought to struggle, but she was pinned almost entirely beneath the weight of his body. She could feel knuckles and nodules of bark pressing into her flesh; she could feel his leg forcing its way between her thighs, bruisingly. His lips passed from her mouth to her neck until she began to shout out, whereupon he forced his mouth once more over hers to stifle her and then, hard and awkward, he dragged down his trousers, pulled up the pure white pleats of her dress and forced aside her underwear. Arlette screamed noiselessly into the hot, hard cave of his mouth. She clenched her eyes closed and concentrated on a point five minutes from now when this would be over, when she could go inside, wash, sit, cry, go home.

As he climaxed his body softened against hers and he brought them both down into the bed of dry leaves. Arlette sat with her back still against the tree, Gideon's head buried first in her shoulder and then in her lap. He breathed heavily, in and out, and Arlette stared deep and dark into the sky, feeling the awful hot wetness inside her. It had all taken about thirty seconds.

After a moment, Gideon lifted his head from her lap and smiled at her, an incongruous look of childish wonder. 'Oh, my darling,' he said, cupping her cheek with his hand. 'My precious darling. Thank you.'

Arlette blinked at him and said, 'What?'

'Thank you. Thank you for letting me show you how I really feel.'

Arlette could think of no words. Instead she nodded, just once.

'A momentous day!' Gideon cried out, suddenly getting to his feet. 'A marvellous day!'

She watched mutely as he pulled up his trousers, put away his damp penis, buttoned up his fly, brushed away crumbs of autumn leaf from his clothing. 'Here,' he held his hand down to her and she took it. He pulled her up to standing and watched her tenderly as she pulled down her skirt, brushed away more crumbs of autumn leaves.

'Oh, here,' he said, 'you have some dirt . . . let me . . .'

She stood numbly as he carefully brushed some clods of dry earth from the back of her dress. 'Such a beautiful dress,' he muttered sweetly. 'We mustn't let it be spoiled. There.' He smiled at her triumphantly. 'You look perfect. No one would ever know.'

She nodded again, feeling the rancid trickle of warm liquid in the gap between her underwear and her stocking tops. 'I need to clean myself,' she said.

'Of course. Yes. Of course. But first, I feel I absolutely have to mark this occasion somehow.' He pulled apart his jacket and took something from his inside pocket, something small and metal that gleamed dully in the darkness. Arlette caught her breath, fearing that the ordeal may not yet be over.

'Here,' he said, pulling open the penknife. He started to gouge out lumps of the tree behind them. 'Here, a lasting memorial. Our little secret.' Arlette stood in abject silence as Gideon chiselled away at the wood and then he brought out a box of matches and lit one up. 'See,' he said, putting one hand gently on to her bare shoulder.

Arlette peered at the tree.

She shuddered and turned away.

'Don't you like it?'

She said, 'I'm going inside now, Gideon, to clean myself. And after that I shall be going home.'

'But, Arlette,' he said pleadingly, 'the party. What about the party?'

'I don't care about the party.'

'But – what shall I tell Leticia? What shall I tell Lilian? All your friends?'

'I have no idea, Gideon.'

She picked up the hem of her beautiful white dress and she walked back across the lawn, her legs trembling, her hands shaking, and she headed through the servants' entrance in the basement, to the nearest bathroom where she scrubbed herself raw.

*

Dear Mother,

I am so sorry not to have written you a decent letter for such a long time. I cannot tell you how busy my life is here in London. I work so hard and play so hard and on the rare nights I'm at home with nothing to do, before I've even picked up a pen, I'm already halfway to sleep. I hope you are well. It's been a glorious summer. Did you spend much time on the beach? I did think of you, often, and those long days we used to spend together. It all feels like such a long time ago now . . .

Well, my news, such as it is: I have spent this summer conducting a remarkable love affair. With a musician. I can't tell you much more about him, other than that he is a gentleman, and that I love him very much. He is away at the moment, performing in the North with his orchestra, but next Monday he will be returning and I cannot breathe with the anticipation of seeing him again. The period of his absence has almost reduced me to madness. For the past week I have not left my room apart from to go to work; I am truly a recluse. And this week, more than any other since I left you on the quayside just over a year ago, I have missed you more than words can say. I have lain in bed at night and dreamed of you, wanting to lie in your arms and have you stroke my hair, like you used to do when I was small. Because, Mother, the most awful thing happened to me last week. I am not sure I can put it into words without feeling the pain of it all over again, maybe I can tell you, maybe I can't, but a man, a man I loved platonically and with deepest affection, a man I considered to be the best of all possible people and a true, genuine friend, violated my trust, violated my body, in the most heartless and animal of ways. I cannot think too hard and too long upon the details of this incident, and I am sure you would not wish to hear of them. I have told no one, not even my closest friends, because I am scared of how they might react. But I feel constantly now on the verge of hysteria. I feel dirty, I feel like all my joy in life, my trust in humanity, my hope for the future has been snatched from my hands and torn to shreds.

Oh, Mother, I am desperate, I am destroyed. Every time I close my eyes I feel his mouth on mine, I smell the scent of his skin, I panic, my heart races, as if I am locked in a box, as if I have been buried alive. The air turns to dust in my mouth, I can't eat, I can't sleep, I am destroyed, Mother, I am *destroyed* . . .

Arlette breathed in deeply, caught a sob at the back of her throat, ripped the pages from the notepad, screwed them into a small tight ball and hurled them at the wall. Then she began afresh.

Dear Mother,
    Yet again the social and professional whirl of my

life prevents me from writing to you properly. Yet again I must just dash you off a few paltry and insufficient lines to tell you that I am very happy, very well and missing you very much. The summer has been marvellous, and now autumn is upon us and I have been in London for more than a year. Where did the time go to? Well, Mother, I must dash, I am expected at a party and my friends are calling for me. I will write again next week.

All my fondest love,

Arlette.

She pulled the sheet carefully from the notepad, folded it very precisely, and slid it into a lavender-scented envelope, which she addressed to her mother. Then she walked slowly across the room and collected the discarded ball of paper, pushing it deep and dark into the bottom of her wastepaper basket. A moment later she retrieved it from the wastepaper basket, and laid it in the wash basin, where she set it alight with a match and watched it burn itself away to a small pile of blackened ephemera.

45

Godfrey stood on the doorstep, his suitcase at his feet, his overcoat held over his arm, his hat in his hand. Miss Chettling was looking from Godfrey to Arlette and back again, her face a picture of anguished uncertainty.

'Miss De La Mare,' she began tremulously, 'this gentleman says that he is here to see you . . .?'

Arlette looked at Godfrey, her love, her joy, her future, and she gulped back a cry of misery.

'Godfrey,' she said stiffly, 'what are you doing here?'

'My dear,' he said, 'I was worried. I had expected to see you at the station.' The smile on his face was strained and slightly embarrassed. Arlette's heart lurched.

'Yes, indeed, did you not get my note?'

'No, I did not.' His smile faltered a fraction and he squeezed his hat nervously between his beautiful fingers.

Arlette swallowed down a sob and said, 'Oh dear. I posted it on Friday morning. I had hoped . . .'

'Oh, now, that is a pity. Was there a change in your plans?'

'Well, yes, there was, there was . . .' She paused and

said, 'Miss Chettling, I would like to talk to Mr Pickle in private, if that's possible.'

Miss Chettling looked momentarily shocked and then recovered herself. 'Yes,' she said, 'if you're sure.'

'I am, thank you, Miss Chettling.'

Miss Chettling tiptoed back up the stairs and Arlette turned to Godfrey.

'Shall I come in?' he asked.

'Um, well, I'm not sure that's necessary, Godfrey. I just . . .' She wrung her hands together and stared at the ground, at the gleam of Godfrey's patent shoes, at a cobweb embedded between the bricks in the doorway. She felt her stomach contract and expand, and forced the words from her mouth, dry and painful as a stone. 'The thing is, Godfrey, my circumstances are somewhat changed. I, um, I no longer.' She swallowed hard and cleared her throat. 'I am no longer in a position to . . . I think we will have to finish this.'

'Finish this,' he repeated.

'Yes. You and I. I can't. Not any more.'

'I'm not sure I understand entirely.' He blinked at her, still smiling.

'Oh, Godfrey,' she exclaimed, 'please don't make this harder than it needs to be! I can't see you any more. Things have changed while you've been gone. Irreversibly. I'm so very sorry.'

His big eyes glistened and she saw him gulp. He passed his hat from one hand to the other and said, 'I see. And in what way have things changed?'

'I've taken up with a new man,' she said, bile rising at the back of her throat as she released the awful words of truth.

'Oh,' his brow twitched. 'And am I allowed to know who this new man might be?'

'It is Gideon,' she said tersely.

Godfrey turned his gaze from Arlette and up to the sky, as though the answer had been up there all along. 'Yes,' he said, nodding just once. 'Yes. Of course.'

'Why would you say that?' she asked. 'Why "of course"?'

Godfrey laughed bitterly. 'Oh, my dear,' he said. 'Do you really need to ask?'

'Well, yes, clearly I do, otherwise I should not be asking.'

He sighed and stared at Arlette with a mixture of fondness and irritation. Then he put his hat back upon his head, picked up his suitcase, bowed his head at Arlette and very slowly turned and walked away.

Arlette watched him for a moment. Every fibre of her being wanted to chase after him, wanted to hurl herself at him, wanted to kiss him, to hold him, to bring him inside, to her room, to her bed, to her life for ever and ever. But then she remembered: that avenue had been closed to her four weeks ago against a tree in Leticia's garden. That avenue had been closed to her when Gideon's sperm had entered her body and fertilised her egg, and although no doctor had yet confirmed the terrible truth, Arlette knew. Her monthly curse was two weeks late. Her breasts were large and tender. And there had been, for the past twenty-four hours, a peculiar taste in her mouth, a taste of metal and dirt.

And no, it was not Godfrey's baby. She had still been bleeding when Godfrey had left for Manchester; they had not had encounters of that type since before her last curse. And even then they had been careful, had employed techniques to ensure that conception would not take place. As they always did.

It was Gideon's baby inside her. She knew it. She felt it. She hated it.

She watched Godfrey until he was but a toy figure in the distance and then he turned the corner and was gone.

She called at Gideon's house that afternoon, dressed as a far plainer woman than the one he had last seen in white knife pleats and a marcel wave. The house that she had first entered as a virgin, with Lilian as her escort, the house that had charmed her with its vagueness and its clutter, now looked ominous in the dark gold October light. She felt nausea rise from her stomach to the back of her throat, not knowing how she would feel when she saw his face again, heard his voice, watched those lips turn up into his oafish smile. He opened the door to her half dressed, his hair lank behind his ears, his eyes full of sleep. He blinked at her, and then there it was, that smile, Gideon's smile. Childlike, pure, slightly confused.

'My God,' he said. 'Arlette! How wonderful! I thought you were cross with me.'

Arlette could barely think straight; her words jumbled up and rearranged themselves inside her head. She breathed in deeply and pulled them back together, and she said, 'Gideon. I believe I am pregnant. I believe it is yours.'

Gideon said nothing at first. He merely ran a hand through his hair and stared at her.

'But surely not,' he said with a hoarse laugh. 'I mean, we made love only once.'

Arlette closed her eyes and inhaled, trying to calm herself against the twin assault of his misuse of the words 'made love' and his blatant ignorance about matters of a reproductive nature.

'It only takes one . . .' she said, unable to find a word to complete her sentence that would in any way be an accurate reference to what had occurred between them. 'It only needs to happen once,' she finished.

He rubbed at his stubbled chin and nodded at her, as though grateful in some way for the clarification. 'I see,' he said. 'Well . . .'

'I have an appointment tomorrow with the doctor. If I am right, if I am pregnant, then you are to marry me. Immediately.'

'Marry you?' he asked, his eyes sparkling with amusement.

She nodded, once.

'Why, of course. I mean, Arlette, as you know, I adore you, I –'

'This has absolutely nothing to do with love, Gideon. Far from it. I am pregnant, with your child –'

'Are you sure?' he interrupted. 'Sure that it is mine?'

'Yes,' she snapped, unwilling to enter into an explanation. 'I am sure.'

Gideon smiled and rubbed his chin, chewing over the prospect happily. 'Well, well, well,' he said.

'I am pregnant. With your child. I will have to give up work. I have already given up Godfrey. You will marry me and be a generous and kind father and husband. You will care for us both and ensure that we have everything we need. In perpetuity. But, Gideon, you will never, *ever* lay a single finger of yours upon my body again. I will not so much as feel the touch of your breath against me. Do you hear? And if you do I will tell everyone what happened at my birthday party. Absolutely everyone. And I will leave out not a single disgraceful detail. I will also take away your child and make sure that you never see it again. Do you understand?'

Gideon stared at Arlette and nodded dumbly.

'Goodbye, Gideon,' she said. 'I shall be in touch. And keep Saturday free.'

'What for?'

'For a wedding,' she said. 'Of the most inglorious variety.'

46

1995

Someone had been sick on Betty's front step. It was bright yellow and smelled of fish. She stopped breathing and stepped over it gingerly. It must have been deposited there after the street cleaners had left – fairly recently, in other words. While Betty was awaking and showering and getting ready for work other people were stumbling around, throwing up on doorsteps.

Amy was taking the children to her best friend's house in the country at lunchtime, so Betty had the afternoon and tomorrow morning off. She could barely wait. She'd been working for Amy since only Tuesday but with the ten-hour days and the rather eventful evenings, it felt like much longer.

'Nice,' said John, sauntering towards his pitch with a big cardboard box in his arms and gesturing towards the pile of vomit.

Betty blanched at the sound of his voice. It was the first time she'd seen him since the morning after she'd slept with Dom.

'I know,' she said, sneering. 'Gross.'

John put the box down on his stand and turned his back

to her while he untaped it and started pulling out records. Betty stood for a moment, feeling she should say something, something to bring them back on track.

'Are you cross with me?' she asked eventually.

John turned and glanced at her over his shoulder. 'No,' he said. 'Not at all. Why, should I be?'

She shrugged. 'I don't know,' she said. 'You just seem a bit . . . *offish*.'

'Well, you know, that's me. Brightly by name, miserably by nature.' His voice was tight and cold.

'So we're OK, are we?'

He shrugged. 'Course we are. Right as rain. Have a good day now,' he said patronisingly, before turning again and sauntering away from her.

Betty waited a beat, to see if he would turn and give her one of his smiles, the ones he saved just for her that made her feel like she'd won the lottery. But he didn't. She sighed and headed for work.

'Now, listen,' said Amy, sliding her arms into a battered leather jacket and pulling her hair out from the back collar. 'Tomorrow night. I'm having a party. Here. Like, huge big fuck-off thing, OK? Party starts at eight, but I'll need you here earlier, to settle the kids, say about six o'clock. Once they're in bed you can come and join the party, but stay sober, yeah. Someone will have to be able to drive a car in an emergency. And then I'll need you to stay overnight. OK? And do the kids on Sunday morning. Maybe even into lunchtime.' She pulled up her sleeve and looked at her watch. 'So, I'm off to the salon. I'll be back at twelve. Dom's popping over. He says ten, but I don't know, *who knows*, maybe not at all.'

'Oh,' said Betty, her heart starting to race, 'any particular reason?'

'He says he wants to see the kids. But if you could somehow get him outta here before I get back, I would love you for ever. I've got crazy heaps of shit to do and I am *not* in the mood for seeing his pitiful face. I told him just an hour, so you don't need to feel bad about kicking him out. But don't say anything to the kids, OK? Don't wanna get their hopes up and then have them dashed because Daddy Dearest is comatose in some skanky blond's bed. Right, *kids*!' she yelled over her shoulder. 'Mommy's going out for a coupla hours. Betty's here. Be good. Love you!' She didn't wait for the children to acknowledge her parting words, just slung a bag over her shoulder, grabbed a bunch of keys and hurtled out of the house.

Betty took a deep breath and headed into the kitchen. Donny was eating a bowl of Cheerios and Mina, the maid (who Amy always referred to as though she were a kindly houseguest, just there for the fun of it, rather than a paid employee), was spooning mashed banana into the baby's mouth. Acacia, the toddler, was wandering around with an unbuttoned Babygro on and a milk bottle hanging from between her teeth. The maid smiled gratefully at Betty when she saw her walk in and passed her the bowl of mashed banana, before going to the kitchen sink to wash her hands.

'Morning, guys!' said Betty.

'Morning,' grumbled Donny, who was not, Betty was coming to learn, a morning person.

'Morning, Acacia!' She smiled at the toddler, who beamed at her, and in doing so lost her grip on the milk bottle, which fell to the floor, squirting milk in pretty much a full circle across the floor.

'Oh-oh,' sang Betty, pulling off sheets of kitchen roll and mopping it up. 'Oh-oh.'

'Silly Cashie,' said Donny, smiling.

'No,' said Betty. 'Cashie's not silly. Cashie's just smiling. Aren't you, my lovely? Just smiling at Betty.' Acacia smiled again. And then weed on the floor.

'Oh!' said Betty. 'No nappy. Mummy left you without a nappy!' She beamed and grabbed some more kitchen roll. 'Oh, look at that, look at all that wee-wee.' Acacia wrinkled her nose at Betty and smiled again.

'Naughty Cashie,' said Donny, banging his spoon against the kitchen table in delight. 'Naughty, naughty Cashie.'

Astrid, seeing what her big brother was doing, grabbed her plastic spoon and began copying him, banging her spoon against her bowl of mashed banana, bang bang bang, until the bowl dropped off the table and onto the kitchen floor, turning one hundred and eighty degrees in its descent, depositing gooey banana all over the floor. Seeing her breakfast disappear out of sight, the baby began to cry. Betty took a deep breath. What sort of idiots had three children, she thought to herself. What sort of ridiculous fools would fill up their beautiful house with people intent on spilling stuff and pissing everywhere?

She breathed in once, twice, three times and then she rose up onto her feet, her hands full of balled up, piss-soaked kitchen roll and smiled her Happy Betty smile. 'Oh,' she said, brightly, 'never mind. Never mind.' And then she turned to the sink to rinse out a cloth and jumped an inch in the air when she saw Dom standing in the doorway.

'Morning all,' he said, pulling his hands from his pockets and sauntering in.

'*Daddy!*' cried Donny, leaping to his feet and sending a spoonful of Cheerios flying across the table as he did so.

Dom grabbed Donny and threw him in the air, then held him aloft on his shoulder like a football trophy. Donny smiled triumphantly and squeezed Dom's head between his hands.

Betty smiled and said, 'You're early.'

'I've been waiting round the corner,' he said, 'waiting for the Wicked W –' he stopped himself, 'waiting for Mummy to go.'

He looked dishevelled, and even from halfway across the room, Betty could smell stale alcohol emanating from him. 'Have you slept?' she asked.

He smiled sheepishly and shook his head. 'Nah,' he said, 'we, er . . . well, we got the sleeper last night, turned into a bit of a party, not much sleeping, let's put it that way . . .'

'Ah.' Betty nodded sagely. 'So, how long have you been waiting round the corner?'

'About an hour,' he shrugged, 'maybe longer. My mate owns the pub round the corner. He let me hang out there.'

She nodded again.

He looked at her wide-eyed with innocence. 'He's been mainlining me strong coffee.'

She gave him a look that said she didn't care, she wasn't his wife, she wasn't his mother, it was up to him how he lived his life.

In response he threw her a puppy-dog look and said, 'Any eggs in the fridge?'

'No idea,' she said, 'I've been here only two minutes and I've spent the full extent of that two minutes clearing stuff up off the floor. Why don't you have a look?'

He lowered Donny to the floor and shuffled towards the fridge. Betty dropped to her knees and mopped up the mashed banana, then the milky Cheerios.

'So,' she said, standing up, 'how did it go? The secret location?'

'Waste of time,' he said. 'Total waste of time. Gav didn't show. Tommy spent the whole time on the phone to his missus. And me and Bryce just played poker and drank schnapps.'

'Oh,' said Betty.

'Yeah.' Dom pulled a sliced loaf out of the bread bin and took out two pieces of bread. 'Exactly.'

He dropped the bread into a big shiny toaster like the ones they have in Italian cafés and started noisily pulling drawers open and shut. 'Frying pan?' he asked.

'No idea,' Betty said. 'Didn't you used to live here?'

'Live here? Yes. Cook here? Not very often. A-ha,' he said victoriously, 'found it!' He pulled open the door of the big pink Smeg fridge and stared into it. 'So,' he said, 'lovely Betty. How've you been?'

'Fine,' she said.

He reached into the fridge and brought out a box of eggs. He peered at it and said, 'Use by the fifteenth of June. What date is it today?'

'It's the sixteenth,' she said.

'What do you reckon? Can I eat these?'

'Of course you can,' she said, wiping mush from the baby's mouth.

'Coolio,' he said, juggling two eggs in the air and just about catching them again. 'Don, wanna crack an egg?'

'Yeah!' said Donny, immediately grabbing his step and pulling it over to the hob. 'Can I crack both of them?'

'Course you can, mate, course you can. Betty? Want an egg?'

'No thank you,' she said primly.

'Suit yourself.'

Betty watched Dom bouncing around the kitchen, hyper as a child, spilling things, treating Donovan as if he were a toy, unable to work out how to light the gas, burning the toast, leaving crumbs in the butter, splattering the hob with hot oil, and she felt suddenly intensely annoyed. It was like every time she saw him he was acting out a different role. She thought of the guy she'd spent the night with three days ago, the calm, thoughtful guy who'd cooked her a roast chicken as if it was the simplest thing in the world, who'd seduced her so smoothly and convincingly. Then she thought of the drunk idiot in the Groucho, the one who'd squeezed her bum and called her 'the nanny' to impress his stupid friend. She thought of the time she'd seen him screaming down the phone at someone, hard and aggressive, through his back window, and then she thought again of the blurred photos on the front page of the *Mirror* a few weeks ago. It occurred to her, suddenly and over-poweringly, that she had absolutely no idea who he was. Right now he was acting out the role of the crazy dad, the fun guy who showed up unexpectedly and created havoc. And she didn't like it, not one bit.

Finally he sat down at the kitchen table with a plate of toast and eggs. He grabbed a bottle of ketchup and showily, ostentatiously, covered the whole lot in red sauce, like he was trying to prove he was a real regular guy, the salt of the earth. 'There,' he said, rubbing his hands together and smiling, 'look at that. Lovely stuff.'

Betty pulled Astrid out of her baby seat and put her on her hip.

'So,' said Dom, 'what are we going to do today?'

The question was directed at everyone in the room.

'Football! Football!' shouted Donovan.

'Excellent idea.'

'Erm, listen, Dom,' Betty began. 'Amy said she'll be back at twelve and that she didn't really . . . that it would be good if . . .'

'Yeah. I get it. I'll be gone by then. Don't you worry.'

'Actually,' she continued, 'maybe it would be better to keep the kids here. You know? Keep them at home. It's only a couple of hours.' She fiddled with the hem of Astrid's dress while she spoke.

Dom stared at her blankly for a moment and then he said, 'What? You think I'm going to steal him?'

Betty grimaced. 'No, of course not. Just you might get carried away, you know, forget the time. And Amy wants to get the kids straight in the car when she gets back. I think she'll be really cross if Donny's not here.'

Dom laughed a false, hollow laugh and said, 'I am capable of telling the time, Betty. I'm not a complete moron.'

'I never said you were.'

'Well, yeah, but you *implied* it.'

'No, it's just, you know, you haven't slept, you've been drinking . . .'

'Oh, for *fuck's* sake.' Dom slammed his hands down on the table and Betty instinctively put an admonishing finger to her lips. Dom raised his eyebrows at her and then folded his arms across his chest. 'What is this?' he barked. 'I've got two *effing* wives now. Jesus.'

Betty glanced at the children to make sure they weren't too perturbed by this exchange and the ripe language but they seemed unfazed, and it occurred to Betty, sadly, that they were probably used to it.

'It's not that,' she said in as mild a voice as she could manage. 'It's Amy. I work for Amy. I have to follow her rules.'

'You do not work for Amy,' said Dom, darkly, 'you work for me. Who do you think pays your wages?'

'Amy. . .?'

He rolled his eyes. 'Oh, really, you think so? And tell me, when was the last time Mighty sold a million records, eh? When was the last time Mighty sold out a stadium tour? You think Amy Metz paid for this place?' He gestured around the room. 'You think Amy Metz is paying to get her hair dyed, as we speak? You think she pays for anything?'

Betty shrugged and stroked the baby's hair. 'I never really thought about it.'

'Well, there you go.' He pushed his half-eaten plate of food away childishly. 'Think about it for just one moment, and you'll see that I pay your wages and therefore you work for me.'

Betty gulped. She could feel tears rising up through her body and she swallowed them down painfully.

Dom sighed dramatically and put a hand on Donny's head. 'But,' he began, 'if Mummy says you can't go out and play football with Daddy then I suppose we'll just have to do what Mummy says.'

'No!' screamed Donovan. 'No! I want to play football!'

'Sorry, mate,' said Dom, casting a meaningful glance in Betty's direction. 'The women don't want us to, and us poor blokes have to do what the women say. Otherwise we get our willies chopped off.'

Donovan stopped crying for a minute and stared at Dom, aghast. 'Really?'

'No,' said Betty, 'of course not. But Mummy wants you in the car when she gets back and so football will have to wait for another day.'

'No!' he screamed again. 'No! Now! Football now!'

Dom kissed Donny on his head and gave Betty another dark look. 'I think I'd better leave,' he said.

Betty grimaced at him. 'Why?' she said. 'Couldn't you just play football in the garden?' She looked through the sliding glass doors to the sixty-foot lawn with half-size football goal beyond.

'No!' shouted Donny. 'I want to play in the park. With Daddy.'

Dom simply raised an eyebrow at Betty and got to his feet. 'Sorry, mate,' he said to Donny. 'Fun's over. I'll see you soon, yeah.' He kissed him on the mouth. 'And you, girls, love you all.' He kissed Acacia and then he leaned in towards Betty to kiss the baby, and she reeled at the smell of his vaporous breath, the stale cigarette smoke clinging to his clothes and a blob of egg yolk in the corner of his mouth drying to a crust.

'Where are you going?' she asked.

'Oh, a few things to sort out, you know. Gotta find Gav. Gotta get a kip. I'll see you soon, yeah?'

She nodded mutely, while Donovan sobbed quietly behind her.

She watched Dom unpeel Donovan from his leg at the front door and squeeze it closed behind him, almost trapping his son's fingers as he did so.

Betty turned back to the kitchen. The room was in

chaos: cracked eggshells littered the work surface, the oily frying pan was still on the hob, there were crumbs of burned toast everywhere, and Acacia, still without a nappy, had at some point, without anyone even noticing, done a poo on the floor.

Donovan ran back into the kitchen, his face puce with fury, tears coursing down his cheeks and screamed at Betty, 'Why didn't you let Daddy take me to the park? I *hate* you!' before stamping up the stairs and slamming his bedroom door behind him.

Betty brought the baby close to her face and kissed her scalp tenderly. 'Naughty Daddy,' she whispered softly in her ear. 'What a naughty, naughty Daddy.'

And then she put the baby down, pushed up her sleeves, and set about hosing down the kitchen.

47

1920

For her wedding Arlette wore black. Minu was her maid of honour and Gideon's brother Toby was the best man. They married at Chelsea Town Hall during a torrential downpour that marked the end of the mellow early days of autumn, and arrived for a sombre lunch at a Chelsea café like a band of drowned rats. Arlette and Gideon were toasted with tumblers of warm whisky and they ate gristly lamp chops with cold mashed potatoes, which Arlette promptly threw up in the gutter when they left the restaurant an hour later.

Gideon offered to carry Arlette over the threshold of his cottage but she told him not to be a fool and stamped into the house crossly, drank another tumbler of Scotch and went straight to bed.

When she awoke the following morning, she experienced, as she had every morning since the awful night of her twenty-second birthday, a brief moment of forgetfulness, of feeling how she used to feel, of being the Arlette who had a stellar career in ladies' fashion, who lived in cosy Bloomsbury lodgings with her best friend, who loved a man called Godfrey Pickle and would one day have his babies.

And then, as her eyes slowly opened, so too would her memory. And then her stomach would convulse and a sob would rise up through her, and she'd have to clutch herself to stop herself screaming out loud at the horror of it all.

Her doctor had offered her the services of a 'good woman' in Russell Square, but Arlette had shaken her head forcefully.

'No,' she said, 'no. I could not do that. It is a baby. It needs me.'

He had nodded once and said, 'And I feel sure you will provide well for it. You seem to be a fine and very mature young woman.'

'Yes,' she agreed primly. 'I am.'

She could hear Gideon, now, rattling around in the kitchen. She stared at the wall, blindly, brushing away a single tear from her nose. A moment later there was a soft knock at the door.

'Come,' she said.

Gideon stood in the doorway, dressed and clean, holding a tray.

'I have brought you ginger tea,' he said. 'I have been told it is very soothing for morning sickness. And some unbuttered toast. Will you be going to work today?'

Arlette nodded and sat up in her bed. 'Yes,' she said, 'I shall work until I feel I am no longer able to do so.'

'Good,' he said, laying the tray on her bed-stand. 'And how did you sleep?'

'I slept well, thank you,' she replied.

'That's good,' he said, standing slightly awkwardly above her bed with his hands in his jacket pockets.

They were silent for a moment, until Gideon cleared his throat and said, 'Well, I shall leave you to get ready. I have lit a fire downstairs so there is plenty of hot water. If you need me for anything, I shall be upstairs in my studio.'

'Thank you, I'm sure I shall be fine.'

Gideon smiled tightly and turned to leave. But halfway to the door he stopped and turned back. 'Your name,' he began nervously, 'will you be Mrs Worsley?'

'No,' she said. 'I will be Mrs De La Mare. I should not wish to replace my father's surname with any man's name, least of all yours.'

Gideon looked injured, but then rallied and said, 'But the baby . . .?'

'The baby shall have your name.'

He smiled then and left the room, closing the door quietly behind himself.

48

1995

John Brightly was not on his stand when Betty got back to Berwick Street at twelve thirty. A man was holding an Ultravox picture disc in his hand and looking anxiously up and down the street. He looked at Betty as she stopped to take out her front door key and said, 'Excuse me, do you work here?'

She smiled. 'No,' she said, 'sorry.'

'Oh.' The man looked disappointed. 'Right. It's just, I've been stood here for about ten minutes now, wanting to buy this single, but there's no one here.'

'Oh,' she said, 'that's strange. I know the guy who runs this stand and he never leaves it unattended.'

'Right,' said the man, distractedly. 'It says five pounds on the label. Can I just give you the money? And you can give it to him when he comes back?'

Betty stifled a smile. The man seemed oddly anxious to buy an Ultravox picture disc. She couldn't imagine what he wanted to do with it. 'Er, yeah, sure,' she said.

'Great.' He passed her a crumpled note and in return she slid the single into a paper bag and handed it to him.

He tucked it lovingly into a flight bag slung over his shoulder and scuttled away.

Betty watched John's pitch from her front window for a while after she got upstairs. She made herself some lunch and ate it by the kitchen window, peering down every minute or two. Then she sat and wrote a note that said: 'John, I sold a single to some guy for a fiver. Ring the bell when you get back and I'll give you the cash.'

She ran downstairs and tucked the note under the leg of a display stand on the table and then went back upstairs to smoke a cigarette, leaving both doors open so she could hear the doorbell.

She glanced across at Dom's house. There were no signs of life. Dom had either crashed out in his clothes or he was out somewhere getting up to no good. She thought of the two of them, sitting framed together in that window three nights ago, she thought of him telling her that he wished he'd met her first. She thought of how she'd felt, filled with longing, and then the shock of his soft lips against hers. And then she thought of the scene in Amy's kitchen just now, and shuddered.

There was still no sign of John when she looked out of her window again a few minutes later, so once more she headed downstairs and spoke to the man who ran the pitch next door, selling toiletries.

'Excuse me,' she began.

The man looked at her with annoyance, before his face softened into a lecherous smile. 'What can I do for you, beautiful?'

Betty pointed a thumb at John's stand. 'Any idea where John is?'

'Bloke in the hats?'

'Yes, you know, he's here every day.'

'Yeah, yeah, I know who you mean. Far as I know he just popped over the road, you know, call of nature.'

He gestured at the scruffy pub opposite, the heavy metal pub that Betty had never ventured into and always walked past very quickly with her head down.

'Right,' she said. 'OK.' She decided to give him five more minutes, then she would try to find him. She sat on his stool and counted down the minutes and then, when he had still failed to reappear, she took a deep breath and headed across the road to the pub.

The pub was quiet on this sunny Friday lunchtime and she headed straight for the bar, ignoring the curious gazes of the handful of solitary men in denim waistcoats, the line of tattooed arms propping up the bar. She smiled at the unhappy-looking barmaid and said, 'A guy from the market came in here about half an hour ago. Hasn't been seen since. Would you mind just checking the men's toilets for me?'

The barmaid raised a pencilled-in eyebrow and said, 'Go and look yourself. I can't leave the bar.'

'Fine,' said Betty, 'good.'

She followed the signs to a scruffy door at the back and breathed in. She knocked once, quietly, and then twice, louder, and she pushed open the door and found John collapsed on the floor, half in and half out of the solitary cubicle, his arms spread out in front of him as though he'd been trying to catch himself. There was a trickle of dark brown blood running from his hairline to the floor.

Betty shouted out and dropped to her knees. There was a slight sheen of sweat on John's forehead. He felt very hot, almost feverish and his breath sounded laboured.

'John! Oh my God, John! Help!' she called out towards the door. 'Someone help! Call an ambulance!' But it was pointless, the jukebox was booming out heavy metal. Then she remembered her mobile phone in her bag. She pulled it out and dialled in 999, her other hand touching John's throat, feeling for breath. She answered the operator's questions: yes, he was breathing; no, he wasn't blue; yes, there was a head wound; no, it didn't seem to be deep. In under a minute she heard the faint sound of sirens outside on the street.

'It's OK, John,' she whispered, stroking his hair, that thick dense hair she'd dreamed about touching so often in the past. 'It's OK. The ambulance is here. We're going to the hospital now. They'll make you better, don't you worry. Don't you worry, John Brightly.'

The door flew open and a female paramedic appeared. 'Betty?' she said.

'Yes, yes.'

She got to her knees next to John. 'And this is John?'

'Yes,' said Betty, 'John Brightly.'

'And you're his friend?' She put a hand to his throat for a pulse.

Betty nodded.

'I'm Jackie,' she said, feeling his forehead. 'He's very hot.' She put a thermometer into his ear and stared at it. 'Fever,' she said. 'Has he been unwell?'

Betty shrugged. 'I don't know,' she said. 'He wasn't the last time I spoke to him.'

'And when was that?'

'Wednesday,' she said. 'Although I saw him this morning and he looked OK. But I didn't really talk to him.'

'Hmm.' Jackie put the thermometer back in her pack and called through the door to another paramedic waiting outside. 'We're going to need a stretcher, patient concussed. And also high temperature, 42.2 Celsius, he'll need something to bring it down.'

The male paramedic disappeared.

Betty said, 'What do you think happened?'

Jackie sat back on her heels and said, 'I think he fainted. Cracked his head on the sink there.'

'Do you think he'll be OK?'

'Hard to say. I don't know how long he's been like this.'

'About half an hour,' said Betty, anxiously. 'Maybe longer.'

Jackie winced. 'That's a long time to be out. But he hasn't lost much blood.' She sucked in her breath. 'We'll run some tests. We'll see.'

A stretcher arrived and Betty waited outside the toilets while the two paramedics strapped John onto it.

'Can I come?' she asked, following beside them, John's hot floppy hand held in hers.

'Of course you can.'

'Where are you taking him?'

'UCH.'

In the back of the ambulance they took John's temperature again and covered him over with a metallic blanket. It seemed remarkable to Betty that someone so extraordinarily warm could feel so lifeless. She kept his hand in hers and talked to him. 'Sold a single for you,' she said, 'an Ultravox picture disc. I mean, seriously, who wants an Ultravox picture disc in 1995? I thought maybe he was going to make a wall clock out of it. Or maybe *mould* it into a fruit bowl, or something. Anyway, he was really happy. And I've got your fiver. Which I will give you when you *wake up*. Which you must do *very soon*, please.' She smiled at him and squeezed his hand. 'And I've told the toiletries guy to keep an eye on your pitch, so don't worry about that. And I have your hat safe in my bag.' She pulled open her bag to show him his hat. 'So now all you have to do is open your eyes and say something. OK?'

The ambulance squealed around a corner and Betty held onto her seat. A moment later they were pulling up at the back end of the UCH and John was being put onto a trolley.

The trolley was pushed down corridor after corridor, through sets of flapping plastic doors until he was taken away from sight into a cubicle behind curtains and Betty suddenly found herself alone, on a plastic chair, staring at a poster about tetanus injections.

Betty sat on that chair for nearly fifty minutes before finally a doctor appeared.

'I'm his friend,' she said, jumping to her feet, 'the man, in there. Is he OK?'

The doctor smiled and said, 'He will be.'

'Can I see him?' she asked.

'No,' he replied. 'Not yet. He's conscious now, but he's got a very bad infection. We think it might be pneumonia. We're waiting for the bloods to come back. If it is we'll need to keep him in overnight, get some heavyweight antibiotics into him. And also keep an eye on him after the concussion.'

'But does he seem all right? Can he remember what happened?'

'Yes, he appears to be fully *compos mentis*. But we'll keep an eye on him anyway, just to be sure.'

'And the pneumonia – I mean, how would he have got that?'

'Similar to flu,' said the doctor.

'Could he have got it from living in a damp flat?'

The doctor shrugged and put his hands into his trouser pockets. 'Definitely,' he said, 'yeah. In extreme circumstances, when the damp's really bad, the spores from the mildew can cause all sorts of health problems.'

Betty nodded. 'Does he know I'm here?'

'Er, yeah, I think so. I think he knows there's someone here. Once he's settled on a ward, you can go and see him. We're just waiting for a bed. Shouldn't be too long.' He smiled and then turned as if to leave before turning back and saying, 'My name's Richard, by the way, and you are . . . ?'

'I'm Betty,' she said.

The doctor fixed her with a look set somewhere between delight and desire and said, 'That is a truly awesome name. Good to meet you, Betty,' before tucking his hands back into his pockets and sauntering away.

Betty blinked after him in surprise. She felt unsettled and not at all happy that John Brightly was being treated and diagnosed by a man who used the word 'awesome' and hit on his patient's friends.

The next hour ticked away slowly and incessantly. Betty fiddled with her phone and managed to work out how to send a text message. She sent it to the only other friend she knew with a mobile phone, Joe Joe.

'I'm in the hospital with John from downstairs. He knocked his head. How are you?'

A message appeared thirty seconds later. 'I am good, baby, how are u. And poor John, kiss him from me! We all miss U!!'

Betty imagined Joe Joe in his Wendy's uniform, typing to her from the staffroom with a large Pepsi in his spare hand and someone else sitting opposite him eating chips and reading the *Sun*. Another world, she thought, another life.

'Miss you too,' she replied, 'xxx.'

She found a game on her phone, Patience, which she played until the battery started flashing at her. Then she read a copy of *Take a Break* magazine, got herself a bag of crisps from a vending machine, and had a cup of tea in a polystyrene cup. Finally John appeared in the corridor, being pushed in a wheelchair, looking sheepish and shell-shocked.

'Hello, trouble,' he said croakily.

'You can talk,' she replied.

John laughed.

'My first day off this week and I've spent most of it in A&E,' she said.

'Then you're a fool,' he said.

Betty laughed then, and before she'd thought about what she was doing she'd taken his hand in hers. 'I must be,' she said. 'Felt sorry for you.'

He had a row of stitches on his temple and was attached to a drip that followed them on wheels up the corridors towards the lift.

'You look good,' she said, as the lift doors closed and they started their ascent to the ward.

'Yeah,' he said, 'I bet I do.'

'No, I mean it, you do. Compared to how you looked two hours ago.'

'When I was spread-eagled on a toilet floor, covered in blood and sweating profusely, you mean?'

'Yeah.' She squeezed his hand and smiled. 'Exactly.'

'How did you find me?' he asked.

'Toiletries man.'

'Micky.'

'If you say so.'

'Good old Micky.' The lift doors opened and the porter pushed John down another corridor.

'You know that's it now, don't you? You have to move. You cannot live in that flat for a minute longer.'

John shrugged. 'Usual issues. No time.'

'Well, then stay with me.' The words were out of her mouth before she'd even thought it through. 'I'm hardly there. You're hardly there. It's so convenient.'

'Er, Betty, you live in a studio flat.'

'Yes, I do. But I have a sofa.'

'I'm six foot two.'

'Well, then I'll call your sister, you can stay with her.'

'No way!'

'Then stay with me. My flat is small, but it is very warm. And very dry. And I can get you things, you know, glasses of water. And bowls of soup.'

'You're mad,' he said.

'Of course I am,' she said. 'But I'm also practical. And this makes total sense.' The porter stopped at the nurses' station on the ward and talked to the nurse behind the desk. Then John was taken to a bed in the corner of the ward where Betty and the porter helped him onto the bed.

'I'll think about it,' he said, patting her hand slightly patronisingly. 'But listen, for now, while I'm stuck here, I need to ask you a really big favour. Could you pack up my pitch? Micky will help. The keys to my van are in my jacket pocket.'

'Where's your jacket?'

'On my pitch. Under the table.'

'Right, and where's your van?'

'Underground car park on Brewer Street. I'm really sorry. This is all a fucking hassle.'

'No. It's fine. It's not a hassle. I can sort it all out. I've got nothing else to do. Honestly.'

John looked at her and then he patted her hand again, fondly this time.

'I could store your stuff in my place.'

'And again, I remind you, you live in a studio flat.'

'There's room,' she said. 'I can make room.'

John paused for a moment and then smiled weakly. 'Why are you being so nice?' he asked.

'Why wouldn't I?' she replied. 'I think we already ascertained that we hold each other in high regard. I'm just being a friend.'

He looked at her curiously, as if he was trying to work out a puzzle. Then he smiled again and nodded. 'That would be brilliant,' he said. 'Totally brilliant. Thank you.' He squeezed her hand and Betty felt her stomach roll over unexpectedly.

'You're welcome,' she said.

'And talking of being friends, I did something for you earlier. I went to the library. Did some research. I was going to tell you about it when you got back from work. But I decided to faint in a public toilet and split my head open instead, so –'

'What?' said Betty, excitedly. 'What did you find?'

'I found Gideon Worsley's nephew.'

'What. How?'

He shrugged. 'It was easy. I looked up Gideon in the *Encyclopaedia Britannica* and saw that he had a brother called Toby who was a major-general, brought a battalion through the Battle of the Somme, and it said that he had a son called Jeremiah. I thought, well, how many Jeremiah Worsleys could there be in the world, so I looked him up in the phonebook and there he was, running an antiques shop in World's End.'

Betty stared at him.

'The address is in my jacket pocket.'

'Under your pitch?'

'Under my pitch.'

'Have you spoken to him?'

'No. I thought I'd leave that treat for you.'

A nurse appeared inside the curtained cubicle and took John's temperature. She consulted a clipboard at the foot of his bed and smiled and said, 'Much better. It's right down to normal.'

'Go,' said John.

'What?'

'Go home. Sort my pitch. Get down to World's End. He'll be shutting up his shop soon.'

Betty looked anxiously between John and the nurse. 'Is he going to be all right,' she asked. 'I mean, if I go?'

The nurse nodded. 'He's going to be absolutely fine. Someone's bringing up the anti-bs. We'll keep him in until they've done their job, and to monitor his temperature, but then he'll be fine to go home.'

'So, what, tomorrow?'

'Yes,' said the nurse. 'Maybe. Probably.'

Betty squeezed John's hand one more time. 'You've got my mobile phone number. Call me, if you need me. But I'll be back later. At visiting hours.'

'Don't be daft.'

'I'm not being daft.' She kissed his forehead, firmly, maternally. 'I'll see you later.'

'I won't be expecting you.'

She left the cubicle then, through the curtains, and was halfway to the door when she heard the nurse say to John, 'She's very pretty, your girlfriend.' And then she heard John reply, 'She's not my girlfriend.' Betty stopped, to hear what he would say next, but he said nothing, so she carried on towards the door.

Jeremiah Worsley's antiques shop at World's End was the most enchanting shop Betty had ever set foot in. It still had its original ornate Victorian shopfront and was filled in every square foot with beautiful objects: tables made from swirling green marble and gleaming gold, oversized chandeliers, candlesticks held aloft by pewter ladies, exquisitely detailed marquetry cabinets, and immense oil paintings of bosomy gentlewomen posed with spaniels. It reminded her, almost, of Arlette's boudoir and the atmosphere was complemented by a crackling 78 playing quietly on a gramophone player, a cut-glass English voice singing a sweet song about swallows and swifts and sweethearts.

Behind a large mahogany and marble desk sat a man who looked a little like a toad, or possibly a sea lion. He was large – very large – his girth straining against a striped waistcoat, his hair a mass of oily white curls, his face a terrifying scarlet boil. He was humming gently along with the music and slowly turning the pages of a book about Edith Piaf.

He glanced up at Betty as she entered and said, 'Good afternoon' in a booming drawl that pulled out the last syllable to an almost comical extent.

She approached his desk and he eyed her again from over the top of his book. He sighed, almost imperceptibly, and laid the book down on the desktop. 'Yes, dear lady, can I help you? I'm not hiring at the moment. In fact, I'm probably going to have to sell up and then throw myself from a bridge onto a motorway, given the current economic climate. So . . .'

Betty smiled, glad that she was not about to add to his woes. 'No,' she said, 'I'm not looking for a job, I'm looking for Jeremiah Worsley.'

'You have found him.' He smiled, a touch facetiously.

'Good. Excellent. My name's Betty.'

'Oh,' he smiled, 'a Betty. I have not met a Betty in a very long time. The last Betty I knew was my char. Back in the days when I could afford a char.' He raised a bushy eyebrow. 'So, Betty, what can I do for you?'

'Well, I'm doing some detective work,' she said. 'My grandmother just passed away and she left a substantial amount of money in her will to a mysterious beneficiary.

I've got as far as working out that she was part of the jazz scene in Soho in the early twenties and that she was friends with your uncle, Gideon Worsley. In fact, he painted her.'

Suddenly Jeremiah Worsley's entire demeanour changed. He drew himself up straight in his capacious chair, pulled his slouching shoulders up to his chin, slammed his hands down upon the tabletop and shouted out, '*Arlette!*'

Betty gasped. 'Yes!' she said. 'How did you know?'

'An *educated guess*, dear girl. So, good grief, you're her granddaughter, you say?'

'I'm her step-granddaughter. But we were very close.'

'Oh my goodness, my goodness. Arlette's granddaughter! This calls for a tipple. Can I get you one?' He pulled a decanter from a drawer inside his desk and held out two tumblers.

'Yes, please.' Betty had no idea what she was about to be given, but agreed with Jeremiah that this seemed absolutely the right moment for a stiff drink. This was it, she thought, she was right on the cusp of finding Clara Pickle.

He passed her something brown and fumy and she took a sip. She suspected it might be brandy.

'Well, well,' he said, smiling broadly now, revealing brandy-ravaged teeth. 'So, tell me more. Tell me what you need to know.'

'Everything,' said Betty, her throat burning against the drink. 'I need to know everything.'

'Well, dear oh dear. All I know is family lore. All I know

is that Arlette was my uncle's muse, a lovely-looking girl, it would seem, going by his portraits of her.'

'Did you ever meet her?'

'Oh, no. Good grief, no, she was long gone before I was even born.'

'Gone where?'

'I have no idea. Wherever you found her, I presume. The story goes that my uncle Gideon fell madly in love with her, pursued her, but she was in love with another man. I think, possibly, one of the jazz musicians they were comporting with. And then all of a sudden she had a change of heart, ditched the musician and married Gideon. And then, it seemed, she simply disappeared.'

'Disappeared?'

'Yes,' he said. 'And Uncle Gideon went rather mad after this. Rather unhinged. Stopped painting. Was made to marry his cousin, rather against his will, and then topped himself the night before the wedding.'

'I thought he fell from a horse.'

'Ah, yes, well, that's what it says in the NPG. Yes, the official line. The family history, though, says that he drank himself into a stupor, took some terrible opiate and then took off over the hills without any saddlery on a horse that everyone knew was not to be trusted. Seeking oblivion. Knew that if the booze and the drugs didn't wipe him out, the mad horse would.'

'So Gideon had no children?'

'None that we know of. Although, of course, the lore could be wrong, Arlette might have fallen pregnant with his child – maybe that's why she disappeared. What was the surname of the girl named in the will?'

'Pickle.'

Jeremiah guffawed. 'No,' he said, 'really?'

'That is it. Really. Clara Pickle.'

He stopped laughing and furrowed his brow. 'Well,' he said, 'that makes no sense whatsoever. I think, in that case, the connection ends here. There is no one called Pickle in our family and I have never even heard of the name before. There is obviously another strand to this story that does not involve the Worsley family.' He sighed. 'What a terrible pity.'

'Are there any other portraits?' asked Betty. 'That you know of?'

'Of Arlette? Oh, yes,' he said, 'gosh, yes. Plenty. The estate has them.'

'The estate?'

'Yes, what was formerly our family home in Oxford-shire, and is now a tourist attraction and wedding venue. Gideon's portraits live there now. In the Gideon Worsley Room. Lots of Arlette. You should head up there, take a look.'

Betty blinked. 'Really?' she said.

'Oh, yes. About five or six, I'd say. Including quite a famous one. Here, hold on just one minute . . .' He turned in his swivel chair and hooked a large hardback book out of a shelf with a fat finger. 'Here,' he said, 'this is one of Uncle Gideon's most famous paintings.'

He opened the book up in front of him and then turned

it to face her. He tapped the picture with his finger. 'It's called *Arlette and Sandy*. Imagine that, sixty inches square.' He described a large square with his hands. 'It's utterly mesmerising.'

Betty leaned forward to look at the painting.

It was composed of Arlette, looking very young and delicate, seated on a chaise longue in a loosely buttoned chiffon blouse, leaning with her head against the shoulder of a very handsome black man. The man had a long face, large eyes, a roman nose and was wearing a white shirt under an unbuttoned waistcoat, staring lustily at the artist. It was a picture full of passion and yearning. The sitters looked as though they had just been caught in the act of undressing each other by the artist.

'Sandy,' she said, running a finger across the picture. 'Who was he?'

'No idea,' said Jeremiah. 'A jazz musician, I suppose.'

'But it looks . . .' Betty paused. 'Don't you think, it looks as if they were lovers?'

Jeremiah turned the page to face him and shrugged. 'I suppose it does, rather, but then, you know, anything went, back in the twenties. Everyone was at it.'

'But if Gideon was in love with my grandmother, and Gideon painted this, then maybe this was the chap she was in love with while he was pursuing her?'

'Yes,' Jeremiah agreed, 'it probably was.'

'Wow.' Betty stared again at the noble-looking man with the coal-black skin. And then she suddenly felt a rush of familiarity. 'You know,' she said, pulling the book back to her and staring at it more closely, 'this man, his face. I feel sure I've seen him before. He's not the same man in the National Portrait Gallery, is he?'

'No, no, that man looked entirely different, to my eye, but then, you know . . .'

He chuckled, and she glared at him before he said what she almost definitely thought he was about to say and cut in with, 'I know! I know where I recognise him from. I've got a flyer for a gig from 1920. Sandy Beach and the Love Brothers! Of course. How stupid of me. This is Sandy Beach! He was in the Southern Syncopated Orchestra!'

'The *what* orchestra?'

'World famous. Played for the King. Toast of the town.'

Jeremiah looked at her sceptically, as though she could not possibly know something about jazz that he did not already know.

'My friend's researching them for me. I'm having dinner with her tonight.' She fizzed with excitement. 'This is it. I think we're nearly there. The pieces of the puzzle are falling into place.'

'But Clara Pickle. She's still rather unaccounted for.'

Betty grimaced. 'Well, yes. But I've got a feeling she's just around the corner. I really have. In fact, I know exactly where I'm going next.' She checked the time. It was five o'clock. She just about had time to do it before she met Alexandra. But then she wouldn't have time to go back to the hospital for visiting hours. She sighed. Tomorrow morning, she thought; she could go tomorrow morning.

'Thank you,' she said, 'for your time. Do you have a

card I could take, in case I have any more questions?'

'Yes, yes, of course.' He wheezed forwards, pulled one from a small wooden box and passed it to her. 'And likewise, when you find out about the mysterious Ms Pickle, I insist you call me, or drop by, let me know. I shan't sleep otherwise.'

'I will,' she smiled. 'Definitely.'

'Lovely to meet you, Betty. Goodbye.'

He looked as if he was attempting to rise to his feet, a feat that worried Betty somewhat, so she smiled and said, 'Don't get up. I can see myself out.'

'Good,' said Jeremiah, sinking back into his Jeremiah-shaped chair and smiling with relief. 'Good.'

Jimmy's was a big scruffy basement restaurant, loud as hell, all Formica and plastic tablecloths and sweat-stained waiters running around theatrically as though they were being filmed.

Betty scanned the room for the familiar shock of Alexandra's white-blond hair and then threaded her way through the dense network of tables towards her.

'Hi!' she said.

'Oh, *great*,' said Alexandra, resting her cigarette in a glass ashtray and standing to kiss Betty on each cheek. 'You got my message. So glad.'

'Yeah, I must have just missed you. It was seven thirty.'

Alexandra picked her half-smoked cigarette out of the ashtray and inhaled on it. 'No worries,' she said. 'I'm here most nights.'

443

'You are?'

'Yeah. I'm always forgetting to eat. Suddenly it's, like, seven o'clock, my stomach is literally eating its own lining. And then I think: *kleftiko*.' She smiled and tipped some ash into the tray. 'And you know, I'd spend more in M&S buying the fucking ingredients to make a fucking kleftiko than it costs to eat one here. That someone else has made. Someone *Greek*. Who then washes up my stuff afterwards.' She smiled happily and passed Betty a menu.

Betty smiled at her. 'Do I need to ask what you'd recommend?'

Alexandra laughed and took the menu back, then she called over a waiter and ordered two kleftikos and a bottle of white.

Thirty seconds later the waiter returned with a bowl of pickled carrots and olives and big wrinkly green chillies, which they both devoured hungrily.

'So,' said Alexandra, 'how's the job going?'

Betty shrugged. 'Good,' she said. 'It's fun.'

Alexandra shuddered. 'Three under three,' she said. 'Rather you than me.'

'Yes, but they're not mine. I can give them back.'

'Oh, yes, I know all that,' she said with a dismissive flap of her hand. 'But I honestly don't even think I could do five minutes. I'd lose one. Or, Christ, accidentally kill one or something. I mean, I have no concept of safety around children.'

'One of them choked,' said Betty, 'the first time I was left with them.'

'Urgh!' Alexandra clutched her chest with a bony hand. 'My *God*, what did you do?'

'Heimlich manoeuvre.'

'What the fuck is that?' She looked appalled.

'You know, when you wrap your arms round their chest and squeeze.'

She shuddered again. 'There, you see,' she said. 'If that had been me, that child would now be *dead*. And then I would have to kill myself.' She put her hand to her throat dramatically. 'Not a child person,' she finished sagely.

She poured them each a glass of wine and drank hers thirstily. 'Mmm,' she said, her eyes rolling backwards slightly with pleasure. 'I needed that. Fucking awful day.'

Betty smiled. It seemed from her brief exposure to Alexandra Brightly that pretty much every day was *fucking awful*.

'I've just been to the hospital,' Betty said, 'to see your brother.'

'What!'

'He's got pneumonia.'

Alexandra shivered gently with distaste. 'Oh *God*, how fucking typical.'

'And mild concussion.'

Her face screwed up in horror. 'How awful. What on *fucking earth* has he been doing?'

'Well, living in a damp flat and working too hard, mainly.'

'Good God,' Alexandra said, 'this is why I don't bother with him. Why on *earth* is he still living in that ridiculous flat? London is full of flats. He's making loads of money. It's fucking crazy.' She sighed and pulled another cigarette from a packet in front of her and lit it. She inhaled crossly and then exhaled, letting her face soften. 'Is he OK?' she asked, almost reluctantly.

'He's fine,' Betty said. 'He'll be out tomorrow. And he's coming to stay with me.'

'Oh, that's nuts. He can come and stay with me. There's no reason why you should have to put up with him.'

Betty smiled, slightly embarrassed. 'Yes, I think he'd rather stay with me, closer to work, you know . . .' She drifted off, not wishing to venture any further into the murky depths of their fractious sibling dynamic. 'It's fine,' she finished. 'I don't mind at all.'

Alexandra narrowed her eyes. 'What's going on with you two?' she asked.

'Absolutely nothing,' Betty replied nonchalantly.

'Hmm, I smell more-than-just-good-friends.'

'No,' Betty said, 'definitely not. He's just . . . we are just friends, honestly. He helps me out, and I help him out.'

'*He* helps *you* out?' Alexandra asked sceptically.

'Yes,' Betty replied. 'Just today, for example, he went to the library for me and did some research.'

Alexandra snorted derisively. 'Yeah, right,' she said, 'and I'm sure that was *incredibly* useful.'

'It was!' Betty cried. 'He found Gideon Worsley's nephew. And I've just been to see him.'

'You're kidding me?'

'No. I'm not. He's called Jeremiah and he owns an antiques shop, and he told me loads of stuff about Gideon and Arlette.'

'Like what?' Alexandra looked simultaneously delighted and aghast.

'Like that they were married, that Arlette disappeared, like that Arlette was having an affair with Sandy Beach – you know, the guy on the flyer – and that she ditched him for Gideon, and that Gideon killed himself because he was so destroyed about losing Arlette.'

'Oh God, pure *gold*!' Alexandra exclaimed with her hand to her throat. 'Well done, Johnny Boy. But listen, listen.' She put down her wine glass and put on her reading glasses. 'I have also got some things to tell you.' She pulled some stuff out of a big leather bag hanging from the back of her chair and started to leaf through it. Then she paused and stared at Betty pensively. 'I hope you're ready for it,' she said gently. 'Because if it means what I think it means then it's really rather sad . . .'

49

1921

Arlette never saw the baby. It was taken away from her before she had a chance to set eyes on it. She'd been delirious at the time, full of ether and chloroform, crazy as a street lady, no idea what was happening. The only thing she knew was that her baby had come three months early and was already dead.

'What colour is it?' she asked the midwife as the baby was carried from the room, like waste product.

'Please don't talk, Mrs De La Mare,' she was told sternly.

'Is it white?' she screamed. 'Is it white?'

'Of course it's white,' the midwife snapped at her. 'What other colour could you possibly expect it to be? A tiny white boy. Poor wee soul.'

She strode from the room and Arlette was left alone, her body aching and empty.

A tiny white boy.

Thank God for that.

Thank God for that.

For months she had feared her instincts wrong. A tiny, gritty part of her, quietly questioning the evidence. *Maybe it was Godfrey's*.

But no. The baby had not been Godfrey's. It had been Gideon's. She had not gone through these past four months of wretchedness for nothing.

She put her trembling hands to her belly. It was still full and firm. A cruel illusion. No baby. Just an empty sack. She had known, she had known for days. Where once there had been the soothing, fascinating tumble and kick of a being inside her, suddenly there had been nothing, just a desolate stillness. And then when the pain had begun, she'd known. Known that she would be pushing out of her a baby that she would never hold in her arms.

A tiny white boy.

Francis Worsley. That was to be his name.

She sat up and felt the room spin in circles around her head. The door opened and a man stood in the doorway, a tall handsome man. Her husband. Her rapist. He was crying.

'There,' she said coldly. 'There. It is over. We can end this farce. The marriage will be annulled.'

'Our baby,' he sobbed. Mucus bubbled from his nose.

'I know,' she said. 'It was never meant to be. It was your punishment,' she continued, 'for what you did to me.'

He stared at her desperately, his fist half-stuffed into his mouth to hold back the tears. 'You callous *whore*,' he sobbed. 'You dirty, callous *whore*.'

She stared at him. 'You made a whore out of me, Gideon. All of this is your fault. Every last bit of it.'

'I cannot believe I ever loved you. I had no idea your heart was made of lead.'

She turned and faced the wall, her back to him, her hands tucked beneath her cheek. 'Please go, Gideon,' she said. 'When the midwife says I am fit to be up, I will pack my things and return to the Millers.'

She heard him in the doorway, the damp, ugly noises of misery, his fist beating the wall twice, and then the sound of his leather soles turning on the floorboards and the door slamming closed behind him.

She breathed in hard, sucking down her own desperate sobs.

Her baby was dead.

But her future was reborn.

Most of the orchestra was based in London now – the tour suspended temporarily because their manager had been declared bankrupt and his case was going through the courts – picking up cheques and handfuls of notes here and there, performing in smaller groups around the Soho clubs.

Arlette had kept up with Godfrey's comings and goings through Minu, who still frequented the clubs and parties. It had been painful to be reminded that beyond the walls of her strange Chelsea prison, beyond her empty, loveless marriage with Gideon, life was still continuing in all its silly, glittering, light-hearted glory. Godfrey was still living in his rooms in south London and playing with the Love Brothers, a regular nightly slot at the Blue Butterfly on Coventry Street.

And it was there, exactly four weeks after the stillbirth

of her son, that Arlette went to see what could be salvaged from the pitiful remains of their love affair.

She and Minu sat side by side in a booth, drinking pink gins, gossiping frantically and pretending that the previous six months had been merely a blink of the eye. Minu still did not know the truth about the baby, about its conception. When she had returned that night from the party at the Millers', Arlette had brushed away her concerns, told her that she had been violently sick, too much to drink, maybe, or something she'd eaten. She did wonder if Minu had worked it out for herself, as she'd never questioned the fact of Arlette jumping so quickly and unexpectedly from a torrid love affair with Godfrey into marriage and parenthood with Gideon. But if she suspected anything she said nothing, merely went along with Arlette's charade of being two carefree young gals out on the town.

'My new roommate is not a patch on you, Arlette,' she said reassuringly. 'She is so deadly dull, you know. She attends the Sunday service at St George's and says grace before even so much as a sip of water. I can't think why I ever thought to let her have the room. I was swayed by her looks. So awfully pretty. I thought that a pretty girl would by definition be a jolly girl. I was wrong . . .'

She laughed, and Arlette laughed, and then glanced over Minu's shoulder at the stage where the previous band were taking their leave, bowing and smiling at the applauding audience. She breathed in deeply. Soon, she thought, any moment, Godfrey would be there. Her Godfrey. The only man she'd ever loved. Minu glanced at her and squeezed her hand. Arlette smiled back. One day Arlette would tell Minu everything. But not now. Not yet.

A smiling man took to the stage then, his hands clasped together, his hair slicked back with pomade, a daffodil pinned to his lapel, and said, in a faux American accent: 'Ladies and gentleman, sirs, lords, dukes and duchesses, kings and queens, it is my pleasure to introduce to you, our very own special guests, three of the most celebrated performers from the world-renowned Southern Syncopated Orchestra, and all the way from the sun-kissed isles of the Caribbean, please put your hands together, for Sandy Beach and his infectious Love Brothers.'

Arlette did indeed put her hands together, and she clapped until they rang with pain. The spotlights swung up and the curtains were parted and there he was. Handsome and bright-eyed, his clarinet clutched between his long fingers, in a royal-blue suit and a matching mohair fedora, his foot tapping along in rhythm with the opening bars.

Arlette caught her breath and stared.

She stared and she stared, drinking in every detail of him, knowing he would be unable to see her with all those lights in his eyes, knowing that after tonight she might never see him again.

'He looks well,' Minu whispered loudly in her ear.

'Yes,' agreed Arlette. 'He does.'

After the performance, she and Minu made their way

to the backstage, a place Arlette was by now intimately familiar with. She'd stood in a dozen different backstage areas a hundred times; she knew the smells, the noises, the protocols.

And then, even before she saw him, she smelled him: vanilla and sandalwood, the scent she'd helped him choose in Liberty almost a year ago. She turned and there he was, jacketless, his shirt stuck to his body with sweat, a towel in one hand, a cold beer in the other, a smile from some other just-finished conversation still playing on his lips.

'Oh, my dear sweet goodness,' he drawled, the smile freezing in place.

'Hello,' she said.

He looked behind himself and to the left and right as though the reason for Arlette's presence might somehow make itself known in physical form.

'Well, gosh, hello!'

'You were wonderful tonight,' she continued brightly. 'Truly amazing.'

'Why, thank you, Miss De La Mare. Or should I say, Mrs . . .?'

'No, I am Miss. Still.'

'And you came . . .' he looked again from left to right '. . . alone?'

She nodded. 'Gideon and I are no longer together. I lost the baby. The marriage is to be annulled.'

Godfrey's eyebrows jumped up towards his hairline. 'My goodness, my goodness.' He rubbed his chin and stared at the ground. 'Well, well, what an unexpected turn of events. And of course, I hope it goes without saying that I am truly, *truly* sorry for your loss.'

'Thank you, Godfrey. But it was for the best.'

He glanced at her uncertainly, taken aback by her words.

'The marriage was never consummated, Godfrey,' she whispered meaningfully.

He stared at her again in surprise. 'But . . . ?'

'It was *never* consummated. The baby,' she lowered her voice further, 'it was Gideon's fault. He took advantage of me . . .'

She cleared her throat and flushed red. It was the first time she had told anyone and the words burned like hot coals as they left her mouth.

Godfrey blinked and shook his head, as though mistaken in what he had heard her say. 'You mean, he . . .?'

'Yes,' she whispered. 'At my birthday party.'

His face clouded over then, with anger. 'He . . . he . . .' He turned this way and that, trying to find a place for himself. 'Jesus *Christ*, Arlette, why didn't you tell me?'

'Because it was all such a horrible, terrible mess and I wanted everything to be as simple as possible. Because it was the right thing to do.'

'How could that have been the right thing to do? We were in *love*, Arlette. We were going to be together. If you'd told me, I could have –'

'What, Godfrey? What could you have done? There is nothing you could have done. Hit him? Beaten him to a

454

bloody mess? Then what? I would have had a bleeding husband and I would still have been pregnant. And you might have ended up in gaol.'

'I would not have hit him, Arlette. I have never hit another person in my life. I would have . . .' He ground his hands together as he tried to find inside himself a solution to a problem that had passed. 'I would have just wanted to know. So that I could have held you and taken care of you. So that I might not have spent the past six months in a state of terrible indescribable pain, feeling like a stake had been passed through my heart and left there.'

Arlette took his hands in hers and said, 'It is done now. It is finished. We can go now and dance. Would you like that? To go dancing?'

He lifted his gaze from the floor and towards her. 'Yes,' he said. 'I would very much like to go dancing. Thank you.'

They danced until three in the morning. It was the first time Arlette had danced since her birthday party in September. She felt young and light upon her feet, and for moments at a time it was really possible to believe that the past six months had never happened, that her life had continued as it had been destined to before Godfrey had gone away to Manchester and left her in the untrust-worthy hands of Gideon. But she wanted more from tonight than to dance and to laugh; she had a deep, smouldering need within her to cover over the past with a new layer, to paste over the foulness of what Gideon had done to her with the goodness of what Godfrey could do for her. She wanted to go to bed with him. Desperately. And so when he offered to see her home to the Millers' she said, very firmly, 'No. I would like to go home with you.'

He looked at her curiously. 'I am not really supposed to have lady friends to stay,' he said, in a tone of voice that suggested he might be prepared to risk the wrath of his landlady on this occasion.

'I know,' said Arlette. 'And I have no intention of *staying*, Godfrey. I should merely visit. Very briefly.'

Godfrey smiled at her. 'Not too briefly, I hope?'

'Let us not discuss it for another moment. I honestly feel there is nothing to lose. Nothing whatsoever.'

Godfrey said, 'I could not agree more. Shall we?' He offered her the crook of his elbow and they walked together from the club and into a carriage headed for the murky unknown depths of a place called New Cross.

The sun rose at six a.m. and Arlette saw clearly for the first time the dank starkness of Godfrey's lodgings. They were squeezed, at very close quarters, upon a collapsible bed with a very thin mattress. The room was in fact only half a room, carved in two from a bigger room by a thin wall papered over with a print of damp roses. Godfrey had a sink, through which ran a long crack such that it looked as if it might fall apart at the merest touch. His clothes hung from a coat stand in the middle of the room – 'to keep them as far away as possible from the mould on the walls,' he'd explained. A small window hung with dirty lace looked out over a builder's yard and cold air blew in through a missing pane. As she awoke she felt a vague horror at her surroundings, uncomfortable after a night on the loose springs of the cheap bed, and cold in spite of the proximity of Godfrey on the bed next to her. The room smelled of stale cooking: mushy vegetables and boiled bones. She brought herself closer to Godfrey's body, the only savoury thing in the room, and he tucked his head neatly into the crook of her neck.

The room was ugly and it smelled, but in the years and the decades to come, when she looked back on this watery early April morning in a New Cross backstreet in 1921, Arlette would be filled with deep nostalgic yearning. In her mind, Godfrey's charmless room would take on the air of a magical fairy-tale setting, an enchanted room with real roses climbing up the walls and swallows pirouetting outside the window. Because unknown to her, this would be the last time she would feel Godfrey's body against hers, the last time she would feel his breath in the crook of her neck, his fingers curled round hers, and the last time in her whole life that she would experience real happiness.

She wished she'd known it at the time, wished she'd thought less of the smell of boiled bones and more of the feeling of his satin skin. She wished she had not rushed away so soon, had not been so concerned with the prospect of discovery by a red-faced landlady. And she wished she had said more to him, more than the rushed words of someone who thinks they have all the time in the world. She had not known at that precise moment that she was not living in her happy ever after, that her happy ever after was not going to materialise, that something had gone wrong during the editing process of the screenplay of her life. That while she made her rushed goodbyes, her unnecessary escape to the warmth and comfort of Leticia Miller's house, other things were shifting around, little tiny imperceptible happenings that, during the course of the day to come, were going to hammer the path of her life completely out of shape.

A confused and gin-sodden Leticia was crouching in the front garden of her beautiful stucco house in Holland Park, her youngest son in her arms, her daughter by her side holding the cat, watching it burn slowly, but purposefully to the ground. A dozen firefighters were trying their best to dampen the flames, but already the bones and cavities of the house were clear to see; already it was obvious the house was dead.

'It's *all my fault*!' Leticia was wailing. 'All my fault!'

Lilian merely scowled at her and rubbed the cat's head.

'What happened?' asked Arlette, running from the hackney carriage.

'A burning cigarette. It fell from my fingers onto my discarded clothes. I believe, also, an upended bottle of something flammable may have played a part . . .' She said all of this in a high-pitched voice, tremulous and wistful, as though recounting a lovely dream. She smiled and held her boy closer to her.

'Mother was *drunk*. Out for the count. While her

children slept. The maid sounded the alarm. Thank *God* there was one responsible adult in the house otherwise who knows what might have become of all of us?'

The maid stood to their left, wrapped in a blanket, drinking something warm from a hip flask. The last of the night darkness had left the sky now and the scene was bathed in the stark light of day.

Lilian said, 'I'm going back to Philip's house.' She looked at Arlette. 'Will you come with me?'

Arlette looked from the house to Leticia and then to Lilian. Philip's house next door looked warm and welcoming. 'Yes,' she said, 'if you think they won't mind?'

'Of course they won't. They're the very definition of hospitable. Mother, you should come too, let James get warm, get something to eat.'

'No,' said her mother numbly. 'No, you take James. I'll stay here. Until it's done. I can't go until it's done.'

So Arlette, Lilian, James and the cat headed next door where Philip's parents made sure they were given bowls of steaming porridge and strong cups of coffee, and offered them beds for the nights to come.

'That is so, so kind of you, thank you so much. And, of course, Father has been telegraphed. He'll be home soon, I'm sure. He'll make arrangements for us all. This will be only for a night or two.'

'As long as it needs,' Philip's mother said. 'As long as it takes.' And then she looked at Arlette and said, 'And you, Miss . . .?'

'Miss De La Mare.'

'Yes, of course, Miss De La Mare, you are welcome to stay, too, of course.'

Arlette smiled blankly. The offer was sincerely voiced, but Arlette felt a void behind it, something empty and non-existent. She would stay tonight, quite happily in this warm and welcoming house of strangers, she would stay quite happily the night after, and the night after that. But then what? Mr Miller would return, he would probably move the family into a suite at a smart hotel, or possibly take a short lease on an apartment for them all. Again, Arlette felt sure that she would be welcome, that space would be found for her, but again, there was a darkness behind the fact. Because she was twenty-two years old, she had shared rooms with a girlfriend that she had paid for with her own earned money, she had run a department in a famous London store, she had been married, she had lived in her own home, she had taken a baby to six months' gestation and delivered it dead, she had annulled a marriage and spent the night with her charismatic lover in a boarding house in New Cross, and the days of living off the generosity of her mother's friends seemed no longer to be quite appropriate. She was no longer 'spending some time in London', she was living here, and it was time, she suddenly believed, to put down roots, to stop being a transient, a guest. It was time to start her life properly.

'Thank you,' she said fulsomely. 'Thank you so much. That would be most kind.'

But already she was making plans for the next phase.

Already she was dreaming of the register office wedding, a just-so little blue dress, a small bouquet of gerbera daisies and sandalwood blossom, a raucous party at the Blue Butterfly or the Cygnet, maybe fancy dress, certainly an open invitation to the whole orchestra and all of her friends. She thought of the little house that she and Godfrey could share, maybe on a neat terrace somewhere in south London; she would not mind, some bits of south London were rather nice, or so she'd been told. She thought of a small cosy kitchen and a cat or two. She thought of friendly neighbours, curious about the unusual couple next door, him black, her white, both so pleasant, both so smart. She thought about parties and tours, she thought even about taking Godfrey to Guernsey, where she would march him into her mother's house with pride, pretend that her face wasn't really contorted with not knowing what to say. She thought about babies and she thought about a long cruise to the Caribbean, to visit his mother, with a pair of adorable coffee-skinned tots by their side. She saw it all, clearer than she'd ever seen anything in her life.

She saw her future.

50

1995

Betty awoke the following morning at six thirty, in spite of having turned her alarm clock off the night before in preparation for her first lie-in in nearly a week. For a moment she forgot that she wasn't going to work and almost leaped out of bed. But then she remembered. Amy and the kids were in the Cotswolds. She was free until six o'clock. And then she remembered something else. What Alexandra had told her the night before. About a man called Sandy Beach. Or Godfrey Pickle.

Yes. He had existed. Whoever he was and whatever his role in Arlette's history. He had existed. And he had somehow, although there was no record of it, passed on his colourful name to a woman called Clara. Who may or may not have been Arlette's child. But had, in some mysterious way, been significant enough to her to warrant a sizeable chunk of her inheritance.

The facts and the stories: Gideon Worsley, Godfrey Pickle, the portraits and the houses on Abingdon Villas and Chelsea Embankment, the photos, the programmes, the book inscribed to 'Pickle' – she had it all now, more information than Peter Lawler had ever had at his disposal. But it felt like it had all landed on her lap in the wrong order, like a ripped-up letter that she needed to spread out flat on the floor and find a way to fit together.

She tried to make herself go back to sleep, but it was no use, her mind swirled and spun, laying out the facts this way and that, till she felt almost dizzy with it and jumped out of bed, poker straight and ready to start the day. There was one last thing she hadn't investigated: the address in St Anne's Court, the last known address of Clara Pickle. Arlette had already tried, and so had Peter Lawler. But there had to be another way in, another little clue in there somewhere, to open up the picture. She dressed and left the house.

The building was scruffy art deco. It would have been brand new when Arlette lived in London. Now its white walls were streaked green with mildew and the windows were thick with grime. But regardless of its appearance, the important thing about the building was that it faced directly opposite the address mentioned in Arlette's will and that it appeared, from street level, to be entirely residential.

Betty appraised the building. It was nine thirty, early for a Soho Saturday, but she didn't have time for polite consideration. She had no idea when she would next get a morning off work. She strode towards the entrance of the building, which was slightly recessed from the street, and before she lost her nerve she pulled back her shoulders and pushed the buzzer for apartment number one. A male voice answered, with a bright and robust, 'Good morning!' and she breathed a sigh of relief.

'Good morning,' she shouted into the intercom. 'I'm trying to trace someone for an inheritance and I'm looking for someone who might have lived in this block for a very long time.'

There was a pause and a crackle, and then the jolly-sounding man sighed and said, sounding almost disappointed not to be able to help, 'I've been here for six months.'

'Oh,' she said, 'never mind. Do you happen to know if anyone else in this building has been here longer?'

'Nobody in this building talks to anyone else,' he hissed, camply. 'Stuck-up Londoners.' She noticed then that his accent was northern. 'But there is a very *very* old lady up on the top floor. Smells of wee. She might do you.'

Betty wrinkled her nose. 'Oh,' she said. 'What flat number is she?'

'No idea, love, but if I buzz you in, you could go up and knock on some doors.'

Betty paused. The building was dank and depressing and she didn't really love the idea of an old lady who smelled of wee. But this was as close as she was going to get to some answers, so she said, 'Yes, great, that would be brilliant.' And heaved the door open when he buzzed it.

The interior of the small block was every bit as unappealing as the exterior, and she picked her way up the concrete stairs gingerly. There were only two doors at the top floor, one was painted pink and decorated with plastic flowers and garden gnomes. The other was painted dark blue and had a threadbare welcome mat outside. She looked between the two doors, trying to guess which one might belong to the incredibly old lady, and decided on the blue one, knocking on it gently with her knuckles.

She heard noises behind her door, shuffling and scuffling, muttering and moaning and she held in her breath, suddenly nervous about the imminent encounter. Then she heard catches and locks being pulled across the door before it opened against a chain and she saw a very tiny woman with dyed black hair and heavily pencilled-in eyebrows staring up at her. 'Wrong house,' she whispered. 'You have the *wrong house*.'

Her voice was strongly accented – Russian possibly, or Polish. She went to close the door again but Betty put her hand against it. 'How long have you lived here?' she asked urgently.

'*Wrong house*!' she shouted out again.

'Please!' called Betty. 'I'm trying to trace someone who used to live over the road, for an inheritance.'

'What!' the lady stopped pushing against the door and cupped a hand to her ear. Her fingernails were very long and painted burgundy.

'I'm trying to find someone. For an inheritance,' Betty repeated, enunciating each word precisely.

'No,' said the woman, 'I am not the right person. I do not have any inheritance.'

She went to close the door again and again Betty held it open. 'I just need to talk to someone who's lived here for a long time. Please. Can I just ask you a question or two?'

The woman narrowed her eyes at Betty. 'What is your name?'

'Betty Dean.'

The woman smiled, revealing just three teeth. Betty took in the cavernous, rotten maw with silent horror.

'Pretty girl,' the woman said, peering at her. 'Very pretty girl. Are you on the game?'

'No!'

'Drugs?'

'No! I'm a nanny!'

The woman narrowed her eyes again and finally pulled open the door. Betty's eyes widened at the full sight of her. No more than four foot ten, so thin that every bone in her body was visible through her clothes, she wore a tracksuit made of cream velour with a garish diamanté pattern picked out on the sleeves, and a series of huge medallions around her neck that were so heavy they caused her to stoop. The tracksuit was encrusted in places with old food and other substances which Betty didn't care to ponder on for too long, and she did, indeed, smell very strongly of wee. Her alarmingly dark hair was piled on her head in an unsavoury bird's nest with three inches of snow-white roots.

Betty stayed where she was, feeling quite strongly that she did not want to enter the lady's flat, and instead she smiled encouragingly and said, 'What year did you move in here?'

The lady winced, as though the consideration of such a

fact was physically painful in some way. 'I have been here since 1943. I came during the war. With my baby.'

Betty nodded, silently acknowledging the likelihood of a terrible story behind her words.

'I am seventy-seven years old. Although I look much older.'

Betty shook her head. 'No, you don't, you –'

'I look a hundred. I feel a hundred. I want to die.'

Betty looked at her in alarm.

'Don't be worried about this. It is normal. One day you will be old like me and you will not be pretty any more, and your child will be dead and your husband will be dead and your lover will be dead and you will live alone in this terrible place and you will also want to be dead. *Believe me!*'

Betty jumped slightly and then smiled sympathetically, a slightly inconsequential reaction to her words, but all that she could come up with.

'When you came to live here,' she asked, 'do you remember at all who lived across the road, in those flats above the Mexican restaurant?'

'Mexican restaurant? What Mexican restaurant?'

Betty pointed through the small window on the landing towards the street. 'Down there,' she said.

'Ach,' said the woman, 'the last time I went out there, it was a French restaurant. Everything changes. All the time.'

'And the flats,' Betty steered the conversation back to saliency. 'Do you remember who lived there, before they turned them into offices?'

The woman put her door onto the latch and shuffled towards the window. Betty drew in her breath against her sour aroma. 'Yes,' she said, 'I remember.'

Betty's heart began to race. 'You do?'

'Yes. How could I forget? It was a home,' she said, 'for unwed mothers. Mainly call girls and foreigners. Run by the Church.'

'The Church?'

'Yes. St Anne's. Do-gooders. No place for children, I would have thought. But there were still children in that place up until a few years back. You could hear those babies screaming. One stopped, another started. That one stopped, another one started. All through the night. And then one day,' she turned and smiled again, 'all the babies left, they boarded it up and so it was until they turned it into offices.' She turned back to the window. 'And then, of course, I missed the babies.'

'How long do you think it had been a home, when you moved here?'

The woman shrugged, her tiny bones of shoulders jutting almost out of their sockets. 'I do not know,' she snapped. 'Ask the Church! Ask the do-gooders!' She relaxed her shoulders again and sighed. 'So,' she asked, 'who is it? Who is this lucky person who is going to get your inheritance?'

'I don't know,' said Betty. 'But I think it might be one of those screaming babies across the road. Someone called Clara Pickle. Or Clara Jones.'

'What was her date of birth?'

'We don't know.'

The old lady shrugged. 'Well, then, how are you going to find her?'

Betty stared through the window at the smart offices where Clara Pickle might have started her mysterious life and sighed. 'I don't know,' she said.

'That is a lot of not knowing.' The woman looked at her sceptically. 'Go and talk to the Church.' She tapped her veined temple with one gnarled old finger. 'Get yourself some *knowledge*.'

Betty breathed in huge gulps of fresh air when she left the building a moment later. She tried not to think too much about the lady, whose name she had never asked, tried not to think about her dark, day-to-day life or who cared for her, or how it might be to be so old and care so little for life itself. Instead she headed straight for St Anne's Church on Wardour Street, hoping desperately that her run of good luck was not about to run out.

The church looked odd perched between the bars and restaurants, the gaming lounges and betting shops, as if it had been left there accidentally. A plaque commemorated its reopening by Princess Anne after it had been blown apart in the Second World War. And on this sunny Saturday morning in June, the church and its community centre were buzzing with people and activity in a very encouraging manner.

Betty found the vicar talking with a grimy, tearful man

of the street, who kept sniffing very loudly and wiping his streaming nose against the sleeve of his tattered jacket. She sat and waited patiently for a few minutes until finally the homeless man smiled widely, hugged the vicar to him, picked up a filthy rucksack, nodded at Betty and left the building.

'Good morning,' the vicar boomed, in a soft Scottish accent. 'Are you looking for me?'

Betty nodded and got to her feet. 'Yes,' she said, 'do you have a moment or two to spare?'

'I have many moments to spare. Today is my official day of spare moments.' He beamed.

Betty smiled back and said, 'Do you know anything about a home for unwed mothers that your Church used to run, in St Anne's Court?'

He smiled and held an arm out towards her. 'This sounds like a moment for spending in my office,' he said. 'Do come with me.'

She followed him into a smart office, across a courtyard, located slightly away from the church itself.

'Now,' he said, holding the door open for her, 'we've only been on these premises for a few years but I'm pretty certain that everything came with us. For a long time there was no church here to speak of, just a wreck, so all the paperwork was kept together by necessity. And I do vaguely recall something about the home for unwed mothers. Sit.' He waved at a green chair. 'Tea?'

'Yes, thank you.'

He called through his door to someone in an adjoining

room for two mugs of tea and then turned back to Betty.

'So, tell me what you need to know.'

'I'm looking for a beneficiary. For my grandmother's will. She's called Clara Pickle. And she lived at the address of the home at some point. And that is all I know.'

'Right, so, no date of birth?'

'No date of birth. But I think she might have been mixed race. And her mother's name might have been Arlette. Or might not have been Arlette. And if it wasn't Arlette, then I have no idea what it might have been.'

'And her father?'

Betty blinked. And then she gulped. 'Yes,' she said, 'the father. I can tell you all about the father. His name was Godfrey Pickle. He was a really famous musician.'

The vicar pulled out a large box folder and said, 'Right, let's start at the beginning: 1920. That's when the home was opened. Let's start there and see where we end up. I'll call out names, you tell me to stop if you hear anything interesting.'

It took only about five minutes for the vicar to get to the name Esther Jones.

'Jones!' said Betty. 'That was the other name on the will, Clara Jones! Does it say what her baby's name was?'

He peered at the piece of paper and sighed. 'Let me see, hmm, hmm, yes, here it is. Esther Jones was signed into the home on the twenty-second of October 1921. And she gave birth in November 1921. To, yes, a baby girl. Called Clara Tatiana. She weighed seven pounds and fifteen ounces. Mother and baby both well, it says here.'

Betty felt tingles racing up and down her spine.

'And . . . well, it says here that they moved out in January 1922, and that, oh, this is interesting, it gives the name of the father here. And it's not your Mr Pickle. No, it says here the baby's father was called Edward Minchin. Yes. Edward John Minchin. Of 24 Rippon Road, London SE.'

'But,' Betty furrowed her brow, 'that makes no sense. Why would my grandmother have left all her money to a girl born to two people I've never heard of?'

The vicar shrugged. 'I have no idea,' he said. 'But although you've never heard of them, your grandmother clearly had. And now you have the girl's real name . . .'

She looked at him quizzically.

'Yes. You've been looking for a Clara Pickle or a Clara Jones. But she was neither of those, was she? She would have been a Clara Minchin. Clara Minchin of Rippon Road.' He leaned back into his chair and eyed her conclusively. 'I think your search might almost be over.'

51

1921

Arlette pulled open the box.

Leticia watched her sadly, with her hands knitted together.

'I think your room came out of it quite well,' she said softly. 'Obviously, I don't know exactly what you had in there, but it does seem there was very little damage. Your wardrobe stood untouched, and luckily the door was closed so there may be a slight whiff of smoke, but . . .' She fluttered her fingers together, nervously. 'Oh, I do hope you're not too disappointed.'

Leticia had done nothing but apologise for the past three days. She had vowed never to drink another drop of alcohol. And her husband had vowed never to leave her again. Lilian had vowed to relax now that someone was taking responsibility for her mother, and Philip had vowed to take Lilian to stay in his family's beach-front apartment in Cannes for the whole summer. In many ways the fire had been a blessing. In other ways it had been a tragedy. Family heirlooms turned to ash. Much-loved dresses smoke-damaged beyond repair. All of James's toys burned to nothing. Photographs gone for ever. And also, intangibly, but overwhelmingly, a loss of the sense of gay innocence that had sat over the house and its inhabitants since the very first moment Arlette had set foot there nineteen months earlier. She'd thought it a magical, enchanted place, and now it was a black carcass, and the family who once lived there all robbed of their sense of entitlement and certainty. Now, for a while at least, it was as though they were no different from anyone else.

She reached her hands into the box and pulled out her dressing table set, her hair decorations, a box of jewels, framed photographs of her mother, her father in his uniform, a photo album, bundles of Godfrey's postcards, some delicate underwear, silk stockings, flyers from nights out at clubs, an old cigar box filled with photographs, all in a good state. She pulled out a tapestry she'd been working on, a half-knitted hat, a dozen or so paperback novels and there, right at the bottom, she pulled out a small scrap of muslin. She stared at it for a moment. It had been in the drawer of her bed-stand, where it had lain since she'd first put it there, the day she'd brought it home from Liberty's perfumery. Another world. Another life. She brought it to her nose and inhaled. It smelled, mainly, of smoke, but beneath the nutty smoke, it still lingered: vanilla and sandalwood. The smell of Godfrey.

'Well,' said Leticia, 'are you happy? Has it mainly been saved?'

'Yes,' said Arlette. 'Yes. It's all here. Everything important. Thank you.'

Leticia sat down heavily and brought her hand to her

clavicle. 'Oh thank goodness. Thank *goodness*. Finally, some good news. Finally . . .'

Arlette had not seen Godfrey for three days. There had been so much to sort out here, with the Millers. She had not felt able to swan off and leave them to it. But tomorrow they would be moving into a suite of rooms attached to Mr Miller's London office and a firm of builders had been commissioned to start rebuilding the house. Now she felt it would be perfectly acceptable to move on with her life. And so she prettied herself at the mirror of the room she was sharing with Lilian at the neighbours' house, changed into a fresh dress and headed for Bloomsbury, to Minu's rooms.

'I saw Gideon last night,' said Minu, her hand holding her hair up on top of her head while she fixed it in place with grips.

Arlette blanched at the mention of his name.

'He looked terrible,' Minu continued.

'I can't say that I am terribly unhappy to hear that.'

Minu glanced at her. 'I wish I could understand,' she said. 'You two were once the closest of friends. So easy together. It doesn't make any sense to me that you are now so indisposed towards each other. I feel as if a large chapter of the book is missing.'

She kept her gaze on Arlette for a second or two, inviting her to confide, but Arlette merely smiled and said, 'Love follows no rule book. And what of you? Still no dream of a man waiting in the wings to whisk you away?'

Minu laughed wryly. 'I am afraid not. No. But it serves me well to be a spinster, since my novel is all about a beautiful but lonely girl, looking for love in the city.' She smiled and adjusted her hair. 'There,' she said, 'now I look divine. And so do you. Let's go and find this lovely man of yours and tell him to marry you.'

They arrived at the Blue Butterfly half an hour later to find someone's birthday party in full swing. Judging by the number of diarists in the room and the air of barely contained anticipation, it was clearly the birthday party of someone terribly important. Arlette and Minu leaned conspiratorially towards the receptionist and said, 'Whose birthday, tell tell!'

'Oh, now, girls, I couldn't possibly say.'

'Of course you can!' they teased. 'Tell us immediately!'

'It's Bertie Langhorn.'

'Oh my goodness!' they both cried. 'And he, just this minute, parted from his lovely wife.'

Arlette smiled at Minu and Minu smiled at her. Bertie Langhorn was a famous actor, very pretty, very rich and recently separated from his childhood sweetheart. Minu had had a terrible crush on him for months. Suddenly the night opened up before them serendipitously, ripe with potential for drama and fun. They took each other by the hand and headed into the club, eyes bright as diamonds, hearts full of mischief, neither of them suspecting for a moment what an unhappy turn the night would take by its closing moments.

*

There was a girl backstage whom Arlette had never seen before. At first she thought she might be a cleaner, or a stagehand. But then she saw her coat draped over her arm and her hat held in her other hand, and by the way she was scanning the room, it was clear she had just arrived from the street and was looking for someone.

Arlette paid her no more attention for a moment or two until she heard her asking a passing man if Sandy Beach was available.

'Just finished the encore, love,' said the man. 'He'll be out in a shake or two.'

'Oh, thank you.'

Arlette stared at the girl. She was young, about the same age as Arlette, possibly younger. She had dark blond hair cut into a bob and was dressed simply in a grey tunic dress and flat shoes. Her face was drawn, her eyes were slightly red. She looked as if she had spent a night crying instead of sleeping. Arlette felt a bubble of something odd and sour rise through her. The girl passed her coat awkwardly from arm to arm. She cleared her throat and peered anxiously towards the aisle that led from the stage to the backstage. She cleared her throat again and then Arlette saw her pass her hand gently around her stomach, first a circular motion, then a cupping motion. The gesture was so fleeting and minute that she almost missed it, but the meaning of it hit Arlette fully in the gullet.

Subconsciously she took a few steps back, so that she was standing in shadow. She heard the final cheers from the raucous, champagne-sodden crowds, then she heard the sound of sprightly, triumphant footsteps as the musicians left the stage. She pushed herself deeper into the dark corner and held her hand to her throat as she watched the next few moments unfold.

'Esther! Hello! What a pleasant surprise!' said Godfrey, looking torn between being pleasantly surprised and utterly horrified, his words sounding overly bright.

'I couldn't do it!' she heard the girl called Esther hiss. 'Here,' she delved into her bag clumsily and pulled out a handful of crumpled paper notes. 'Here's the money. Every last penny of it. But I couldn't do it, Sandy. I just couldn't.'

She started to cry and Godfrey pulled her gently into a quieter corner.

'Ssh, ssh,' he whispered gently into her ear. He pulled her close to him and held her tenderly inside his embrace. The gesture was sweet, but Arlette could see fear etched onto his face as he stared over her shoulder at some point of neutrality.

Arlette pulled in her breath and held it there.

'Tell me what happened?' he said to her. 'Was it the doctor? Did you not like him?'

Esther shook her head crossly. 'No! It wasn't the doctor. He was lovely. It was just . . . *the baby*. The baby, Sandy. Doctor said I'm seven weeks in, maybe longer. But I mean, *look*, Sandy . . .' She pulled down at the fabric of her loose-fitting dress to reveal a slight curve. 'I'm showing. Already. I reckon I'm further along than that. I just couldn't, Sandy, I just couldn't. I'm so sorry! So, so sorry!'

Godfrey stroked her hair and shushed in her ear and Arlette didn't wait to hear another word.

The future wrote itself out in bold capitals across her consciousness. That girl was carrying Godfrey's child. Godfrey would stand by her. Probably even marry her. But even if he didn't, that girl's child, unlike her own blighted foetus, would be born breathing and kicking and ready to live a long and full life. That girl's child would spend its whole life being Godfrey's son or daughter, regardless of what happened to its parents. And the life that Arlette had persuaded herself she wanted – the little house in south London, the friendly neighbours, the trip to the Caribbean with the two adorable piccaninnies in tow – all of it turned to ash in her heart, like the contents of the Millers' house.

She stumbled from the back doors of the club onto a cool, shadowy mews, where her dainty heels scrambled and spluttered against the cobbles. She pulled them off and held them in her hands and she ran then, in stockinged feet, down the mews, around the corner onto Piccadilly and into a waiting taxi.

She watched the streets of London through tear-streaked eyes, the golden pinkness of the gaslamps, the glittering façades of nightclubs and bars, the people, so extraordinary in either their finery or their rags, the wide pavements and the shops full of things that nobody really needed.

Everything was bright and clean, nearly every front door and shopfront repainted after the war, every light bulb replaced, every paving stone scrubbed white. London was gleaming but Arlette's heart was dirty.

She thought of her twenty-second birthday, of Gideon's terrible betrayal and the grey months that had ensued in that house on the river. She thought of her baby, taken away to an incinerator before she'd even seen his face. She thought of the Millers' house, so perfect, like a picture-postcard dream of a London villa, burned down to a dirty carcass. And then she thought of that girl, just now, with her bitten fingernails and her swollen stomach and Godfrey's expression of mute terror.

Too much, she thought to herself, too much.

It was over.

Back at Philip's house on Abingdon Villas, Arlette sealed down the lid of the box Leticia had given her that morning and she put it in a trunk. She laid out an outfit suitable for travelling and she wrote three notes: one for Lilian, one for Minu, one for Godfrey. The following morning, while the house still slept, she put on the travelling clothes, she called the houseboy and asked him to call her a carriage to take her to the station and she followed behind him as he pulled her trunk towards the front door. She left the notes, sealed in envelopes, on a circular table in the hallway, and then she climbed into the carriage and let it take her to the station, where she boarded a train for Portsmouth. At Portsmouth she bought a ticket for a ferry to take her back to where her journey had started: to a big, empty house on a cliff, with distant, tantalising views towards the white cliffs of Dover.

52

1995

Someone had called while Betty was talking to the vicar at St Anne's. She didn't recognise the number so she called it back and found herself talking to John Brightly.

'You didn't die in the night, then?' she began.

'Sadly not. No, apparently I am fit for duty. Or, at least, fit to continue with my pointless existence.'

'Well, that's brilliant news, then.'

'I guess so. But listen. Alex gave me your number. She came to see me, tried to talk me into staying at her place.' He paused. 'But actually, if it's OK with you, it would be great if I could bed down at yours. Just for a night or two. While I sort myself out with somewhere new.'

'Yes!' The word leaped from her mouth like a rubber ball. 'Yes. Of course!'

'Are you sure?'

'God, yes! Definitely. And I'm out tonight. Doing an overnight babysit at Amy's place. So you can have my bed.'

'Oh, no, you wouldn't want me in your bed. Seriously, I'm sweating like a pig.'

'Well, maybe not then, but listen, I'm on my way back

now. Can you get there soon, because I've just found out something about Clara Pickle and I need to get to a library straight away.'

'I'm packed and ready to go,' he said. 'I can be there in fifteen minutes.'

'You look better,' she said, greeting him on the landing. 'How's the wound?'

He pulled off his hat and showed her a neat row of stitches.

'Does it hurt?'

'No,' he said, pulling his hat back on, even though he was indoors and it was about twenty-five degrees outside.

'So no lasting damage?'

'Only time will tell,' he said. 'But so far I feel every bit my usual curmudgeonly, antisocial self.' He waved a paper bag at her. 'Enough antibiotics to keep a small nation in good health. So no boozing for me. And monthly check-ups for a few months, just to make sure everything's as it should be.' He shrugged and smiled. 'Drama over.'

'Drama over, and mystery climaxing,' Betty said, picking up her bag. 'I've got to shoot.'

'Can I come with?'

'Don't you have Ultravox picture discs to sell?'

He smiled drolly. 'That was an aberration,' he said.

'It was an abomination.'

'That too. I don't even know how it got there. But no, I think I can probably risk a day off.'

Betty looked at him and smiled. 'Good,' she said, 'because this is going to be a really boring job and I could do with another pair of hands.'

'Right,' she said, flopping twenty London phonebooks onto the table in front of John. 'We are looking for a woman called Clara Minchin. Or CT Minchin. But it's possible, of course, that she married and changed her name. So let's just look for any Minchins. Rippon Road is in Blackheath, apparently, so let's start with the southeast, and then we can work our way up and out of London after that.' She looked at her watch. 'It's two. I've got to be at Amy's at six. Four hours. Should be plenty. Let's go.'

John looked at her and then at the tower of phone directories on the table in front of him and smiled defeatedly.

'Yes, ma'am,' he said.

Betty grinned at him. 'Good,' she said. 'I'm glad we both understand our roles here.' He raised an eyebrow at her and opened his directory, and Betty opened hers.

It was a strangely companionable thing to do together. The library was virtually empty on this sunny June lunchtime, and there was something hypnotic about the rhythmic turning of the pages, the occasional pause to write down a number or to take a sip of coffee from the paper cups they'd brought with them.

'Anything interesting?' Betty asked after a few minutes.

'A few Minchins, nothing conclusive. You?'

'Same.'

They carried on turning the pages, pushing directories to the side once they'd finished with them until suddenly John slammed his hands down on to the directory in front of him and said, 'There's a Minchin! In Rippon Road!'

'What!'

'Yes! Look! Derek Minchin. 24 Rippon Road, SE3.'

'Give me that.' Betty pulled it away from him and stared at the listing. And there it was. In black and white. *Derek Minchin.* 'Oh!' She inhaled loudly. 'Oh my God. This is it. This is it. We're there. Oh my God.' She put her hands over her mouth and stared at John incredulously. 'Let's go,' she said. 'Let's go and phone him!'

John watched her intently as she pushed in the number on her mobile phone outside the library a moment later and she smiled at him nervously. She cleared her throat and patted down her hair, and then she stood up straight when the phone was answered on the third ring.

'Hello?'

'Oh, hello, is that Derek Minchin?'

'Speaking.'

'Oh, hi,' she said, 'I wonder if you could help me. I'm looking for someone called Clara –'

'Yes,' he interrupted, smoothly.

'Clara Minchin,' she continued.

'Clara Davies, these days,' he interrupted. 'My sister.'

Betty blinked. And then she paused as a massive swell of euphoric laughter threatened to overwhelm her. 'Oh,' she said eventually. 'That's wonderful, that's –'

'What's it regarding?' Derek Minchin asked, suddenly sounding suspicious.

'Well, it's kind of a private matter. I wondered if you might have a number for her?'

'Well,' Derek drew in his breath audibly. 'I think you can understand that I might not want to do that. Not without knowing what the matter is regarding. I mean, it's a matter of privacy, isn't it?'

'Yes, yes, of course. Yes. I see that. But maybe you could ask her to call me? As soon as possible.'

'Well, that wouldn't be easy. She's in Benidorm.'

'Benidorm?'

'Benidorm. With my other sisters. They go every year. But I can't go because of my problems, you know?'

Betty had no idea, but said, 'Oh, I see. And when will she be back?'

'They're coming back in tomorrow, I think. Hold on, let me check . . . *Dad*! *Dad*! When are the girls back?'

Dad, thought Betty. Dad?

She heard a muttering in the background and then Derek came back on the line and said, 'Yes. Tomorrow, getting in late apparently. But I'll give her your number, let her know to call you. Is there anything you can tell me, so that, you know, she has an idea why she's calling you?'

'Tell her it's an inheritance.'

'Ooh,' said Derek, 'an inheritance. That'll be nice. What a run of luck she's having. She just won a thousand on the lottery, too.'

Betty laughed. 'Lucky Clara,' she said.

'I'll say,' said Derek. 'So, tell me what your name and number is, hold on, let me just get a pen . . . oh, flipping hell, there's never any pens what work in this bloody house. Here, right, off you go . . .'

She gave him her name and number and then, before she hung up she said, 'Can I just ask you one thing, before you go, about Clara?'

'Try me.'

'Well, this might sound like a strange question – you'll probably think I'm mad for asking – but Clara . . . is she . . . I mean . . . what colour is she?'

'Ha, how funny that you should ask. Well I never, but yes, Clara is a black lady. Yes, she is. Rest of us is white. She's black. And there's a story behind that. If you're interested. But maybe I'll leave Clara to tell you all about that. When you see her.'

Betty smiled. She suspected she already knew.

Betty had taken all three children to a café around the corner from Amy's house, to get them out from under her feet while she ran around frantically organising caterers and sound equipment. Betty breathed out in relief as silence fell upon their table and the three children sat eating happily and quietly. It had been a truly extraordinary, overwhelming day. As she sat here, Clara Pickle/Minchin/Jones/Davies would be enjoying her last evening in Spain, sitting in a bar perhaps, or on the balcony of a sea-facing apartment, drinking Sangria and wishing that she could stay for ever. This time tomorrow she would be on her way to the airport and by Monday morning, she would know that she was the recipient of the contents of the bank account of a lady from Guernsey who'd once loved her father.

A shiver ran down her spine at the prospect.

And then she saw Donovan about to knock a large glass of organic orange juice across the café table and she stretched her arm out to catch it, and as she did so another arm appeared, clothed in black leather and attached to the body of Dom Jones.

'Steady, mate,' he said to Donovan, who immediately jumped to his feet and ran around the table and into his father's arms.

'Daddy! Daddy!'

Betty smiled uncertainly, unsure how this impromptu visit fitted into Amy's vision for the night and also how she felt about seeing Dom again after their fractious encounter the previous morning.

'Don't worry,' said Dom, smiling sheepishly over the top of Donny's head, 'I'm not planning on taking them anywhere. Amy knows I'm here. I've just been to the house and she said it was OK. And listen,' he sat himself on Donovan's seat, with his son held upon his lap. 'I just wanted to say I am so, so, so incredibly, unbelievably sorry about yesterday morning. I mean, really. I was completely out of order. Totally. A total and utter prize . . .' he silently mouthed a derogatory one-syllable word.

Betty smiled grudgingly. 'Yeah,' she said, 'you were a bit.'

'And you were absolutely right to stop me taking Donny out.'

'No!' shouted Donny. 'She was absolutely wrong!'

They both smiled at Donny, who frowned back at them both and stuck his fork grumpily into his eggs on toast.

'No, really. You were very professional. You did your job well. Thank you.'

Betty's smile softened. She shrugged and rubbed her elbows.

'Where's Daddy's egg?' Dom asked Donovan, his mouth opened wide.

Donny slowly and very seriously detached a hunk of bread and egg with his fingers and offered it to his father. Dom gobbled it up and licked Donny's fingers and squeezed his son tight to him. '*Dee*-licious,' he said, kissing Donny's neck and squeezing him again. 'Thank you. And how are my girls?' he asked.

Acacia glanced at him across the table and blew him a kiss, her newest trick, before turning her attention back to her scrambled eggs and mushrooms.

Dom pretended to catch the kiss and drop it into his heart. Acacia looked at him again through her long lashes and sighed, as though her father was truly the most magnificent man in the world. The baby sat in her high chair and smeared ice-cream into the tray with two flattened hands.

'You're so good at this,' said Dom, surveying the contented brood. 'You make it look so easy. When you eventually get round to having your own –'

'Not for a very long time,' Betty interjected.

'No, not for a very long time. But when you do. Lucky kids . . .' His gaze dropped to the top of Donny's head and he smiled again.

Betty smiled. Having her own children felt about as distant a concept as time travel. 'Are you going to the party?' she asked, changing the subject.

'Oh, f – God, no. No way. I f . . . flipping hate all those people. Half the reason we . . .' he mouthed the words '*split up*'. 'Anyway, I've got a gig tonight.' He looked at his watch. 'In fact, yeah, I'd better push off in a minute. But not until I've had a bite of Donny's fairy cake.'

Donny snatched the waiting cake towards him and clutched it at his chest while Dom pretended to try to steal it.

Betty watched him, curiously. He was doing it again, that human chameleon thing. Here he was, sober, apologetic dad, playing by the rules, doing low-key mucking about with his children, before heading off to work.

He caught her staring at him and smiled. 'I want to square stuff with you, Betty,' he said. 'I want to explain myself. What are you doing tomorrow?'

'I'm doing this lot,' she said, gesturing towards his children, 'until Amy can face doing them herself.'

Dom smiled wryly. 'Right, so, late then. Send me a text message when you're heading home. I'll come and ring on your bell,' he said.

'I've got a house guest.'

'Well, come and ring on mine.'

'I'm not sure, Dom . . .'

'Just to talk.' He skewered her with an intense look. 'I just want to talk to you.'

She shrugged. 'OK,' she said.

He smiled, and the smile took the breath out of her. It was real and sincere. It was, she felt, utterly without guile, a rare sighting of the real Dom Jones. And she liked it. She felt an overwhelming compulsion to jump to her feet and squeeze him hard. Instead she laughed.

'What?'

'Nothing,' she said, 'nothing.'

He smiled at her again, that sweet sincere smile and she smiled back. And then, after a round of hugs and kisses and nibbles of various children's fairy cakes, he was gone into the summer evening, off to be a pop star.

The party was a crashing disappointment, lots of people talking about schools and nannies and restaurants with Michelin stars in Chelsea. Betty made her excuses at 11 p.m. and headed up for bed. She peered through the window of her bedroom (a boxroom next to the baby's room) at the street below. The pavement was pooled in yellow light from the ornate Victorian streetlamps, and Primrose Hill itself was bathed in blue, a luscious swell of bucolic splendour rising from the heart of north London. And there they were, like rats in jackets, the paparazzi, hoping for something shocking to splash all over the front pages of the Sunday papers. Betty felt like opening the window and shouting out, 'Go home! They're all really boring!' But instead she climbed into her pyjamas and got into bed.

It took her a while to fall asleep that night, the sounds of the bass from the sound system banging through the bones of the house and into the very marrow of her. She eventually dropped off at about midnight and when she woke up an hour and a half later, her first thought was that one of the children must have set off the monitor and disturbed her, but then she realised there was someone in her room. She sat bolt upright and searched for the light-switch with her hand.

'Ssh,' said a voice, 'it's just me. It's just Amy.'

Betty groaned and croaked, 'What? Are the kids OK?'

Amy took a few steps towards Betty's bed. 'Kids are fine,' she said. 'I just went in and checked on them.'

'Oh,' said Betty, running her hands down her bed-messed hair and rubbing her eyes. 'Good.'

'They look so beautiful when they're asleep,' Amy breathed, perching herself gently on the edge of Betty's bed.

Betty pulled herself up into a full sitting position and moved towards the wall.

'Like angels. You think you couldn't love them any more. You think you're going to die of it. Their beauty. Their innocence. Their little hands curled up into those tiny fists. And then they wake up the next morning, and Jesus fucking Christ, you wonder why the fuck you ever had them.'

She laughed and then sighed. 'I don't really mean that,' she said. 'Of course I don't. It's just, you know, they're all so little and I don't really know them yet, and I know that one day, when they're older – you know, proper little people – I'll be so so grateful I had them, but right now . . .' she sighed again. 'Jeez. I dunno. It's such hard work. Even with my beloved Betty.'

She squeezed Betty's hand under the duvet and smiled into the darkness, and now that Betty's eyes had adjusted to the dark she could see that Amy was drunk. Or if not drunk, incredibly stoned.

'What would I do without you, my wonderful Betty? You know, I do honestly believe that my husband is a humungous prick of the highest order, but he got it right with you. I'll give him that. That was a good call. *Good call, Dom!*' She paused and stared at Betty. 'Thank you,' she said.

Betty smiled awkwardly. 'You're welcome,' she said. 'It's a pleasure. Your children are great.'

'Aren't they?' smiled Amy. 'And you know, shit, I watch you with them and I think, shit, *why* can't I be like that with them? Why can't I just be patient and kind and gentle like that? Like Betty? You're a special girl, Betty Dean. A very special girl. You know, forget the two-week trial. Seriously. I'm sold. I'll sort you out on a salary from Monday. OK?'

Betty nodded. 'Thank you,' she said.

And then Amy slowly lowered her face towards Betty's and kissed her gently on her cheek.

Betty froze.

Amy stroked her hair away from her face.

'Sleep tight, pretty Betty,' she said. 'I'll see you in the morning.'

She paused and stared at Betty dreamily for a moment, before squeezing her shoulder and tiptoeing quietly from her room.

The following morning it was as if the whole thing had been a dream. Amy came down just after eleven, showered and bleary-eyed, dressed in a vintage summer dress and slippers, her Titian hair woven into two plaits. Betty and the children were in the garden playing in the sandpit.

'Good morning, my lovely children,' she called from the kitchen doorway where she was clutching a mug of coffee and a strip of painkillers. 'Good morning, Betty.'

Betty smiled at her brightly. 'Morning!'

'How was your night?'

'Fine,' said Betty. 'Fine. Astrid woke up at three for a bottle, Acacia woke up at four for a cuddle and Donovan was standing in my doorway at quarter to six, ready to start the day.'

'Oh God, poor you.'

Betty shrugged. 'It's fine. I thought it would be worse to be honest.'

Amy popped two pills from the strip and knocked them back with a gulp of coffee. 'You're a star,' she said. 'A total star. I'm taking the kids to Kate's for lunch today, so you can go home then, say about twelve thirty?'

Betty smiled again. 'Great.'

'Great,' echoed Amy.

And then she was gone.

53

1921

Dear Lilian,

Well, to say that I miss you all would be a statement of extraordinary inadequacy. I miss all of you, every moment of every day (except, perhaps, your younger brothers!). I miss London, I miss the buses and the motorcars, the noise and the smell. I miss parties with Minu, and the music. I really do miss the music. How are you all? How are the building works going? I suppose it will be a long time before the house is ready for you all to move back in. But then, an apartment in Hyde Park is likely a fine compensation for you all in the meantime.

I am sorry that I left so suddenly and without proper farewells. And now that I am away from everything, I feel I can share with you the exact reasons for my disappearance. I overheard Godfrey having a conversation with a young girl about their unborn baby. She gave him back a sum of money that he had given her to deal with the situation and told him that she 'couldn't do it'. Now I, more than most, can understand that, as you know. It is no one's fault. I left Godfrey without explanation, he owed me nothing. And this poor girl is just doing what she feels is right. There is no one to blame, no one to be angry with, but Godfrey has to be free to do the right thing with regard to this girl and he won't be able to do that easily with me in the picture.

So, here I am, back where I started. My mother is so happy to have me back. Already my time in London feels like a dream. Travel really is just a momentary pause in the ongoing rhythm of real life. Nothing changes. Not really. But, Lilian, I need you to do something for me. Please would you stay in touch with Godfrey? I want to know that he is well and happy, that his baby comes without any drama, that he finds a way through this. Please? As far as I know he will be in London for the whole of the summer. I still love him so very much, and I know I always will.

Love and best wishes to you all,
Your friend,
Arlette.

Dearest Arlette,

How shocking! Your dilemma is clear and I hate to say it but I think you have done the right thing. Poor Godfrey. Poor you. Poor little baby. It should all have been so very different, I feel.

I did see Godfrey last week. Minu and I went to a Love Brothers show at the Blue Butterfly. He looked very sad, his eyes like the eyes of an orphaned spaniel. I can't tell you.

Anyway, I did talk to him after the show. I told him that you'd written, that you were well. He did not mention a baby, but I did see a young girl sitting in the wings, knitting something in white wool. I took her to be the young lady in question. But I was not introduced. The whole affair seems very much steeped in sadness and consolation.

We are all well. The house is very far from being repaired. I cannot bear to look at it when I return on occasion to visit Philip.

Fondest love to you, my friend,
Lilian

Dearest Lilian,

Thank you so much for your report and I'm sorry I have not written for so long. Mother was taken ill, a bout of terrible bronchitis, and I have spent these last weeks going back and forth to the sanatorium. Thank goodness I was here. I feel more than ever I made the right decision. Although, if I can share with you a terrible truth, every time I think of Godfrey I feel so angry at the world, at my mother, at the unfairness of everything.

Please send more news, of you, the family, and of course Godfrey, whenever you get a minute.

Yours,
Arlette

Dearest Arlette,

Well, I start with joyful news. Philip has asked me to marry him and I have accepted! I will become Mrs Philip Love. Is that not the most charming name, worth marrying for that alone! I will be having a joint twentieth birthday party and engagement party in September. If your mother is feeling better and you can face the journey back to London, it would be so super if you were to be there. It will be a really happy, splendid night. One I feel we could all do with after the many sadnesses of the last year.

As for Godfrey, I have not seen him, but I hear he is off on tour again. And Minu saw him a couple of weeks ago and apparently he mentioned that he has a new girl and a baby on the way. He said it is due in November. But more than that, Minu did not ask and I do not know. He asked after you. She said he still has the sad eyes. And that his music is more piquant than ever.

Sweet dreams, my lovely friend, and best wishes to your dear mother from my dear mother,

Lilian

Dearest Lilian,

Oh, my dear friend! I have been dancing with joy at your news! Philip seems such a good man and you will be the loveliest, sweetest little wife. You already have so much practice in running a home. Where will you live? Oh, I'm sure it will be somewhere utterly divine. You two lucky people, I could not be happier. Whether or not I will be able to make it across for your engagement party remains to be seen. I will most definitely do everything I can, be assured of that much.

I wish that I could write and say that my heart is healing, that I am missing Godfrey less, but that would not be true. My mother and her family are forever introducing me to nice chaps, really, perfectly nice chaps. But I see them, and their bland faces and their small lives – some have never left the island, you know – and I cannot bear for that to be the end of it. There has to be more, don't you think? Well, for me at least. And as long as I shall live, I will always know, deep in my heart, that the best has passed me by, in a terrible chaos of tragedy and bad luck. Nothing will ever compare, I shall live out my life in a state of pitiful resignation.

Best regards, my dear girl,
Arlette

54

1995

'Are you decent?'

Betty stood outside the front door of her flat and waited for a response.

'I am fully clothed,' John shouted out.

She turned her key in the lock and walked in. John was on the sofa in a white polo shirt and jeans, his hair freshly washed and messed up, his feet bare, watching a TV presenter, who'd been at Amy's party the night before, lasciviously interviewing Louise Wener from Sleeper on the television.

Betty laughed. 'Met him last night,' she said drily.

John raised a minutely interested eyebrow at her. He pointed at Louise Wener. 'Did you meet *her*?'

Betty shook her head and John sighed dramatically. 'Shame.'

Betty smiled again and headed for the kettle. 'Tea?'

'Let me,' said John, leaping to his feet.

'No,' said Betty. 'You sit. You're ill.'

'I am not ill,' he said. 'I am recovering.'

'Well, all the more reason to take it easy,' she said, filling the kettle with water.

John sighed and sat down again. 'Listen,' he said, 'I was thinking. It's a beautiful day. And I'm so grateful to you for everything you've done. I'd really like to repay you. I'd really like to take you out to lunch. In fact . . .' he blushed slightly, 'I've taken the liberty of packing a picnic.' He stood up and opened the fridge. 'I got sushi, do you like sushi?'

She shrugged and said, 'I've never tried it.'

'Oh, well, I also got some champagne.'

'But you can't drink.'

He grimaced. 'Champagne,' he said, 'is not drink. Well, not where I come from, anyway. So, smoked salmon and cream cheese bagels, and look . . .' he pulled out a tiny glass jar, 'some caviar.'

Betty blinked. 'Wow,' she said.

'Yeah,' he said, scratching his chin, 'I know. I went a bit OTT, but you know, I never get a day off. This is my first free Sunday in over a year, so I just thought . . . well . . .' He closed the fridge door and looked slightly embarrassed.

'Thank you,' said Betty. 'Seriously. That is amazing.' She was about to say, 'No one has ever bought champagne for me before,' but stopped herself as she remembered that someone had. Dom had. At the Groucho. That awful night when he'd cried those big crocodile tears, squeezed her bum and called her 'the nanny'. She shook the memory from her thoughts and said, 'Where are you taking me?'

'Green Park?'

'Lovely,' she said, 'I'll have a shower and put on a nice dress.'

'And listen,' John called out to her retreating back, 'I want you to know, I've already lined up some places to view tomorrow. I won't be hanging around. OK? In case you were worried?'

Betty turned and smiled at him. 'I wasn't worried,' she said.

If there had ever been a more beautiful Sunday afternoon in the entire history of Sunday afternoons, Betty would have been very surprised indeed.

The sky was an electric blue and scattered with puffy clouds that passed across the sun at convenient intervals as though it was their job to stop sunbathers from overheating. After they'd eaten their picnic on a bath towel and drunk champagne from mugs, Betty and John rented deckchairs, which they turned at angles to face the sun.

'Now, this is the life,' said John, stretching out his legs and smiling into the sun.

'Not secretly wishing you were at a record fair, then?'

'Oh, well, yeah. Obviously I'd rather be in a big dusty hall in the suburbs with a load of lonely guys in stale T-shirts . . .'

'. . . buying Ultravox picture discs . . .'

'Buying Ultravox picture discs. But this will do. This will very much do.'

He pulled a Discman from his jacket pocket and

plugged in some headphones. 'Wanna share?' he said, offering her an earpiece.

'Depends what you're listening to,' she said.

'Ultravox, of course.'

She raised an eyebrow at him and smiled.

He returned her smile. 'What do you want to listen to?'

He passed her a small leather case full of CDs out of their boxes and she looked at him curiously. 'You thought of everything,' she said.

'I certainly did,' he said, watching her leaf through the pages of discs.

'Here,' she said, 'let's listen to this one.'

It was an album by the Chemical Brothers. She chose it because she liked the title, *Exit Planet Dust.*

'Good choice,' he said, looking at her with respect. 'Their first album. Only just came out yesterday.'

Betty nodded seriously, as if of course she knew that, as if she was a big fat muso, just like him.

He put the disc in the player and passed her an earpiece, then he turned up the volume and for the next hour they sat just like that, side by side, their arms hanging at their sides, the sun playing on their skin, the breathtaking, mind-blowing sound of Chemical Brothers, whoever the hell they were, taking them both to another place entirely.

As the album came to a close, Betty opened her eyes and saw John smiling at her.

'Why are you smiling at me?' she teased. 'You're freaking me out. I can see your teeth and everything.'

John pulled his lips down over his teeth. 'I'll never do it again,' he promised.

'Good,' said Betty, folding her arms across her chest.

'So, what did you think?'

'Amazing,' she said. 'Totally.'

'Good,' he said, with some kind of unspoken satisfaction. 'That's good. What sort of music do you normally listen to? I have to confess, I've had a look around your place, not a scrap of vinyl or a CD to be found.'

She shrugged. 'I left it all at home,' she said. 'Didn't think I'd need it.'

'Jesus,' he said, 'different strokes. The first thing I'd pack if I was leaving home would be my music. It would be my "what would you rescue first in a fire" thing. What would yours be?'

She paused and considered the question. 'Right now,' she said, 'it would be Arlette's stuff. Her photos. The book. The flyers. Apart from that, nothing really. It's all just stuff, isn't it? None of it really means anything.'

He nodded. And then he smiled and said, 'One more treat.' He leaned down and pulled a small paper box from the picnic bag. It was tied up with pale blue ribbon and had the words 'Patisserie Valerie' printed on it. He opened the lid and offered it to Betty. The box was filled with pastries, some topped with strawberries, others oozing whipped cream and confectioner's custard.

'Good God,' she said, her mouth hanging ajar. 'Those look amazing. But I mustn't.'

He looked at her blankly. 'What?'

'Oh God, I just can't. I put on so much weight when I was at Wendy's, and now I'm constantly eating with the children and look . . .' She grabbed her spare tyre and showed it to him.

He laughed. 'You weirdo,' he said.

'I am not a weirdo.'

'You are, Betty Dean. I mean, look at you. Just look at you. How can you even begin to think you're overweight? If anything . . .' he stopped.

'What?'

'If anything you were too thin, when I first saw you, in that stupid coat. Like a little shrimp, all bug-eyed and skinny. Now you're . . .'

'What?' she said again, narrowing her eyes.

'Well, you're just about perfect.'

She stared at him.

'*Just about*, I said, *just about*. Don't go getting any ideas about yourself.'

'Oh, it's too late for that, John Brightly, way too late for that.'

He smiled at her and waved the box under her nose again. 'Go on,' he said, 'you know you want one.'

'No,' she laughed, pushing the box away, 'I don't!'

'Go on, get stuck in.' As he said it, she saw a little flash of unadulterated mischief pass across his face. Before she could lever herself from her deckchair he'd picked a cream puff from the box and pushed it into her face.

She looked at him in stunned silence, unsure whether she was amused or deeply offended. She decided she was both, and after wiping most of a cream bun from her face with her fingers and then licking it off, she smiled at John sweetly, lifted another cake out of the box and rubbed it into his cheeks.

'Oh, right. Oh, right!' he said, rubbing his hands together, his eyes shining with delight, before picking out another bun and chasing Betty around a tree with it. He caught her after a moment and held onto her breathlessly, the bun in one hand, her shoulder in the other. She caught her breath and stared at him, imploringly. He stared back at her, triumphantly. And then he lowered the bun and his look turned to something else, something she could not quite interpret.

She wiped some cream from his face and he caught her hand in mid-air. 'Betty . . .' he began.

'What?' she said.

He stared at her, slightly helplessly.

Betty caught her breath.

Then he dropped her hand and lowered his gaze and said, 'Nothing. Just . . . you've got cream in your ear.' He pointed at her right ear and she put a finger in it and wiggled it around.

'Has it gone?' she asked.

'Yes,' he said, with a strange sadness. 'It's gone.'

She looked at him tenderly. 'Are you OK?'

'Yeah,' he said, naughty John gone from sight, laconic John back in his place. 'I'm fine. Here.' He offered her the bun. 'Eat this. For me.'

Betty took the bun from his outstretched hand. She

smiled at him. 'Thank you, John,' she said. 'Thank you for the picnic. Thank you for the champagne. And thank you for the music . . .'

'The songs I'm singing.'

'Thanks for all the joy they're bringing.'

'Who could live without it?'

'I ask, in all honesty.'

'What would life be?'

'Without a song, or a dance, what are we?'

John smiled. 'Indeed.'

The moment drew away from them. And then it passed. Something had nearly happened here today, in the park, with John Brightly. Something that Betty wasn't quite ready for. And neither, she suspected, was John.

'Come on,' said Betty, 'let's go home.'

There was a note in the mail catcher when they got back to Berwick Street half an hour later: 'Betty, come over. I'm in till six.'

Betty glanced at her watch. It was just past five. She saw John looking at her. She had no idea what to say. 'Erm . . .'

He read the note and shrugged. 'See you later,' he said coldly.

'It's –'

'Don't worry about it. He's your boss. Off you run.'

'Yes, but . . .'

John forced a small smile. 'Go,' he said. 'I'll be fine. I'll see you later.'

Betty sighed. This was not what she wanted. But she'd promised Dom she'd hear what he had to say. And it was only for an hour.

'I'll be back at six,' she said. 'Will you be in?'

He shrugged. 'Not sure.'

'Right. OK. Well, I might see you later.'

'Yeah.' He shrugged again. 'You might.'

'Thank you again, John,' she said. 'It's been a perfect day.'

'Yeah,' he agreed. 'A perfect day. I'm glad I spent it with you.'

She stood on the pavement outside her flat for a moment after John went inside. Then she breathed in deeply, smoothed her hair and turned the corner into Peter Street.

Dom was wearing a football strip when he answered the door to her a minute later.

His face lit up when he saw her and he said, 'Thank God, I thought I was going to miss you.'

She eyed the football strip. 'What the fuck are you wearing?'

Dom glanced down at himself and said, 'Charity five-a-side thing.'

'Who won?'

'My team, of course. Thrashed them. Where've you been? Amy said you left hers at twelve thirty.' The question was slightly accusatory in tone.

'I've been to the park,' she said.

He nodded, appraising her gently through his velvety lashes.

'How was the party?' he asked, leading her through to the kitchen.

'It was all right,' she said. 'Not quite the sex-and-drugs-crazed wife-swapper I'd been led to expect.'

'Yeah, well, that's because Amy binned all our mates when I moved out and got a whole new set. Ones who like going to bed at ten o'clock. With a mug of *green tea* . . .'

He opened the fridge and pulled out two cold beers. He offered one to Betty and then passed her a bottle opener.

'So nothing to report then?' he asked, pulling a chair out from under the kitchen table and sitting astride it, as though it were a motorbike.

'No,' she said, wondering why she was here when she could have been in her flat with John. 'I went to bed at eleven o'clock. It all seemed very civilised.'

'Good,' he said, staring at the tabletop. 'Good. Listen. Betty,' he looked up at her, suddenly and dramatically, 'I don't know how to say this, so I'm just going to come straight out and say it. I've been thinking a lot about you lately. An awful lot. I think . . .'

He paused and scratched at the label of his beer bottle. 'I think you're totally brilliant. Totally. I think you're beautiful. And bright. And sexy, I mean, *fuck*, you're sexy.'

Betty picked at some dry skin on her fingernails and waited for it, the moment of truth, the moment he told her that he didn't want to be her boyfriend. And she was ready for it. Because she didn't want to be his girlfriend either. Too much baggage. Too much bullshit. And he looked silly in his football strip. What had happened here that night had been a one-off, just a moment of craziness. She was prepared to accept that and she was ready now for him to draw a line underneath it all.

'And I've been thinking,' he continued, 'about what we were talking about here the other night. About other destinies. You know. About how maybe just because things seem like they have to be a certain way, it doesn't mean that you can't change it. If that's what you want. And so when I was down in the country, with the band, I spent a couple of hours out with an estate agent. He showed me some fucking amazing gaffs. I mean, places that made the house in Primrose Hill look like a shed, you know. And listen,' he leaned towards her suddenly and covered her hand over with his. 'I want to do it. You and me. A big house in the country. Pigs. Ducks. The kids to stay in the holidays. Farmhouse breakfast. The works.'

His hand gripped hers and his soft brown eyes bored into hers, and for a moment Betty was rendered completely speechless.

'Remember I said I wished I'd met you first? Well, maybe I met you last. Do you see what I mean? I met you *last.*'

She nodded and tried to form a response.

'And that's the one, isn't it?' he continued. 'The one you meet last.'

He was evangelised, energised.

'Shit,' said Betty, 'I mean . . . Seriously, I really do not know what to say. At all.'

Dom just smiled at her dreamily. 'It could be so great,' he said. 'Just think about it.'

She stared at him mutely. 'But what about me?' she said. 'What would I do?'

He looked at her strangely. 'What do you mean, what would you do?'

'All day? While you were on tour? When you were away recording?'

He smiled and rubbed his hand up and down her arm. 'Well, that's the beautiful thing, Betty. You could do whatever you wanted. Whatever you bloody well wanted. You could paint. You could write. You could come on tour with me. You could have a baby. You could do whatever the fucking hell you fucking well wanted to do!' He beamed at her slightly maniacally.

She smiled and nodded. 'And what about Amy?'

'What *about* Amy?'

'Well, she might be a bit . . .'

He dismissed her half-formed concerns with a wave of his beer bottle. 'Amy will be fine. At least she'll know, when the kids come to stay, that they'll be in good hands. At least she knows you, she trusts you.'

'She offered me the job.'

'What?'

'Last night. Amy came into my room and told me I was amazing and offered me the job. I think she really likes me, Dom. I think she really needs me. I'm not sure I can just up and leave her.'

He laughed. 'Oh, yeah, right. Amy always makes out that the nanny is like the centre of the universe. It's her MO. Make them feel indispensable and then push them to their limits.'

'I honestly don't think it's like that,' Betty said. 'Really.'

He laughed again and Betty grimaced. She thought about the flat round the corner, John Brightly on the sofa, then she thought about the country pile, the farmhouse kitchen, a room full of easels, a bank account she didn't need to worry about and Dom Jones's beautiful brown eyes staring at her passionately every morning when she woke up.

'I know,' said Dom, leaning away again, 'I know this all seems like I'm rushing things. I've only known you a few weeks. But there's something about you, Betty. I felt it the first time I saw you, in your Wendy's uniform. Something pure. Something good. And I wish I had the time to wine you and dine you and really get to know you. But my life's not like that, my life is, you know, crazy. All these years I've let that craziness rule everything, but now, with you, I feel like I've found the calm, gentle centre of everything. You are, like, my pacemaker . . .'

'Your pacemaker?'

'Yeah,' he said, staring at her deeply. 'Tick, tick, tick. A metronome.'

A pacemaker? A metronome?

He gazed at her blindly for a moment before it hit him.

'No!' he said. 'No. You're more than that. Of course you are, Betty. Listen, Betty, the bottom line is: *I'm crazy about you*. OK?'

OK? Was he asking her or telling her?

She shrugged, feeling strangely unmoved by a megastar telling her that he was crazy about her. 'Dom,' she began, 'I don't know. It's just . . .' she paused, ran her fingertip around the rim of her beer bottle '. . . I've got so much going on here right now. I finally found my grandmother's beneficiary. And Amy, she needs me. I can't let her down.'

He leaned back towards her and grabbed her hands again. 'I'm going to Berlin tonight,' he said. 'I'll be back on Wednesday. Think about it, Betty. That's all I ask of you. Please, just think about it.' He picked up both her hands then, and kissed the hillocks of her knuckles. 'Will you do that?' he said, his brown eyes staring into hers pleadingly.

Betty felt her stomach swish and billow at the touch of his lips against her skin. She nodded. 'Yes,' she said. 'Of course I will.'

'Honestly, Betty,' he said, resting her hands back on the table. 'I swear, this feels like the first grown-up thing I have ever done in my life. Ever.'

He smiled at her and let her go.

John didn't ask where Betty had been or what she'd been doing when she came back to the flat just before six. He merely moved along the sofa and said, 'True romance?'

'Sorry?' said Betty.

513

'*True Romance*,' he said again, waving a mug of half-drunk tea at the TV. 'Have you seen it?'

'No,' she said. 'It never made it to the Mallard on Guernsey. I was gutted.'

She took the seat next to him and collapsed heavily into the cushions, her entire being reeling from the events of the last hour, desperately grateful to John for just sitting here being so perfectly normal.

'Well, now's your chance. I bought it yesterday, some Chinese guy selling stuff off the pavement.'

'How far in are you?'

'I'll start it again.'

'Are you sure?'

'Course I am.' He stopped the film and pressed rewind. While they sat and watched the film replay itself backwards he turned to her and said, 'I meant to ask you something?'

She looked at him questioningly.

'What was the deal with Clara's dad? I mean, we've found her now and clearly she was brought up by somebody else. What happened to her father? What happened to Godfrey Pickle?'

Betty smiled sadly. 'Didn't I tell you?'

'No,' he said. 'You didn't.'

'Your sister told me. It's really sad.'

John paused the picture on the DVD player and turned to face her.

'Go on,' he said.

Betty took a deep breath.

55

1921

Arlette stepped from the carriage and looked up at the imposing apartment block. It stood ten storeys high, facing directly across Hyde Park. A smartly liveried porter helped her across the threshold with her bag and directed her to a lift to take her to the third floor.

It was blissful to be back in London. Blissful and also poignant. She would only be here for three nights: she had a job now on the island, at a dress shop in St Peter Port, and they couldn't give her any more time than that. But three nights were better than no nights at all, and she was just happy she'd been able to come across for Lilian's party.

Lilian greeted her at the door of the apartment and threw herself so hard into Arlette's arms that she almost knocked her off her feet.

'Darling, darling Arlette! Look at you! So beautiful. And wearing such a fine coat.' She admired it at arm's length. 'It's just yummy. Where did it come from?'

'From the dress shop where I work.'

'Ah, so style has finally reached the distant shores of Guernsey?'

'With a little help from me, yes,' Arlette laughed.

'Oh, I've missed you so much. Come in. Come in. Come and see our beautiful apartment.'

Lilian showed Arlette the rooms, all high-ceilinged and bathed in the white-gold sunlight that streamed clear across the park and straight through the tall windows.

'And you're in here, with me,' she said finally, showing Arlette into the last of the many bedrooms. 'Because, I'm rather afraid, we have Henry at home now. And Arthur is back on exeat. But it will be cosy, and it will give us a chance to share all our secrets under cover of night!'

Arlette smiled tightly. She did not want to share secrets. She just wanted to celebrate Lilian's happiness and then go home.

Lilian sat her down in the parlour and sent for tea and biscuits. 'So,' she began, 'the schedule of events is this: on Sunday night we are having a family meal here, at the apartment. Tomorrow night, of course, is the party. So tonight, I thought we could go to a club, maybe. With Minu?'

Arlette glanced at Lilian nervously. 'A club?'

'Yes. If you like. I thought maybe the Blue Butterfly. But never fear. Godfrey is not in London. Right now he is in Scotland. With the orchestra.'

'Oh,' Arlette felt some kind of unspoken anxiety she had been carrying around inside herself since she'd first planned this trip to London ebb out of her at these words. Godfrey was in Scotland. She would not be seeing him. She felt both relieved and deflated. 'Well,' she said, 'that's probably good.'

'Yes,' agreed Lilian, 'it is.'

'And what of the girl?' she asked. 'Any news of her?'

'Yes,' said Lilian conspiratorially. 'Minu had a letter from Godfrey a few days ago; her parents have thrown her from their home.'

Arlette clasped a hand across her mouth. 'Poor girl,' she whispered.

'Poor girl indeed.'

'And where is she now?'

'Godfrey told Minu that she is staying in Soho, while he is away, at a home for unwed mothers.'

'Oh, how sad.'

'Yes. But he'll be returning in early November, in time for the birth. He said he will find them rooms, that he will marry her.'

Arlette felt an agonising stab of sorrow pierce her heart at these words. She'd known it would happen. It was why she'd left London. But to hear the words, to know as fact that someone else would be spending the rest of their life with the man she loved, that someone else would live in the small house with the friendly neighbours, would take the coffee-skinned toddlers back to St Lucia on a majestic cruise ship. She held back a guttural sob and forced a tiny smile. 'Good,' she said. 'That's good.'

A clattering emanated from the hallway and Leticia and the three boys hurtled into the room. All of them were ruddy-cheeked and smiling, even Leticia, who had more colour in her face than Arlette had ever seen her carrying before.

'Glorious Arlette!' cried Leticia at the sight of her. 'What a splendid, splendid treat! Welcome! Boys,' she called out behind her, 'look who's here. It's Arlette!'

The three boys peered at Arlette disinterestedly, apart from Henry, who threw her a very strange look indeed and said, 'Well, well, well, I thought we'd seen the last of you.'

'Henry!' Leticia chastised. 'There's no need for such rudeness. Really.'

Henry merely grimaced and disappeared.

'Henry!' called Leticia. 'Come back here right now and apologise to our guest.'

'Oh, really,' said Arlette, 'it's fine.'

'No,' said Leticia, sternly, 'it is not fine. Come back here right now,' she called again, 'or I will be talking to your father and your allowance will not be making an appearance in your bank account this month. Now, Henry!'

Arlette almost jumped at the authoritative tone of Leticia's voice and she looked at Lilian in surprise and vague amusement.

Lilian smiled and whispered, 'Such changes, Arlette. Such changes.'

Henry reappeared in the doorway and stared at Arlette sulkily. 'I apologise for my comments, Miss De La Mare. Now, if you will excuse me, I have some tiresome domestic chores to attend to.'

He disappeared and Leticia smiled at Arlette. 'Such terrible boys,' she said. 'I am taking them in hand. They will be the most charming boys in London by the next time you visit!'

'I am sure they will,' said Arlette. 'And possibly they will also be uncles.'

Leticia put a hand to her heart and gasped. 'And me then a grandmother! Well, well, well. What a silly thought. But also so terribly exciting. Now, I must leave you girls to catch up. I have some last-minute party arrangements to discuss. So lovely to have you back, Arlette. Such a treat.'

She left the room and Lilian looked at Arlette and shrugged. 'Well,' she said, 'sometimes bad things do happen for a good reason.'

Arlette accompanied Leticia and Lilian into the West End the next morning, where Lilian was having the last fitting for her party dress and looking for new hairpins with which to ornament her hair. Arlette left them in the dress shop and took herself for a walk through streets that had once been her second home. It was another bright September day, golden and crisp, just like the day last year when she'd walked to the river with Godfrey, when he'd told her he wanted to be with her forever, just before he'd gone to Manchester and left her to her fate with Gideon Worsley.

She found herself wandering carelessly, but maybe somewhere deep down, purposefully, towards Soho. She'd asked Minu last night about the home for unwed mothers. St Anne's Court, Minu had told her. Just opposite the new flats.

She didn't have a plan, she just wanted to see. See what someone looked like with Godfrey's baby growing inside them. She crossed over Soho Square, tatty and tawdry on this bright Saturday morning. Drunks and opium addicts stared at her horribly through glassy eyes and she averted her gaze, walking briskly and with purpose. St Anne's Court was a short road, equally dirty and sordid, but there, as Minu had said, was the shiny new block of flats, built in the modern style, all gleaming granite and streaky marble.

Arlette stood before the building and looked at the house opposite. On the ground level was a tiny shop selling supplies for cripples and injured soldiers. Above were three floors, all grimy-windowed and unwelcoming. There was no signage to suggest what the building was used for, just the number 12 engraved into the mantel. She watched the building for a while, until, after a moment a young girl scuttled out, hiding her blooming stomach with a bag held across herself. She scuttled back again a moment later, holding a paper bag from a pharmacy to her chest, and Arlette crossed the street urgently towards her.

'Hello,' she said.

The girl looked at her in horror.

'I'm sorry. I don't mean to alarm you. I'm just . . .' She stopped, suddenly aware of the stupidity of her actions. 'It's just,' she continued, 'there's a girl staying here. She's called Esther. I wondered . . .'

'Esther Jones or Esther Murray?'

'I'm not sure,' said Arlette. 'The one who's engaged to a coloured man.'

'Ah,' said the girl, knowingly, 'yes, Esther Jones. What about her?'

'I'm a friend of her fiancé's. I was just, he asked me to check up on her, while he's away. To make sure she's all right.'

'Well, you're not allowed in there,' she said. 'No one's allowed in there. But I can tell her you were asking after her. If you like?'

Arlette stared at the grimy building and then back at the grimy girl. There was another world behind those walls, a world she could not come close to imagining.

She shook her head and said, 'Thank you. But no. It's fine. As long as she's all right?'

'Yes, she's fine. Her and the baby. Fighting fit.'

'Good,' said Arlette, tears blurring her vision, 'that's good. Thank you for your time.'

And then she turned and headed back through the dirty streets of daytime Soho towards the glittering dress shop in gleaming, glorious Mayfair.

56

Telegram

Arlette STOP Call immediately STOP Hyd 2362
STOP I have news STOP Call as soon as you can
STOP
Lilian

Arlette read the telegram, once, then twice. She felt no
urgency. Just curiosity. 'I have news.' It could mean
anything. She did not hurry to the exchange. She felt
there was no need. Instead she folded the note, and tucked
it into her purse, with a half-formed plan to visit the
exchange on her way home from work, to where the
telegram had been delivered.

But the telegram sat in her purse, calling to her, as the
day passed. Why a telegram? she asked herself. If it was just
family news, would not a letter have sufficed? Eventually, as
the nagging feeling intensified, she asked her manager for
an early break and she made her way through the bustling
streets of St Peter Port to the main exchange.

The telephone was answered by the operator in Lilian's
apartment block. 'Hyde Park Mansions, to whom would
you like to be connected?'

Arlette asked for the Millers' apartment and the telephone in their flat was answered by the maid: 'Good afternoon, Millers' residence, how may I help you?'

'I would like to speak to Miss Lilian Miller.'

'And who shall I say is calling?'

'This is Miss De La Mare.'

'Just one moment, Miss De La Mare.'

Eventually Lilian came on the line and Arlette felt herself tense up at the prospect of what she was about to hear.

'Darling Arlette,' said Lilian, her voice choked with tears.

'What?' snapped Arlette. 'What is it?'

'It has been on the news, but I thought it may not have got as far as the Channel Isles.'

'What, Lilian, what?'

'Oh, it is too, too sad. The most dreadful thing. The orchestra . . .'

'The orchestra?'

'Yes, Arlette. The orchestra have drowned.'

Arlette paused, taking it in, trying to make sense of something that sounded, in Lilian's mangled words, faintly comical. How could an orchestra drown?

'The SS *Rowan*. It went down last night. Off the coast of Scotland. There was a collision with another ship. The orchestra were on board, Arlette, nearly all of them.'

Arlette blanched and sunk to her knees. The operator looked at her in alarm. '*Comment va, Mademoiselle?*' she asked in patois.

'Godfrey?' Arlette said.

'I have no idea; they have not yet released any names. But the whole ship went down, Arlette. The whole ship!'

Arlette breathed in and brought herself up to standing again. No, she thought, it simply could not be true. No, Godfrey would not have been on the ship. He would have been on his way back to London, to marry Esther Jones, to see his baby arrive in the world. He would not have been on the ship.

An image passed through her consciousness as she listened to Lilian sniffing and wailing in her Hyde Park apartment. It was an image of water, dark blue, dark as ink, and a man passing down through it, a smart suit floating from his body like the tendrils of a sea anemone, his arms spread out, his eyes open, the eyes of Godfrey Pickle, dead, but smiling as he drifted downwards, smiling and at peace. And then like an afterthought, drifting down behind him, a golden clarinet, glinting and glittering in the water, following him down to his watery grave. And she knew then that he was dead. Felt it inside herself, sharp as a knife, yet soothing as a lullaby.

Of course, she thought, of course.

She smiled then, the saddest smile she'd ever smiled, and said to Lilian, 'It's all right, Lilian. It really is. It's all right. We'll wait for news. Just wait for news.'

But she already knew there was no good news. The love of her life was dead. And his baby would have no father.

When it was confirmed three days later that eight

members of the orchestra had perished in the icy seas off the coast of Scotland, and that one of them had been 'world-renowned clarinettist Godfrey Pickle, otherwise known as Sandy Beach', Arlette sat in her room for a whole day and screamed until her throat was raw.

57

1995

Betty barely slept that night.

Candy Lee had a visitor downstairs and was screaming and banging walls, and the pub over the road had its doors wide open because it was such a warm night and the street was full of the sound of Iron Maiden and long-haired men wearing eyeliner. And, of course, on top of the usual night-time Soho cacophony, there was the sound of John Brightly, on the sofa down below, moaning quietly in his sleep and shouting out every now and then words that sounded like gobbledegook.

But more than the noise was the internal monologue hammering away in her head.

As she lay there, trying and failing to sleep, Clara was in a taxi coming home from the airport. And, as she lay there, trying and failing to sleep, Dom Jones was on a plane coming in to land at Berlin airport.

He'd given her the details of a farmhouse in Gloucestershire he'd looked at on Thursday. 'Take it,' he'd said, 'stare at it. Dream about it.'

She pulled it out from under her pillow now and switched on a torch, not wanting to wake John. The farmhouse was called St Luke's House. It was part Georgian, part Edwardian and, as she leafed through the details, she saw that it was utterly enchanting in every way, from its bleached blue stucco façade, to its vine-filled orangery, its full-length dining hall with buttressed ceiling and coat of arms, and its sweeping lawns that cascaded down towards fields of corn and rape.

From below she heard Candy Lee reaching her climax and she forced her pillow over her head until it was over. For a moment it was quiet and she turned her attention back to the details of the house. But then it started up again and she felt herself filled with a kind of primal rage.

She had not, she realised, for the full eight weeks of her time in Soho, slept through a whole night without interruptions. And if she did ever manage to sleep through a whole night without interruptions, she had been awoken at five o'clock by the rubbish trucks. And if she had ever managed to sleep through the five a.m. visits from the rubbish trucks then she had been awoken at six a.m. by the first of the market traders arriving to set up their stalls. The trucks and the traders she could stomach. Candy Lee wailing and banging on walls she could not. And so, before she'd had a chance to think through what she was doing, she'd pulled on a cardigan over her pyjamas, climbed down her ladder, tiptoed past John Brightly and marched downstairs to bang on Candy's door.

It took a moment or two for the door to be opened and when it finally was Betty did not know where to look.

There was Candy, dressed in a feathered bolero, leather chaps and PVC boots, her breasts hanging out over the top of a cut-out bra. She had a glass of champagne in one hand and in the other – and this was more remarkable to Betty than anything else about her appearance – a half-smoked cigarette.

'Beautiful Betty!' Candy beamed at her.

'You're smoking,' said Betty.

'Yes!' said Candy.

'But, I thought you were asthmatic?'

'I am! Betty! Come in! Finally, you came to see me.'

'No,' said Betty, suddenly flustered, 'listen. Candy. It's midnight. I've got to be up early in the morning for work. I've had a really, really, really long day. Could you please, *please*, PLEASE keep the noise down?'

Candy wrinkled her face up. 'Noise? What noise?'

Betty blanched, really not wanting to spell it out. 'The, you know, you and your friend.'

'What friend?'

Betty grimaced. 'You know, whoever you have staying with you tonight.'

'Betty! I have nobody staying with me tonight. I am alone, Betty.'

'But the . . .?'

'What, Betty?' Candy smiled at her disarmingly.

'All the . . .' She paused. 'All the shouting. And banging. You know.'

'Oh, Betty, that is just me! Pleasuring myself! There is nobody else. Look,' she pulled her door open wider and

Betty peered in just far enough to see that the entire flat was painted lurid lipstick pink. 'Look!'

'Right. Yes. I believe you. It's just. Well, nothing. I'm just tired and I want to sleep and I'd really appreciate it if you could . . . do . . . be a bit quieter.'

'I tell you what, Betty,' said Candy, her body-language suddenly becoming more hostile. 'You stop smoking outside my window,' she waved her cigarette around wildly, 'I stop being loud. Yes?'

Betty sighed. 'But, Candy, you're smoking. I don't understand.'

'Yes! I am smoking. I am not *passive* smoking. Big difference, OK?' And then, before Betty had a chance to work out any kind of reasonable response to such an unreasonable declaration, the door was slammed in her face.

Betty stood there for a moment. She rubbed her hands hard down her face. She shook her head from side to side. And then she turned and headed back upstairs.

John was still sleeping as she passed him on the sofa. She stopped and looked at him for a while. The moon was shining down onto him and he looked strangely pained, the muscles of his face knotted up under his skin. Instinctively she put a hand to his cheek, cupping it gently to soothe him. His eyes flickered open and he smiled at her.

'Betty?'

'Sorry,' she said, 'I didn't mean to wake you. You just looked so anxious.'

He smiled and yawned. 'I think you'll find that's my natural state of being.'

'No,' she said, not wanting to play that game any more. 'No. It's not.'

He looked at her quizzically.

'I've seen it now,' she said, 'the real John Brightly. In the park, chilling out, larking around with cream buns. You can't fool me any more.'

'Damn,' he said. 'Cover blown.' He brought himself up to a sitting position and Betty sat down next to him. 'What are you doing awake, anyway?'

'Candy Lee,' she sighed through a yawn. 'Bringing herself to countless extremely loud orgasms. In sexy lingerie. Jesus. I think I'm done here, you know. I think I'm finished with Soho. My mother was right. It's not a place to live. My contract's nearly up and I really think I might have to move on.'

John glanced at her anxiously. 'Oh,' he said flatly.

Betty smiled at him. 'You sound disappointed,' she said.

He shrugged. 'Well, you know, I've got used to having you around. Where are you thinking of going?'

'Oh, shit, I don't know.' She ran her hands down her face, thinking of St Luke's House. 'I have no idea.' She inhaled loudly, and then she said: 'Dom Jones just asked me to live with him.'

John blinked. 'What?'

'Earlier, when I went round to his. He told me he's crazy about me and he wants to live in the country with me and become a new person.' As the words left her mouth she felt the full ridiculousness of them and she laughed wryly.

'You're kidding me.'

'No,' she laughed again. 'I'm not. Look.' She brought the particulars for St Luke's House down from her mezzanine. 'He wants to buy this and move me in. He wants to be a "grown-up".'

The two of them sat side by side staring at the particulars for a minute, both trying to form a suitable response.

'So, that morning,' began John, 'you know, when you were coming in, early . . .?'

'Yes. I slept with him. I slept with Dom Jones. You were right.'

John groaned and let his chin fall into his chest. 'Oh, Betty,' he said.

'I know,' she said. 'And I know you said I would and I said I wouldn't, but honestly, John, he can be so lovely . . .'

John raised an eyebrow sceptically.

'Really. He can. And then other times he can be such a prick, and I do really like him, though I definitely don't think I love him. But look at this place!' she waved the paperwork. 'Just look at it! I wouldn't have to work again. I wouldn't have to worry about money . . .'

'You wouldn't ever be able to trust him. Ever.'

Betty sighed and stared at her feet. 'I know,' she said. 'Of course I know. It's just. Christ. He's a pop star. He's a genius . . .'

John snorted.

'Well, some people think he's a genius. And Arlette lost her chance to spend her life with a world-famous musician. She had that opportunity taken away from her and now it's being offered to me and I kind of think it's like history repeating itself and I'd need a really good reason not to take it.'

It was silent for a moment and Betty stared pensively at the carpet beneath her feet.

'I can think of a really good reason.'

She looked at him curiously. 'What?' she said.

'This,' he said.

And then he brought her face towards his with warm strong hands and kissed her on the lips.

Betty stared at him. She blinked, once, and said, 'You kissed me.'

He nodded.

'Why?' she said. 'Why did you kiss me?'

He groaned and got to his feet. He paced towards the window and stared at the street below.

'No, really,' she continued. 'Why?'

He turned, abruptly, and stared at her. 'Never mind,' he said quietly. 'Forget it ever happened.'

Betty put a finger to her lips, touching the spot where John Brightly's lips had brushed against hers. She was numb from head to toe. First Dom, then Candy, now John. She tried to think of something to say, but failed.

'I'm really sorry, OK?' said John. 'Bad timing. I just thought . . .'

'What?' said Betty.

'I don't know what I thought. But clearly I was wrong.'

'No,' said Betty. 'No, it's just . . .'

'Don't worry about it,' he said, 'go back to bed. Get some sleep.'

'No, I want to . . .'

'Seriously, Betty, go to sleep. Forget about it. Please.'

She stared at him for a moment, at the strong set of him, the shape of him silhouetted through the window, the fall of his shoulders. She had no idea what had just happened and no idea what it meant. But suddenly she was tired. She had nothing left to give to the day.

'Good night, John,' she said, climbing up her ladder.

'Good night, Betty,' said John, still staring through the window.

The following morning, John was gone and so were his meagre possessions. Outside, his stand was empty. Betty sighed and headed for work.

Monday was Donny's day at nursery so Betty dropped him off there, and then she took the two girls to a Tumble Tots class in a church hall in Hampstead, and it was there, while she sat with Astrid on her lap, watching Acacia climbing up a mountain of soft multicoloured cubes, that Clara Davies called her.

'Hello,' said a woman with a strong London accent. 'Is that Betty?'

'Yes,' said Betty, 'it is.'

'Oh, hello, this is Clara. Clara Davies. I got a message, from my brother Derek, to call you?'

'Yes!' cried Betty. 'Yes!' She grabbed Astrid and the phone and took them both to a quiet corner of the hall.

'He said something about an inheritance.'

'Yes,' said Betty, 'that's right. I've got some news for you. I wondered if it would be possible to meet up with you?'

'Well, yes, maybe. But I'd need to know more. I mean, who's it from?'

'It's from my grandmother,' said Betty. 'You didn't know her. But she knew your father. A long time ago.'

'My father?'

'Yes, not Edward Minchin. Your *real* father.'

'Oh, my word. My goodness. How peculiar. My real father.'

'How much do you know, about your real father?'

There was a small silence on the line and Betty moved Astrid onto her other knee.

'I just know that he was a sailor. From the Caribbean.'

'A sailor?' said Betty.

'Yes. A "boss-eyed, scurvy-riddled sailor" as my father used to describe him.' She laughed wryly.

Betty inhaled. 'Right,' she said. 'Listen. Can I meet you? I've got so much to tell you. And I've also got something to give you. Something my grandmother kept for a very long time.'

Clara Davies sighed. 'I suppose,' she said. 'Although I just got back from holiday, I've got so much to do . . .'

'It will only take a few minutes,' Betty said. 'I can meet you anywhere.'

Clara sighed again and then she said, 'Yes. All right then. Come here. What time?'

'I finish work at seven o'clock.'

'Come here at eight then. I'm in Battersea. Do you know it?'

'Actually,' said Betty, thinking of her visit to Peter Lawler's widow all those weeks ago, 'yes, I do.'

She hung up a minute later and put her hand into her bag, checking for the small ancient book that was now, finally, after seventy-four years, about to be reunited with its intended recipient, and she smiled.

58

Telegram

Arlette STOP Godfrey's baby born STOP A girl
STOP Clara Tatiana STOP Healthy and well
STOP That was as much as they would tell me
STOP
   Minu

Arlette folded the telegram and she smiled. Thank God,
she thought to herself, thank God. A small chink of light
had forced its way through the darkness. The baby was
safe. Her mother was safe. A small part of Godfrey
remained.

She thought of the baby constantly over the course of
the next few days. She tried to picture her, wondered if
she would have the tight dark curls of her father or the
smooth brown locks of her mother. She wondered how
dark she would be, what colour her eyes were. She passed
the children's clothes shop in St Peter Port every day and
eyed the bootees and the mittens, the tiny hats and hand-
knitted layettes.

She stared into perambulators and gasped at the
tininess and preciousness of new infants. She thought

about the baby so much that she ached with it. And she knew that tied in irrevocably with her obsession with the idea of Godfrey's baby girl across the Channel were her own unformed feelings about the baby she had carried and lost nine months ago. The tiny blue scrap who she hadn't been allowed so much as to glance upon. She had been glad at the time, glad to be spared the fate of a loveless, sexless marriage to a man she despised. But although her head had made sense of it all, her heart still yearned for the thing she'd been expecting that had not materialised: the baby in her arms.

Her obsession grew as the days passed. She caught the eye of a black-faced sailor in a St Peter Port alleyway one evening at dusk and for a moment she was tempted to take him from the street into a room and to make with him a baby just like Clara Tatiana, a baby like Godfrey's, a beautiful brown baby. The thought passed in and out of her consciousness like a bullet, gone before she'd acknowledged it. But she feared herself growing mad with it, with this need to be involved, to be a part of Clara Tatiana.

And then one day, a week after Clara's birth, she walked into a bookshop and she said to the man who sat behind the desk wearing a threadbare suit and broken spectacles, 'Excuse me, but do you have any stories for children, about a little black girl?'

The man looked at her aghast and removed his broken spectacles. 'About what, Mademoiselle?'

'About a little black girl,' she repeated. 'A storybook.'

He replaced his spectacles and huffed and puffed and said, 'What an odd request. No. I'm sure we don't. Although, if you're not fussed about gender, I could offer you this . . .' He pulled a book from a shelf and passed it to her. The book was called *The Story of Little Black Sambo* and featured on its cover an illustration of a coal-black boy with a mop of matching hair and legs like string, holding a green umbrella and beaming brightly with vivid yellow teeth. Arlette recoiled. The image was alarming and unsettling. 'No,' she said, 'no, that's not right at all. I was hoping for something a little more . . . *realistic*.'

The bookseller put his hands into the pockets of his old suit jacket and rocked back on his heels. 'What on earth do you mean?'

'I mean, I mean . . .' she faltered. She didn't know what she meant. What she wanted, she supposed, was a book about a little girl who looked exactly like the fantasy girl she'd spent all week creating inside her own head. 'Oh, nothing,' she said eventually. 'I just want a book for a little girl. A book she could grow to love as she grew up. A book she would like to keep for ever and read to her own daughters.'

'Well, then,' said the bookseller, 'you couldn't go too far wrong with this. It's one of our bestsellers. Has been for years.' He put another book into her hands. *Pollyanna*. The character on the front of the jacket was far from black, but she was lovely to behold, a joyful girl clutching a basket of flowers, swinging through a sun-dappled meadow. It was bright and uplifting, just what a girl born into a grimy

Soho almshouse to a father she would never meet might like to own.

'What is the story about?' she asked, turning it over in her hands.

'It is about,' he said, 'a very *glad girl*.'

Arlette paid for the book and watched as the dusty man wrapped it and tied it with ribbon. When she got home she wrote carefully on the inside cover and then, before she rewrapped it, a thought occurred to her. She pulled out the drawer on her dressing table and she put her fingers to the very back. From there she pulled out a tiny square of muslin. She put it to her nose and breathed in deeply, taking in the smell of Godfrey Pickle one last time, before sliding it in between the pages of the book, wrapping it and sending it to the house on St Anne's Court.

Dear Miss De La Mare,

I thank you for this gift. I cannot aksept it. Sandy is gonn and his dorter is now sum one elsis. We won't tork of him agin in our hows. Please do not bother us agin. You are not welcum.

Yorse,

Esther Jones

59

1995

Clara Davies lived in a tiny cottage off Battersea High Street. She was tall and elegant, with wiry silver hair, which she wore tied back in a bun, and was dressed in black trousers, a black T-shirt and a turquoise belted cardigan. On her feet were red patent pumps with gold buckles.

Betty stared at the pumps in surprise, thinking how much Arlette would have liked them.

'Betty?' she said, in a rough London accent, that didn't quite match her elegant appearance. 'Lovely to meet you. Come in.'

She held the door open and Betty entered. 'I'm really sorry I'm late,' she said, brushing her feet against the doormat, 'I work as a nanny and my boss was a bit late home.'

'Never mind, never mind, you're here now.' She led her into a tiny living room where a tray of tea and biscuits was neatly laid out. Everything in her house was perfect: floral curtains, antique pine furnishings, a smoke-stained fireplace, a vase of yellow tulips and pictures everywhere of children and grandchildren, of holidays and Christmases and good times.

Clara poured her tea into a chinoiserie cup and passed it to her. She looked like Godfrey, Betty thought, or at least she looked like the portrait of Godfrey that Gideon Worsley's nephew had shown him in that book in his shop. She had the hooked nose, although much smaller and neater, and the heavy-lidded eyes. She was strikingly, remarkably beautiful even in her seventies and Betty's eyes then rested upon a studio portrait, in black and white, of Clara in her youth.

'Is that you?' she asked, pointing at it.

'Oh, yes. That's me all right. Back in my heyday.' She laughed warmly. 'Had that on my Z-card.'

'Z-card?'

'Yeah, you know, my modelling card.'

'You were a model?'

'Yes, well, sort of. Not much call for mixed-race girls in my day. But I did a bit of that, a bit of singing, bit of acting. I was a regular little showgirl, really.' She chuckled and poured herself a cup of tea.

Betty smiled at her. 'You were very beautiful,' she said. 'If you were modelling today . . .'

'Yeah, I'd probably be on the front of *Vogue* or something. But that's that. That's the way it was. Life moves on. I've had a good life so I can't complain about anything really. Though the money these supermodels make these days, I could have done with a bit of that.' She laughed out loud and Betty, at the mention of money, pulled out her handbag.

'So, listen, first things first. This inheritance.'

Clara's eyes lit up. 'Well, yes. All very mysterious. Are you sure you've got the right Clara Davies?' She laughed again.

Betty laughed too. 'Yes,' she said. 'Quite sure. Although the name on the will is actually Clara Jones. Or Clara Pickle.'

'Clara *Pickle!*' She laughed even louder then. 'What sort of name is that?'

'Well,' said Betty, gently, 'that's the name you'd have had if your father hadn't died.'

Clara put her hands to her throat and roared out laughing. 'Oh my goodness,' she breathed, 'Clara Pickle. Can you imagine! Clara Pickle. Well, I had a close escape there then, didn't I? I always thought Minchin was bad. But *Pickle* . . .'

'Godfrey Pickle. That was his name.'

Clara stopped laughing and became more serious. She narrowed her eyes at Betty and said, 'How do you *know* all this? Who are you?'

'I told you, my grandmother was a friend of Godfrey's. I think . . .' she paused, passed her hand over the book in her handbag '. . . I think they were lovers. I don't know. She never mentioned it while she was alive. But she hired a private eye to find you, when she was alive.' She shrugged. 'And also, at some point she put you in her will. So whatever their relationship with each other, it must have been important in some way.'

Clara nodded, her teacup still held in her hand where it had been suspended for the past minute.

'And anyway,' Betty continued. 'At some point, while my grandmother still had her health, she sent this private eye some bits and pieces from her time in London – photos, flyers – but it seems that the investigator died before he ever managed to find anything to lead him to you. His ex-wife had been sitting with all this stuff in a box for years, wondering what to do with it.'

'And then you came along?'

'Yes,' smiled Betty. 'The will states that you had to be found in a year, and if neither you nor any of your successors were found within that time, then, well, the inheritance would revert to me.'

Clara's eyes widened. 'My God, you daft ha'p'orth, why did you find me?' she laughed again, loud and rich.

'Legally incumbent and all that,' Betty replied. 'If you'd ever found out that you'd been mentioned in this will and no one had made any effort to find you, you could have sued. Me,' she finished, with a small laugh. 'So I came over in April and set out to find you. And eight weeks later, here I am.'

Clara put down her teacup and smiled at Betty. 'Maybe a new career for you then. Private investigator.'

Betty smiled. 'Maybe,' she said. 'So, listen then, here it is . . .' She pulled out the will and passed it to Clara. 'Proof, that I'm not a nut-job.'

Clara read the will, slowly and silently. 'What's this?' she said. 'St Anne's Court. Soho?'

'It used to be a home,' Betty explained, 'for unwed mothers. I think it's where you were born.'

Clara put a hand to her heart, as though finally, the significance of this meeting was making itself felt.

'And who are all these other people?'

'That's Jolyon, my stepfather, and Alison is my mum.'

Clara carried on reading and smiled as she read Arlette's closing line about jazz and dancing at her funeral.

'She sounds like a fun lady, your grandmother.'

'Well, no, she wasn't. Not really. She was quite proper. Quite stern. Didn't really like anyone. But she did like me,' Betty said. 'She liked me very much. I think . . .' She paused, a thought occurring to her, fresh and new. 'She always used to say she'd wanted a girl. I think, in her heart, she always felt she should have had you.'

A small silence fell and Betty sipped her tea.

'So,' said Clara. 'The big question . . .'

Betty put down her cup and sat up straight, glad to be pulled out of her reverie and back to the point in question. 'Yes,' she said, 'well, according to my stepfather, the sum of money in the bank account she stipulates is around about ten thousand pounds.'

Clara gasped. 'Well, I never,' she said.

'But there's also some pension funds and saving schemes and a lot of other stuff that he's still sorting out from her estate. It could be a lot more than that.'

Clara gasped again.

'And there's something else.' Betty reached back into her bag. 'I found this, in Arlette's wardrobe. I realised when I saw the inscription that there was a connection with the girl in the will, so I brought it with me.'

She passed the book to Clara, who stared at it tenderly.

'Look,' said Betty, 'look at the inscription.'

Clara opened the book and read it. A sheen of tears came to her eyes. 'How lovely,' she said. 'What a lovely, lovely thing.' She flicked through the book and smiled. 'It's so old,' she said, 'I've never seen such an old book before.'

'I've had it valued. It's worth only about forty pounds, but could be more now that we know the story behind the inscription. That would add to its value. Because there's so much to this story, Clara, so much I don't think you know.'

'Shall I get us a glass of wine?'

Betty smiled and nodded.

Clara brought the wine in two small glasses and handed one to Betty. She also put a bowl of salted nuts on the table between them. 'So,' she said, 'tell me what you know.'

'Well, why don't we start with you telling me what you know, so that I don't spring anything too shocking on you.'

'Well,' said Clara, gently running her hand up and down the book on her lap. 'I really don't know anything. Just what I said. My mum was taken somewhat against her will by a "dirty black boss-eyed sailor". That's what my dad told us. Just the once mind, sat us all down when I was about six, when I asked why I was black and the others weren't. Sat us all down and told us that. Told us never to mention it to Mum, said she couldn't talk about it, even now. Said he'd taken pity on Mum, and married her even with the black bastard baby. I mean, you can see why I didn't want to dwell on it too much, can't you? You can see why we didn't talk about it.' She stopped and looked up at Betty questioningly. 'So,' she said, 'go on . . .'

Betty took a deep breath. The woman sitting in front of her was seventy-three years old, she'd had children and grandchildren, she'd lived a long, full, colourful life and it seemed insolent, in a way, for a stripling like Betty, a girl who'd done nothing and gone nowhere, to be rearranging the entire skeleton of this fine woman's history.

'Your father,' she began, 'was not a sailor. He was a musician. A clarinettist. He played with a world-famous jazz orchestra. Your father played in front of the King of England. He played in every city in this country. He had London at his feet. Your father was not a boss-eyed sailor. Or a rapist. He was a legend.'

Clara stared at her.

'Here,' she said, 'here are some photocopies that they did for me at the Soho Historical Society, of flyers and stuff. And here's a photo of the orchestra. Godfrey's not in that picture, unfortunately; it was taken before he joined.'

Clara fingered the photocopy gently, her eyes shining with pleasure. 'Oh my, look at them,' she said. 'Aren't they a fine-looking group of fellows? In their smart suits. I mean, gosh, I had no idea there were all these black fellows in London that long ago. I had no idea at all . . .'

She looked up from the photo. 'Are there any pictures of this Godfrey fellow? Of my . . .?'

'Your dad? Yes,' Betty said, holding another photocopy to her chest. 'I have got one. Are you ready?'

Clara gulped and nodded. 'Ready as I'll ever be,' she said.

Betty passed her the Love Brothers flyer, the piece of paper that had gone from London to Guernsey seventy years ago, then back to London in the post to Peter Lawler, and then sat for years in a box in a flat on Battersea Park Road before being passed into her hands, and now, finally, being given to the person in the world to whom it would mean the most. Betty felt a chill run down her spine and she watched Clara intently.

Clara didn't say anything for a moment. She sat, with her hand at her throat, her other hand holding the corner of the flyer. Her eyes filled with tears and then she looked up at Betty and said, 'Him, in the middle?'

Betty nodded.

'Oh my,' she said. 'Oh my. He's . . .' She pulled a tissue from the pocket of her cardigan and held it to her eyes. 'He's ever so handsome, isn't he? What a handsome, handsome man. My word. My word.'

She stared at the flyer in silence again. 'He looks like me,' she whispered after a moment. She looked up at Betty and said it again, louder. 'Don't you think? He looks just like me?'

'He really does,' agreed Betty.

'Is this the only picture you've got?'

Betty nodded. 'Although . . .' she began.

'Yes?'

'Well, from what I can see it looks like my grandmother also had an affair with an artist while she was in London, an artist called Gideon Worsley. He has two portraits hanging in the National Portrait Gallery, including one of my grandmother.'

'Well, I never.'

'He painted a lot of jazz musicians from around that time. And I met his nephew last week and he showed me a picture of a portrait of both of them. Your father and my grandmother. Apparently it's hanging in the estate where the artist grew up. In Oxfordshire.'

'My word.'

'Would you like to go and see it? It's open to the public.'

Clara laughed nervously. 'Well, yes. Gosh, yes, I'm sure I would. I think. But,' her face darkened, 'my dad. I mean, my real dad, the one who raised me. He's so old now. He's ninety-five. I just think, well, he mustn't know. It might kill him, you know. All these years, he's done everything for me, all these years, he's been the best dad, always been my hero, you know. I want to go and see this painting. But, please, don't ever let my dad know. Will you?'

'No,' said Betty, 'of course I won't. Never.'

Clara smiled with relief. 'Thank you,' she said. 'Thank you. For everything. For this,' she gestured at the flyer, 'and this.' She gestured at the will. 'You know, all my life, I've thought it was a miracle that I could have come into this world through such dark happenings, that I could have had the genes of such a bad man, yet my entire life has been like a fairy tale, you know. Met the man of my dreams, had the job of my dreams, two beautiful daughters, two wonderful sisters, my funny brother, my sweet, sweet parents. Never wanted for anything, never known a day's pain or sadness. I always wondered how it could be – that maybe I had a fairy godmother, you know, or a guardian angel, someone looking over me. And now it all makes sense. My father was a special man . . .' She paused thoughtfully for a moment and then looked at Betty. 'I mean, I assume he's dead. This man. This Godfrey Pickle?'

Betty nodded. 'He died a month before you were born. He was twenty-seven. He and the orchestra were on a ship to Scotland. It collided with another ship in the fog. Eight of them died. They never found your father . . .'

Fresh tears sprang to Clara's eyes. 'So Godfrey and my mother, were they . . .?'

'I don't know that story, unfortunately. There's only one person who could tell you the truth about that.'

'Dad.'

'Yes.'

Clara sighed. 'Ah well,' she said. 'Then that is a story I will never really know.'

Clara put all the paper into a neat pile on the coffee table in front of her and sighed again. 'Well,' she said, bittersweetly, 'well I never. This is like *Surprise, Surprise*. I keep half-expecting Cilla Black to walk in and burst into song!'

She laughed and picked up the *Pollyanna* book and as she did so, something fell from between its pages onto her lap. She picked it up and looked at it. 'Whatever is that?' she said, holding it up to Betty.

It was a small square of muslin, slightly yellowed with age. Clara held it to her nose and inhaled. 'Mmm,' she said, 'it smells kind of perfumey.' She passed it to Betty, who also smelled it. And as she did so it was as if she'd been swallowed up inside a tidal wave of nostalgia and memory. She was there, in Arlette's boudoir, sniffing all her scents, the overwrought brown fragrances in delicate glass bottles with silver filigree casings and tiny glass droppers. And she saw herself, as if it were two minutes ago, reaching for the dropper of a bottle of something green and fresh-looking, and Arlette saying, '*Ah, now that one, Betty, is not a lady's perfume. That is an aftershave. A scent for a man. Have a sniff, tell me what you think.*'

Betty dropped the perfume onto her tiny wrist and inhaled. 'Yummy,' she said. 'It smells like being on holiday.'

'Well, yes,' Arlette had smiled, 'exactly right. Sandalwood and vanilla. I got it shipped over specially from Liberty. It reminds me so very much of another time and place. It reminds me so much of Godfrey.'

'Who was Godfrey?'

'Godfrey was a friend of mine. A very long time ago. And that is how he smelled.'

Betty had not needed or asked for any more detail than that, and until this precise moment she had not remembered the conversation at all.

But now she passed the muslin square back to Clara and she smiled and said, 'That was how your father smelled. Sandalwood and vanilla. From Liberty.'

Clara smiled too, sniffed the square one more time, deeply and intensely, and put it in the pocket of her cardigan.

'Thank you,' she said. 'Thank you for finding me. I am really ever so grateful.'

Dom's plane landed at Heathrow at ten o'clock on Wednesday morning. At ten twenty-seven Betty's phone rang. She was at the kitchen table in Amy's house painting old toilet roll tubes with glitter paint.

'I'm back,' said Dom. 'When can I see you?'

'Now,' said Betty, wanting to get this done. 'I'm at home, with the kids, come now.'

'I'll be there in an hour,' he said. 'I missed you.'

Betty didn't reply.

'You're blond again!' were Dom's first words as he strolled into the hallway at eleven thirty.

Betty put her hand to her hair and smiled. 'Yes,' she said. 'Amy paid for it. At her hairdressers.'

Dom rolled his eyes. 'Ah yes,' he said, 'buttering you up nicely.'

Betty smiled and said nothing but his reaction to Amy's treat merely cemented her commitment to the decision she'd made on Sunday night.

'It was a nice thing to do,' she said.

'Well, yes. It was. And you look stunning. But don't be fooled. She has a hidden agenda, remember that.'

Betty narrowed her eyes at him. 'I think,' she said, 'that the only hidden agenda Amy has is to provide decent childcare for her children. And the only reason why the other nannies never lasted more than four months was because they weren't good enough. And I am.'

Dom raised his eyebrows at her and put up a pacifying hand. 'OK, OK,' he said. 'I'm just trying to put you in the picture, that's all.'

'Dom,' she said, 'I am in the picture. I am standing right in the middle of the picture looking at it from every angle and all I can say is that while I respect you as a musician and as a father and as an employer, you are a really, really awful ex-husband.'

He threw her a look of horror.

'Seriously. I mean it. You put three babies in that woman, one after the other, and then you let yourself be dragged into a filthy toilet by some "ugly girl", because you have no control over your "little fella",' she stared meaningfully at his crotch, 'and *then* you spend the next two months blaming your wife for everything when it is your wife who is running around like a headless chicken trying to hold everything together. And somehow you have managed to persuade yourself that things would be different with me. But they wouldn't. I am not the answer, Dom. Really. I'm not. No woman is the answer for you. Because any woman you end up with would become Amy in the end. And you would never ever be faithful. And I am not so desperate to live in the lap of luxury that I would want to spend the rest of my life wondering who you're in bed with or how much you're drinking or whether you're going to come home and be nice Dom or not nice Dom. And besides . . .' she paused for breath, inhaled, smiled softly, 'besides all of that, Dom, I don't love you.'

He stared at her agog.

'So thank you, Dom, for the kind offer, but I'm afraid I won't be taking you up on it. I'll be staying here. In London. Working for Amy. And I'll just be,' she smiled again, 'I'll just be – the nanny.'

The monitor on the kitchen counter crackled into life then and the sound of Astrid waking from her morning nap filled the air.

'Donny and Acacia are in the kitchen,' she said, 'they'd love to see you. Can you stay?'

He nodded at her mutely. 'Er, sure,' he said. 'Yeah. I'm not in a hurry.'

'Good,' said Betty, heading up the stairs. 'I've just boiled the kettle. Maybe you could make us a pot of tea?'

She walked away from him then, up the stairs and down the corridor, a smile of satisfaction playing gently on her lips.

60

Ten Days Later

'Ah, Miss Betty Dean, welcome, welcome, welcome!' Jeremiah Worsley walked towards her, his feet crunching against the gravelled driveway, a big red hand outstretched, smiling widely. 'Welcome to our humble abode.'

Humble it was not. A picturebook Jacobean manor house set in a wooded vale; crenulations, candy-twist chimney stacks, box-cut yews, a moat and gargoyles. One of the prettiest houses Betty had ever seen.

'Allow me to introduce you to George Worsley, my nephew, and his wife, Kitty. They run the estate now, poor buggers,' he laughed heartily.

Betty shook hands with the couple who looked like they'd stepped straight off the cover of *Country Life*, right down to their ruddy cheeks and the pair of chocolate Labradors skittering around their wellington-booted feet.

'Hellair, hellair,' they both said, 'how wonderful to meet you, Betty.'

'Likewise,' she said. And then she turned to the minibus parked in the driveway behind her. 'I've brought quite a party,' she said, 'I hope you don't mind?'

'Nair nair, not at awl,' said George, 'after all, this is quite a momentous event.'

The door of the minibus slid open and Betty introduced its passengers as they disembarked.

'This is Jolyon, Arlette's son, and Alison, my mother. This is Alexandra Brightly, a friend of mine, who helped with my search. And this,' she held out her hand to help her from the bus, 'is Clara Davies, Godfrey's daughter.'

Jeremiah, George and Kitty's faces blossomed at the sight of their guests. 'So lovely to meet you all, so utterly thrilling.'

'Such a beautiful house,' said Clara, staring upwards and around herself in awe.

'Thank you veh much,' trilled Kitty. 'It's a total pain, awbviously, but worth all the sweat and tears. Anyway, come in, come in, do.'

The party followed Jeremiah, George and Kitty through breathtaking room after breathtaking room. They gave a perfunctory commentary as they passed through each: blue room, red room, green room, sitting room, library, billiards room, like a full-size tour of a Cluedo board.

And then they came to a stop outside a room with a plaque outside that said: 'The Gideon Worsley Room.'

'Well, then, here we are,' said Kitty, rubbing her hands together. 'As you know, Great-uncle Gideon was a well-regarded portraitist of the post-war generation. Something of a black sheep, he found his way to London after the war and lived an unconventional life: a meagre cottage, bohemian friends and a taste for the exotic. Two of his portraits hang in the National Portrait Gallery, and five hang here, at his ancestral family home. The rest are in private ownership around the world. So,' she glanced from Jolyon to Clara, 'are you ready?'

Clara and Jolyon smiled at each other and nodded.

'Here it is,' said George, removing a red velvet cover with a flourish, '*Sandy and Arlette.*'

Betty caught her breath and held it as the cover came away. And then she gasped. Her hand went instinctively to her throat and she turned to catch Jolyon's reaction. 'Well, well, well,' he said, shaking his head slowly. 'Well, I never.'

Betty turned then to Clara. She too had her hand to her throat and was staring at the painting with her jaw ajar.

'Wow,' said Alexandra.

'Incredible,' said Alison.

'Good grief,' said Jolyon.

'Quite something, isn't it?' said Jeremiah, smiling with satisfaction.

'It's awesome,' said Alexandra. 'I want it. How much will you take for it?'

Her joke broke through the air of stultifying shock and everyone laughed softly.

Jolyon moved closer to the painting and squinted at it. 'It's incredible,' he said, leaning in closer. 'Utterly incredible, I mean, look at Mummy. *Look at her.*' He turned incredulously to both Betty and Alison. 'She looks so . . . *sexy.*' He flushed violently red as the word left his mouth. 'Remarkable,' he continued. 'Just remarkable. I can't believe you did it, Betty. You really did it.' He eyed her proudly. 'What an achievement. My God. And all this history. All this colour. This drama. Imagine,' he said, dreamily, 'if we'd just placed an advert and no one had replied and we'd never have known any of this.' He shook his head sadly at the thought. 'Thank you, Betty,' he said. 'Thank you so much.'

Clara was sniffing and dabbing at her eyes with a tissue. 'I'm sorry,' she said as Betty put an arm around her shoulder, 'it's just, you know, *wow*. My daddy. Such a fine, fine man. I just want to touch him, you know, I want to stretch out my hand and just *touch him*.'

George pulled a camera from a bag around his neck and said, 'Would you mind awfully, Jolyon, Clara, just a photo, just for us, of the two of you, next to your respective parents?'

They looked at each other uncertainly. Clara said, 'Not for publicity? Not for anything official? My father, my real father, I don't want him to –'

'No, I assure you, just for us, for the family, for posterity.'

Jolyon and Clara posed then, one on either side of the painting, smiling shyly, Arlette's son, Godfrey's daughter, neither the child that the couple had dreamed of making together, but their children none the less. Betty took some photos with her own camera and with Clara's, and Alison took photos with hers. It was a sweet, perfect moment, as the sun streamed in through the stained leaded windows and a small group of disparate people made some kind of resolution with themselves and the truth of their pasts. A weird kind of family connection was being made here today, a connection not of blood, but of shared history.

Betty stood back for a moment and surveyed the scene. She imagined for a moment Godfrey and Arlette watching from somewhere high above them all, from somewhere high behind that hot, round summer sun. She saw them and they were smiling.

John Brightly did a double take when he saw Betty walking towards his record stall the following morning.

'You're blond again,' he said.

She ruffled her hair with her fingers and smiled. 'I certainly am.'

He nodded. 'I like it.'

'Good,' she said, pushing her sunglasses up into her hair.

'I thought you'd moved out.' He gestured at the door behind them with his eyes.

'Yeah. I did. I have. Last Friday. I would have said goodbye, but you weren't here.'

He shrugged. 'Yeah. Yeah . . .' he petered off.

'What happened to you?'

He shrugged again. 'Nothing much. Just needed to, you know, regroup. Find a new flat.'

'And did you?'

'Yeah. I did. A nice place. Top floor. Dry. Clean. You know.'

'Whereabouts?'

'Notting Hill. Well, yeah, North Kensington, more accurately, but I can walk to the tube in under ten minutes.' He rearranged a stack of records, mindlessly. 'And you,' he said, eventually. 'What about you? Where are you living now?'

'I am living in Zone *Three*,' she said with a grim smile.

John winced sympathetically.

'Tooting Broadway. Sharing a flat with a girl called Celia. Found it through an ad in *Loot*, you know, like a *real* Londoner. Nice quiet block. Nice quiet neighbours. Half an hour on the Northern line to work. No one's been sick on our front step. *Yet*.' She smiled and rocked back on her heels slightly.

'So you decided against the rock-chick lifestyle option?'

She snorted. 'Of course I did.'

He looked at her curiously. 'Hmm.'

'Hmm what?'

'Nothing,' he said. 'Just, you know, that night, you sounded like you were seriously considering it.'

'Well, yeah. I was. For about thirty seconds. Until somebody gave me a good reason not to.'

He glanced at her with surprise. Then he turned back to his record stall as if the conversation was over.

'It's my birthday today,' she said. 'I'm twenty-three.'

'Oh,' he turned to her and smiled. 'Wow. Well. Happy birthday to you.'

Betty took a deep breath, readying herself for her next question. 'Is that kiss still up for grabs?'

He stared at her in amazement. Then his face softened. 'What,' he said, 'you mean, this one?' He leaned down and kissed her.

'Yes,' she said, pulling away from the kiss. 'Yes, that one.'

John Brightly smiled at her, one of his lottery winner smiles, and said, 'Oh, all right then, but only because it's your birthday.' And then they wrapped their arms around each other, there, in the swirling, pungent chaos of a crazy Soho morning, and they kissed each other as if there was nobody there to see them.

Acknowledgements

Thanks to Kate Burke, my lovely shiny new editor, for the superb brainstorming session which helped bring Arlette's story fully to life, and for finally letting me have a photograph on my cover, like a big grown-up writer. And massive thanks to Susan, Jen, Najma, Claire, Georgina, Selina, Rob, Andrew, Richard and everyone else at Random House who works so hard on my behalf.

Thanks to all my friends on the Board, life without you doesn't bear thinking about. And thanks to all the staff at Apostrophe for letting me sit for hours over a laptop and a double macchiato without ever asking me what on earth I was doing.

Thanks to Jonny Geller, my trusty and wonderful agent.

Thanks to Jascha, my trusty and wonderful husband.

And thanks to all my lovely followers on Twitter and fantastic friends on Facebook. I hope it doesn't sound daft to say you make me feel like part of a big online family.

The character name of Minu McAteer was given to me by Maggie McAteer, the winner of an auction in aid of the brilliant Peter Bowron Catteshall Stroll which raises funds for the children's hospice charity Shooting Star CHASE (www.catteshallstroll.co.uk). Thank you, Maggie, I really hope your niece enjoys her namesake (once she's old enough to read!).

Notes on the text

The Southern Syncopated Orchestra was a real orchestra. As far as possible I have stuck to the facts regarding the orchestra and their lengthy tour of the United Kingdom during 1919–1921. Everything else – the clubs, the musicians, the socialites and the journalists – is pure fiction. And any historical errors are entirely of my own making.

Getting to Know
Lisa Jewell

Read on for an exclusive piece by Lisa on the writing of *Before I Met You*, reading group questions, a Q&A, and Lisa's tips for aspiring writers.

Lisa on
Before I Met You

I had no idea when I began writing *Before I Met You* that it would end up being a dual-timeframe mystery. The book started life as a simple romance, but by the time I'd brought Betty to London, set her up in her Soho studio flat, given her a job at Wendy's and introduced her to her two love interests, rather terrifyingly, I ran out of steam. I no longer wanted to write a romance! I wasn't, as they say, *feeling it*. So I sent off the first hundred or so pages to my editor, after which we spent a rather intense hour on the phone trying to work out how to give the story legs and wings. It was during this conversation that I had a sudden image of a faded black and white photograph of Betty's recently deceased grandmother, young and glamorous in swinging 1920's London, and immediately I could see what I needed to do.

I envisaged Arlette being part of the post-war London jazz scene in the late 1910s, but wasn't entirely sure that jazz had made it to London that early. Serendipitously, the first web page that came up when I ran a Google search for jazz in 1919 was a BBC article about the Southern Syncopated Orchestra. As I read the article I felt shivers of excitement. The last piece of the jigsaw had revealed itself. So I took Arlette from the early chapters and gave her a remarkable back story and, in the process of doing so, gave her granddaughter Betty a wonderful mystery to solve.

The book wrote itself from that point onwards. I didn't do any preliminary research into the period (apart from reading a book called *Under My Own Colours* by Susy Kestler, the granddaughter of one of the original members of the Southern Syncopated Orchestra). I'd never written in a historical period before and I really wanted to do what I always do when writing, which is just to jump in feet first and let the characters take the lead, rather than getting distracted by other people's stories. Instead, I researched as I wrote, as and when the narrative needed it. I have no idea if my 1920 chapters would stand up to intense scrutiny by a historian (I very much doubt it!) but I certainly hope I've captured the flavour and feeling of the times. The post-war years in London were quite a remarkable period in social history. The younger generation were peeling off layers of stale Victorian values and the city was full of free thinkers, liberals and bohemians. I would love to have been a part of it – the clothes! Particularly the clothes! – but have had to make do with just writing about it instead.

I also loved writing about the Britpop years. I fell in love with my husband in 1995 so it was almost a given that I would set Betty's love story bang in the middle of Blur v. Oasis, shaggy haircuts and the advent of mobile phones. Writing about a world without mobile phones and the internet was quite liberating. As a writer you have many more options available for stretching out the suspense when the reader can't say, 'Well, why didn't he just Google it?' Or 'Surely she would have called him by now?' It was fun to write about payphones, telephone directories and handwritten notes put through letterboxes. And it's much more satisfying to put a character on a bus across London to research something rather than to sit them in front of a laptop.

I absolutely loved writing this book, and that is genuinely the first time I have been able to say that about a book since *Ralph's Party*. I really hope the pleasure I took in writing it shines through and that you have enjoyed reading it.

Lots of love,

Lisa

x

Reading Group Questions on *Before I Met You*

- Once Betty arrives in Soho, she feels quite overwhelmed by what has happened recently. How do you think you would feel if you were in her situation, and decided to embark upon a journey on your own and out of your comfort zone?

- There are a number of differences between Betty's life in the 1990s and Arlette's in the 1920s. But what are the similarities? Do you relate to either one of them in particular?

- In moving to Soho, Betty gains a lot of life experience in a short amount of time. How do you think she has changed throughout the novel? How does this compare to Arlette?

- When Arlette breaks up with Godfrey, she lies to him. Do you think this was the right thing to do? Should she have told him the truth about Gideon straight away?

- Betty continues to see Dom even though she is warned against him. How did you feel about Dom? Did you trust him? Would you have stayed away from him?

- The fire at Leticia's house is described as both a blessing and a tragedy. Do you agree? Do you feel it was more one than the other? Why?

- What do you make of Amy's relationship with Dom? Do you feel sorry for her?

- Do you think that Arlette regrets her time in London as it has caused her so much sadness? Or do you think she feels it was worth it to meet Godfrey? How would you feel?

- Betty spends her time in Soho with both Dom and John Brightly. How do the two of them compare with each other? Do you think that Betty makes the right choice?

- Arlette goes through a lot of upset during her story. Does knowing what has happened to her alter your viewpoint of the Arlette we meet at the beginning of the story?

Q&A with Lisa

• **Which writers or books have inspired you?**

As a child I read anything and everything, from the children's classics to Dickens to *The Thorn Birds, The Grapes of Wrath* and every single Agatha Christie ever published. I read four or five books a week, so on a deeply fundamental level I have been inspired by a huge and eclectic raft of writers. More specifically I do love Nick Hornby and Maggie O'Farrell, both of whom make what they do look so easy. It was a conversation with a friend about *High Fidelity* that resulted in me writing my first book and you don't get much more inspiring than that!

• **What made you want to become a writer?**

Reading made me want to become a writer. I had a vague idea about being a journalist as a child but life took me far away from that, and by the time I was in my twenties I was a secretary. I'd married young and started reading a lot again and my husband told me he thought I'd be able to write a book that other people would want to read. After that marriage broke up I signed up for creative writing lessons to see if he was right. He was.

• **What's the best thing about being an author?**

On a practical level it is so nice not to have to wake up every morning and go to the same place and see the same people and do things for someone else that you're not really that interested in. I love working from home and making my own schedule. On good days it is possible for me to do a whole day's work in an hour. Then I get to have fun. It's also a brilliant job to have when you've got kids, as you can work your days around them and not miss out on anything. Beyond the practical, though, I do love it when I'm talking to someone who's really full of themselves and they ask me what I do and I tell them I'm a published author. It's very satisfying!

• *Before I Met You* is your tenth novel. Have you found that your writing has changed since *Ralph's Party* (1999)?

I hope so. It's hard for me to be objective. My readers would probably be better placed to comment on that. I definitely have to try harder and harder with each book to avoid repeating myself, which results in new ways of using language and describing things. I have also discovered the joy of a proper storyline. My first few books were very much jumping in blindly and seeing where I ended up. These days I'd rather have a structure in place and a solid concept behind the characters.

• How did it feel to write about two very distinct time periods at the same time? Was there one you preferred over the other?

I definitely preferred writing the scenes set in 1920. I think it was the sense of walking across fresh ground, writing about places and things and people I'd never written about before. Also, Betty's story was chopped and changed and moved about as the book found its shape, whereas Arlette's story was new and shiny and barely needed any work doing to it, so I could just focus on the detail and the sense of time and place.

• Do you follow a particular routine when you write?

It does tend to change a lot, but at the moment I am enjoying having both my children in school and having the run of the house again. Before, I used to have to rush to the gym to get my youngest in the crèche and then rush to the café to meet the child minder, then cloister myself away in my room at the top of the house. Now I'm free as a bird, currently writing this in the kitchen. Such joy! But I do most of my writing in the café next to my gym. I like the white noise and people-watching and not having any access to the internet. They also make much better coffee than me.

• Which character in *Before I Met You* did you enjoy writing most?

I enjoyed writing about Betty and Arlette in equal measure. After writing a few somewhat dark and complex characters in my previous two or three books, I really wanted to write about simple, uncomplicated souls, whom other people are naturally drawn to. Betty and Arlette were like the tent-poles in each of their narratives – good and strong and there to support the story and the other characters. I wanted their motives to be clear and uncompromising, a stark contrast with some of the people they come across. Of the smaller players, I did love writing Betty's Soho neighbour, Candy Lee. I actually created her on a day when I was in rather a bad mood, mainly to cheer myself up!

- **Your fans often comment on how much they love your characters and how easy they are to relate to. How do you make them so 'real'? Do you base them on people you know or are they purely fictional?**

All my characters are entirely fictional. But also entirely real. They do just tend to arrive in my head fully formed and then I just have to find a good name for them (I'm anal about names) and decide what to do with them. There's no trick to it. At the risk of sounding a bit airy-fairy, it just sort of happens.

- **What is your next novel about?**

It about Colin and Lorelei Bird and their four children, Megan, Bethan, Rory and Rhys. They live in a chocolate-box cottage in the Cotswolds in a rose-covered idyll. Until one day, when the children are all young adults, something tragic happens that nobody can find an explanation for and the family slowly starts to implode. The book begins in the aftermath of Lorelei's death, many years later. She had become estranged from her family and was a compulsive hoarder. Will her family find any answers to the mysteries of their past inside the crammed rooms of their childhood home? And will they find a way to become a family again?

It's a proper family saga with a massive great secret beating darkly at its heart. I wrote it really fast and didn't change anything as I was going along. It comes out in July 2013.

Lisa on Being a Writer

How I got into publishing

I never for a moment thought I would end up being a published author. In my early teenage years I had this romantic idea of working as a journalist for the *NME*. That clearly didn't work out and I ended up working in fashion retail instead. Then at some point in my early twenties I had this vague idea that someone should write a book about women like me in their early twenties, which nobody seemed to be doing at the time. But it wasn't until I was in my late twenties, when I had just been made redundant from my job as a secretary, that I seriously considered the possibility of writing a book.

It was the Nick Hornby novel *High Fidelity* that inspired me. It was the first time I'd read a book that really spoke to me, that made me think, 'Gosh, maybe it is possible to write a book in accessible language about ordinary people who live in London, and maybe I don't have to wait until I'm 55 years old and have had lots of life experience.' I mentioned this crazy concept to a friend and instead of laughing at me, she made me a bet. She said, 'Write three chapters and I'll take you out to dinner.' So I wrote the three chapters and she did take me out to dinner. But she didn't leave it there. She persuaded me to send the three chapters out to agents. This I did, purely to mollify her – I did not believe for a moment that what I'd written was good enough to be published. And so, when the rejection letters started to arrive I was unsurprised and mildly delighted. I had rejection letters! From literary agents! What fun! I only began to take things seriously when the last letter arrived and it was from an agent who wanted to see the rest of the book.

I moved in with my boyfriend and took a part-time job. Within the year I'd finished the book and given it to the agent.

She made me virtually rewrite it and then got me a book deal. A *two*-book deal. This meant that not only had I written one whole book, but now I had to write another. This was the moment that it first hit me. The playful bet with a friend was over. I was a writer now.

My top tips for writers

I would never have had the confidence (or sheer brass balls!) to push myself to write my first book if it hadn't been for my friend making me that bet, my husband insisting I could finish it when the agent liked the first three chapters, and everyone around me egging me on. Now that's something I can do for other people and I never get bored of giving people advice about writing.

My five tips for writing are pretty simplistic:

Number One: Read. Don't read the way you normally read, don't immerse yourself in the book. Instead, really look at what the author's done, in terms of moving the story along, in terms of building up characters, in terms of making the dialogue natural. Really learn from it.

Number Two: (And this is really important) Disavow yourself of any romantic notions about the process of writing. Don't imagine for a minute that it's going to be fun or that it's going to be easy. It's going to be neither of those things; it's going to be one of the most challenging things you'll ever do in your life. It's very, very difficult to write a book, even one that's easy to read.

Number Three: Start.

Number Four: Keep Going.

And Number Five: Finish.

Those last three things may sound obvious but most people never manage to get that far. You'll be leagues ahead of the game if you can just push through to the magic words: The End.

Once you've actually written a book, it's also a bit of a numbers game. The same friend who challenged me to write a book all those years ago subsequently went on to write her own novel. In the meantime she moved back to Australia, left her manuscript with me and asked me to keep sending it out. And so I did. Every week I'd pick another three agents out of the *Writers' & Artists' Yearbook*, take the three chapters up to the post office and post them off for her. I think I probably sent her manuscript out to about thirty agents and received thirty rejection letters until one day a letter arrived from a slightly crazed agent saying it was the most brilliant book she'd ever read and she wanted to get it published immediately. Which she did. So I would say, while it's important to have realistic expectations, patience and tenacity and just keeping on going are equally important because it only takes one person to love your book and you're halfway there.

What it's like to be a writer

There are lots of things I love about being a writer. I will tell anyone who asks that it is the best job in the world. It occurred to me shortly after I started writing full-time, after ten years working in offices, that it was the first time I'd felt like a proper grown up. Office jobs, it seemed to me, were really just an extension of school, with prescribed times for eating and arriving and leaving, all the rules and regulations, bullying and favouritism and politics. When I started writing I was genuinely in charge of my own time for the first time in my life. I did not have to talk to anyone I did not like or do anything I did not want to do. It was so liberating and I am still delighted every morning when I wake up and know that my day is my own. It's also a great job to have as a parent. I am able to take my children to school in the morning and to pick them up in the afternoon. I can go on school trips and take time out to see shows and assemblies and I never miss out on anything. Spending half my day being a mother and the other half being a professional writer is a very nice balance.

The other best thing about being a writer is telling people that I'm a writer. It's incredibly satisfying to walk into a social situation to face someone you've never met before and get to that dreaded question, 'So what do you do?' and to be able to tell them that you do something that is a dream for a lot of people. It's always terribly interesting for the person you're talking to as well. Suddenly, you've opened the door of this secret world to them – everyone always wants to know how many books I've written and where I find my ideas.

But apart from the lifestyle, which is clearly pretty great, there is also the process of writing itself. Try and imagine you've got this vast world inside your head. You're controlling all these people; you're controlling their destinies, and you've got no one you can talk to about it. Nobody knows what's going on in this world in your head except for you. You are the managing director of all managing directors. It can be quite wearing at times having sole responsibility for this thing. But it is also incredibly exhilarating. Especially when it's going well. The feel of the book coalescing, like a clay pot on a wheel, the golden moment when you suddenly get it, you know where it's going, and the euphoria of finishing, of putting that last full stop in place and knowing that you have accomplished something amazing.

But for me, I would say probably the best thing about being a writer is the publication process. The little steps that build towards the moment your book hits the shops: the initial feedback from your publishers; looking at artwork; editing; writing the acknowledgements; feeling the freshly printed book in your hands for the first time; the weekly sales figures being emailed to you on a Tuesday afternoon; reviews and comments from readers; seeing your book on a shelf in a bookshop. It honestly never ever gets boring. I am so lucky to do what I do, and I remember that every single day of my life. If anyone ever hears me moaning about my job, slap me.

The Truth About Melody Browne

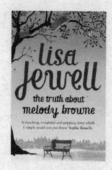

When she was nine years old, Melody Browne's house burned down. Not only did the fire destroy all her possessions, it took with it all her memories – she can remember nothing before her ninth birthday. Now in her early thirties, Melody lives in a council flat in the middle of London with her seventeen-year-old son. She's made a good life for herself and her son and she likes it that way.

Until one night something extraordinary happens. Whilst attending a hypnotist show with her first date in years she faints – and when she comes round she starts to remember. At first her memories mean nothing to her but then slowly, day by day, she begins to piece together the real story of her childhood. But with every mystery she solves another one materialises, with every question she answers another appears. And Melody begins to wonder if she'll ever know the truth about her past . . .

arrow books

Lydia, Robyn and Dean don't know each other – yet.

They live very different lives but each of them, independently, has always felt that something is missing.

What they don't know is that a letter is about to arrive that will turn their lives upside down.

It is a letter containing a secret – one that will bind them together, and show them what love and family and friendship *really* mean . . .

ALSO BY LISA JEWELL

The House
We Grew Up In

Meet the Bird Family.

All four children have an idyllic childhood: a picture
book cottage in a country village, a warm, cosy kitchen
filled with love and laughter, sun-drenched afternoons in
a rambling garden.

But one Easter weekend a tragedy strikes the Bird family that is so devastating that, almost imperceptibly, it
begins to tear them apart.

The years pass and the children become adults and
begin to develop their own quite separate lives. Soon it's
almost as though they've never been a family at all.

Almost. But not quite.

Because something has happened that will call them
home, back to the house they grew up in – and to what
really happened that Easter weekend all those years ago.

CENTURY

Get to know
Lisa online

Be the first to hear Lisa's news and find out
all about her new book releases at
www.lisa-jewell.co.uk

Join the official Facebook page at
www.facebook/lisajewellofficial